Praise for Barbara

T0288225

'Never portentous, never trivial, marvelously come----- ------------
of pathos, this is surely among the most powerful collections of stories
produced in New Zealand. Its unerring economy of effects suggests at
times the quality of a Flaubert, a Patrick White, a Grace Paley.'
Ian Reid, *Listener*

'. . . this must be one of the sharpest collections in English since Carver's
Cathedral in 1984 . . . Barbara Anderson's stories are about love, grief
and everyday emotional erosion . . . They are freighted with experience,
fresh with insight, told with a mature economy . . .'
Michael Hulse, *Guardian Weekly*

'In breathtakingly honest and funny prose, Anderson creates a world that
simply jumps with life and meaning, with joy and disappointment and hope.'
Kirsty Gunn, *Herald*

'An acute, unusual novelist whose clipped, quirky prose has earned her
comparisons with Grace Paley and Raymond Carver.'
Nick Hornby, *Times Literary Supplement*

'A quite irresistible writer with a microscopic eye for telltale detail – and
a dazzlingly accurate ear for dialogue as it is really spoken.'
Dirk Bogarde

'Economical, probing, and original, Anderson is an immaculate stylist.'
Joy Mackenzie, *Sunday Star Times*

'She is a novelist of great talent, well qualified to write black comedy. But
she has, too, the comprehension of human incomprehension, the pity for
human pity, that makes it possible to write tragedy.'
Penelope Fitzgerald, *Times Literary Supplement*

'Her stories and her skill in crafting them are superb. Above all, her stories
are great fun to read.'
Paul Day, *Waikato Times*

Novels by Barbara Anderson

Girls High

Portrait of the Artist's Wife

All the Nice Girls

The House Guest

Proud Garments

Long Hot Summer

The Swing Around

Change of Heart

Collected Stories

Barbara Anderson

Victoria University Press

VICTORIA UNIVERSITY PRESS
Victoria University of Wellington
PO Box 600 Wellington

Copyright © Barbara Anderson 2005

First published 2005
Reprinted 2006

National Library of New Zealand Cataloguing-in-Publication Data

Anderson, Barbara, 1926-
Short stories. Selections
Collected stories / Barbara Anderson.
ISBN 0-86473-498-0
I. Anderson, Barbara, 1926- Short stories. II. Title.
NZ823.2—dc 22

Printed by Astra Print, Wellington

Contents

I think we should go into the jungle is for Neil.

The Peacocks / Glorious Things is in memoriam
Dorothea Turner 1910–1997.

Acknowledgements

Grateful thanks to the editors of *Landfall*, the *Listener*, *London Magazine*, *Metro*, *Soho Square*, *Sport*, the *Timaru Herald* and *Vital Writing*, and to Radio New Zealand and the BBC.

'Discontinuous Lives', 'Up the River with Mrs Gallant', 'Shanties', 'Poojah', 'The Girls', 'One Potato Two Potato', 'Egypt is a Timeless Land', 'Commitment', 'Tuataras', 'Feeding the Sparrows', 'I Want to Get Out, I Said', 'Rollo's Dairy (Jake and Deedee)', 'It is Necessary I Have a Balloon', 'Subalpine Meadow', 'School Story' and 'Fast Post' were collected in *I think we should go into the jungle* (VUP, 1989; Secker & Warburg, 1993).

'The Westerly', 'We Could Celebrate', 'Living on the Beach', 'I Thought There'd Be a Couch', 'Balance', 'The Grateful Dead', 'The Peacocks' and 'Glorious Things' were collected in *The Peacocks* (VUP, 1997).

'The Westerly', 'We Could Celebrate', 'Living on the Beach', 'The Right Sort of Ears', 'I Thought There'd Be a Couch', 'Real Beach Weather', 'Balance', 'The Grateful Dead', 'Day Out', 'Glorious Things' and 'So Lovely of Them' were collected in *Glorious Things* (Jonathan Cape, 1999).

'Peppermint Frogs', 'The Daggy End' and 'The Man with the Plug in His Nose' are previously uncollected.

Discontinuous Lives

I am pouring the tea at my cousin's house after her funeral
and there are many special requests. — No milk please, just a
dash, is there a stronger one, where's the sugar. But that is how
it is wherever I am pouring so why not at a funeral. We have
brought extra cups. There are green ones with primroses,
wine coloured ones with gold rims and Andrea's blue and
white. Most people have one by now, the women that is,
the men have whisky. Amber curls in each glass for comfort
for that is how it is at funerals, though maybe a sherry later
for some of the girls. Another cousin, Maureen, says into
my ear as I turn my head checking for cupless female hands
— That's Morris Baker.

— Morris who? I say, then remember. — Morris Baker!
Where?

— Over there, Maureen points.

— But it's a woman!

— Didn't you know? A pseudonym.

— No! Goodness me, how extraordinary, and I have
to regroup, my cousin's silver-plated teapot left hanging
because I am so surprised, like when I found Auden's 'Lay

9

your sleeping head my love' was written to a man, to say nothing of Shakespeare's sonnets. Why not, and many men have most beautiful hair but it is a different head I see laid human on that faithless arm, and now Morris Baker.

Morris Baker is a large woman, deep bosomed. It finishes not far above her belt having swelled out at the usual place. She wears an expensive easy-care which has small purple and black checks. Her dark grey hair is swept back from her strong features and her expression is serene and what on earth is this world famous novelist (albeit of yesteryear) doing at Diane's funeral on Bluff Hill, I gasp.

— Didn't you know? says Maureen again. — She was born in the Bay, at Clive.

— No indeed. Fancy that. Fancy *A Man in Grey, A Nettle Graspd, Whither Stranger* and all the rest of them coming from *Clive*, for heaven's sake!

— No no no, says Maureen rescuing the teapot which has begun to dribble onto Diane's brown carpet of which she was so proud. — They left years ago, went back to England, her parents were English, they got fed up. It must have been after you left. I can remember when she went. What a party, she was a beautiful girl.

— And still is. How amazing, I must meet her. Why is she out?

— There's a brother or something. She lives in Burford now, you know in England.

But this cannot be. I lived in Burford for years and if anyone came from New Zealand, let alone a famous novelist (I was there in yesteryear) I would have met her because everyone would have said — There is another New Zealander living in Burford you must meet her.

Whether you want to or not.

— Perhaps it had an E or something, says Maureen.

— Yes perhaps, though I am puzzled.

By now people are coming back for second cups and I am pouring again and reboiling the kettle and Morris Baker has to keep.

We stack the cups on the steel bench, looking out over the grapefruit tree which did well for us all because Diane was generous. — We'll do them later we say, nodding wisely at the cups and saucers and each other. We know what to do. I wipe my hands on a tea towel I sent Diane from Burford which has a picture of Anne Hathaway's cottage on it and move back to the front room which is crowded with my cousin's friends and relations. A neighbour shows me the spot where he found my cousin. — It was *there*, he says pointing. — There. I stare at the carpet beneath his craggy finger and nod. — Yes, I say. Yes.

There is quite a lot of noise by now. — Diane would be pleased we say, but do we know. We know she liked people and parties. — Where would I be without my friends she would ask as we arrived with another jar of soup to stuff in her refrigerator and always on New Year's Eve she let her hair down but we still don't know. Like when middle-aged children say at a parent's demise, Mother would hate to have been a nuisance. Have they seen it in writing.

Morris Baker is by the window, the neighbour is pointing at the carpet, Morris Baker is nodding. I move over quickly, my hand outstretched. — Hullo, I'm Elaine Wilkinson, I just want to say I've always loved your books. Morris Baker is pleased. She puts down her empty cup which we must have missed and holds out her hand. I remember from Burford about women shaking hands, it does not happen in Napier so much though occasionally, prizegivings for example. Her hand is warm and soft, the bones beneath are strong. If Morris Baker shakes hands like this in Burford the ladies must be surprised and I bet she does. She smiles at me, a beautiful warm wide embracing smile. Her eyes are large and brown and I am delighted to meet her and this shows as we beam at each other holding hands.

— Which book did you like best? asks Morris Baker.

— *Whither Stranger*, I say. — Yes that is my favourite, she replies.

— Tell me what you meant at the end did Rupert . . .

Morris Baker flings back her smooth coiled head to laugh deeply. — Ah no, she says, you mustn't ask me that, how do I know.

There is too much noise.

— Come into the spare room, I say, so we move to the door into the hall, touching people gently to show respect for my cousin Diane who is dead.

The hall is narrow and empty, there are coats on the hooks and a beater which someone brought for the cream but didn't need lies on the carpet. The telephone my cousin loved sits round-shouldered and silent, grieving on its table.

My cousin was not a believer. She was bonny and blithe and good and gay and saved me when I returned from Burford in despair, having tried matrimony and failed.

Morris Baker and I have reached the spare room. It is very simple. Every penny my cousin Diane had she earned in the library, unqualified and cheerful. There are two single beds covered in glazed chintz 'all over' pattern of pink rosebuds and blue ribbons which loop and scroll to encircle each bud. She made these on her ancient Singer inherited from Auntie Dot when the more affluent were converting them into wrought-iron Outdoor Tables. She frilled the valances and attached them firmly so that the crass hot pink of the sprung base was hidden. She ran up the curtains. All this I know and ignore as Morris Baker and I sit one on each bed knee to knee though mine are higher and we continue our in depth discussion of Morris Baker's books.

— I always thought that you left the ending of *Whither Stranger* so *unresolved*, I say.

— Well of course.

— Yes I know. I mean I know you meant to but . . .

Morris Baker laughs an in depth gurgle of pleasure. She stabs a hand down the front of her dress and produces a small white handkerchief. I am not to be put off.

— I know you meant to I say, leaning forward with my hands on my knees, but I still think . . . I mean we don't even know if Rupert *stays*.

Morris Baker dabs at the end of her dry nose with her handkerchief.

— I have left you, that is the reader, she says, imaginative space.

— Yes I know and I like that, I say, — but don't you think that in this case you might have just . . . The unspoken word 'cheated' stains the silence. I have gone too far. I am now an anxious placating figure, a shadow of that switched on bibliophile whose behind creased the roses opposite Morris Baker's.

But Morris Baker is an old pro, a trouper, she takes the rough with the smooth, she wins some she loses some, she rides with the punches, she takes it on the chin and comes back fighting.

— How can you, she says smiling with large white teeth (I envy to gut bitterness those with the white sort) — How can you say in the same breath that you like imaginative space and yet you feel I've cheated by leaving you, the reader, just that.

— Goodness me! I gasp. I didn't say that.

— No you didn't say it, says Morris Baker, but I heard it.

This is better than ever. Morris Baker is an opponent worthy of the steel of one who has slogged through extramural English and a hard time we had of it I'm here to tell you.

— What I meant was, I say laughing with my yellow teeth for amiability, what I meant was that I think there is a difference between the author leaving the reader imaginative space and just not knowing . . . Again the words melt and fizzle. The cut and thrust of literary criticism is one thing, a tea pourer being rude to a famous author at her friend's funeral is another. How can I say '. . . not knowing how to finish'.

— Not knowing how to finish, says Morris Baker.

I toss my head to show how merry my laugh is. The curls bounce in the three-sided mirror attached to the dressing table. I look away quickly and focus instead on three mats embroidered by my late cousin which lie upon its horizontal surface. The larger one lies in the middle, a smaller supporter graces each side. Embroidered upon each is a lady in a crinoline. Three faces are hidden by poke bonnets, three flesh-pink mini hands hold parasols, six tiny feet wade among buttonhole stitch forget-me-nots, lazy daisies, and blades of single stitch grass. The two smaller mats have proportionally smaller ladies but the blossoms of their flowering fields are the same size. Each mat is edged with crochet in a colour called ecru. As a diversion from Morris Baker's acuteness I heave myself up from the bed and hold up the large mat.

— Diane made these, I say.

— Good Lord, laughs Morris Baker.

This comment has the small shock of a cobweb in the face. It clings. It won't do. I brush it away.

— Tell me about your life, I babble. When did you leave the Bay? What was your real name?

— Beryl Hollings, she says.

The years slough off, a crumpled discard. — Beryl, Beryl, I scream, seizing her hands. — I'm Elaine Nimmo! We are hugging and laughing and laughing and, No, Go on, Of course, Of course, I knew I knew you, we lie, but not quite, I did have a feeling. We laugh some more, touching for warmth, touching for contact, touching for old times and remembering and for the wonder of our lives and reunion after so long when we had almost forgotten we existed, the other one that is.

They were different the Hollings, being English for a start.

And they weren't at Clive as Maureen said, just Greenmeadows like we were, but too far to bike so Beryl and I played together on parent-arranged visits, the worst sort.

— Aw hang Mum do I have to go, it smells. It is not the smell which worries me but I don't know how to express unease, and hope to touch a sympathetic chord. My mother dislikes smells. — It *whats*? — Smells. — Nonsense! My mother lifts her head momentarily from her bedmaking demonstration. Her hands continue their origami-like pleating and tucking of the blankets; she insists on hospital corners. — What a fuss pot, she laughs. I spot the contradiction, but though hospital corners may defeat me I know about answering back.

The Hollings house did smell; a close, layered smell, airless and nicotined. The French doors never opened onto the wide verandah except for the huffing exit of Dinky the canker-eared spaniel.

They had brought their things with them from Home and crammed them into the small square rooms. The Drawing Room was the worst. A mahogany bureau faded beside a brass-bound sea chest (male) and a small davenport (female). Occasional tables teetered at a touch. There was no room to move. — No space, no space, moaned Mrs Hollings, drifting and dreaming of height and width, of gentler suns and softer airs. She cut up cucumbers and 'applied' them to her pale skin. She did what she could.

Captain Hollings was a small explosive man described by my Uncle Bob as a no hoper and thus watched with interest as he stumped about clutching a stick for support. He had lost a leg in the war. Where? How?

The Captain rose late. His pretend leg, its attachment end slack-jawed and empty, waited beside his disordered bed as he made a good breakfast and Beryl and Mrs Hollings scurried in and out with replacements in response to his roars. — Marmalade! — Toast! Dinky lay at his feet, a golden lump beneath the eiderdown, buried deep in his foetid smell.

After several false starts Beryl and I became friends. My father and I swept up the drive in the Buick, hammered the bored lion's head knocker against the door till Mrs Hollings, distracted and unnerved by any summons, yanked the door open, her fingers fluttering against her mouth for protection. She apologised for everything, anything, the stuck door, her apron, the lack of decent rain for the farmers, her very existence. She made me want to cry. My father waited hat in hand and departed as soon as possible. Beryl appeared behind her mother and stuck her tongue out at me in greeting. Her mother's hunted glance fell on us. — Well now chicks what would you like to play? There was no need to answer. We skidded to the heavy-lidded chest in the back hall full of the

Captain and Mrs Hollings' discarded finery, presumably also shipped from Home. I wore black velvet and a solar topee. Beryl sailed along the concrete paths in front of me trailing green lace, clumping along in ankle strap Minnie Mouse shoes, her head high as we progressed towards Making Up, our discontinuous unwritten lives beneath the lemon tree.

— Where had we got to? she asked on arrival, adjusting the set of the peplum above her knees.

— You're still in the cave, I said. — I haven't broken free yet.

— Well hurry up, said Beryl, sitting down in butter box confinement.

Our real life was carefully hidden at school. We were in the same class, with Miss Lynskey who taught me right from left and ran a ballot for the class monitor. We voted according to sex and sycophancy. I voted for Beryl who voted for Ann Henare who voted for Glenys Ashwood who voted for the next girl up.

My visits to the Hollings increased in frequency. Happy, wreathed in night smells, we lay in our narrow beds telling. — I'll tell if you tell. I flaunted my double-jointed thumbs. Beryl skited her tap steps. We swapped comics, *Dick Tracy* for *Phantom*. We investigated Romance, our stomachs flat on the sun-baked verandah. ('She has dirtied her face to hide her beauty,' cried the Sultan. 'This shows intelligence. A rare thing in a slave girl'). We attached one end of a long rope to a hook on the verandah wall. — You turn, bossed Beryl. I swung the other end yelling — Apple jelly jam tart/Tell me the name of your sweetheart/A,B,C,D . . .

Beryl jumped, then tripped sprawling on the hot wood at M. — Mervyn, I squealed, — Mervyn Colley's your boy. Mervyn with purple painted school sores who squinted in the front row and still couldn't see. Beryl's bush of black hair shook as she leapt at me. I turned to flee and cannoned into Mrs Holling's wet apron.

— Elaine, she gasped, winded. — Beryl, look who's here.

We stared at my cousin Diane in her frock with apples on it, five years younger, smiling and golden. We untied the rope, hooked it round her shoulders and ran her deep through the garden behind the garage to the lemon tree. Her cheeks were pinker than ever from the enforced gallop. She glowed with pleasure, proud to play with the big kids. Beryl moved to me, stiff fingers shielding her secret.

— The Ward of the Sultan is in our power! she hissed.

— Yes!

— We'll tie her up.

— Yes! Yes!

— For ever. Beryl's usually pale face was scarlet. My legs were hot with excitement. My cousin smiled, safe as houses. Beryl seized one end of the rope and we twirled the captive around twisting and tugging, one at each end. — She is our slave. — Yes! — For ever! My heart was bonging, too big for its space.

— She can take your father's toast in! I screamed. Diane's smile faltered. She tried to reach out a hand to me. Beryl slapped it back and tugged harder on the cords. — Eelaine, panted my cousin.

— And help him on with his leg! shouted Beryl.

— No! squealed the terrified child. We dragged the struggling kicking bawling four year old to the post of the clothes line and slammed her against it, my knee in her stomach my hands busy while Beryl loosed and retied the rope. We cobbled the ends together, our fingers tense and eager. My pants were wet with mob violence, my throat harsh with blood lust. Diane's eyes never left my face. — Eeelaine! Eeelaine! she sobbed. 'The bleating of the kid excites the tiger.'

— Shut up I said, my face stiff with rejection.

— Mum! screamed my cousin with the hysterical despair of the betrayed.

— Belt up! said Beryl, her hands tugging at the knots.

— Or we'll sock you! I yelled, jumping up and down in damp chilling delight.

All this Morris Baker and I remember as we sit facing each other in the still room and our relationship shifts and slides and does not resettle. Author and reader, admired and admirer have vanished from my cousin's sparsely-furnished lovingly-furbished spare room. The room is empty. There is no sound.

Morris Baker's strong left hand, the nails pink and curved, touches her powdered cheek. The hairs on her arms are no longer dark like they used to be. Her ear lobes are rounded and puffy, modelled from play dough, the chunky gold earrings too heavy for old ears. Her handkerchief is a tight ball.

— Do you remember . . . says Morris Baker.

— Yes, I say. Yes, I do.

Up the River with
Mrs Gallant

Mr Levis invited them to call him Des. And this is Arnold he said.

Mr Kent said Hi Arnold.

Mrs Kent said that she was pleased to meet him.

Mrs Gallant said Hullo, Arnold.

Mr Gallant said Good morning.

Mr Borges said nothing.

Des said that if they just liked to walk down to the landing stage Arnold would bring the boat down with the tractor.

Mrs Gallant said wasn't Mr Gallant going to leave the car in the shade.

Mr Gallant said that if Mrs Gallant was able to tell him where the shade from one tree was going to be for the next six hours he would be happy to.

Mr Kent said that he was going to give it a burl anyway and reparked the Falcon beneath the puriri.

Mrs Kent told Mrs Gallant that she and Stan were from Hamilton.

Mrs Gallant told Mrs Kent that she and Eric were from Rotorua.

Mrs Kent said that she had a second cousin in Rotorua. Esme. Esme. She would be forgetting her own head next.

And that she supposed she should wait for Stan but what the hell.

Mrs Gallant smiled at Mr Borges.

Mr Borges nodded.

At the landing stage Des said that he would like them to take turns sitting in the front and perhaps the ladies?

Mrs Kent remarked that the landing stage looked a bit ass over tip.

Arnold said that the landing stage was safe as houses and would the lady get into the boat.

Mrs Kent said Where was Stan.

Mr Kent said Here.

Mrs Kent asked Mr Kent where he had got to. She hopped across the landing stage, climbed onto the boat and into one of the front seats. She said that it wasn't too lady like but that she would be right.

Mrs Gallant followed.

Mr Kent and Mr Gallant climbed into the next row.

Des said that Arnold was on the Access Training Scheme and doing very well but it was difficult to fit in the hundred hours river time in a business like this and that he hoped that the customers would have no objection if Arnold came with them and drove the boat back because of the hundred hours.

Mrs Kent said that she would be delighted anytime.

Mr Kent said Well.

Mr Gallant asked how many passengers the boat was licensed for.

Des said that it was licensed for seven passengers.

Mrs Gallant smiled.

Mr Borges said nothing.

Arnold said Good on them, climbed into the boat and sat in the back row with Mr Borges. Mr Borges smiled.

Des started the motor and picked up the microphone. He said that the river was approximately ninety miles long and had been called the Rhine Of New Zealand. It had been used as a waterway since the time of the first Maoris.

Perhaps the busiest time on the river, he said, was the end of the nineteenth century and the beginning of the twentieth until the Main Trunk was completed. River boats plied, freight and passengers were transported in thousands and in all that time there were only two deaths which must be something of a record.

Mr Gallant said that he hoped that it would stay that way.

Des invited him to come again.

Mrs Kent said that Mr Gallant was only kidding.

Mr Gallant said No he wasn't.

Mrs Gallant said Eric.

Des said that he was born and brought up on the river. He had lived on the river all his life and he knew the river like the back of his hand and his aim was for every one of his passengers to learn more about this beautiful river which was steeped in history.

Mr Kent said that Des would do him.

Mrs Kent said Hear Hear.

Mr Borges, Mr Gallant and Arnold said nothing.

Mrs Gallant said that it was a lovely day.

Des said that she wasn't running as sweet as usual, probably a few stones up the grille.

Mrs Gallant asked What did that mean.

Des said Stones, you know, up the grille.

Mrs Gallant said that she realised that.

Mr Gallant smiled.

Mrs Kent said that they had a lovely day for it anyhow.

Des said they certainly had and to take a look at the flying fox across the river. He explained that the alignment of the posts was very important indeed.

Mr Gallant said that it would be.

Des said that otherwise she could come across but she wouldn't go back. On the other hand if it was wrong the other way she would go back but she wouldn't come across.

Mr Gallant said Exactly.

Mr Kent said it was all Dutch to him Ooh Pardon.

Mrs Kent said that the young man wasn't Dutch and that Stan needn't worry.

Mr Kent said Then what was he?

Mrs Kent said that yes the day certainly was a cracker.

Mrs Gallant smiled.

Des said that the cooling system wasn't operating as per usual either. Usually she stayed at twenty. That was what he liked her at. Twenty.

Mrs Gallant said that it was at seventy now was it not.

Des said Yes it was.

Mrs Gallant said Oh.

Mr Gallant laughed.

Des said that they certainly would like Pipiriki.

Mrs Kent said That was for sure.

Des moored the boat at the Pipiriki landing stage. Everyone climbed out. Des put a large carton on an outdoor table and said they could help themselves to tea or coffee.

Mrs Gallant said that she and Eric would only need one tea bag between them as they both took tea very weak without milk.

Des said that Mrs Gallant needn't worry as he had provided two tea bags each per person as usual.

Mr Gallant said that she was only trying to help.

Mrs Kent asked if there was a toilet.

Arnold pointed up the path.

Des said that after lunch they should go up and look at Pipiriki. Pipiriki House had once been a world famous hotel. It had burned down in 1959. He said to have a good look at the shelter and to go around the back as there were some flush toilets.

Mrs Kent said that now Des told her and they both laughed.

Mrs Gallant said What shelter.

Des said A shelter for tourists you know trampers, that sort of thing.

Everyone liked Pipiriki very much. After an hour they climbed back into the boat.

Mr Kent said that he wished some of those activists could see all those kids happy and swimming.

Mr Gallant said Why?

Mr Kent said to look at that one jumping there. That he hadn't a care in the world.

Mr Gallant said that that was hardly the point.

Mrs Gallant said Eric.

Mr Gallant said Hell's delight woman.

Mr Borges smiled.

Mrs Kent said that they used to live near Cambridge but that they had moved in to Hamilton when the boy took over.

Mrs Gallant said Was that right, and that she wished they had been able to land at Jerusalem.

Arnold said that he could go a swim.

Des said that he had been going to have a good look at her yesterday but that he hadn't had a break for so long and that he just hadn't felt like it.

No one said anything.

Des said that anyway he had had another booking in the end as things had turned out.

The boat leapt and bucked high in the air.

Mrs Kent said Ooops.

Des said that that showed you what happened if you let your concentration slip even for a second with a jettie. She had hit a stump.

Mr Gallant laughed.

Arnold asked if the Boss would like him to take over.

Des and Arnold laughed.

Mrs Gallant said to look at that kingfisher.

Mrs Kent said Where.

Mrs Gallant said There. That Mrs Kent was too late. That it had gone.

Des pointed out many points of interest and said that no she certainly wasn't going too good.

Mrs Gallant said that hadn't the temperature gauge gone up to eighty or was she wrong.

Des said that no she was not wrong and that he had better give her a breather and stopped the boat. He said it was probably the temperature of the water, it being a hot day.

Nobody said anything. The boat rocked, silent on the trough of its own waves. The sun shone.

Des said that that should have cooled her down a bit and started the boat.

The temperature gauge climbed to seventy.

Des said that that was more like it and that there had

been a Maori battle on that island between the Hau Hau supporters and the non-supporters.

Mr Gallant wondered why they had chosen an island.

Des said that Mr Gallant had him there and swung the boat into a shallow tributary of the river. He told Arnold that they had better check the grille and how would Arnold like a swim.

Arnold said that that would be no problem. He climbed around onto the bow of the boat and said that they would now see his beautiful body. He removed his shirt and told Mrs Gallant and Mrs Kent to control themselves.

Mrs Kent yelped.

Arnold faced the vertical cliff of the bank, presented his shorts clad buttocks and shook them.

Everyone laughed except Mr Gallant and Mr Borges.

Mr Borges stood up quickly, took a photograph of Arnold's back view, and sat down again.

Arnold jumped into the water and swam to the back of the boat. Des fumbled beneath his feet and handed the passengers various pieces of equipment for Arnold to poke up the grille. The male passengers handed the things on to Arnold with stern efficiency.

After some time Arnold said that he had found three stones up the grille.

Des said that that was good.

Arnold said that they were not big buggers though.

Des said Never mind.

Arnold handed the equipment back into the boat and did a honeypot jump from the shallow water into a deep pool.

Mr Kent said See?

Arnold swam to the bow of the boat and heaved himself into the boat.

Mr Borges took a photograph of Arnold's front view.

Mrs Gallant said that they were lucky that Arnold had come with them.

Mrs Kent said that Mrs Gallant could say that again and would the boat go better now that Arnold had removed the stones.

Des said that he hoped so.

Mr Gallant laughed.

They stopped several times on the return trip for the boat to cool down and as she was not going too well Des sometimes had to make several sweeps before she could pick up enough speed for her to lift up over the rapids. Des said that normally at this stage, when she was less than half full of gas he could fling her about all over the place no sweat.

Mr Gallant said that they must be thankful for small mercies.

Des swung the boat in a wide spraying circle and pulled into the jetty at the old flour mill. They climbed the hill. Des carrying the afternoon tea carton. After tea Des said that he would tell them about the old flour mill and the river in general. Everyone expressed interest. They trooped into the warm shadowy old building and Des began.

After half an hour Mrs Kent asked whether Des would mind if she sat down.

Des said that although perhaps it was technically more correct to call them river boats he still thought of them as steamers though strictly speaking they weren't steamers for long.

Mrs Kent sat down.

Mrs Gallant sat down.

Mr Kent looked as though he was going to cry.

Mr Gallant closed his eyes.

BARBARA ANDERSON

Arnold sat outside in the shade.

Mr Borges joined him.

After three quarters of an hour Des said that he hoped they had all learned something of the river.

They climbed down to the river in silence.

Des said that as she wasn't the best perhaps if Mrs Gallant and Mr Kent would like to sit in front.

Mr Gallant muttered something about sensible arrangement of ballast.

Mrs Kent asked Des why.

Arnold said it was because he liked the good-looking girls in the back with him.

Mrs Kent told Arnold to get away and climbed nimbly into the back seat.

Mrs Gallant said nothing.

They set off with Des at the wheel. The temperature gauge rose above eighty. Des asked the passengers to look around their feet for a tool which would enable Arnold to take another poke up the grille without getting out of the boat.

Mrs Gallant said that there was a pipe thing here if that was any help.

Mrs Kent gave a startled cry and said What was that smoke.

Mr Gallant said that that was steam.

Mrs Kent said that it was red hot that pipe thing there.

Mr Gallant said that he was not at all surprised.

Arnold said that she would be right.

Des said that she had better have another cool off and stopped the boat.

The boat limped to the original landing jetty two hours later than planned. The passengers collected their belongings without comment and trailed up the hill.

Des told Arnold that he could bring the boat up.

Arnold said that Des was the Boss.

Mrs Gallant remarked that it had been a very interesting day and that wasn't the river beautiful.

Mrs Kent said that yes it was but that she had felt so sorry for the poor chap.

Mr Gallant said God in Heaven.

Mrs Gallant remarked that she saw that Mr Kent's car was in the shade.

Mr Gallant said that it probably had not been for the first six hours.

Mrs Gallant said that that remark was typical absolutely typical.

Mrs Kent said that they used to have Jerseys but the boy had switched to Friesians.

Mr Kent said that he had been happy enough with Jerseys but that there you were.

Mrs Kent said that they just want to be different and that it was quite understandable.

Mr Kent said that he had never said it wasn't.

Mr Borges said nothing.

Arnold appeared on the tractor, pulling the boat on its trailer. He parked it in the shed and appeared with a Visitors' Book. He invited the passengers to make their crosses.

Everyone laughed except Mr Gallant and Mr Borges.

Des said that he would give her an overhaul tomorrow that was for sure.

Mrs Kent signed the book and wrote Lovely day under Comments.

Mr Kent signed and wrote Ditto.

Mr Gallant signed his name only.

Mr Borges signed and wrote Sweden.

Mrs Gallant missed the signing. She stumped across the bleached grass and stood gazing at the river.

It said nothing.

Shanties

I sit in my caravan in the El Dorado caravan park and I think I am a very lucky woman. I think of those shanties we saw on the roadside.

I am very fond of my caravan. The man I bought it from painted it himself. He was a professional house painter of the old school, no spraying. The brush marks don't show or anything but it looks, well it would have been better sprayed. It is the shape of a Walt Disney cloud, rounded at both ends. But blue. Inside it is punk pink. Very compact if a bit tatsy but caravans often are, they seem to bring out the kitsch. The vendor showed me his product most meticulously. He pulled out the drawers. He unrolled the awning. We squatted together, heads close as children with jokes while we inspected the underpinnings. I kicked the tyres. He was selling it because he'd bought it as a spare room for his daughter who didn't come. She was in Brisbane and she wrote to say she was coming, but . . . His voice trailed away. I didn't pursue it. I couldn't do anything and I didn't want to start thinking negative thoughts about my elliptical pie in the sky. I could see he was glad to get rid of it though.

The caravan park is well run by the caretaker, Mr Kelson. Most of the residents are long-term. We're long-term they say. Nothing fly-by-night with us though that remains unsaid. Some are so long-term they have pretend fences which define their territory. Mr Laski's is a one foot high white picket. One has a path to the door bordered with matching river stones painted white. Many of the homes have names emblazoned on their sleek sides. Rio Bella Vista has a glimpse of the river. Roll Your Own next door to me will never cruise again because Mrs Millrod is a widow and Cyril did the driving. Mrs Millrod is the victim of some crippling disease. She is very small and has to turn her head sideways to smile up at me. For some reason this makes even her 'Good morning Julie' seem wise, knowing. She is uncomplaining and cheerful in her little girl dresses and doesn't ask questions. I am thinking of painting Run Away on my mobile home but would they get it? Or El Deserto? Better just to say my husband . . . Yes, well, what? My husband and I . . . Some sort of caravan park Queen's Message for God's sake. The thing is, it's not only the things that happen, it's the explanations required. The new persona which must be created, the screen relit behind which I dance.

*

The hotel suite was vast. Mike tipped the man who delivered the luggage and turned to her, stroking a hand over his seal coat hair. She was bouncing on the enormous double bed in her petticoat, her shoes abandoned in the middle of the room, their heels angled. — Bit of a scream, she called. — What? he said. — The whole thing. Us. Here. Everything. He lay down on the other side of the King Size, a yard across the furrows of the quilted bedspread. She stopped bouncing and snatched her narrow feet to sit cross-legged, calves flat on the bed, supple and trim as a worked out Jane Fonda. — I mean *look* at it! She stared at the muted pastels of the overstuffed chairs, the decorator prints on the walls of the opulent anonymous room. — It's so huge . . . We could hold a levee why not? Her hand covered her mouth in a caricature of stifled laughter. She laughed at her jokes, her faux pas, at bloody life itself. He dropped his shoulders and breathed out.

    — Julie.

    — Yes?

    Phrases slid into his mind. — I've slaved for it. — For God's sake, woman. — Why don't you . . . — Why can't you . . .

    Were abandoned. — Nothing.

    Her head lifted, scenting the frustration behind his silence.

    — The firm's paying, he said.

    — I didn't mean *that*, she said. The corners of her mouth twitched. The attempt to suppress her laughter, to humour him as though he was a fractious child, infuriated him further. He rolled over to the edge of the vast bed. He should go through the draft of his speech. See Brett. He loosened his tie. Yawned. The air conditioning wasn't perfect. — Don't forget the laundry, he muttered. — No. She was reading the house magazine of the hotel chain. — Listen to this. The Hotel Ponceroo is situated in central downtown Washington with easy access to . . . Can it be central and downtown at the same time? He closed his eyes. — Yes, he said. — Yes, it can, he told the darkness.

He jolted upright at her shriek, his heart lurching. She stood at the window, her feet half buried in the carpet, a six foot bath sheet wrapped around her body. Her hair was wet, her mouth open with delight not terror. She was pointing out the window. — Look at that! He dragged himself off the bed and stumbled over. She had pulled back one of the curtains on which peonies, birds of paradise and chinese temples melded in corals and greens. It revealed a concrete service area lined with garbage cans. A rangy cat stalked its beat, planting each pad with care. Mike stared down, clutching the window sill. — What's wrong with it? he said. — No, no. She pointed again. — *That!* A neon sign on the roof of the building opposite flashed red white red white across the bleak scene. — Eddie's Condoms! Eddie's Condoms! Eddie's Condoms! — Isn't that *mar*vellous! she cried. He stared at the sign, his eyelids heavy as safety curtains, hating her. — It's just so . . . Oh I can't explain. Like that weight lifter who 'rips his glutes'. So *mar*vellous! she said.

*

I have been lucky also in finding a job. This is a country town and it has problems and the worst is lack of employment. People stand around. There is an air of . . . decay is too strong a word. Even the multi-coloured plastic streamers above the used car lots seem listless. The place used to bustle and throb with energy like a farm generator I knew. Mr Barber made his own electricity which seemed a God-like activity. A generator crouched at the back of his garage waiting to stutter into creation.

I have a job in the local canning factory. I sit with the other women at the ever coming conveyor belt as the peas roll by and we remove shreds of leaves, tendrils, all the waste scraps of a pea crop. All day our hands move rhythmically in sweeping arcs, our fingers are nimble and selective, our heads are turbanned in green. We spy for purity. We judge. We are efficient and sharp-eyed. Nothing extraneous escapes us. Once I found a feather in a can of chicken soup but that was in another country.

I am not reticent with the other women. Fouled-up relationships flow by like the peas, but nobody picks at them. There is a lot of laughter as we sit on the splay-legged plastic chairs in the canteen. We had to help Em up the day she christened the conveyor belt the steel eel.

*

The aircraft slipped down onto the runway. He glanced across her and nodded. A good landing. His smile was that of a fellow conspirator, eye contact, closed lips. She smiled back then began stowing her mess of clutter into a string kit of all things. As the plane braked to a stop a team of uniformed workmen ran onto the tarmac to align the steps. They ran bent double as though intent on avoiding detection. Three young women in green lily gowns held ropes of flower garlands. A band struck up an oompah of welcome as Brett appeared to check the cabin luggage. His upper lip twitched beneath the ragged sandy moustache. — And the little one. Right then? He beamed at them, his face proud. The door opened and the heat blasted in. Mike bent his head, then straightened quickly to run down the aircraft steps, hand outstretched to clasp the hand of the senior member of the group waiting to greet him. Julie followed, her linen suit a crumpled disaster, the orange string kit bumping her knee at every step. — I think the aircraft's got a flat tyre, she told the welcoming committee.

Unlike Washington, the air conditioning was faultless. Brett was taking notes, the ballpoint in his left hand pecking at a small pad. — Oh yes, he said. — One more thing. The helicopter. Doors on or off? They want to know which you prefer. — Oh. Off I think. Mike glanced across at Julie who was upended over a suitcase on the floor. — Definitely, she said. She straightened up from her head down bottom up scrabbling and looked distractedly around the suite.

— What is it now? said Mike.

— My blue belt.

He looked at the easy-care non-iron hanging around her like a sack. Her lack of vanity used to fascinate him. He dismissed the thought quickly. — It doesn't need a belt, he lied.

— It does, but what the hell. The jungle won't care.

— We're not going to the jungle. I told you we're . . .

— You said I think we should go into the jungle and I said speak for yourself and you said . . .

— That was yesterday. We went. You didn't.

— I know I didn't. She stood on one foot as though practising balance. — No jungle?

— We go *over* the jungle, said Brett, ever helpful.

— Ah. She raked a hand through her hair. — It's just the snakes.

— The snakes aren't going to bounce up at you.

— Not to a helicopter. No. She sounded genuinely amused. Probably was he thought sourly.

— No doors eh? That's great. So what is it today?

— Why don't you read the flaming programme?

— Because I've lost the flaming programme. She smiled.
— One of our programmes is missing. Shot down with the belt.

His shoulders sagged. — Today we visit a hydroelectric project. We drive to the airport. We fly for two hours to an outlying island . . .

She looked puzzled. — No doors?

— God in heaven! The two hours is in a fixed-wing aircraft. The helicopter is just the last half hour. He snatched the programme from his open briefcase and flapped it at her, jabbing an accusing finger at the print. — See!

— Yes, she said.

The drive to the airport seemed endless. The driver manoeuvred through the chaos of city traffic onto a motorway which lead through an industrial hinterland of grey. The grass verge beneath the hoardings was lined with squatter's shanties built from straw mats, cardboard, an occasional length of corrugated iron. Nobody was visible. They must be at work. But where were the children? She turned to ask Mike, as if he would know. His eyes were closed.

— Mike?

— Nnnn?

— Nothing.

The car sped on.

She tried to work out the advertisements, most of them obvious. Delighted women gazed with rapture at cakes of soap. Children stretched eager arms to toys forever beyond their reach. A giant Pink Panther gesticulated with writhing neon limbs above a garage. Factories became fewer.

They left the motorway and drove through a suburb. Tropical trees soared above them, their branches touching across the road. Weathered stone walls covered in cascading pink and orange flowered creepers hid the houses beyond. Women with straw brooms whisked the unblemished footpaths. The driver glanced at her in the rear vision mirror and smiled his gap-toothed smile.

Most of the party slept in the fixed-wing aircraft. Mouths hung open, an occasional snorting snore woke its sleeper. Technical magazines slipped to the floor. Mike's rough pad was open on his knees as he stared at the jungle searching for words. Julie slept beside him, her head heavy on his shoulder. Eventually Brett moved forward touching the back of each seat. — Ten minutes, he said.

The reception at the tiny airport was a miniature of their arrival in the country two days before. Heat struck the tarmac and was reflected back. Officials greeted them, wives were introduced. Everyone smiled; nervous smiles, hopeless smiles, smiles of jaw-cracking intensity. Different slender young women placed garlands around the same bent necks. A large corsage of white and pink orchids was pinned to the front of Julie's sack-like garment by the smallest garland lady. Photographs were taken. They moved across the shimmering runway to the helicopter which squatted nearby. — Outside or in? Mike asked her. — Outside. The pragmatism of helicopters; up, along, down. No messing about.

The young pilot checked their safety belts, smiling and gentle. The smile snapped off, his face was blank and tough as he climbed into his seat and started the engine. They lifted rapidly. Julie stared down at the viridian landscape. People below pointed and waved, paddy fields became patches, farmers working on the terraced hillsides became toys then disappeared. The wind rushed by tugging and ripping at her corsage as she leant out. After a few minutes the whole thing broke loose and hurtled downwards. Her laughter tossed after it. — I've lost it! she shouted at Mike. — What? — Never mind!

She thought of the falling flowers. Imagined them drifting down, spiralling gently till they brushed the ground at the feet of a farmer, his wife, a spellbound child. Undamaged, a gift of no value, but perfect. A sign. In reality of course they would hurtle downwards, self-destructing, crashing to a pulp. The wire could damage even. Mike leant over to her. — *What've* you lost, he yelled.

*

— What're you doing at Christmas, Julie? Em asks on the way back from the canteen. What I'm doing at Christmas is holing up, burrowing deep as a mutton bird into El Deserto, so I have to think quickly.

— Uh, I say for time. — Come to us, she says. I want to tell her how it happened but there is no time and anyway I can't remember. I want to tell her I can't remember.

I remember leaving, I can see the shape of the broken bit on the bottom step as I lugged my suitcase, but I can't remember a lot of it. We had a major row I remember that. We didn't often have them. We were more subtle. After ten years we knew how to slip the knife in. Expert anatomists, we operated with wrist-turning speed, our triumph the shock on the face of the loved one, the lover who didn't know he/she had been stabbed till the pain. We used the tools of the intimate; old sour jokes, resurrected pomposities, small meannesses. You can't hone those weapons on strangers.

I can't remember how it started even. It was the Sunday

after we got back from that place. I can see the colours. Dark blue sweatshirt, old white shorts. Something about fruit juice cartons and how you can never get into the things. I can see the orange oblong in his hand as he shouts at me. See myself crouched behind the table, clutching the life-support formica. Hear the noise ricocheting around the Living Decor Kitchen as I duck his blistering rage and slam it back.

Mr Kelson, the caretaker, is employed by the absentee owner. I admire Mr Kelson because he is so tidy. He is neat and trim, his work shorts knife-pleated. Rubbish is anathema to him. If it is small enough he stabs it with a spike then scrapes the spike clean against the side of a small cart he made himself. It is almost a child's trolley but not quite. He trims the edges of the grass alongside the concrete paths with a wheel like a giant pastry cutter on a long handle then stows the shavings in his cart. Again it looks almost fun but not quite. Mr Kelson shakes me by the hand and wishes me a Merry Christmas. His hand is hard and bony, cool to the touch. He wears a cap with Hawaii Hotcha printed on it in red, a gift from his son who has made it (lifestylewise) in the States. Mr Kelson shoves it back on his head, the yellow duck's bill peak aims at the blazing sky. He looks at me thoughtfully. — I hope it goes off all right for you, he says. — Christmas and that.

Christmas is over now so I am relaxed, lying prone on my pink bed reading an article about where people go to buy the best of things they wish to buy in Auckland, when Mike comes up my step. I fall upright. — How'd you know I was here? I hiss. We stare at each other, two cornered animals.
— Oh God, he says.

— Christmas is over, I say.

He looks blank. — Christmas?

I have been wary over Christmas.

— All that food, he says still staring.

My mind skitters, skids, runs down. I hear my voice.
— Where did you go?

— Sandra's.

I believe him. Sandra the sister, the wife and mother, presiding calm and munificent over mountains of hot food, her hands busy with portions, her eyes begging seconds from her torpid husband, her tense skinny children.

My knees start to shake. I flop onto my bed. Mike sits on the divan. Our knees almost touch. His slip-on shoes are new, shiny and black as jackboots. A blowfly buzzes, flinging itself at the tiny window. I open the window and flop it out.

— Get out, I say to Mike.

There is a knock on the door. We stop shouting. Mike looks at me. My house. I open the door. Mr Kelson stands outside. Beside him, no higher than his chest, is Mrs Millrod, her sideways face worried, her hands clasped tight against her flowered front.

— Everything OK then Julie? says Mr Kelson.

— Fine. Fine, I say. — This is my husband Mike. Mrs Millrod my neighbour. Mr Kelson the caretaker.

Mike is already on his feet. He shakes Mr Kelson's cool hand. He steps down onto the beaten grass to greet Mrs Millrod. Her joy beams up at him. Mrs Millrod. Mrs Millrod.

Conversation is relaxed. Mike admires the condition of El Dorado. Mr Kelson says it's not easy with the casuals. Mike says he can understand that. Mrs Millrod smiles. They leave soon, after more handshakes, more smiles. Their departure is muted, tactful.

I have to say something . . . — Do you remember the shanties by the motorway in that awful place?

The pupils of his eyes have contracted in the sun.

— I didn't mean it, he says. — I didn't mean it.

The hand on my shoulder weighs a kilo.

— Julie, he says.

I am tired beyond words. I am drowning in a deep river of sleep. I almost yawn. The effort of swallowing the thing exhausts me further.

—Forget it, I say. — Forget it.

Poojah

When I was a small child our neighbour Miss Messerson took me by the hand and led me into a large bedroom in her house next door where she lifted me up to show me the body of her mother as she thought I would like to see her as Mother looked so beautiful. I have little memory of this experience other than a sensation of wishing to be elsewhere. Not an uncommon childhood sensation.

It surfaced, for example, every Christmas when we were taken to do poojah to Baby Jesus at an ivy-covered house in the Cashmere hills. The house belonged to Mrs Carter. The best part was the stone frog on the entrance porch, more throttled by ivy each year, but available for stroking if requested. It had to be sought out by Mrs Carter's daughter Mildred.

We shuffled in with our parents, my father solemn, my mother smiling. We wore our best clothes which I could recognise today. For several years I wore a white summer jersey knitted in moss stitch embroidered at the plain yoke with pink worm roses, and a white pleated skirt. My brother wore blue shorts, a white shirt, a miniature navy blue spotted bow tie and the expression of an enraged bull. He was a heller, my brother, and very beautiful. His curls rioted, his eyes blazed, and his dark lashes were so long they became a nuisance later when he had to wear glasses. Perhaps that was part of his problem, but impaired vision or not, Duncan was 'difficult'. We were both under duress at poojah. He from rage, I from embarrassment.

When we had all assembled, shuffled our feet, found the frog, we mooched in and greeted Mrs Carter. The room into which we were herded was small and dark, the heavy velvet curtains pulled against the blazing sun. A huge Christmas tree touched the gabled roof, the air was thick with incense. Mrs Carter, whose ankles were so swollen she could scarcely walk, sat filling a wide chair in the shadows to the left of the tree. I know now because I have been told that she was a wise, well-educated woman of a kindly disposition. I saw the smile but it was no help. She was the spider occupant and we were trapped in deep scented misery.

Mildred Carter did the marshalling. When I heard of 'marshalling yards' during the war I thought of Mildred. What age was she? Forty, fifty? We had no way of knowing and anyhow it was irrelevant. She was grey all over. Her grey hair sprung outwards from her small head. Her dress was also grey. She wore no make-up and her smile wore thin as the afternoon progressed. But she had a fair turn of speed which she demonstrated whenever Duncan or Evan Morrison made a break for it. One or the other (they never combined their talents as far as I can remember) would fling himself down the parched grass slope, screaming, but there was no escape. Cornered, they would be 'led' back by Mildred, who never even puffed, and handed over to their respective mothers for mopping up while their respective fathers stared thoughtfully into the middle distance and I wished to be somewhere else.

Day after day, week after week through the hot summer the ceremony continued. There were usually no more than one or two other families present with their offspring as Mrs Carter disliked crowds. Mr Morrison, large and jokey, was always present when we were with his gentle wife and Evan; six years of skin and bone and quivering tension. Sometimes the bland Parkins were there with their stolid twins who seemed unravaged by the proceedings. Sometimes the creaking Dr Perry and his sad wife, and daughter Jane who we had to be nice to. — *Why* Mum? — Sssh Duncan.

— Everybody here. A statement of fact from Mildred, not a question. She adjusted the needle of the gramophone and the choir of King's College Cambridge burst into the heat and incense with the injunction *Oh come all ye faithful*. The parents stood with their backs to the wall, their children either rebellious, or resigned or calm (and who could tell which). Sometimes a baby cried, always Evan whimpered.

— Now, said Mildred. — Who will poojah first? You Patricia? Good girl. Patricia would toss back her thick hot plait, take the censer from Mildred's outstretched hands and kneel in front of the nativity scene assembled at the base of the Christmas tree. There was a camel with a nodding head. Nothing was to scale. The Christ Child lay big as a shepherd. A lamp was the same size as a Nubian King, a tiger smaller than a lamb. Styles differed also. Attenuated figures handcarved in Germany stood or lay alongside strange garish-coloured animals from Mrs Carter's East. I would like to say that this eclecticism symbolised for me the whole world but this was not so. I thought it a mess, and a hot mess and I wished to be gone, especially when Mildred turned to me with a smile and said — Beth? Assisted by a poke between the shoulder blades from my mother I fell on my knees. I realise now that poojah is a Sanskrit word meaning a ritual act of worship. We were meant to make the sign of the cross, then, helped by Miss Carter, strike the censer three times against its base — and say in clear tones, — Happy Birthday, Baby Jesus. I never achieved the clear tones but I did better than Evan who panicked yearly. — Happy slappy, happy . . . Maam, he screamed, stumbling to his feet, the smoking censer abandoned on the carpet to be snatched up by the nearest adult as he blundered to bury his shamed head against his mother's thighs, to feel the stroking hand, the Sssh Evan. It's all right. There, honey, there.

Duncan did better. In later years when I was still longing for extinction he grasped the censer and made poojah with grace and dignity. I merely thought he'd sold out.

Tea happened afterwards in another shadowed room. Why was it called the House of Sunshine, when the sun was so rigorously excluded? We followed Mrs Carter, who hobbled on two sticks. We trailed through dark passages, up a flight of steps to the dining room to be greeted by the black variety of Christmas cake which no child will eat and animal biscuits which we considered beneath us but ate anyway. I suppose our parents were there. Evan Morrison usually pinched me in a friendly way on my behind. Though perhaps I am confused, it may not have been friendly at that age, but he is not alive to ask. Once we escaped and rolled down the bank clutching our yellow pigs and pink lions watched by the startled Parkins. But only once.

What was it all about? A simple celebration of the Adoration by two devout High Anglican churchwomen, in which we were all invited to join, especially the children. But

Poojah

why poojah? Had they lived in India? Presumably, but why the amalgam? And why were we never told?

All I know is that when we piled into the stifling car and my father drove home, his eyes straight ahead, and my mother sang:

I fell into a basket of eggs
And all the yellow splashed over my legs
Yip I addy I ay, I ay
Yip I addy I ay

I never felt happier in my life.

The Girls

All the girls could kill. Their father taught them. — Stand
astride grip with the knees yank the head, knife in. Speed's
the thing. They smell blood.

All the girls did too. Blood, the sour smell of concrete
and later the stench of guts. A gantry with a pulley was
positioned above the sump. There was a tap with a length of
blue hose attached. A naked light bulb hung from the ceiling,
the shadows were sharp. Years later when Ellespie saw an
interrogation scene in an old black-and-white she smelled the
shed and moved her lover's hand from her thigh. His beard
loomed. — What's wrong? She shook her head and stared at
the face of the victim which filled the screen.

The killing shed was an exact square of concrete blocks. It
squatted beside the woolshed in direct line with house.

— Couldn't you screen it or something their mother said.

— Plant a bloody rose on if you like said their father but
she never got round to it.

She came from Argyll, a small woman with thin ankles
and tiny paw-like hands. He fell without volition, a sinker
plummeting. She maddened him, called him insane names,

seemed amused, teased him with distance and flair. Sometimes in despair he could almost imagine grabbing that red-blond bush of hair, twisting it at the back, jerking.

— You'll have to marry me Elspeth he said.

She did, and hated everything about the place: the mountains which lay too near, slanting in long diagonals against the sky; the trim little cottage which became less so as the hot pink paint faded to blush and the tide of grime mounted.

She chanted the Highland expatriate's song to herself, grinding it into her mind. 'Yet still the blood is strong, the heart is Highland. And we in dreams behold the Hebrides.' Except that the blood was not and the dream an ache in the mouth.

Why did she marry him then? She knew her own mind, a source of interest and pleasure to her, so why had she drifted into it? Not because he insisted, demanded, standing with legs tensed as though he might spring at her. — I don't think I love you, I mean . . . He slammed his hands together. — Love! Christ, I've got enough for a harem he said.

She tried with the girls. — I did try. She had dreamt of a romance in which she starred as Mother; of lovable infants tumbling at her feet, not four lean and hungry whippets. Shona, Fiona, Ellespie and Jean.

He slaved on the place which was barely a viable unit. Shona heard and told them. — The farm's barely a viable unit she whispered. Oh, they said. He was a hard worker. Elspeth, even her mother in a brief disastrous visit, granted him that dour colonial accolade. She watched him one evening as he fed the dogs from the dog tucker safe which stood on four legs beside the chopping board. His knife slashed and hacked, she could see it glinting in the dusk as the dogs strained at the ends of their chains, their barks screaming yelps, their leaping bodies twisted. He had been out since six that morning with one brief marauding stop at the house for food. Elspeth's mother watched in silence till each dog had been flung its share. She turned from the window and plonked stiff-kneed on the flowered sofa, pulling the knitting needle from the coil of hair on her neck. — He's honest, he's a hard worker, you married him now get on with it she said.

Elspeth knew she had tried to shatter the cool mother tradition she had been born to. Had tried to break the mould, which unless smashed, sets each daughter in her mother's attitudes. As soon as she pushed each daughter out to scream its arrival into the world, she tried. She cuddled each newborn, as emaciated as a Christ child in a fifteenth century Dutch painting. She suckled each grabbing mouth. She smiled and cooed at each set of grey eyes which stared unblinkingly at the centre of her forehead. And she gave up.

She took to little rests. As long as the girls could remember mother had a rest each afternoon. After lunch, once she'd got him out of the house again. Shona, Fiona, Ellespie and Jean, called Jinny, learnt early that you got them out of the house, though Dad leapt always, his hand reaching for his yellow towelling hat from the top of the fridge as she stacked the dishes and covered them with a tea towel, tucking in the corners because of the blowies.

— Look after Jean she said as usual one day in the school holidays. — I'm going to have a rest.

— Ssssh Shona warned as they crept beneath the bedroom window.

— Ssssh snarled Fiona and Ellespie, lips contorted against

wrinkled noses with the effort. Jinny picked up the cat which emitted the ghost of a burp. It followed them across the chaffy grass most afternoons to the woolshed where they played involved and hierarchical games. — And Jinny can be the baby they said. Jinny rebelled. She was punting her behind along the oiled floor beneath the wool sorters' table crooning to herself. Her scream brought them running. She had gouged her hand on the rusty shearing comb which hung from her palm. Shona yanked it out, blinked at the beads of blood welling to streams, picked up the hiccoughing child and ran. She was half way across the home paddock before she remembered. When Elspeth came out she found them all waiting on the back step, Jinny asleep in her sister's sharp arms, a stained tea towel around the hand.

— Why didn't you wake me!

— Shona's pinched face was blank. — You were having a Rest. You said!

— Mad . . . Mad.

Ellespie wanted to know what her mother did there. The girls were down at the creek after school, hunting for koura and she was sick of it, turning over stones and nothing there. — I want to go to the toilet she said. — Go here said Fiona. — No. She left them squatting in the chill water and ran up the hill, skipping the cowpats with precision. She dragged an empty apple box from the wash house, scrambled onto it and peered in. Her eyes met those of her mother who lay on her side of the bed, eyes open wide, wide. Ellespie toppled off the box and ran. Not even reading!

This one's the reader, Dad told Miss Pennelly, his hand on Ellespie's shoulder at school evenings to discuss progress. Their mother had gone too, originally.

— The Scotch, not Scottish, Scotch, have always known the importance of Education. Their public school education, and I mean *public*, is the best in the world. Bar none she told them firmly. — My mother is Scotch said Ellespie. — Scottish corrected Miss Pennelly. Ellespie let her have it.

But again she drifted from them. As it were. — You go Stan. Not tonight. I couldn't. She smiled up at him, her hair bright as sparks under the lamp though dimmed to faded ginger by day. He stood silent, hair slicked back. All ready. A muscle at the left side of his mouth jerked sideways as he shrugged into his whiskery sports coat. — All right you lot. Into the car. Not you Jinny. He lifted her from his feet, clenched her to him for a moment then handed the kicking child to Elspeth. — I want to go too! Legs threshing, stick arms thrust upwards to deny purchase, Jinny 'performed'. Elspeth dropped her on the floor and picked up the fair isle pattern as the door shut. She kept them all in jerseys. — You're too little she told the sodden heap bawling at her feet, her words drowned by the noise of the Chrysler's gears crashing as it slammed down the track.

All the girls had to earn the right to work with him.

— I'll show you once. Right? he'd say, and they nodded. Many things they knew because they had always known, the same way they knew the door at the Farmer's Co-op with the powder puff and mirror was theirs and Dad's the one with the top hat. They knew which way each gate opened, how to saddle up, whether it was a stray sheep on the Tops, or that plant thing. How to feed out. He yelled at them, his face twisted with rage, if they did anything stupid. He never praised them, except Jinny. Occasionally there was a wink as the last pen filled or they were cut out in the sheds. Or as they jolted home in silence, the scent of horse sweat heavy in the air. Killing was the last thing he taught them, when they were about fifteen.

Ellespie was older. — I don't want to. I just don't want to. Shona and Fiona had their own knives by now which hung in the shed for when they were home.

— You don't have to Ellespie said her mother. She pressed the palm of a hand against her back hair and pushed it into shape.

— It's completely barbaric. I can't think how I ever allowed it.

— You were probably having a rest Mum said Jinny.

— Don't cut your toast Jean. Break it.

— Why?

— Because. Elspeth demonstrated, her little paws tearing the toast into large pieces.

— Of course she has to learn said their father. He was puzzled; searching his wife's face for a clue. — What would you do if I was ill?

Elspeth laughed, toast crumbs spurting from her lips.

— You! You wouldn't know how.

So Jinny the smallest, wiriest of them all learnt next. She reminded Ellespie of a game little Shorthorn calf. Tough orange curls bunched above her forehead. Although nimble, she seemed to stand four square, planted, her eyes steady in her pale face. She came back from the shed the first time in silence. — What was it like? whispered Ellespie. The grey eyes stared as though identifying her. Every freckle showed.

— All right said Jinny.

When they left school Shona and Fiona flatted in town. Shona had style, an unexpected bonus. She cased her angular body in luminous trousers so tight they seemed painted on. Pelvic bones jutted either side of the concave dish of her stomach, her hair was swathed and hidden in scarves. Scarves like those worn by where-are-they-now actresses, though most are dead. Gloria Swanson say. She worked as a receptionist for two years (The Doctor will see you now) then married a young thruster from Christchurch who was giving the place a go to consolidate. Elspeth was slightly in awe of her eldest child. — Shona is a strong woman she said and you could make what you liked of it.

To the end of their days Shona and Fiona remained essential to each other. A matrix of trust and ambivalent memories united them. Happy? Unhappy? They discussed it endlessly. Spent hours telling each other things they already knew.

— Jinny was the rider of course said Shona.

— Oh of course said Fiona.

— I never was.

— No you weren't.

— Still it was fun wasn't it? tried Shona.

Fiona considered her verdict. — W-ell she said.

— I mean a lot of it.

— Oh yes, a *lot* of it.

They wrote frequent letters telling each other what the recipient was doing, as though she had no way of knowing otherwise and would find the information useful. 'It is Thursday and you will be busy with the party for Doug's conference,' wrote Fiona. 'Wednesday so you'll have your spinning group,' replied Shona. Shona 'slipped away for a few days with Fif,' whenever she could manage to park the children.

— Do you think it would have been better if she'd left?

Gone back? she asked one day, her breath puffing a drift of icing sugar from the top of Fiona's Blow Away Sponge. Fiona took a long sip of tea and replaced the cup in its saucer before replying.
— Well there you are. She sighed in elegaic sorrow for all remembered childhoods. — Who's to say? she said.

Fiona had married a high country farmer. She took her knife with her just in case. If Bruce or the shepherd or whoever couldn't kill. But of course it never was needed and rusted, wreathed in fluff behind scuffed shoes, deep in the back of the master wardrobe. Years later she wrapped it in newspaper and took it to the farm tip because of the children. It gave her a weird feeling as she flung it from her. That poem. King Arthur's sword, a hand coming up from the lake. The sword though would otherwise have sunk, whereas she had to clamber onto the uncertain surface of the tip to bury the knife. She covered it with over-age or unidentifiable objects from the deepfreeze clean out which had shared the wheelbarrow ride up from the house. Then lightened, at ease with the world, she pushed the empty barrow down the track in time for the school bus, singing *Jesu, joy of man's desiring* to the surrounding hills.

Shona's knife stayed in the shed. She seldom mentioned the farm. People were surprised. — You! On a farm?

Jinny used hers. She remained on the farm which she never had any intention of leaving. She was sweet as a nut, ageless as unticked time. As her mother drifted further further away her daughter took over the housekeeping as well, such as it was. She slammed a joint of mutton in the oven when necessary. She swept the kitchen floor when the thistle seed puffs in the corners had accumulated to tremulous quivering heaps. She and Stan sat together each evening. Elspeth was in bed by eight. They gave up the television. The picture, never the best because of the mountains, now lurched continuously, rolling them into its world of home life and splattered violence, its marvels of nature, sport, and innovative advertising.

— It's a good advertisement though, said Jinny one night before they flagged the whole thing away in disgust. They stared at a lavatory seat lid quacking between rolls. — You remember a talking lavatory seat.

Stan located his matches and relit his pipe. — You remember the talking seat he said. — Not the product. So it's not.

— Mmm said Jinny. She put out a hand, palm upwards in silent expectation of his box of matches.

The next day she nailed a loop of leather strap either side of the fireplace so she and Stan could hang their feet as they dozed, smoked or listened to The Weather. Shona and Fiona never discussed with Jinny what would happen, you know. Later.

Ellespie never had a knife. It hadn't seemed worth it though she learnt eventually. She continued reading and went North to Training College. The lines on her father's forehead creased in concentration when she showed him the letter. He snapped his glasses back in their case. — Why d'y'want to go up North? he said.

Ellespie felt as though she had been caught red-handed, the jam spoon dripping on the storeroom floor.

— Oh well she said. — You know Stan.

— Know what?

— See the world. All that.

He drove her to the bus in silence but that was nothing new.

*

Everything about it was good. The tugging wind trapped and cornered by buildings, steep short cuts bordered by Garden Escapes, precipitous gullies where throttling green creepers blanketed the trees beneath. And Bruno. Occasionally if she woke in the night when he'd yanked the duvet off her she thought of Stan, how he seemed impervious to heat or cold, an automaton programmed for work.

— My father doesn't trust city men she told Bruno one day. — Christ in concrete he yelled with delight. — Where've you been! It's like living with someone from the Lost City of Atlantis. She twisted the sludge coloured mug so the crack was on the other side. — I don't know about the Lost City of Atlantis she muttered. — I've got a book about it somewhere he said.

He had a book about everything. They lay in bed all Sundays reading, swapping occasionally. — Read this bit. — The man's a wanker. — Yeah but . . . His arms were beautiful hairy triangles to support his thrusting head.

— God I'm hungry he moaned. It was a test, a gamble. Who gave in first, who crawled groaning from the low bed to pull on something and grope to the dairy. She had seen Dustin Hoffman in *Kramer versus Kramer* zip his jeans like that. Not looking.

On Saturdays if they weren't reading or making love they went to the gym. They sweated with the righteous, each cocooned in her/his personal individualised workout programme. Self-absorbed as Narcissus they searched for themselves in ten foot mirrors, faces blank or contorted with loathing not love. They heaved and grunted, pulled and swung. Tab the flab. No gain without pain. Stan, Stan, it's me.

Bruno despised joggers. — Yon Cassius hath a lean and hungry look he roared. She looked it up in the Dictionary of Quotations under Cassius. — Give me men about me that have muscles! He seized her, squashing her nose against his Save the Whales. She loved him heart crutch mind and belly. He was a huge man, a towering hairy giant. His shape filled the doorway outlined in flame from the light in the hall as he groped to the bed and fell on her. — Where's the light. — It's shot she gasped. — Oh well I guess we'll make it. When she thought of Bruce and Doug, oh well never mind.

She wrote careful letters home. — A friend of mine Bevan and I went . . . Bevan, I call him Bruno, says . . . Jinny answered in her large looping scrawl. — Who's this Bevan/Bruno? Stan wrote occasionally, painful lined one-pagers. — It's been hosing down since Mon. But we need the feed. How are your studies? All the best. Dad.

They were discussing abortion in the abstract when the telephone rang.

— I don't approve of it said Bruno, slipping a new insole into his gym shoe.

— You don't what? she said.

— I said I don't . . . He stood up. — OK, OK. I'm coming he snarled. He clumped to the telephone hobbling on one shoe and lifted the receiver.

— Yeah. Yeah she's here. Hang on. He turned and waved the receiver vaguely in the air.

Ellespie slid along the dinette seat. — Who is it?

— Didn't say. He handed her the receiver and plonked down again to concentrate on his insole, smoothing it in place with careful splayed fingers.

— Ellie here.

— Ellespie? The voice was faint. The line bad.

— Jinny! Toll calls, like kisses, were for crises. — What is it? she said.

— Dad. He rolled the truck.

— Is he all right?

— He's dead, the flat voice answered.

— Jinny! gasped Ellespie. Bruno's head lifted. — I'll come straight away.

— You don't have to. Not straight away. Shona and Fif. They're . . .

— I'll come tonight.

— OK. Thanks.

— Jinny?

— Yes.

— How are you?

— I'll meet the plane then, said Jinny. — Unless I hear.

Jinny picked her up at five o'clock. The foothills were unattainable golden lands, the mountains hidden by cloud. The Airport was a paddock equipped with aeronautical essentials. It's air of makeshift impermanence was enhanced by the knowledge that the slab-like hut (office, lounge, conveniences) was opened only once a day for the arrival of this plane. As she came down the steps Ellespie saw Jinny scowling into the sun, hands thrust deep in her pockets. She didn't move to meet Ellespie, kissed her, but avoided her sweeping hug. She picked up her sister's small pack and they marched meshed in silence to the car. This is totally one hundred per cent insane thought Ellespie. — Tell me about it Jinny she said a few minutes later as the Holden swung onto the farm road.

So Jinny told her. How he needn't have gone to town

on Tuesday. Not really. There was nothing vital. Where it
happened. That turn by Berenson's woolshed, I'll show
you. How Stan climbed out, he must have thought he was
all right. I mean he stopped Ivan in the paper car, told him
about the rolling. Ivan had seen the truck anyway, recognised
it of course, checked it was empty. Dad had seemed OK, Ivan
said. He died ten minutes later. Ivan had been very decent.
Everyone had. Rushing over with food. There had been a
postmortem and all that. A haemorrhage of the brain. It can
happen like that sometimes they said. Jinny's voice drained
on, her eyes pulled straight ahead.
    — And how's Mum?
    The eyes flicked at her for a second.
    — Just the same.
    — But does she . . . ?
    — It's hard to know.
    — Jinny does she know he's dead?
    — Oh yes said Jinny. — She knows he's dead. She sits with
him.

    — I have all the arrangements in train Jinny said later, her
mouth grimacing to emphasise the euphemism. — Guess
what the undertaker said! Her laughter was a crow of delight.
Ellespie shook her head in silence.
    — He squeezed my hand said Jinny, and said he regretted
we had to meet in such tragic circumstances! God in heaven!
Do you reckon they do a course?

She told Ellespie that they would have the morning together
before Shona, Fiona and husbands appeared, having made
child minding arrangements. But her room was empty when
Ellespie opened the door early next day.

Ellespie sat with her mother who seemed pleased to see her and asked after her children. — I've always liked the Air Force she said. — There was a camp near us at home. Absolute charmers. Yes. She sat serene and vacant, even her knitting fingers stilled. — Have you seen your Father she said suddenly. — Yes said Ellespie.

She made macaroni cheese hoping she remembered correctly that it was Jinny's favourite not Stan's. She removed his towelling hat from the top of the fridge and hid it in the woolshed behind the pine logs, then corrected this absurdity and put it back.

The coffin rested on small trestles. It stood in the closed-in sunporch beside the lumpy divan, level with the Indian cotton curtains she had made last time. Ellespie gazed at the effigy of her father which lay cushioned in white satin.

The skin was dragged tight over the beak nose, mounded eyelids sealed the eyes. Ellespie stared at the face against the shiny stuff and thought of Jinny.

At twelve thirty she went into the living room. Her mother was sunk in the rioting flowers of the sofa, her hands folded over the Journal of Agriculture open on her knees at Poultry Notes. Ellespie touched one of the still hands. — I'll be back soon Mum she said. I'm going to find Jinny. Her mother's sandy eyelashes blinked. — What's for lunch? she said.

Tracks fanned out from the back door. To the killing shed, the vegetable garden, the garage. Jinny's old roan was tethered to the fence by the shed, his head hanging. Ellespie ran across the paddock and fell in the door. Jinny was leaning against the wall smoking a cigarette.

— Hi she said.

Ellespie's shoes scuffed the concrete as she moved to her.

Relaxed, indolent, Jinny flicked the butt down the sump and heaved herself upright. She shrugged, the slightest lift of the shoulders. — Oh well.

At the door she turned to Ellespie.

— Come on, she said.

One Potato
Two Potato

Nancy and Helen spend the summer in each other's pockets. Helen's grandmother tells them so. Long bleached days pile up behind them, flat as the town in which they live. An Irish colleen, Nancy's father calls her, stamping the foot-operated automatic pressing machine — press, phouugh, suck, clang — PRESS. Nancy hears it sometimes in her dreams, a lullaby for a motherless child, another of her father's endearments. He sings Nancy with the laughing face though this is sometimes muddled with Jeannie with the light brown hair. He owns the only dry cleaning shop in the town. A dusty lancewood slants in the window, a river of sweat clamps the shirt to his back. Helen's mother, Mrs Ellison, is clean and thus a good customer for things she can't wash. — You'll tell me, Mr Davenport won't you? Promise you'll tell me when I reach the stage of throwing food down my front? Mr Davenport stares and promises.

He likes Mrs Ellison. All his ideas of a fine woman are melded and joined in her contoured form. She doesn't flop about in the heat like some of them. In fact she gives up scanties in the hottest weather but who's to know. She seems so certain so real. In a sense she comforts him for the nervousness he feels about his inability to remember his dead wife Kath. Well he *remembers* her of course but somehow . . . He shuts his eyes and sees her small head sunk in the pillow. Hears her voice calling. Don. Don. But it all went on too long. He can't remember her clearly enough before then, not when she was well that is, laughing, running even. It worries him. He feels cheated and watches Nancy with particular care as she leaps through life. — That's my girl he cries at the Main School Athletic Sports. — Have a go then Nance! And Nancy wins always, legs flashing, black curls damp on her forehead as she snatches the lime-green bottle from Helen's hand at the finishing line. — Don't drink it Nancee it's sou-er, warns Helen, but Nancy loves the stuff, flinging it down her throat till she chokes, wiping the back of her hand across her mouth like a boy.

They have known each other since Nancy slithered her bottom around the vinyl floor of the shop. Later they played together, dressing and undressing blank-faced dolls and avoiding Mr Davenport's feet. If he could see his way clear he would press the crumpled scraps of garments. Their eyes level with the clamping press, Nancy and Helen waited. — But Dad it's . . . — That's it Nance. It was better than nothing, they could see that, but the doubt remained.

Dolls fade; bikes increase the girls' range. Nancy skims back and forwards across the town to play at the Ellisons. She is welcome as Helen is an only.

Mrs Ellison's face wilts at home. The effort of keeping things nice is unremitting. Clothes flap on the line in segregated precision, a stray sock tossing among the skirts is repegged where it belongs. As soon as the clothes are dry Mrs

Ellison snatches them from the line, flaps them slaps them till they lie subjugated and flat in the basket, all billowing flight extinguished. Sighing, Mrs Ellison heaves the cane basket up the back steps and begins damping. She sprinkles water from her hand, flipping the parched clothes in endless baptisms from an enamel font. Then she irons.

Mr Ellison is rarely visible. Occasionally if Nancy stays late she hears him enter the front door, hears his fluting call. — I'm home. Mrs Ellison says nothing. She stamps the iron at the board. Her husband walks into the kitchen, stroking black strands of hair across his scalp.

— Oh there you are.

— Where did you think I'd be?

—I think I'd better be off Mrs Ellison.

— Right Nancy.

And Nancy leaps to her bike and pedals home so fast the pedals spin from beneath her feet. — Dad Dad I'm home! She buries her head in his hairy beautiful neck. — Give us a chance matey he says, moving the beer to his other hand.

Mrs Ellison's mother, Marjorie, often sits with her daughter during the ironing. She sits upright on the kitchen stool, hands attentive in her lap, her feet encased in navy shoes which mould themselves to her bunions. Occasionally she sags then slaps herself upright again. Her own husband died in his prime, far too young, carried away by incompetence at the hospital. A photograph in the lounge shows a man like a tree trunk holding a blurred Helen. Helen is apprehensive of her grandmother. — Shut your mouth child. And Helen tries, snorting through her blocked nose till she bursts and she and Nancy fall about in helpless delight. — There's no call for that says Marjorie, but this is worse and Helen and

Nancy rush out the back, bare feet scudding. Mrs Ellison
still irons. Marjorie hitches up her skirt, stretches out her
legs, peers at them then smooths her skirt down again. She
picks a green thread between thumb and forefinger, rolls it
into a tiny ball and drops it surreptitiously onto the floor. It
doesn't show.

 — They tell me you've moved him out she says.

Mrs Ellison licks her fingers and flicks the iron. The spit
hisses to nothing.

 — Who told you that she says.

 — I heard.

 — It's all over town too I suppose that he snores so hard
I can't get a minute's sleep. Her face is hot, her hands
busy.

 — Your father snored.

 — Not like him.

 — Worse.

 — Never.

Newly ironed clothes have the cleanest smell in the world.
There is no sound but the hissing sweep of the iron.

 — Moved him out snorts Marjorie.

Mrs Ellison snaps off the iron. — He's got a lovely room,
all redecorated you want to see it? Her mother is on her feet
jerking her skirt into position. She gives herself a little shake.
— Yes, she says. The progress upstairs is followed by Nancy
and Helen who have trailed in for a drink from the tap.
There is silence as they climb the figured carpet except for
the murmured skipping chant Nancy has on the brain. One
potato two potato three potato four.

 — Mine's done up too says Mrs Ellison. She flings open
the door of the master bedroom, a large room filled with
light. Nancy has not seen this room before and is pleased

with the dressing table set on long spindly legs, its top covered with bottles which scatter the light. Nancy fingers one. Helen concentrates on trying to breathe through her nose. Her grandmother is silent, registering the fact that there is now only one single bed in the room. Its bedspread is quilted birds, its eiderdown restuffed and puffed. — Never in all my days says Marjorie.

Now Mrs Ellison is showing a smaller room. Her husband's fly-tying equipment is neatly arranged on a small table. A miniature vice holds the hook of a Hammill's Killer. The body is formed from red wool twisted and tied with yellow, the side feathers are grey partridge dyed green, tied in killer fashion, a fluff of black squirrel fur for the tail lies beside the vice. Hairy Dogs, Red Setters, Mrs Simpsons, and Grey Rabbits are arranged in boxes made for the purpose which lie behind the vice. Mr Ellison is one of the best amateur fly-tiers in the district and his creations are much in demand and sworn by. Helen likes to watch him working but Nancy finds it boring and Mr Ellison finds Nancy a Fidgety Phil. Mr Ellison's knobbled fingers weave and poke, his sharp-pointed scissors snip at the exact spot, strands of appropriately coloured wool hang around his bent neck. He whistles 'If I had a rose from you/For every time you made me blue/I'd have a room full of roses', and is happy. A cigarette lighter in the form of a miniature Toyota car sits alongside his ashtray. You press the wheel and flame spurts from the bonnet but Nancy has seen this before. Mr Ellison's sister brought it back from Japan. It is unexpected on several counts.

The room is refurbished with red curtains slashed with brown. A disintegrating cane chair piled with floppy cushions sits in front of the table. — He won't let me get *rid* of the thing says Mrs Ellison, giving Mr Ellison's string-binding job on the back leg a nudge with her open-toed sandal. It does mar the decor but Marjorie is not interested.

— Your father would never she says. — Outside girls, says Mrs Ellison and Nancy and Helen are glad to.

— One potato two potato three potato *FOUR*. Five potato six potato seven potato *MORE!*

Mrs Ellison and her mother return to the kitchen. Marjorie would like a cup of tea but Mrs Ellison is still smarting. She resumes the ironing in silence.

— Do you blind bake your Rough Puff? asks Marjorie. Mrs Ellison glances up from Nancy's summer gym.

— For the bottom you mean?

— Yes.

Mrs Ellison gives the gym a quick shake and hangs it on a hanger on the back of the door. — Always, she says firmly. — Don't you?

But Marjorie is not caught out. — Oh yes, she says. — I don't know about this new stuff though. It sogs whatever.

— I never have any problem, says Mrs Ellison.

Marjorie gives in. — How about a cup of tea? she says. Mrs Ellison glances up from a pink towel in simulated surprise. — Oh if you *want* one she says.

— I'll make it. Marjorie knows her own mind. — Where are the afghans? she says.

— In the cupboard.

The eager hiss of steam continues.

One of the reasons Helen is apprehensive of her grandmother is that she must see her almost every day. She is taking piano and bikes around to practice on the upright Bentley in the front room of the box-like house where Marjorie lives alone.

Family wedding groups line the walls, women stand sheathed like arum lilies beside large men. In one of the photographs Helen is a flowergirl. She is not a success. Her mouth hangs open and she gazes at her posy as though it might explode. Helen senses that her grandmother wants something from her but she is unable to work out what and this makes her nervous. One of Marjorie's treasures is her collection of old seventy-eights. Bing Crosby oozes and warbles through the still house. 'I'm dreaming of a white christmas' he confides. Marjorie is adamant. — They don't make music like that now she tells Helen.

Helen swoops her bike around the corner of the house and finds her grandmother sitting on the back porch drying her hair. It is long and falls over her shoulders in streams. — You look like a princess, Gran! — Rapunzel, Rapunzel let down your golden hair but yours is silver she says, pleased to find life imitating books. Her grandmother stares up at the skinny child, her speckled hand touches Helen's face for a moment. Then she stamps herself upright and twists her hair into a french roll. Her hands move deftly right left one two; the pins stab in. — It's dry now she says.

Mrs Ellison has organized a cottage at the beach. Helen's hands are twisted in supplication. — Please. Can't she come Mum?

Mrs Ellison is bland, — I'm very happy to have Nancy at any time you know that.

— Well? Helen shuts her mouth, breathless with hope.

— What if Mr Davenport asked you to stay at Turangi again? You said you were homesick.

Helen is silent for a moment but desperation drives. — I needn't go.

Her mother stares. — What would you say? How would you get out of it she asks.

The Turangi experience resurfaces. Helen sees herself as though she is circling above the scene like the blowfly which droned around the centre light each night as she snivelled into her lumpy pillow — homesick for what?

Mr Davenport went to the pub while Helen and Nancy read comics in the Holden. He brought drinks out for them, laughing and teasing his girls as they snatched at the dripping cans. Once a mate took the orders, a smiling man with a good solid gut beneath his T-shirt. He yelled across the vast car park to Mr Davenport who cupped a hand to his ear in exaggerated concern for clarity. — Fanta for a pretty girl and a *what*?

There was something about the place, felt in the air, trapped in the cobwebby corners of the bach. When Mr Davenport looked at her like that. When Nancy climbed into his bed in the icy mornings and she hung back. Come on Hen, he said, it'd freeze a brass monkey out there, hop in. But Helen remained shuffling her bare feet on the coir matting. She watched Mr Davenport scratching the exuberant black hair which sprouted from the neck of his striped pyjamas. He stared at her. His voice was gentle.

— You'll swallow a fly one day Hen you know that?

— I want to go home mumbled Helen.

— All right Mum.

Mrs Ellison smiles. How about the girl Barwick she says.

— No.

Helen thinks of Nancy. Of how she runs. Sees her hair always in a mess, snagged and tangled at the Baths after lengths. Sees her outside the Aztec Milk Bar that very day as she steps across the gutter to the footpath, a dancing movement, toe turned out like Miss Stringer at Ballet, not that either of them go. Nancy wouldn't be seen dead.

Nancy is still in Helen's mind as she skids her bike to a halt at the Ellison's back door after practice. Mr Davenport is standing close to her mother. He jumps, snatches a handkerchief from his pocket and scrubs his face. — Deliveries, deliveries, he mutters through his blue Eskay.

— Nancy told me you'd dropped deliveries. Helen is positive. — As from last month. She told me.

Mr Davenport is delighted. He laughs loudly. — Well there you go. Just a few specials.

Mrs Ellison is also laughing. — How many she says.

Mr Davenport flings his arms in the air with joy just like Nancy. He is panting with shared laughter. — Wouldn't you know eh wouldn't you know. He hugs Helen. — You'll do me he says. He riffles her hair then turns and runs around the corner still laughing.

Mrs Ellison's laughter stops. — Oh well she says and moves to the stove.

One potato two potato three potato *FOUR*. Helen has got it on the brain now.

The telephone rings trilling down the hall as Helen comes in from practice next day. She lifts the receiver and stands silent as a man's voice breathes at her.

— Is your Mum there?

Helen clutches the receiver tightly.

— No, she lies.

She listens with her shoulders hunched as Mr Davenport's words stream on. Her hand moves to the back of her neck.

— No, she says. — No. Don't. She drops the receiver back

71

and runs into the kitchen. Her Mother is poking the joint. She slams the oven door shut and straightens up with the skewer clenched upright in her hand.

— Who was it? she says.

— Wrong number. Helen knows the lie is hopeless. She scents defeat, sees Nancy leaping away. Mrs Ellison drops the skewer in the sink and turns to her daughter. — Helen? she says. It is a statement of intent. The light from the dying sun is blinding. Helen moves slightly.

— A man, she says.

— What did he want?

— Sexual intercourse, says Helen. — On the telephone.

— On the telephone! Mrs Ellison throws back her head and laughs. Helen's legs are heavy, her arms hang. She stares unhappily at the strong cords of her mother's outstretched neck.

Mrs Ellison is still laughing. She laughs and laughs and laughs. Tears spurt from her eyes. She flops onto the kitchen stool and wipes her eyes with the patchwork oven mitt. Helen's mouth hangs open, her eyes are on her mother's face. She is saved.

— Oh my God gasps Mrs Ellison. — On the telephone.

Egypt is a Timeless Land

The young man beside her was determined she should see them. He seized her hand and pointed it at the window as though this would achieve contact.

— See? he said. — See? Look. There! He was almost prostrate in her lap as he leaned across, willing her to see, insisting with force that she didn't miss the pyramids. The hair in his ear was soft and downy. His face was solemn with the intensity of his commitment.

— You're not looking he said, his face a foot from hers.

— I am!

— Well?

She squinted past her husband in the window seat.

— There, do you mean?

— No!

Peter's eyes lifted from *War and Peace*. He always read it on long air trips. Invaluable. Time flies, he told people. He smiled at the young man. — Give it up, he advised.

There was something far below on the brown flatness. A sort of geometrical smudge, two or more.

— I see them, she cried. — There!

— Yes!

Sheila and the young man Grant (in computers, business trip) leaned back and smiled at each other with relief.

— Thank you, she said. — I'd never have spotted them.

— Oh well, said Grant. — That's OK.

She put her hand on the hefty thigh stretching the trouser fabric beside her. He glanced at her then moved the leg slightly. She was staring straight ahead at the back of the seat in front of her.

Grant seized his other ankle with both hands and jerked the knee to his chin several times, then repeated the process with the leg from which she snatched her hand. — Pity to miss them, he said, pausing for a moment to reassure the face beside him.

— While they're there, said Peter from the battle of Borodino. He glanced across at Grant as though seeing him for the first time in ten thousand miles. — Did you see that a bit fell off the Sphinx? he said.

Grant leant forward in excitement. — Now? he gasped.

Peter shook his head and picked up his book. — Months ago, he said. — Huge. Four hundred tonnes. You'd better be quick.

Grant looked at him warily. There was no response. Sheila smiled. Grant continued his in-flight exercises, his face tense with the concentration of one who knows he is on to a good thing.

Peter yawned hugely and shifted his buttocks.

The drinks trolley appeared from the pantry, clanking beneath the prepared face of an air hostess. — Thank God muttered Peter. Grant didn't drink but he could go a Coke.

*

Only the canteen staff trapped behind glass and carbohydrates seemed calm. The first-years sat on tables, their scarves discarded on the floor among spills and pieces of sodden bun. Someone screamed, the sound slicing the background din.

Peter pushed the debris to one side of a littered table and tore off his jacket. His striped cotton shirt was soft and beautiful. He flopped onto the chair, rubbing his hands. — Aah, he said. — This is the life.

Sheila watched his jaws clamp the rubbery bun. The unclamped bit parted like joke lips. Mock cream seeped out, stained with crimson. — Junk, she said.

— I like it, he mumbled.

— You shouldn't!

— Try and stop me, he said, licking his fingers.

— OK.

He pulled a grey handkerchief from the pocket of his corduroys, slapped it against his mouth, then shoved it back. His smile was wide, generous to her imperfections.

— You try too hard, he said touching her cheek with one sticky finger.

She had come down to Dunedin at the beginning of the year, virtually hand in hand with Tom Rallings. They had been joint Head Prefects at High, led blameless academic lives and opened the Leavers' Ball, clasped alone and together on the empty floor for the first surge of the Leavers' Waltz. Their parents were friends. Until Sheila's father died they played euchre week by week in each others' cluttered houses. Sheila and Tom knew they were lucky. Lucky to be clever, lucky to have won Scholarships, lucky oh especially lucky to have each other in their mothball-scented homeknits to hug and confide in, and what would they have done if they hadn't.

— Throw them *away*, for heaven's sake, said Jill, her first roommate at the hostel.

— But what about the moths!

— Bugger the moths. Jill dropped lean and dangerous onto her moccasin heels and began snatching the white balls from among the woollens in the bottom drawer. — Four! God, I'd rather have the holes anytime. She threw the things down the lavatory where they melted to scented sludge.

Tom was residual, lingering from home, part of her familiar knobbly past. When the sun shone his parents sat side by side on a collapsing sofa on the front verandah acknowledging the world with a wave, a lifted hand.

— Yes, they replied. — Yes. Tom's away now, down south, getting his letters.

He was unable to get into a hostel and lodged with a bitch in London Street. The food was bad, his room pokey, but it had a desk and a view of a patch of grass. He watched the male blackbird and its mate, which he had always thought was a thrush until Zoology 1. He admired their ability to wait, head cocked sideways waiting for the strike. In the meantime he had Sheila.

They were both surprised when Peter Rossiter picked her from the pool. Tom was left, but not without resources. He found Jocelyn all by himself and life continued.

Sheila's mother was not pleased and told her so in the August break. — What have you got against Tom anyhow?

— Aw Mum said Sheila, rubbing the chilblain on her heel. Do shut up and take that *thing* off your head why can't you, she thought, but that was how Mrs Greer did her hair, and very useful it was too, her Curl Tidy. She also had a Breeze Bonnet for the main street where the wind was a whetted knife. Sometimes Mrs Greer wore a navy blue beret with her blue and white striped jersey. She looked like a leery matelot. Sheila was an only daughter after two sons but by no means a gift. A challenge rather, as no woman can expect perfection in male offspring.

Peter won her. He squatted in front of the open fire on Uncle Harry's pouf, arms hugging his knees in *Boyhood of Raleigh* attentiveness to her recent widowhood. — When you're on your own with boys you know, it's not easy, said Mrs Greer. Her round face was belligerent as she stoked the fire, scrabbling and stabbing at its core.

— I'm sure you're right said Peter. He put out a hand for the poker. — I'll do it. She declined his offer. — They make a mess of it see. They just wiggle and the whole flaming thing falls through, she explained.

Peter leant forward. — I *see*, he nodded.

Mrs Greer gazed at his thoughtful face. A lock of hair fell across his forehead as he told her of his night shift job in a Dunedin bakery and his problems with the smalls.

— At that stage, four o'clock in the bloody morning, he said, just when I thought it was all over, he produced the smalls!

— The whats? said Mrs Greer.

— The smalls.

Too difficult. Mrs Greer begs for help, her face anxious. Loving the story, she wants it all. — What are the smalls? she insists.

Peter is on his feet demonstrating. He is dabbing icing on small cakes, slipping a stab of jam between puffs, a blob of mock cream deep in the throats of pastry cornucopias. Mrs Greer can just see his long arms stretching, his hair flopping, his floury hands. She loves him.

Sheila loves him later when he creeps down the icy hall

past Mrs Greer's snores. — This place is like the South bloody Col, he mutters as she welcomes him onto her slumped wire-wove.

He liked Woodville. The shop verandahs which waited for shoot outs, the bar doors which swung. The decor of the Daisy Lee Milk Bar exceeded his hopes, though the Banana Split was a disappointment, as was Glenda's hairstyle. The classic style for Milk Bar ladies, he told Glenda (who was one tough lady according to Sheila's brother John) is piled high in front and hanging down at the back. Glenda didn't thump him. She touched her back hair and smiled.

— Have you ever thought of Christchurch? asked Peter sprawling across the counter. But Glenda knew that one day her prince would come and so he did eventually. Terry Auburn from the Coast.

Sheila finished her degree. She had intended to do Diatetics but the money was better in teaching and they were saving. They married the week Peter qualified. The wedding was all right — well, all right. Peter's parents were divorced. His mother, a shy almost speechless woman, lived in Dunedin and came up nervously with Peter. Peter's father and his new wife Sandra flew up from Christchurch and had to be collected from Palmerston by a groomsman. Everyone did the best they could, though it did make the wedding photographs a bit lopsided as Sandra insisted. — I'm not *invisible* am I? she said adjusting the rake of her hat outside the church door.

The bride and groom sat at the top table flanked by the bridal party. Sheila leant forward reaching for an asparagus roll. — I'm having an asparagus roll, she told Peter. She turned to him quickly, her face half hidden by the stiff tulle.

— Peter, she said. Have an asparagus roll. But his mouth was full of sausage and pastry and he couldn't even smile.

When Sheila won the Scholarship Miss Egerton tried to talk her out of Home Science. — I've nothing against Home Economics, she lied, shaking her puff of thin gold curls, but with your brain . . . You could go *on.* — You can go on in Home Economics, said Sheila. She had no intention of going on, other than to a perfect marriage and sublime motherhood, and Home Economics provided the best resource material available for working towards her goal.

They rented a derelict cottage in Mount Victoria. Sheila ran up curtains, she upholstered and resprung, she painted and transformed when she came home from school each day. She was like something out of an ancient request session, waving Peter farewell from her gingerbread trellis fence each morning, running to kiss him as he bounded up the steps from the money market each evening. They made love on the floor, the kitchen table, in the shower. They were inventive.

And then Simon made three and Sheila never worked again.
 And the parties, oh the parties, and the candles and the fun. She could adapt any recipe. — It's my training she said modestly. Her guests relaxed, motoring through the *Terrine aux foies de volaille* (Yours? Yes. Ttt.) in the knowledge that Sheila would make them well fed and Peter would make them informed and cheerful for he was both and such attributes are transferable.
 But she tried too hard.
 — Fuck the Hollandaise! cried Peter when he found her tense and stiff-fingered, surrounded by empty eggshells and

something yellow and curdled in a double boiler beside the baby's bottle.

— I can't serve the Haplens your bloody trout without Hollandaise, she said rounding on him, the wooden spoon raised.

— Why not? He knew he was on shaky ground.

— Because trout is the most tasteless fish in the whole bloody world and you catch it and I fight with it, she said slamming back to the stove.

He considered kissing the back of her neck but decided against it.

She rescued the sauce with an extra yolk.

— Delicious, murmured Donald Haplen, slipping the fork between pink lips. — Tell me Peter, he said after a pause for mastication. — What do you make of this positive discrimination?

— Oh essential, said Peter. Candlelight suited him. It emphasised the beak of his nose, the bones and hollows of his cheeks. — Essential, he repeated firmly.

— I don't agree at all, said Shona Wooton who had a mind like a man. She'd been told. She drank without favour from Peter's wine glass and her own. He made no comment, bending forward to obtain her permission each time he refilled the glasses. It was difficult to catch her eye. It returned to her glass accompanied by a pretty little flutter of surprise each time she found it replenished.

— The opportunities are there, she said, touching the corners of her mouth with a napkin. — Equal education. It's all *there.*

— When I was teaching at Mangere, said Sheila, who had something to say but was swept away to the hostess bin.

— But surely Peter, in your position, said Donald, his

hand engulfing his wineglass, you must see the *results* of such insanity. Can't read, can't write, can't spell!

— Would you put all that down to positive discrimination? enquired Peter, pushing back his hair. Wise Peter, who is informed and keeps calm and is liberal.

And what about Viet*nam*? cries Joanna Haplen.

The babies, ah the babies. All she had hoped for and more. When Sheila thinks about that time, the years melt to a warm fecund haze of loving and being loved and being essential and minding and caring and knowing how lucky she was. Where was Peter? There, but cackhanded and useless really. Useless. She could do it in half the time and did, her body dipping and twisting to do up Simon, put down Vicki, change and feed Jack and love every minute of it as she should and did.

Peter read to them of course. His head formed the apex of a familial pyramid on the sofa; long father, small intent children, loved books. They tried the new words, testing for taste. Peter was amused when they preferred the meticulous detail of Giles' cartoons to the pale dreamy illustrations of the children's literature Sheila kept up with. He read aloud to each successive baby from his own reading, the infant cradled in the crook of his arm waving starfish hands; Dostoevsky occasionally, when he was giving the guy yet another final chance, but usually hefty paperbacks, in-depth biographies, or sagas at a sweep. The children amused him and he was pleased they seemed to be developing a sense of humour.

— I can do a joke, said Simon.

Peter, horizontal on the sofa, put down *American Caesar* with courteous attention.

— Great, he said. — Tell me.

— Ha ha ha, said Simon.

— Very funny, said Peter, picking up the open book.

— Go and tell Mum.

His son stumped off. Peter heard his solemn Ha ha ha from the open plan kitchen of the new house, but the reply was inaudible.

— What's funny about this one, Dad? — Hang on, said Peter. He hunkered down onto the carpet beside Vicki and the discarded *New Yorker* from the office. A frizzle-faced woman was placing something equally frizzled on the plate of a disheartened looking man beside her. 'I think it's nature's way of telling me to stop cooking,' said the caption.

— It's rather difficult to explain, honey, said Peter. — The lady is tired of cooking.

— Why? said Vicki.

— Just sick of it, I guess. Not like Mum, said Peter, tickling his daughter till she squealed.

They went for picnics. Peter sat in the car and relayed the best bits of *The Goon Show* to Sheila as she ran in and out to the house with cartons for him to stow in the Datsun with meticulous care.

He assumed the horizontal as soon as possible on arrival, thankful to be at one remove from the sodding garden. Sheila stared at the wide sea. I am bossy. I do too much. He supports us all. I nag.

— Where's Jack!

— What? said Peter from beneath the decent sun hat so difficult to find.

— Jack! She was on her feet, leaping across the sand. — Jack!

Simon and Vicki glanced up from their industrious

nimblelegged digging and watering, their togs minuscule and damp around their thighs.

— Here, said Vicki.

— We've buried him, said Simon.

Jack waved, an involuntary gesture. His infant smile was calm. He was covered to his nipples with damp sand. The back of his neck beneath her nuzzling mouth was warm and pleated.

— My darling, my darling, my sweetest love, she muttered.

— I'm sorry. I'm sorry.

— For God's sake, said Peter, lifting the hat for a moment, what are you sorry about now?

She flung herself into everything connected with her dream. Play centre and PTA offered grist. She enjoyed being with people who cared, who were determined to fight, to accept nothing but the best, who gave their time, their effort and outrage to benefit their young. She became Chairperson of both. — Drunk with power, muttered Janet Mill after her defeat over the bus trip to Bushy Park. Of course it wasn't too far, and they must see the kakapo. — We have cars, Sheila explained to Janet who was angrily zipping up her padded windjacket, but a lot of parents haven't.

— Is that right? said Janet.

Simon and Vicki enjoyed Cubs and Brownies until the uniforms were bought and they got sick of it. Sheila spent her days leaping in and out of the car, stowing, fetching and carrying for endless lessons and activities they were good at and which must therefore be encouraged.

— Relax said Peter.

— You spoil them, said her mother. — Where's your own

life? Let the little buggers go by bus. What are you?
— If they have the talent . . . Sheila knew she was right,
armoured in unselfishness.

The children loved staying with Gran even though there
wasn't an electric blanket in sight and the lavatory was
freezing. Its walls had been painted blue and later pink and
there were interesting patterns where the blue resurfaced.
Mrs Greer insisted they travelled to Woodville by bus, as
though this would strengthen moral fibre. One at a time, as
Gran wasn't the girl she used to be, my word. The Manawatu
Gorge with the river swirling below meant they were nearly
there. The cliffs were tied back with wire to keep the rocks
under control.
Gran fried bread and eggs and bacon and sausages and
fritters and to hell with cholesterol which she was appalled to
discover Jack knew about when he was six. — Don't forget
the Daisy Lee, said Peter every time one of his offspring
departed for a holiday with Gran. But it had gone long ago,
turned into a video parlour which didn't last either.
Large uncles with homespun wives welcomed them onto
the farms they managed and fed them home-killed mutton
in warm kitchens. Uncle Frank's had a framed reproduction
of Winston Churchill beneath a high hat, his face clamped
around a cigar, two fingers signifying victory.

Where had it all gone? How had it happened?

Sheila insisted on meals together at the table. (— Sitting up
like vultures. Vicki.)
— A meal is a social occasion, she told them, matching
stubborn face to sullen.

— You try too hard, said Peter into her ear as he turned off the televison.

Simon, who was between flats, sat on a high stool in the kitchen picking at his bare feet. She looked at them in amazement, peels and snatches of yellow parchment skin lay on the cork tiles, his big toes were double-jointed personnel.

— Simon!

He lifted his head. — Yeah?

— What on earth are you *doing*?

His smile was gentle but dangerous. — Picking my feet.

— Well stop.

— Why?

She seized a cloth and opened the oven door. — Because it's disgusting.

— Why?

— Oh shut up, said Sheila, slamming the casserole onto the heat resistant mat on the table. And clean up that mess.

— Some social occasion, yawned Vicki all over the coleslaw.

— Don't be rude to your mother, said Peter, touching his daughter's Pre-Raphaelite tangle of blonde curls. He took the coleslaw from her hands, placed it on the table and patted the back of the chair beside him. She sank down and lifted her head to smile at him.

Sheila clung to Peter in bed at night as they lay beneath the duvet which was always too hot, whatever they said about stroking the feathers down to the bottom. — Why does he? When will they? Why don't they? she begged.

— Relax said Peter. He stroked her till she obeyed, then rewarded her.

His tolerance was wide. He shared the odd roach with Simon as long as Simon aired the room. — Your mother wouldn't like it. His long tapered fingers stretched out to his son in supplication, his snorting laugh was infectious. They had the same taste in comedy and late late horror films, stretched side by side in comfort long after Sheila had huffed off to bed. Nothing shocked him, no joke went too far. Simon and Vicki liked him.

Jack was five years younger than Vicki. A child worried since infancy, his eyes, deep set and blue as Peter's, were troubled. His hair curled as tightly as Vicki's but the colour was a dusty brown. He had his mother's concern to lay hold on life, to get it right. They sat in companionable silence for hours as they drove up to see Mrs Greer who was warmer than she had ever been in her life in an overheated Rest Home in Dannevirke. They were at ease together. — Ma, he called her. — Ma, look at that.

She ran with quick scurrying steps from sofa to chair, snatching one unplumped cushion after another, slapping it into shape and repiling it in a confused harmony of apricot and strong pink against the back of the sofa.

She increased her Meals on Wheels to twice a week.

— How would you feel if I asked you to drive today? she said to Simon who was between jobs as well as flats this time. — Trapped, he said. — Do you have to have your hair tied up in knots like that? You look so *stuck*.

Sheila would never have asked Vicki, who passed every LL.B. exam with languid ease and treated her mother with the contempt she deserved.

— Why don't you do something *real*, Mum? she said one day when the washing machine in her flat had packed up.

— Real like what? said Sheila, clutching the protective colouration of the washing pile to her.

— Something *real*. Sexual Abuse Help Foundation say.

— I do!

— Just money. You're not on the roster.

— Look at me, cried Sheila. — Would you want *me* to . . . ?

— You're just fluffing about, interrupted Vicki. — It's the same with Amnesty. You don't *do* anything.

— I give money. Collect.

— *Collect*. The scorn resurfaced. — You don't even read the magazine.

— I do.

— You burn it. I never see it. I didn't know it existed till the other day.

I will not tell you about the double amputees. I will not describe how the man described how he was blindfolded, given a sedative, how he heard one hand and one foot hit the ground at the same moment. I will not tell you how he said he still has nightmares. As though it could be otherwise and what help is it to the sedated that I share them.

She shoved the washing into the hole and added the soap.

Vicki pressed the button.

Sheila's eyes itched unbearably. — I want to tear them out of my head, she told the hand-stitched lapels of the consultant's three piece suit. He rose quickly, the rounded belly suddenly at eye level. — Come, he said. — Let me examine them.

— You have inadequate tears, insufficient oil in them to lubricate the eyeball. I will give you some drops, said the man, — which will alleviate the problem.

She worked up the story a little. She was always glad of non-controversial material, much of which showed her in a slightly ludicrous light. Simon and Vicki were not interested. Jack patted her arm and told her she could be Miss Inadequate Tears. His siblings groaned. Peter had missed it.

The dim little story trickled away but Jack remembered it. — Hi Inadequate, he greeted her as he crashed up the steps to dump his schoolbag at her feet. — There y'go, Inadequate.

He was more confident. The Seventh Form, he told her, was piss in the hand. He had always been a solitary child, sitting at the kitchen table while she cooked, making them cups of tea in a red pot, licking basins and wringing her with sad tales of rejection by peers which required bracing anecdotes of sticks and stones and ducklings and swans. Suddenly she was surrounded by hairy men in short pants who scarcely glanced at her as they loped through the kitchen shouting for Jack.

She was delighted. — Isn't it marvellous about Jack?

— Nnnn? said Peter. The leader was useless again. Rhubarb rhubarb and the summary tied up with pink ribbon. Pompous clown. He should write a letter. Dear Sir, With regard to your sewage outfall leader, with regard to your leader on sewage outfall . . .

— Jack. He's so happy.

— Good on him.

— I am tired, she told the family doctor, watching his fingers as they stroked the computer keyboard.

He swung round to give her the benefit of his full attention.

— Tired, he said. — That's no good.

— I have never been tired. Never. I can't decide things.

— What sort of things?

— Anything. Which vegetable. Which meat. Pathetic things.

— Do you sleep well.

— No.

He nodded and made a note on the pad supplied by Bayer.

— And? he said.

— I feel all shivery. I forget things.

— What sort of things?

She never had liked him. — Everything, she said.

— Such as?

— I can't decide things, she told Peter.

— Join the club, he said.

She worked on it. She took more exercise, charging up the hill each day like a bee on heat. (Jack.) She considered the gym. She stopped the evening sherry and felt colder than ever.

She put a pad by the bed for essential things she might remember in the night and examined it in the morning.

'Potatoes,' she deciphered. 'Chocolate hail. Get up.' She flung the crumpled scrawl from her as though it was infected.

She ran around the gorse covered hills of Cairo in a dream.

— I have lost my bag, all my papers, my passport, she told the three people who crouched in her brother Frank's cowshed. — Do not bother us, they said. — Which is the way to Cairo? she begged. — I have lost my bag. — That way, said one, pointing up the farm track. — No that way, said the tiny woman in stripes and an organdy collar. — I have lost my bag! she screamed.

Peter shot upright, his hand snatching for the light.

— God in heaven! He blinked at her through lank hair.

— You don't look too hot, What's up? He patted the mattress. — Lie down. There, there, he said giving a quick heave on the duvet before subsiding.

— What's the matter with me? she asked next time. — Is this what they mean by nervous collapse?
He laughed. — I haven't heard that expression for years.
— Breakdown then?
— Such upsets are common in women your age. Though of course I'm no expert, said the smug child.
— Why!
— You are depressed.
— How can I be depressed! Look at Jane Carson. (Tragedy, real tragedy, death and bitter grief.) She's not *depressed*.
— Mrs Carson is a very strong woman. There was silence as they thought of Mrs Carson. He made another note.
— We'll get you an appointment with Nigel Braithwaite as soon as possible. He leant back in his swivel chair, gave a swirl in the direction of the door and stood up. — Medically, he said, you are depressed.

— Nigel Braithwaite wants to see you as well, she told Peter.
— Why? He looked up from the bed, his hand hidden by a shoe.
— I don't know.
— OK. He leant forward and tugged at the laces.
— When? he said, his voice muffled.

They sat side by side in the cramped waiting room. Peter picked up a magazine. — Not many places have *Punch* now, he said. — Too bloody Brit.

They all looked quite sane. An older man. Two women, one plus Sheila. The younger woman lay slumped beside a pallid child with breathing problems. The toes of the mother's track shoes turned up like a blunted jester's. White sheep trekked across her red jersey. The child sucked its thumb, the mother yanked it out without a glance. The child sucked its thumb. The process was repeated. They waited.

The psychiatrist sat miles away scribbling in longhand on a large pad. Sheila kept hefting her chair closer. There were no pictures.

— How can she be depressed if she says she's not depressed? asked Peter. — She's not a fool.

He didn't answer. He kept asking about her parents.

— I can't decide things. I'm cold.

— Sheila's always been such a competent person, said Peter.

Nigel Braithwaite explained about the pills. — Don't worry if they leave a dry taste, a dry *feel* rather. In the mouth.

They picked them up from the local chemist on the way home.

The pills were marvellous. The improvement astonishing.

She was making Hummus for Peter's birthday. ('This well known chick pea dip for nibbling, especially with warm pita bread.')

Peter folded the paper to the entertainment page. — Aah, he said.

— What?

— Nothing. He put down the paper, reaching for his pocket diary and consulted a page. — Ah, he said. — Good. He glanced at his thin oblong watch. — Would you like a drink?

Her face was anxious, her lips pursed above her licked finger. — It always takes more lemon than they say, she said.

He paused on his way to the cupboard. — What?

— Nothing. He lifted the sherry bottle. She shook her head. — No, not with those pill things.

Hummus, Lamb with prunes and apricots, Spicy lentils with zucchini, Eggplant salad, Spinach salad with yoghurt and Coriander bean balls for the feast. 'These interesting little morsels are very tasty although a little messy to hold, so make sure you have plenty of paper serviettes to hand. They can be prepared a day in advance. Do grind your own coriander seeds for this recipe (in a coffee grinder or similar), as the intoxicating fragrance of coriander quickly dissipates.' She rolled another little morsel between her fingers then dipped them in lemon juice as recommended.

Next day she reread the recipe for Lamb with apricots and prunes. It sounded disgusting. Why on earth had she . . . The Eggplant salad was easy, the Spicy lentils with zucchini had better be good. She dried her hands and reached for the next recipe, Spinach salad with yoghurt. She opened the refrigerator and scrabbled in the hydrator. Nothing. Her hands panicked. She backed out and slammed the door. Sheila is such a competent person. She seized her parka from its hook by the back door, grabbed her change purse and keys and skittered down the steps to the garage. Just accept it. Don't fuss. Everyone forgets.

She stood in front of the racks of vegetables which were still sparkling from Bob's sprinkler. The spinach was five dollars seventy a kilo. But the silver beet might be too coarse.

Competent. Competent. The drops of water were beads of silver, meeting, running together, dripping as she stared. There was a puddle on the floor beneath the broccoli. She began swaying very slightly from side to side, her hands clenched around her purse, the keys at her wrist on a wooden bead bracelet. She was shaking, her lips clamped together as she moved from one shelf to another feeling her way to the door. Bob glanced at her, his bald head shiny beneath the flickering miniature TV on the wall. — You OK then, Mrs Rossiter.

They were very kind. Jay took her hand, led her out the back and sat her on a hard chair by a large sink full of spinach. He made a cup of tea. The medallion from his last visit to India swung forward on its gold chain as he handed her the mug. — Just take it quietly, he said. There were discarded lettuce leaves on the floor, over-ripe fruit in boxes, a single light.
— Thank you, Jay, she said. How old are you?
Twenty two. His teeth were perfect. — I'll ring Mr Rossiter? What's the number?
— Number?
— For his office.
— Why?
— Once he hears we've got you in the back room he'll be up like a rocket.
She smiled, her hands balled against her chest with the effort of remembering — Seven double six two five seven.
He stood at the telephone beside her, his arms smooth and brown. She clutched herself and began rocking backwards and forwards in a steady rhythm. Jay glanced at her and nodded his head. — OK thanks, he said and put down the receiver.

— He's not in the office.
— Why?
— They don't know.
— They must know.
— He's not there. His face was unhappy, the skin beneath his eyes looked bruised. — I'll run you home in the truck. No sweat.
Something was ringing in her head. — I've got the car. There's nothing wrong with me.
— Come on then, he said. — No sweat.

Peter sat in still contentment as the lights came up and the audience, mostly matinée loners, drifted out. What a man, he thought. A oncer. A genius. A birthday treat. Sheila had never liked him, she thought him heartbreaking. And two more to come. A Chaplin festival, dumped midweek at the Paramount. He stretched, heaved himself upright in the murky light and groped his way out, side-stepping the queues for the next session. And there had been virtually no publicity.

The bus was full. The driver seemed enraged, lurching and crashing to a vicious stop at the red lights, hurling his standing cargo backwards at the green. The squat little woman beside Peter lost her balance and clutched his arm.
— Pardon me, she muttered, her eyes milky blue beneath her knitted tea cosy hat. Peter smiled. He felt tempted to tell her it was his birthday, that he'd just seen a marvellous film.
— Dirty bastard, she snarled at Peter's chest, nodding her head in the direction of the driver's back. — He'll be old soon. Then he'll know eh. Peter's smiled widened. She reminded him of Mrs Greer; her gallant rage, her uncertain stance, her woolly hat. At the next stop she clung harder than ever until

the bus stopped, then edged her way down the giant steps. The hat bobbed, she lifted a tiny pink hand in salute. — Taa, she said. Peter waved, hanging on with one hand for safety.

It was dark as he walked up the street. One or two fires were lit, the smoke ascending straight to heaven in the still air. The concrete steps to the porch were steep, the white paint on their edges worn. He must try and con Simon into repainting them. His mind flicked to the film. He saw the genteel gestures, the fastidious finger sprinkling imaginary salt at the imaginary feast. He put down his briefcase, steadied it between his legs, dragged out his key and opened the door.

— Hul*lo* he called into the silence. He strolled into the kitchen and glanced around the mess of Middle Eastern feast preparation. — Hullo he called again.

She was sitting on the sofa in the dark.

— Hullo, she said.

Peter suggested the trip two months later.

Sheila turned off the toaster and dug out the slice with a knife.

— Why? she said. She plonked the toast on Peter's plate and sat down.

He bowed his head in thanks. Because I went to the flicks.

— *Why* have you never liked Chaplin? he said munching.

She leapt from the table. He was on his feet, the toast in one hand, his mouth bulging. He clamped her wrist with his other hand and shoved her against the bench.

— OK. I didn't know you were so ill. *Talk* about it for God's sake. I went to the *flicks*!

She moved her head. — You're spitting toast.

95

— Sweet Christ, he shouted. — Table manners! You've got a table manners mind.

— Yes, she screamed. — Yes. I have!

But he came back to it. He had to do something. He came home with travel brochures, photographs of bright delights in flat folders. — It's a good time, he said. — The dollar won't stay at this rate.

— I don't want to, thanks, she said. — I'm not being, you know, I just don't . . .

He took her hand and examined it as though it was something interesting, stroking a ridged vein back towards the wrist with the forefinger of his other hand.

— Give it a go, he said. — What about Egypt?

She picked up her mending. (Women don't *mend* now. Vicki.) She bit off a length of cotton with the quick snipping movement of her teeth which always jarred him, then threaded the needle, holding it up to the light, squinting through her bifocals at the minute hole.

— Egypt? she said, stabbing the needle at a black shirt which had lost a button.

Her father had rolled in from the pub singing his party song. It was years before she discovered it was a hymn.

> There is a happy land
> Far far away.
> Where saints in glory stand
> In bright array.

The rollicking sound echoed down the hall to her bedroom where she lay in bed with tonsillitis clutching a decadent hot water bottle. He clattered into the room in his work boots and flopped on her bed. He dumped a book on the eiderdown, narrowly missing the remains of her bread and milk. — There you are sweetheart, he said, botching an attempt to kiss her forehead and landing in her hair. — Bought you a present. He belched. — Because you're my little sweetheart that's why.

Not birthday, not Christmas, because she was his sweetheart he had bought her this beautiful book, *The Bible designed to be read as Literature.* Muddy black and white photographs of the Holy Lands and Egypt were distributed amongst the text.

'Egypt,' said the introduction, 'is a timeless land. These photographs were taken in the Twentieth Century but the scenes and scenery are unchanged since Biblical Times. The river and bullrushes are identical to those where Pharaoh's daughter and her handmaidens found the infant Moses. Methods of agriculture have not changed over thousands of years.' Camels plodded, water wheels turned, oxen pulled. The pyramids were not mentioned.

Her mother snatched the book and banged it against her apron as though beating dust from it. She glared at Sheila. — You know where he'll have got it don't you? she said. (She always called him He.) — The pub, that's where. It'll have fallen off the back of some bloody truck and he's been taken for a sucker again. Oh! The sound was a guttural explosion of disgust. — Designed to be read as literature my oath.

— Mum, whispered Sheila, her hand outstretched. — Let's have it, Mum.

— Yes, said Sheila, her hands hidden in the folds of the shirt.
— Yes. I'd love to go to Egypt.

Peter even made the travel arrangements. He consulted Sheila, treating her wishes with consideration. He spoke a lot about the travel agent Sharyl: her competence, her knowledge, her huge earrings. They took the ten-day package with optional extras. — We'll see how we go, said Peter.

The plane landed into dry baking heat and confusion. They waved farewell to Grant across the seething terminal and eventually found a taxi. It hurtled through the streaming, screaming streets at high speed, the driver's hand hard down on the horn. Sheila assumed he knew what he was doing. — Look! Aren't they beautiful, she said pointing to two heroic figures in djellabas striding through the dust. — Why are there no fezzes?

— They went out after Farouk, said Peter, clinging to the seat. He preferred driving.

— Why?

— I'll tell you later, said Peter who was concentrating.

She leant back against him. — I should've read more of the modern stuff, she said.

The hotel had seen better days, an expression which pleased Peter. Sheila looked at the wide wardrobe which touched the ceiling, the enormous bed beneath the used-looking cover. — You get in first, she said. — In case something's died in the bottom. She put her arms around him and rubbed her head against his shoulder.

They were woken at four forty-five by the call of the Muezzin. They were right. It is haunting. She lay staring at the grey slit of sky. Come all to church good people, good people come and pray, to another God. The sound was plangent, hanging in the silence after the call had ceased. Peter shambled out of bed to the bathroom and walked straight into the plate glass door with numbing force.

They sat at a window in the dining room eating croissants and sipping café au lait. The hotel lay on a tributary of the Nile. She watched a man far below in a small felucca. He stood at the stern and flung out a fishing net as in the photograph captioned 'I will make you fishers of men.' The net sailed out, settled a moment on the brown water, then sank. Life designed to be read as literature.

— Look. She showed Peter. — I've seen that before.

— Good coffee, said Peter, glancing around for refills. He smiled at her. — Where?

— I had a book. She had never told him about her father.

— Ah.

— It is timeless, she said, lifting her head to glance around the room. — There's Grant. She raised her coffee cup in greeting.

Grant, spruce and breakfasted and ready for the next flight, marched to their table.

— Coffee? smiled Sheila. Grant shook his head. Peter was still looking for more.

— How did you sleep? asked Sheila.

— OK, said Grant, sitting down beside Sheila in his tight trousers. — I could've done without the whatever at five a.m. He had one finger between the pages of a paper back. — I've been reading, he confided. — My God, their religion was pretty weird. You know they thought they had to take everything with them? Whatever they'd need, want even. Did you know that?

— Yes, said Sheila.

— It says here . . .

— Ah thanks. Peter held out his cup to the crisp waiter bearing a silver-plated coffee jug. Sheila shook her head.

— It says here, said Grant, laying the book flat on the table, that they found an entire huge room full of mummified cats, each in its own little casket-type thing so that they could you know . . .

— Have one to hand? smiled Peter.

— Yeah, said Grant. He shuddered. — A room full of mummified cats for Christ's sake.

Sheila's fingers gripped the table. — But why shouldn't they? Her voice was high. — They might want a cat, she insisted. — You don't know! They might need one. Why shouldn't they have a cat? she demanded, staring at the scrubbed, startled face.

Peter put down his cup quickly and turned to stare out the window.

The man in the felucca had hauled the net in from his last cast. Although he was far below, Peter could see the thin body tense as he gathered the net once more, then flung it in a wide sweeping arc out across the water.

Commitment

David is obsessed by sex. Terri is not obsessed by sex, nor indeed by anything. She wishes to be obsessed by something. Committed. She wishes to stand up and be counted because commitment is all and she is not committed and bugger it.

Terri drains her coffee mug and replaces it on the Berber in our living room. She leans back defiant and uncommitted in the bean chair. She hits the chair angrily with the flat of her hand but the beans have nowhere to go. Terri's beauty is angular, she moves well, each action flowing from the one before. Her legs arrange themselves with grace, the angles sharp, flat kneecaps obvious beneath flesh smooth and brown as an egg. Her hair is black and hangs forward but she can flick it back in one sweeping swing and does so. Now she hooks a strand behind her right ear and glares at me.

— You're not committed she says.

In fact I am. Totally. So recently it is still contained.

She changes tack slightly. — It's because women have been brought up to please she says.

— Balls. I stand up, not sinuously. I roll out of my bean chair onto my knees and more or less take it from there.

Once upright I head for the divider of the open plan kitchen. I slam a teaspoon of Greggs in each mug and fill it from the saucepan on the stove because the kettle is still waiting to be picked up. I watch the boiling water swirl the instant into brown sludge bubbles, then move with caution back through the beached toys and hand her a mug with a large red S snaking up it.

Terri puts it down in silence, pulls a cigarette from the packet outlined on the front of her shirt, leaps up and bangs a frisking hand quickly over herself, one, two and behind searching for her Bic lighter. She finds it and flops down knowing the amorphous shape of the bean bag will yield to receive her.

— We are conditioned from birth! she says, wide-eyed as though she has just found this tablet new carved. — Fed myths. Maternal instinct for example. We have to get rid of these myths!

— Okay. I am bored with Terri's conversation and consider her statement tactless in the extreme. I stare out the picture window and count the telephone wires, a process I have found soothing since childhood when, trapped in the dentist's chair owing to thin enamel, I counted the wires as they shimmered and danced beyond the window distorted by the moving air above the gas flame on Mr Falner's round glass table. Sixteen there were.

— Do you want this baby? demands Terri. Twelve. Terri is leaning forward for emphasis, her elbows denting the thighs below her brief shorts.

— Yes I say.

— There you are see! Terri's finger jabs through the exhaled smoke. — You won't admit it. Why shouldn't you *say* you don't want it?

I maintain my bloated dignity.
— We've only got two I mutter.
— How will you manage without your salary? What about the mortgage?
— Oh shut up I say.
Terri regroups. — And you're so hopeless at it she says.
My face flames. I might burst. — We've got to love one another! I shout.

Terri and David are our best friends, a situation forced on us in a sense, though not entirely, by the fact that we are neighbours and David and Sam are colleagues. We know each other very well. They know as I do that Sam scratches himself when agitated. We have camped together, swum naked, so each man knows which garment each woman gropes for first when dressing. By common consent these intimacies lie buried.

Sam is an amiable man and for this I am grateful being diminished and muddled by anger at a personal level. He loves children. I mean all children. He is a better student than I am of the anthropology of children, of their nature, chants, rituals, taboos.

— This old man he played one, he played knick knack on my drum, he bellows as the Cortina spins along the motorway, its radial tyres shooting the water sideways into splayed fountains. Tom and Mick yabber in the back. Predatory as wekas they dispute Leggo pieces. Sam attempts diversion.

— Look! Look kids! he yells. — The wipers are conducting! He turns them faster. This old man hots up to hysteria.
— This old man he plays one he plays . . .
— Just watch the road I moan.

— I am watching the road. I am *driving*.
The snarls in the back have gone underground.
— Let's all sing I cry.
— And he played upon a *ladle*, a *ladle*, a *ladle* I hoot in imitation of the fruity baritone. — And his name was Aiken Drum.
But Tom has achieved the piece. Mick bounces on buttocks stiffened by rage. He roars.

I went to Sunday School as a child. We assembled for instruction in the Church Hall. With Miss Harty. Her tongue was purple because she licked her biro, her gentleness a balm. Each attendance was enhanced by the award of a card depicting a text. *Love thy Neighbour* was particularly attractive. Wreathed with forget-me-nots two dismembered hands clasped each other in eternal amity. My mother also stressed the virtues of neighbourliness. — Don't touch the coconut bumblebees she told my eager hand. — They're for Mrs Esdale. No no not the sponge. That's for someone else.

An Englishman and his wife rented the cottage next to Uncle Fred's bach one summer. My mother placed six downy peaches on their sharp leaves and handed me the willow pattern. — Run in with these to Mr and Mrs Ormondsley. I trailed across the paspalum bearing gifts and knocked on the weathered door. It jerked open as Mrs Ormondsley tugged. A puff of rouge had slipped on one cheek. — These are for you I mumbled. — Oh she said in embarrassed surprise, pale hands reaching to receive. — How kind. Thank you. I turned to skid home. As the door closed I heard her husband's booming bittern cry. — Good God. Are the natives being friendly?

*

It is Saturday evening and David and Terri have arrived with two sixpacks. We sit on the deck and I hope Mick will not appear trailing his piece of blanket and wanning a dring.

David and Sam are discussing their colleague Charles who also lectures at the medical school. They don't like him.

— The bastard's got legs on his stomach from crawling. Count the times you've seen him at it! Just count *up*! says David, flinging himself back in the director's chair with force.

— Man's a total shit. Sam pulls the tab from his can and drops it back inside. He leans forward, squinting into the can with interest.

— I like him says Terri.

The two men swing to her in outrage.

You never know with Terri. She has an empirical selection process. The judgemental litmus paper she uses to test if people are within the pH range of her approval seems to follow no known rules. Those outside the range are irrelevant. I love her.

— He's very intelligent she says. — An interesting talker.

— Oh he can *talk* snaps David.

Terri's chin lifts.

David consolidates. — In a minute you'll be saying he interviews well!

Terry sweeps into a sulk. Her hair falls forward.

— Do y'know David continues, I don't think I've ever had a *sandwich* with the bugger that he hasn't quoted Medawar. Not once.

— Well there you are. Sam is pleased with his friend David. — You've put your finger on it. The man hasn't an original thought in his head. Can't think . . .

Their delight in each other expands in the evening air. David sums up. — The man's a lightweight. Second class brain.

In my sad sorrow I see the organ being reslotted lower on the intellectual tennis ladder.

This brain is not sloppy like those on butchers' slabs but firm like the one at the DSIR. Mr Burke took the whole class to an Open Day. I remember the human brain. It sat, a dirty convoluted ivory carving in a shallow dish of formalin on which floated specks of dust. The capillaries etching its surface were threads of black. I stared at it for a long time. One day I will die. One day I will not exist. It was an educational visit.

Rangitoto deepens to blue-black. David's extended foot scoops the remainder of the pack within reach of his hand. He pulls out a can and lifts it up. Our heads nod or shake in answer to his raised eyebrow. The rhythms of our shared times continue.

Later though as Sam and I edge around each other in the bathroom I find that some of his love for David has leaked. He is muttering pejorative statements about him as he cleans his teeth and I slap Ponds on my dry skin.

— Why've you gone off him? I ask, slamming the stuff under my chin with the back of a hand.

Sam spits; slurps water from the tap into his mouth, spits again then swirls the water around the basin with the heel of his hand. He straightens to tell me.

— I didn't like what he said about Lange he says. He bangs a towel about his face.

— He's said exactly the same thing about Bassett.

Sam glares at me over the towel. — Bassett's a different thing again he says. — As you very well know.

106

I have assumed Bassett's iniquities. My eyes blink from behind his spectacles. My lips are pursed in his anger.

We fall into bed.

I will explain later. Sam will understand.

I haven't had a chance yet. Terri and David are with us again even though it's their turn because I haven't got round to organising a baby-sitter. As part of my commitment that we must all love one another I have made an effort with the food. Proper yeast dough in the pizza. Salad of mixed leaves. Fennel.

But the evening does not flower.

Sam, usually so amiable, is edgy. He has heard a rumour that the American scientific journal to which he has submitted his latest paper now demands 'acceptance fees' for the articles it publishes. This infuriates him, especially as he has no way of knowing if the rumour is true. Or that the paper will be accepted. He scratches frequently. He returns to the topic like a tongue to a lost filling. He drinks more than usual, he mutters imprecations, he bores.

After the real cofee he stands up. — You haven't seen the orchids lately have you Terri? he says.

— Yes says Terri. She also is restless. David, who lectures in Body Systems, has just delivered one of his periodic bursts on the precise physiological and anatomical effects of cigarette smoking. Terri's hands move in her lap.

— That new cymbidium's out says Sam. — Come and see it.

Terri is not surprised at this invitation.

— OK, she says, unfolding herself from the bean chair. She drifts after him as he moves across the kitchen to the back porch. The back door clunks.

David smiles at me. He is a nice man David. I have always said so.

— Shall I put something on the stereo he says. I nod.

— How about the old Kreutzer? — Mmmmm I say. We sit in companionable silence as the music surges around us and I wish I liked the noise more. I lean back and we smile at each other.

Terri and Sam are away a long time but I don't mind because of my commitment. Nor does David. He moves to sit beside me on the sofa. His simian face is kind. His charm laps me.

— Pregnant women turn me on he says. I understand this. I wish to stroke the long silky black hairs on his wandering arm. I need to make sure that they all lie the same way. It is essential. I have felt this necessity before but never as keenly.

Sam and Terri appear around the free-standing brick fireplace, having come in through the front door. Sam is talking over his shoulder to Terri. Their appearance is that of two actors whose entrance indicates a wealth of shared experience offstage.

David's hand has moved down again to my stomach. I grimace wildly. — Get off I mouth. I bounce agitatedly in a futile attempt to dislodge the hand. It has a life of its own this hand, as autonomous as those of *Love thy Neighbour.*

Sam swings round.

— Take your hand off my wife! he shouts.

The anachronism leaves us all speechless with shame for Sam. I heave myself into a more upright position and redrape the erogenous zone. My eyes are down for Sam not for me. I am very intent on my pleating fingers. The hand has gone. The Beethoven has finished.

The best defence is attack. — God you're a prick! David shouts, leaping up. — You get Ann like this. He glares down at my stomach, now suddenly erogenous free. — You ask me here, bore me shitless, disappear for hours with my wife then come back and abuse *me*! His voice rises at the temerity of the man.

Terri has moved to the uncurtained window during this outburst. Three pairs of eyes turn to her. She is the needle of our emotional barometer. What will she do to set us fair again? Nothing. She stares out into the dark as though she is reading it. Her back is beautiful. The atmosphere sparking. I love her.

— I'll get some coffee I say, banal as a TV ad. I start heaving myself up from the sofa. Pushing up with my hands I give a little levering kick with my feet as I reach the edge.

— No! David's firm hand on my shoulder topples me back. — We're going. Come on Terri. The flared hems of her satin trousers swing as she turns. She is silent. It is extremely effective.

They sweep across the Berber to the front door, escorted by a flourish of attendant lords and ladies. A tumbling dwarf.

The door is not slammed.

— Wow I say.

Sam turns on me.

We get to bed somehow. Sam is so enraged he is almost sobbing. — The man's a shit! he says again. The sibilant hate spits out. — Sam I say. He jumps into bed and rolls over immediately. Silver from the street light edges the curtain. It doesn't matter. It doesn't matter. Wisdom unfurls inside my head like one of those Japanese paper flowers in a glass of clear water. They came in shells, Japanese pipis. If I had one I could demonstrate and Sam would understand. Instead we lie side by side after our hard bruising game ticking like time bombs. Our feet touch the base board. The silence skids around the dark room. I open my mouth several times. I am about to explain it all. — Sam I say. His breathing thickens into explosive nasal snorts. He lies on his back, his mouth wide open in a silent shriek. He sleeps, one connubial arm flung across whatever it is that lives inside me.

Tuataras

They fascinated him, the hatching tuataras. Inch-long dragons pecking their way to a wider world. Shells are expected to enclose endearing and vulnerable balls of yellow, grey, or black fluff, but these were different. Leathery, wrinkled like dirty white gloves, the discarded ones resembled something unattractive and crumpled in the bottom of a laundry basket. Each shell had a number written on it with a felt pen. Charles Renshawe opened the inner glass door of the incubator and picked up 18 with care. The occupant had made little progress since his last inspection. The minuscule eyes stared, their sudden blink startling as a wink from a blank face. They peered at him above a jagged rim, the body still completely enclosed.

Charles despised anthropomorphism in any form. Dogs with parasols teetering on their hind legs, advertisements in which chimpanzees jabbered their delight at cups of tea, made him very angry. — What happened to the Mesozoic reptiles? he asked the head.

He replaced the egg quickly, closed the double doors of the incubator, then turned to watch the juveniles which had hatched during the last week.

They were housed in a display case the base of which was covered with a deep layer of dry compost. The tuatara-hatching project was the work of one of his brighter honours students and had been almost too successful. — We'll have them coming out our ears soon, Doctor, said Mrs Blume, crooning and pecking at the computer in the back room.

Charles relit his pipe yet again and counted them. Still eleven. The juveniles were exact miniatures of the adult forms except that they had no upstanding spines along the midline of their backs. Three of them had red dots between their eyes, the identification system of another student's research. This too pleased Charles. Class distinction among the archaic reptiles.

You hardly ever saw them moving. Their immobility was one of the things which fascinated him. He stared at one which was standing on three legs, willing it to ground the fragment of claw. He thought of the toads he had seen on an overnight stop in Guam on his way to present a paper at a Royal Society conference in Tokyo. They had appeared from this tropical dark, dozens of them, to squat motionless on the floodlit concrete path beneath his host's window. Suddenly one would move. Hop. Hop hop hop. Hop. Hop hop. Then resume its rock-like squat, immobile as a programmed chess piece between moves.

Charles glanced at his watch. He had had his five minutes. He gave a faint sigh, turned off the light and returned through Mrs Blume's office to his own shambles. He sat at the desk which was submerged beneath piles of examination papers and resumed his marking. He worked steadily for an hour, ballpoint in hand, ticking, marking, deciding.

His laugh crashed through the silence of the still building, an explosion of pleasure as he rocked back in his chair. He had used the metaphor 'a dishcover of membrane bones' in an unfortunate attempt at clarification in a second-year lecture. He remembered standing in front of a hundred faces, the Asians and their tape recorders intent in the front rows, the rest a haze, a sea of uninterest. Every one of the papers already marked had chanted back the inane phrase. This candidate wrote with authority about a dishcloth of membrane bones. Charles read on, his heart sinking. You would think they would pick up something. At least have a glimmer. Hopeless. Hopeless.

At two a.m. he gave up. He stretched his arms above his head in capitulation, yawned wide and marched out of the mess and locked the door.

He lay very still when he woke next morning, then shut his eyes again quickly. Marking, he thought. That's all. Marking. Then he remembered. Last night had been bad. Very bad. So bad that he had picked up the pile of papers and retreated to his office at the University leaving Rhona red-faced and outraged at the table, abandoned among the chop bones and wilting salad. Charles heaved himself up in the bed. His thin hair stood up from his head in a caricature of fright, his myopic eyes searched with his groping fingers for the spectacles on the bedside table. No sound. Rhona must have finished in the bathroom. Her knuckles tapped against his door. — Out, said his sister, stumping back along the passage to her room.

She was still a good-looking woman. Her fine papery skin lay virtually unlined across the 'good bones' of her face. Her grey hair was puffed and gentle about her face except when Ashley did it too tight. — Don't worry, Charles said. — It'll grow out. — All very well for you, replied Rhona, her eyes snapping. And of course it was all very well for him, it had no effect whatsoever, even if she had had it dyed purple as she'd once threatened to do.

Rhona had been the toast of the town when towns still had toasts. She had appeared frequently among the photographs on the Social Page of slim girls 'escorted' by haunted-looking young men with jug ears. Her face, even in the smudged print, was flawless, her eyes large, the corners of her mouth curving upwards with pleasure. And she was friendly too, and generous. Often she would hiss at one of the young men hovering around her, Go on, go and dance with Leonie. She's been there all night. And the youth would retreat and return to be rewarded by a smile, that smile.

As the years passed the lesser toasts married, their nuptial photographs splashing through the pages of *The Free Lance*. 'Broad acres united', sang the caption beneath the bucolic groom and the hysterical-looking girl clinging to his arm. 'Titian bride' followed 'Twins unite in double ceremony', and still Rhona was unmarried. Nobody could understand it.

Charles was not interested. He was grateful to his sister for being a success and thus freeing him from responsibilities often hissed upon other young men. — And look after your sister. Especially the Supper Waltz. He flatly refused to go to dances. Mrs Renshawe, a strong-minded woman, threatened, cajoled, pleaded. Charles wore her down. 'I am not going to the Combined Dance.' 'I am not going to the Leavers' Dance.' 'I am not going.' Endless scraps of paper bearing such messages haunted Mrs Renshawe in the ball season. They greeted her from every box, container, drawer. They confronted her as she reached for an ivory tip, fluttered from the inside of her rolled napkin, lay beneath the knives in the knife drawer, even, she found once with a slight shock, fell from inside the toilet roll. Defeated, Mrs Renshawe decided that Charles would be better copy as an embryo intellectual. And besides he was a boy.

Charles fulfilled his mother's predictions. A good student, his interest in Zoology was quickened in the sixth form by one of the few effective teachers left behind during the war. Mr Benson was 4F, unfit for active service. He taught science, taught it well, and Charles was hooked. He enrolled at Otago as soon as he left school and majored in Chemistry and Zoology before going Overseas for post-graduate study.

It never occurred to Charles not to go home from Dunedin each holiday. He was quite happy in Hobson Street. He was quite happy anywhere. And besides, he knew he was not staying. He drove his mother about the town, opened the door of the Buick for her as he had been instructed since childhood, stowed her parcels with care, smiled at her when she had finished her shopping and asked with a professional backwards chuck of his head, Home, Mum? He accompanied his father to the Club occasionally, but not often. He stood around politely as his father played snooker in the Billiard Room with Neville Frensham, and the light glinted on the bottles in the bar and the tension heightened and Charles thought what a balls-aching waste of time it all was.

Neville Frensham was a stockbroker in the same firm as his father. Younger, but not a great deal. He and Mr Renshawe walked home together after work and his father often asked Frensham in for a drink. Charles remembered the man, relaxed, at his ease in a large chair, the evening sunlight falling on the hand which held a full glass. Mrs Renshawe sat smiling at him from a smaller chair. She liked large, decisive men with firm handshakes. Charles and his father sat on the padded window seat with cushions at their backs. Rhona, calm, still, beautiful, was perched on the edge of a spindly unpadded thing. She proffered nuts while Charles poured the drinks, the women's gin and tonics in small cut glasses, the men's whiskies in things twice the size; strong, hefty containers you could get a grip on. He saw Mr Frensham shake his head in rejection at the nuts. He patted his stomach, smiling up at Rhona.

— And do you know what he said? he asked. Welcomed after toil, Mr Frensham was enjoying himself. Four pairs of eyes watched him, four faces were attentive. The saga concerned a friend of his son's, a lad about seventeen, to whom Mr Frensham had offered a whisky. He had then enquired about diluents. — And do you know what he said? — He asked for ginger ale! exploded Mr Frensham. He rocked back in his flowery chair, a wary eye on his glass. — I ask you! Shock was registered. Excessive from Mr Renshawe milder from his wife. None from Charles, who was refusing to play. His usual chameleon-like attribute of melding into any social decor seemed to have deserted him. He stared moodily into his beer. Rhona's smile blessed them all.

— Well you can imagine! Mr Frensham gave a little kick with both feet in his excitement. — I'll give you a whisky if you want one, I said, but I'm damned if I'm going to let any callow youth ruin my hard-found whisky with lolly water. I told him! He got short shift from me.

— Shrift, said Charles.

The bristling bad tempered eyebrows leapt at him.

— Pardon?

— The word's shrift, said Charles.

He always enjoyed seeing Rhona, who was now more beautiful than ever. Her pale skin seemed to be illuminated from within. He supposed her capillaries must lie close to the surface, but had the wit not to say so. They had the ease together of those who expect and require nothing from each other. She was still rather notably unmarried.

The next day they trailed upstairs after Sunday Lunch, Rhona in front, Charles two steps behind. She stopped and gripped the newel post on the landing.

— Charles, she said.

— Yes, he said, his eyes on her hand.

— Come along to my room for a minute.

— OK.

It was a pleasant room, low-ceilinged, a small window framed with flowered curtains. He watched the leaves blowing about on the striped lawn below them. His father appeared with the hand mower and began shaving the stripes. Charles pulled the curtain slightly to screen himself, and smiled at Rhona. She took no notice.

— Sit down, she said, patting the bed beside her. The bedcover was the same flowered pattern of poppies, daisies, and cornflowers. A pastoralist's nightmare he thought, and opened his mouth to say so.

— Charles, said Rhona.

— Yes? he sat down beside her and crossed his legs. The bed tipped them towards each other. Charles moved slightly.

— Charles, I want to tell you something.

— Yes, said Charles.

She seemed remarkably agitated. She scrambled up onto the pillow and hugged her knees, wrapping the Liberty's skirt tight around them.

— Aren't you going to ask me what it is? she demanded.

— You'll tell me, he said.

— Oh! The gasp was a rasping intake of air.

— I'm having an affair with Neville Frensham.

— Oh, said Charles.

— Is that all you've got to say! Her blues eyes seared him. His skin prickled.

— He's married isn't he? said Charles miserably.

— Of course he's married, you clot. That's why it's an affair.

An affair, thought Charles. Good heavens. And with that sod. He thought of that hand, that stomach.

— Why are you telling me? he asked.

— God knows, said Rhona, and burst into tears all over him.

She went Overseas soon afterwards. Charles was home when they farewelled her on the *Rangitoto*. They inspected the cabin she was to share with her friend Penelope, large, fair, a good sort. Rhona's side of the cabin was deep in flowers, hot spikes of gladioli were piled upon her bunk, the tiny inadequate shelves spilled over with pyramid-shaped 'arrangements' in posy bowls. Charles watched his sister's face as she read the card attached to a large bouquet of fleshy white orchids.

— Whoever sent those, dear? said Mrs Renshawe.

— The girls from the office, replied Rhona. Charles removed his spectacles, blew on them and wiped them with care. When they left the ship Rhona clung to him, sobbing, hiccoughing with the abandoned despair of a lost child. Mrs Renshawe was puzzled.

Rhona did various jobs in London. She was sacked from Harrods for suggesting to a customer who complained of the high price of the handkerchiefs that perhaps she should shop elsewhere. She trained at an exclusive interior design shop and developed the languid hauteur required. She was hardworking, used her initiative, and they enjoyed her slightly flattened vowels. She lived with English girls which pleased her mother. — What is the point, Mrs Renshawe asked her friend Rita, of going twelve thousand miles across the world to flat with Penelope Parsons?

Rhona wrote cheerful letters home which told nothing. Charles read them and was glad she was happy. They exchanged postcards. He collected all the interesting ones, the bottle at Paeroa, the floral clock at Napier, diners with their mouths open stuffing food at the Hermitage. Rhona replied with reproductions of naked male sculptures from the Louvre, the Uffizi, wherever. 'Wish you were here.' Charles liked her.

She came home occasionally. She was now elegant as well as beautiful. She was invited to meals with all her married friends and played on floors with her many godchildren to whom she gave expensive English-type presents. Corals for the little girls to wear with their party frocks. Large Dinky Toy milk floats and rubbish collection vans which the little boys did not recognize, and which had to be explained and demonstrated by Rhona from England.

She came home when their father died, and two years later when they moved Mrs Renshawe into a home. — I'm not coming home to look after her, she said, glaring at Charles. — Good God, no, he answered. — And you can't can you? — No, said Charles. He had done his best but fortunately it was not enough.

Charles stayed on, rattling around in the Hobson Street house where he had lived since he returned to take up his appointment in Wellington. He gardened, he visited his mother, he invited people for meals. — Anyone who can read can cook, he said, though the hard part was having it all ready at the same countdown. He enjoyed his work and was good at it. He was glad his mother had given up on grandchildren.

He and Rhona never discussed Neville Frensham. He wondered whether to tell her when he died, but did nothing. Someone else would and anyway it was forty years ago. Good God.

He was astounded when Rhona's letter arrived. 'I am returning to New Zealand. Presumably it's all right by you if I come to Hobson Street. Mother can't last much longer and I should be there. Anyway, I want to come home. Very odd. Obviously I'll take over the cooking etc. It might be rather fun. Two of us bumbling towards extinction together. Much love, Rhona.'

Charles thought hard, his mind scurrying for solutions. He thought of cabling 'Don't come. Have made alternative arrangements.' Or just plain 'No. Don't.' But how could he? Under the terms of their father's will she had an equal share in the house. And anyway, how could he?

She came. She stayed. She moved into their mother's bedroom, a large room with a fireplace in one corner, a dressing table on which Mrs Renshawe's silver brushes still sat, a high bed covered with a crocheted bedspread and a long box thing covered in flowered cretonne. When he carried Rhona's suitcases up she had touched the box with the tip of her small pointed shoe. — Good God, she said — the ottoman. What on earth would *Zaharis Interior Design* say? She flung her squashy leather bag on the bed and flopped down beside it. She stared up at Charles with something like panic. He was puffing slightly. — Mr Parkin begged me, she said. — They didn't want me to leave you know. Then why the hell did you, thought Charles, disliking himself. He put an arm around the slightly padded shoulder of her Italian knit and pressed slightly. She buried her fluffy grey head against his jacket for a moment and sniffed.

— Oh well, she said standing up, silver bangles jangling. — Is there any sherry?

But things got worse. He could have told her. He should have told her.

Charles stumped down the stairs, his right hand touching the wall lightly at intervals in a gesture imitated by his students. He turned left through the hall and padded into the kitchen. Rhona was sitting at the table with her back to the sun in the chair in which he had always sat, reading the paper.

— Good morning, said Charles.

— Hullo. She didn't look up.

He lifted the small blue and white striped teapot from the bench. — Old or new? he said. She glanced up briefly.

— Old, she said. Charles opened the window and emptied the teapot onto the rose beneath. He pressed down the red flag of the Russell Hobbs kettle. A plastic bag, its contents weeping and bloody, lay beside it. Charles poked it.

— What's this?

She glanced up, frowning. — What?

He poked again. — This.

— Plums, said Rhona.

— Ah.

BARBARA ANDERSON

Charles made tea, poured himself a cup and pulled out a chair which raked loudly on the faded green vinyl. A blackbird sang, defining its territory. He glanced out across the sunlit lawn. There it was as usual, singing its proprietorial heart out from the spindly kauri in the next door garden. Charles sat down and helped himself to cornflakes, refolding Rhona's open packet of muesli and placing it on the bench. — Which is the whole milk? he asked. Head down, still reading, Rhona handed him a jug embellished with the crowned image of George VI. She had finished her breakfast and was smoking the first of her day's cigarettes. She was a tidy smoker, meticulous in the removal of butts, the emptying of ashtrays. Unlike Charles whose pipe dottle and matchstick-filled messes overflowed throughout the house.

He poured milk onto the cereal and attacked the mush with quick scooping movements of his spoon, herding it into his mouth. He bonged a striped cotton napkin at his face and reached for the toast.

— Any chance of a piece of the paper? he asked.

Rhona swung into action, slapping and tugging at the paper as though it was putting up enormous resistance. Still clutching the overseas news page she handed a crumpled heap to Charles.

— Thank you, said Charles, smoothing and refolding the thing. They read in bristling silence for a while.

— I heard on the radio that Lange's not going to Paris, he said, raising a tentative flag of truce.

It was shot to ribbons. — Would you, snapped Rhona.

— In the circumstances?

— Perhaps not, said Charles.

Rhona snorted, flicking her ash into the small brass ashtray with a quick decisive tap. She finished the cigarette and

122

ground the glowing butt into extinction, then heaved herself up against the unstable plastic table. It rocked, slopping milky tea into Charles' saucer. She emptied the ashtray into the Pelican bag beneath the sink and reclosed the door. She remained planted in front of the sink, a strong white arm clasping the stained blue formica either side of her. Charles, from the corner of his eye, saw her put her head in her hands. Oh God he thought dully. A miasma of dread enclosed him, paralysing action, thought, threatening his very existence as a civilised thinking being.

He made an enormous effort. — What's the matter, Rhona? he said.

Rhona swung around, her pearls clasped about her plump neck, her hands clasped in agony. — It's so bloody *awful* here, she said.

Charles glared at her. Who was she to stand in his familiar old-fashioned kitchen, to breathe its slightly gas-scented air and mouth such antediluvian, anti-colonial crap?

— Are you pining for dear dirty old London? he asked.

Rhona's eyes blinked with surprise. Charles was surprised himself.

— Yes, snapped Rhona. — Yes, I am.

Charles felt rage thickening in his throat. Stronger even than his interest in the Comparative Anatomy of Vertebrates was his feeling for the land forms, the fauna and flora of the country where he grew up. When he had been a postgraduate student in England many of his New Zealand contemporaries had worked and schemed for the glittering prizes of Overseas Appointments. Charles, more able than most, had regarded these men (there were no women) as unusual genetic aberrations who could not be blamed for their imperfections. He knew he was going home and did so.

— And you're so *boring*! continued Rhona, angrily banging her wrists in search of her handkerchief.

Charles breathed out, a liberating puff of relief. — I've always been boring, he said.

Rhona slammed back to the table and crashed her behind onto the unstable silly little chair opposite him.

— Don't you care? she demanded.

— Not in the slightest, said Charles.

She thumped the table with her closed fist.

— And I suppose you're proud of that! Proud of your Intellectual Honesty! she cried. Her face, usually a pleasant sight, was mottled, despairing, damp.

— I don't bore me, said Charles mildly.

To his horror, just when Charles thought he had cushioned the trauma, siphoned off the excess, set things on an even keel again, Rhona for only the third time in his experience, burst into tears.

— You're only half a . . . She gasped. — Only half *there*!

She disintegrated before him. She laid her rounded arms on the plastic table and howled like a — like a what? Charles had never seen anything like it in his life. He stared at her. What should he do? Slap her? God forbid. Ice? Wet towels? He slipped sideways from his skittery little chair and tiptoed from the kitchen.

He felt bad about it. Very bad. Twice in twenty four hours he had abandoned a suffering human being. Charles was not an uncaring man. He gave to things. Not only to any conservation scheme however bizarre or impractical, but also to humanity. His donations to the City Mission had been regular and substantial. They had asked him to join the Board but he had declined owing to pressure of work. They quite understood.

He felt miserable all day. He chaired a Scholarship Board meeting with firm detachment. He continued with his marking, refusing as always to count how many papers remained unmarked. He lunched in the Staff Cafeteria, sitting with his salami and tomato roll, staring across the tossing windblown harbour a thousand miles away. He exchanged pleasantries with Mrs Blume who was suffering from a completely unjustified excess of work, but there you were.

He had not visited the tuataras all day. He finished his last second year paper and leaned back, reaching out a spatulate-fingered hand for the striped tobacco pouch on his desk. He tamped the tobacco into his Lovat Saddle pipe with a nicotine-stained forefinger, wiped the finger on the carpet, and lit up, puffing his pipe with the catharsis of release. After a few minutes he pushed his chair back and ambled out of his office, through Mrs Blume's room into the small laboratory which housed the tuataras.

His fingers quivered as he opened the inner glass door of the incubator. He had timed it well. Before him the tuatara which last night had been a shell, a half head with eyes, climbed out from the remnants of its shell. With a backwards flick of its fragmentary left rear leg it tossed the shell aside. The movement reminded Charles of a stripper in a Soho dive thirty years ago as she kicked aside the irrelevant sloughed-off garments beneath her feet. Charles clutched the sides of the incubator. He felt weak with pleasure. Infinitely tender he picked the newly hatched tuatara up from the incubator and enrolled it among its associates in the compost. It did nothing. It just squatted there, planted on its four angled legs, occasionally moving its head very slowly to one side or the other. Charles picked up a piece of waste paper from the bench on which the incubator stood, pulled out his ballpoint and wrote, 'Have removed No. 18 (contents of) from incubator. In display case. C.R.' He slipped the note into the incubator door as he closed it.

He stood back. A transfusion of happiness flowed through him. He had thought of something. He hurried back to his office, giving Mrs Blume no more than a perfunctory nod. He would do something. Show his concern, his love almost. He reached for the telephone and dialled his home number.

— Rhona, he said into the quacking receiver. — Would you like to see the juvenile tuataras? The babies?

Feeding the Sparrows

— Start where you like then, start where you like she says. Tell me about your life.

What was it like then when I first fed them, scurrying and leaping down the twisted paths of the Gardens leaving caches of crumbs by the rugosa roses, the Holland monument, Dick Seddon himself for God's sake.

Green days forty years ago I say, when I was young and something carving out a career as the lad, the sweeper-upper the packer-into the putter-out of wholesale groceries and believe me they are legion. I could show you caverns of food, cool rooms of cheese with salami alongside, Nescafé drums shaped for caterers. And a Gourmet Range, though thought little of by the bread and butter trade who were our bread and butter say what you like. The only lad they ever had to pick up a broom unasked Farrer said, and where did it get me. What's the virtue in picking up unasked other than to show that you don't have to be asked. Better to leave the broom lying and not take the whole sodding world on my back because that's what I did, I see now, and the birds too as you know.

Sixteen and hefty with it. Strong lad wanted and got. Not my first job either. That was sorting for blows in a factory. There was a sign where we whinged and queued for pay. — Work hard eight hours a day and don't worry and in time you may become the boss and have all the worry. And all the money and a house in the hills and a car with a musical horn the sod.

I felt, I see it now, that no one else could do anything properly. Not just as well as me. Almost at all. Whatever it was — the broom I snatched from the floor, the shelves I monkeyed up desperate to stock the top stuff though all of it within reach of the smallest dairy owner and some are small my word, the sari ladies. That was why, I think now. That was why, though it's hard to say. The books I read no one read, the poems that stay in snatches upset the others if I said them. There's not much poetry in a suburban branch so it's down to the Central and you have to be quick in the weekend for a chair in the sun from the winos.

I heard them at work talking through the years. I heard them saying sodding storeman for God's sake. — Not number one junior to Jesus. — Look Denny I can stack, any fool can stack. I can lug cartons Denny, I got m'letters. — Piss off, y'wanker, get off my back, all that they say and more but still I feel and still I know and still it is inside eating me that they can't, not properly. Not unless I see it, not unless I watch them. Better if I've done it myself then I know.

I know what they mean though. I see myself. I stand at the check-out and the wooden trolleys line up packed teetering high for the dairies, low for the private customers, and my eyes are everywhere. I take the goods off for the girl at the computer to sweep with her ray gun and I see my face in the mirror behind the check out and it looks like the worried face of someone maybe a relation. There is black hair in the neck of a white shirt sprigged with brown and a heavy duty red apron over it and the face of this man is anxious and his hair shoots off his head and it is leaping straight upwards black and anxious and he chews his lip this guy. — Calm down says Diane or May or whoever. — Calm down Denny. But they whisper, Really kinky eh.

The same in the Canteen if you can call it a Canteen, a room at the back. I get an instant from the machine and I have a cheese scone always the same from The Lilac next door and I read Prufrock from the back pocket of my shorts, summer and winter under the red apron though I take that off in the canteen. — I grow old . . . I grow old . . . I shall wear the bottoms of my trousers rolled, and I see the old guy in England at the seaside never the beach like here. Always I do the same each day. I sit down and I place my Rothmans on my right side hand and my Bic lighter opposite and my scone plate in front of my book behind that flat for reading and the cup at my right hand. I lift each thing up and put it down several times and no one else comes to my table which is how I like it, and Jeeze they say but let them it is how I like it.

— The birds she says.
— Yes?
— You fed them?
— Yes.
— For how many years.
I have been asked so many times I know straight off.
— Forty, I say.
— And when did you . . . ? Her eyes are green. Her hand is still.
— Start on my back?

— Yes.

— Thirty years ago.

— And the couple from the Embassy?

I say nothing.

— When did they?

So I say it again, all I've said again and again and again. It was my own way. I made it up. It was mine. I knew if anyone saw they would try and they wouldn't do it right, so when I thought of it I took my bag of crumbs in behind the shed. I get off the bus at the shelter, Glenmore Street, the covered one with fretwork, cross the street on the crossing that's what it's for, why not use the thing, and down the dog leg past the azaleas. Make sure no one is in sight and slip behind the mower shed, you know, where they keep the mowers. I knew if anyone saw they'd try and I knew they'd get it wrong. I bend down see like this, back quite flat and very carefully I put the crumbs on my back and the sparrows are strung out waiting on the guttering each morning, well almost, for thirty years. I am very quiet, there is no sound but the birds or sometimes a creak from the tin roof. When I am still they come down and peck the crumbs from my back and I feel the gentle bill pricks through my parka though you know there's never a hole. The slightest noise even on the path say and they hoosh up and the pecks stop till quiet again and they return. Ten minutes I give them no more then I stand up and they shoot off in all directions they know it's over, but they come back when I'm still to peck the crumbs from the ground.

This day I am feeding them, the smell of moss damp in the air. April it was and I know there is someone else there even though I don't hear because the birds fly up. Still down I turn my head and I see four trouser legs, two dark grey and two light grey and I know it is them, the man and his wife from the Embassy.

— Then?

I have seen them often on my way home. I walk across the bridge though it wasn't there when I started at the warehouse. I have seen them walking hand in hand in the gardens for years in their Mao suits smiling. It was his suit which was lighter grey. Her hair was clamped to her head with dark clips, her walk was a shuffle. People liked them holding hands and smiling, everyone smiled back, the joggers, the strollers, the kids even, in prams.

So when I saw the legs I knew but it didn't make it any better. I stood up and stared at them not smiling. They smiled and bowed and crept away still hand in hand down by the side of the shed but I felt sick you know sick, and I was right.

They must have been practising. A fortnight later I came up the main path through the cemetery on my way home. I wanted a leak so I hopped behind the old fashioned roses. (And what were they doing anyway that morning behind the mower shed?) He was bent over, the little guy his back flat his hands on his knees and she was sprinkling crumbs on his back and they were two chattering and sniggering kids with secrets.

— And?

The sparrows shot off as I yanked him upwards with one hand hefting the back of his Mao collar and flung him forward on the concrete. He crashed face downwards, arms and legs sprawled like a free fall and she screamed and rushed to him, keening and crooning, I suppose his name. She lifted his head and saw his face and ran away screaming and I stayed there with him till it was quiet and the birds came back.

I Want to Get Out,
I Said

Her mother sat very straight beside the empty driver's seat. Mary leaned forward and inspected three tiny sacs of loose skin on the back of the neck in front of her.

— You should have them off, Mum.

— What?

— The things on the back of your neck.

— They're not doing any harm.

— They're not doing any good.

— Be quiet, Mary. Her grandfather sat motionless, an assemblage of crumpled clothes, a smell of cigarettes and airless nights.

Mary ground her behind deeper into the back seat and started out the window at the dust. Who did he think he was? Some deposed Emperor for God's sake, instead of which . . . She moved nearer the window to avoid contact with his hairy jacket but his shape flowed after her, overlaying her side of the car.

— I'm getting out.

— It's very dusty.

— I know it's dusty. I want to get out.

Her mother's sigh drifted through from the front seat.

— It's not my fault.

— I didn't say it was.

— Nobody could expect two punctures.

— I would have thought you could. On a road like this.

— You wanted to see the forest.

— Not much.

— You said.

— All right, all right I said.

Her grandfather heaved his right buttock from the back seat and extracted a flattened cigarette packet from his trouser pocket. His trembling fingers lit a cigarette then held the match to Mary's face for her to blow out. She could kill him, quite seriously she could kill him.

— I want to get out, I said.

Her mother made an odd little sound, somewhere between a grunt and another sigh. She opened the car door and heaved herself out, shaking her cotton skirt from behind sticky knees. She held the front seat forward for Mary, then stamped her jandals on the road, causing plumes of dust to rise around her purple ankles.

— It's very dusty. She stared up through the towering trees.

— We've seen them anyway, she said.

It hadn't started too badly.

— There's no reason why we can't do things as a family just because, her mother had said. — I'll do the driving, well mostly, and you and Sam can take a turn. If you want to, on the . . . The sentence remained unfinished, the unspoken 'easy bits' left hanging. It was the first summer since their father had left. He had come home from the paint shop one lunch hour as Mary and her mother sat at the kitchen table sorting plums.

— Dad. Her mother's head lifted as though she had caught his scent, not the sound of his boots on the concrete. He kicked open the fly door, nodded at them as he dropped the red plastic lunch box on the table and strode the few steps to the bathroom. Silence flowed after him, widening.

Mary's mother bent her head and studied each plum more carefully. Jam? Bottling? Eating?

He came back after some time, the sculpted waves of his grey hair still damp from the comb. With one leg he pulled a chair out from the table and dropped onto it without a backward glance. He picked up one of the ripe plums and turned it over and over, staring at it as though it might tell him something.

— Sandra and I are going to Oz, he said.

— Sandra who?

— For Christ's sake! Is that all . . . ?

— No no Jim I meant . . . I didn't mean . . .

For months afterward her mother behaved like a sheep which had blundered into the wrong race and become separated from the rest of the mob. Any attempt to understand the calamity which had befallen her was useless. She seemed befuddled, a bewildered old ewe banging a woolly head against the rails. All she wanted was to be back with the other girls. Together again. Discussing how Des wouldn't look at beetroot, and as for Jim, they all knew about Jim's eating habits. And his other habits. Mary knew, while still at school. Her mother, that true cliché of the deserted wife, was the last to know. She never blamed Jim, she didn't blame her friend Sandra, she just knew that somehow it had all gone wrong. She had missed some sign, some friendly signal which should have alerted her. Her eyes filled often with hot easy tears. — We were so happy though, she said. Mary wanted to shake her. To shout and scream that it wasn't her mother's silly fault if her husband dumped her for Sandra fat Hatton.

Her grandfather had always been there. His presence seeped through the quiet house as he sat calm and benign in the one comfortable chair in the sitting room. He moved slightly, unbuttoned his cardigan or lifted a foot and replaced it as Jim crashed up the back steps each evening, slamming the fly door which sent its shuddering clatter through the rooms.
— G'day Pops.
— Good evening.
Still.
— Go a beer?
— Thank you.
No one knew his reaction to Jim's departure. He tried to comfort his daughter, patting her shoulder with tentative little movements of a long-fingered pale hand.
— There. There.

Mary's brother Sam also kept his own counsel. He was sixteen when his father left, a tall gentle boy who spent a lot of time lying prone beneath the 1957 De Soto he was stripping on the concrete beside the circular clothesline. As Mary stepped between his outstretched legs one evening, she heard him grunt. She put down her heavy office bag.
— Yeah?
— Hang on. He rolled out from under the chassis of the

dismembered car and reached for an oily rag. He began wiping each finger.

— Well.

He looked at her, squinting into the sun, a streak of oil above his upper lip.

— Do you want to go up north? he said.

They listened to the thudding chatter of the Fitzgerald's old mower gathering itself together, then the change in tone as it was propelled into action. — No, said Mary.

— Well?

— We have to.

— Aw shit. He wiped a final finger. — You know what he'll be like.

— Yes.

— Well then I said.

— She wants to.

— Why?

— Ask her.

His eyes were slits.

— Stuck in the car with him.

— Yes.

— All that bloody way.

— Yes.

He said nothing more, but dropped his head till he lay full length on the concrete, then rolled quickly beneath the car. A hand came out groping for the transistor. Mary bent to move it to him. She touched the sole of one grimy foot with the toe of her strappy sandal, opened the fly door and stepped quickly inside. It snatched like a greedy hand.

It hadn't been too bad. Not so far. There was little chat in the car, and no radio. Power lines looped and slid by,

measuring the Escort's mile after mile after mile progression
to the north. Ice creams sank in cones, licked into nothing.
Comfort stations were inspected. Occasionally her mother
came out quickly, puckered lips pressed rigid in rejection.
— Drive on Sam, she said. Her father sat glaring ahead with
myopic eyes.

— I've never seen the kauris, he said. — Funny that. I
once lived . . . The pause lengthened. — Yes, he said.

The mosquitos struck at Paihia. Sam held out a thin arm.
— They don't bit me.

His grandfather continued anointing himself with care.
— They do, he said, — but you're not allergic to them.

— I'd know if I'd been bitten.

— What's that then?

— What?

— There.

— That!

— It would be lovely if we had a boat, said his Mother.

The sun poured over Mary's shoulders the next morning
as she watched her mother pay the motel bill, smiling and
bobbing at the emaciated woman behind the desk. Through
the open door she saw her grandfather light a cigarette. The
woman lifted a brass urn of blush-pink artificial orchids,
rubbed the formica beneath it with the closed fist which
terminated the twisted ropes of her arm, and put it down
again. Her tan had leached to fawn.

— It gets in the drapes, she said. — I'd rather have ten non
smokers any day. It's the drapes. Mary's grandfather peered
at her. — Drapes?

— Thank you. Thank you. His daughter took his arm and
guided him to the back seat of the car. — Off you go Sam.

The Escort spurted forward. It leapt at the cattle stop, knocking the hibiscus which offered its red plate-like blossoms to the sun.

— Sam, said his mother.

Miles later the car swung left.

— Is this right?

— Yes.

— Oh.

The gravel road deteriorated, small stones sprayed from beneath the wheels, dust rose in swirls around the shimmering heat of the car.

— I'll drive, Sam, said his mother.

Sam's hands tightened on the wheel.

— Sam.

— Put your window up, Sam, said his grandfather. The sneeze was a volcanic, roaring explosion. — Handkerchief! He flapped an angry hand at the box of tissues Mary handed him. — Useless! Useless! he gasped, then grabbed a handful and made quick bonging movements all over his streaming face. Discarded tissues drifted to the floor. — Dust, he said.

— Dust. The car slewed in the gravel and lurched forward, hobbling.

— Puncture, said Sam.

They piled out of the car in silence. Mary helped Sam unload the boot. The pile of holiday gear grew, incongruous and hateful among the grey daisies on the verge. A bird sang in triumph above them as Sam dragged out the spare tyre and bounced it on the road. — Pretty shot, he said, as he attacked the hubcap of the failed wheel.

They were more talkative for a short while after the first puncture, the survivors exchanging brief smiles. Sam's mother brushed his neck with the back of her hand. He sat well back in the seat, his arms stiff as he swung the car into the curves. The temperature rose. The car lurched to the right again as the spare tyre collapsed.

Sam set off for Dargaville bowling the first punctured tyre in front of him, a parody of a Victorian children's book illustration. A car seethed past, obscured in its own dust storm. Mary's grandfather closed his eyes. The dead match fell from his fingers onto the shredded tissues.

— I want to get out, said Mary.

Her mother clambered out and held the front seat forward. Her grandfather's eyes opened.

— We're all in the same boat Mary, he said.

They piled the luggage back again and the three of them retreated to the forest. No one could call it bush. The thin stream of insect sounds stilled for a moment. Her grandfather found a small patch of rough grass against a massive trunk, turned around several times, then collapsed against it like a sack emptying. Mary's mother sat bolt upright, her feet and knees together. She gazed upwards through the endless branches, searching for a sign.

A horn tooted. They peered out cautiously. A blue car had stopped. Sam leapt through the cocoon of dust from the front door to the boot, which he banged with his fist. The driver moved his right arm and the lid opened wide, a giant robot ready to disgorge. Sam pulled out the tyre and clutched it to him.

— He knows you, Grandad, he shouted.

The driver was a thin man with bent shoulders. He heaved himself out of the car, blowing air from rounded lips in tiny puffs. He steadied himself against the bonnet with a splayed hand of freckled fingers. His bald head was also freckled, half ringed with a fluff of faded ginger curls above the ears. His shirt hung loose, aglow with orange palms. Every movement of his body, including his smile, was slow.

— Long time no see then Lester, he said.

A bird lifted high above them.

— Listen, said Mary's grandfather. — Listen.

Rollo's Dairy
(Jake and Deedee)

—He's good though isn't he? said Mrs Fussell.

Her puff cheeks creased as she smiled at the man sitting motionless in the cane chair beside the counter. She bent with a confiding creak until their faces were level.

— Yoo hoo Mr Rollo, she said.

Eyes blank as an empty screen, the man stared back at her.

— Hullo, he said.

— When you think of some of them, I mean. Mrs Fussell snapped upright as Jake punched the till with emphasis, moving slightly to avoid the shooting drawer.

— Yeah, he said. — Not bad for a hundred and ten.

— A hundred and . . . Oh, I'll tell Rex that one, promised Mrs Fussell. Chuckling with pleasure she hitched and slung her various carrier bags into position and teetered across the vinyl to the safety of the Have a Nice Day rug at the doorway.

— Of course Deedee's so lovely with him, she said.

Jake watched her as she stood beneath the old fashioned wooden awning of the dairy waiting for the lights to change. Even when the thing said Cross she still skittered about, nodding and bobbing her thanks to the tiger drivers clamped behind their wheels. She was especially grateful to the tightlipped women, their sleepy children, even, he felt, their enormous dogs. Jake had a sudden vision, so sharp, so ecstatically bright that he clutched the rim of the counter for a second. He saw himself tripping Mrs Fussell with a thrust of his leg, the left one, saw her spread-eagled on the crossing, flattened, her pink bloomers. He glanced down at the leg, blameless in walk shorts, socks, sandals, blew his breath out slowly and shook his head

— Okay Pop? he said.

The man nodded

— Okay Buster? he said to the child in the padded playpen. The baby lifted his arms. — Da da da, replied his son.

Jake made a joke about it once. Twenty-one years old. One wife. One Father gone gaga at fifty. One dairy. Two mortgages. One and a half kids. Where did I go wrong? Deedee loved it, curling up beside him on the lumpy sofa in the back room, her shape convex beneath her Live Cargo maternity shift, her mouth slightly open. She had read an exposé of sexism in International Airlines and learnt with interest that Asian air hostesses are instructed to part their lips slightly when attending to male passengers, as this is known to be both provocative and flattering. The article didn't say to whom, but Deedee rather liked the damp pouting look when she tried it out in the Coca Cola mirror above the sofa.

— It's because you couldn't resist me, she said.

Jake thrust his legs out in front of him then hooked one sandal across his knee and examined the sole. — Yeah, he said. Deedee laid her Sonata Gold rinse against his chest.

— Because I'm so beautiful, she said.

— Yeah.

— Why is it?

He placed two small stones on the glass topped table by his right arm and continued the examination of the sole with the concentration of a mother chimpanzee grooming her baby.

— Because you're so beautiful, he said.

— Stroke me, said Deedee, heaving herself onto her back.

Jake tried to work it out as they lay in bed together in the room over the shop, Deedee's sweet breath puffing at him occasionally across the giant pillow they shared. 'Why have two. I like being close.'

She had always liked being close, ever since they had biked to school together when she was in the third form. She had none of the sharp-elbowed wariness of most of the girls when confronted with the opposite species. Not that she actually did anything the boys did, or nothing Jake could remember, his eyes staring at the flicker from the neon sign below the window.

There was a good hole in the Tuki Tuki that year, deep, natural, no dam needed. They had fixed up a rope to the willow, the usual thing, but that was the best year; a trunk across a narrow inlet, a floating log, the lot. Deedee wouldn't swim because of the slime. — Ooh ooh the feel of it, she squealed, hands fanned across her face to shield the horror. — And the smell! It did smell; a cloying green stench but that was part of it, part of the whole thing and the heat and the splashing shouts and the baked hay-like grass on the banks. Each name familiar, carved till death. Names echoed in those of the boys who nudged and elbowed at the counter in front of him though there hadn't been a Darryl like the new kid round the corner. Hem, Wayne, Wayne had always been there, Grant, Mick, Shane, Kevin. And Deedee, watching and applauding all of them, but especially Jake. It got so he'd glance to check before he swung wide on the rope.

So she was his girl. As inevitable as growth, an extension, one more thing Jake was good at. With his usual amiable lack of effort Jake had the whole thing sewn up.

He was beautiful, his mother had always known this and wondered how it had happened, considering. A true North Country woman, she never admitted the fact even to herself. But when she was sure no one was looking she watched the grace of his hip-rolling walk, the light springing leaps as he ran upstairs. He was her only child. She always called him my son. Never ours.

She had met Jim Rollo when they were both working at the Wairakei hotel. She came from Leeds on a working holiday, waitressing on tables six to ten. Jim assisted in the golf pro's shop. He was a large man whose nobbly wrists shot from the sleeves of the long-sleeved shirts insisted on by the management. He was pleasant, that was the main thing about him, a nice man, especially compared with some of the more lecherous tourists. Her memories of fumbling courtship were filtered through dense clouds of steam from the Geothermal Bore.

They married and moved south to Hastings. Jim had hoped to buy a sports shop but the price was prohibitive — an arm and a leg, an arm and a leg. They settled for a dairy opposite the park where they worked from eight till seven, seven days a week, for seventeen years.

Jean Rollo's death shook the customers. — But she was so

bright! they said. And so she was, bright, quick, attentive and clean. What more could they want. Her death destroyed Jim Rollo. — We were a team, son, he told Jake endlessly. It's like an arm gone. Or a head, thought Jake sadly, staring at the meticulous records of accounts and invoices in his mother's small neat writing.

She had never intended Jake to take over the dairy. With his beautiful body and his sport (summer and winter, Eleven, Fifteen), she saw him as a Physical Training Instructor. She had watched them once on a visit to Dunedin. The trainees were leaping a wooden horse in the grounds of the Training College. They warmed up in acid green track suits then discarded these on the icy benches so they could move even more easily in shorts and singlets. Jean Rollo watched them contract their bodies, tense themselves, spring into a run, a larger spring, up, over to drop down the other side light as cascading silk. She stayed staring for half an hour. A school first, she thought, then who knows, a university? Anywhere. Everyone wants them now. She had never told her plan to Jake. It was a secret to be revealed, like the acknowledgement of his beauty, when the moment allowed.

She died sliding to the floor one day beside the deep freeze, the sound of the packet of Stir Fry clattering to the ground Jim's first intimation of tragedy.

Jake went straight from school to help his father. He soon found he was running the place. Sighing deeply, his father glued himself to the sofa and the television in the back room. It wasn't Alzheimer's, the doctor insisted. — Then what is it? demanded Jake, begging for a name. — Nothing really . . . I mean nothing with a long name, said Dr Francis, shambling about his surgery. — Here's his head, his heels are coming, Mrs Rollo used to say.

Dr Francis ran his practice with efficiency and compassion for his patients' pain. He knew better than most that many die young and fair but it was not for this reason that he longed to retire, to mooch endlessly after a golf ball accompanied by the distracted chatter of the sparrows in the macrocarpa shelter belts. — You know Dot, he had confessed to his wife that morning at breakfast, I'm so bloody sick of sick people.

— Nothing, said Dr Francis again. — He's just signed off.

— But he can't! stormed Jake.

— I'm afraid he can Jake.

Deedee was marvellous. She popped in to help with the orders every afternoon on her way home from school. It drove Jake insane when he heard his father explaining endlessly to her the finer points in the lives of the flickering figures on the screen. — That woman's a snorter Dee, he would say. — The one with the figure. She's trying to steal her own daughter's husband. Can you imagine any mother doing that? Jake heard through the red, black and yellow strips of plastic curtain his father's tooth-sucking contempt and Deedee's commiserating murmur. Once he couldn't stand it another minute. — Deedee! he shouted. — Where's the Mohlenbergs! The curtain slapped as she came running, placating, adorable. Why then did he feel she and his father were somehow . . . not together, that was insane. He didn't, he didn't, not with Deedee's hand slipping cool and intent beneath the belt of his walk shorts. — God, I love you, he said. — I know, said Deedee.

He could never have managed without her. He knew that. All the legal stuff. Power of attorney when it became essential, refinancing the mortgage, everything. How did she know so much? Not from her father, the useless clown. Nor from her mother, a gaunt silent woman who cleaned at the hospital. Her green uniformed figure biked with high lifting knees past the dairy twice a day. If she couldn't avoid it she lifted one hand to Jake, but normally she rode steadily, her eyes fixed straight ahead on the blue Kawekas in the morning, the cut out shape of The Peak on her return.

Deedee's kindness to the husk of Jim Rollo never faltered. It was all so weird. He could walk, dress, and feed himself. He had always taken care of his appearance and continued to do so, brushing his hair with those double hair brushes like the Duke of Windsor or something. He changed rooms with Jake soon after Jean died. — I can't stand it son, the double bed. His bedroom remained meticulously tidy, two *Golf* magazines placed neatly on the bedside table beside two *Autocars*. Nail scissors, tweezers, the brushes, were always in the same position on the tallboy. Behind them stood a small photograph of Jean taken twenty years ago. She looked like a little girl at her first party, her hair fluffed up around her face, her smile apprehensive.

Jake knew, not that he'd ever been told, that Wayne felt he'd been trapped into it by his wife Sheena. Jake had never felt that. He remembered the first time, when he and Deedee were still at school. She had opened her legs wide and welcomed him. Afterwards she sat up, dabbed her legs with her handkerchief, then rinsed it in the river with matter of fact composure. She beamed at him, her doll-sized cottontails in one hand as she brushed the grass from her bottom. She turned, standing on one leg as she pulled on her pants. The two cheeks matched with such breathcatching perfection that Jake fell on his knees, nuzzling. Deedee was shocked. — Jake! She smoothed her blue summer uniform and patted the crushed grass beside her. —Lie down, she said. Jake picked up a dead branch and heaved it at the Tuki Tuki. — Come on, said Deedee. — Lie down.

He was nineteen when they married, Deedee seventeen. She took over the ordering, running the reps with charm and steel. They all loved her, even Benchley in paper goods. He would slap his drooping corduroys, so different from the young guys' gear, and say, Deedee, I love you. The toughest teenage pro in the business.

Jason was born nine months later. Deedee loved being pregnant. Jake knew she would and was glad for her. He showed her a photo in *Woman's Own* of a pregnant film star sunbathing in a bikini. — That's like you, he said. — I don't sunbath in a bikini at nine months! — No, but you Luxuriate in Your Pregnancy, don't you? See. It says here. He stabbed his finger at the print. — Well, you're meant to. It's natural, isn't it? said Deedee, stumping through to the back room. — Hell yes, said Jake.

She had gone to the obstetrician for a routine examination. Jack was stacking the soups, tomato, vegetable, when the phone rang.

— This is Dr Petherton's surgery, said the crisp voice.

— What? said Jake.

— Dr Petherton has sent Mrs Rollo to hospital in an ambulance. The membrane has ruptured.

— What!

— Dr Petherton suggests you make arrangements to get to the hospital right away, Mr Rollo. When Jake slammed the van into action he found he still had a Watties Tomato in his hand. He flung it across the seat and sat fuming at the red light.

Jason was born two hours later. Dr Petherton, half in love with all his golden girls, told Deedee she could make a fortune from a best seller entitled *How to Have a Baby*, by Alison Rollo. He said he'd be happy to write the foreword.

Deedee called the child Jason. — It's neat isn't it? Half yours and half mine. Aren't we lucky! she said scooping her left breast from the cross over top of her nightgown and fastening the button mouth around it as though this was another thing she had known for ever.

Why couldn't he revel in it all as she did? He knew you were meant to, knew how lucky he was. After the delivery he wanted to cry, to weep and weep and weep alone. Deedee was sweating, exhausted, beautiful in the joy of their shared gift.

— We could call him Alicob if we did it the other way, he said.

— Nutter, said Deedee proudly. He called the baby Ali for a while but the name didn't stick although it suited the child. He was a big baby. The down covering his large head changed to thick black curls, his skin was olive, his eyes dark, his expression dreamy. He was a solemn child, and seemed possessed of enormous indolence. Jake realised that babies normally were but he was puzzled by the fact that almost from the beginning Jason lolled at the breast with his eyes open. There seemed no attention to the matter in hand. — Shouldn't he shut his eyes or something? asked Jake. — Why? asked Deedee. Why indeed.

She was still feeding Jason at ten months when she found she was pregnant again.

— I think I'd better stop feeding him, she said sadly.

— Yeah, said Jake. — I reckon.

— I hate to do it. It seems so unfair, said Deedee, snatching

Jason from his padded playpen and burying her head in the nape of his neck.

The padded playpen-cum-cot was an unexpected and handsome present from Deedee's parents. It reminded Jake of a miniature boxing ring, just the shape of course. Every aspect of the thing was designed for comfort and protection. It was blue, the padded mattress base also blue with a scattering of bright yellow daisies. Deedee had attached various rattles and small fluffy toys around the rim. Jason lurched from one to the other chewing plastic rattles or miniature bears without discrimination, occasionally crashing backwards with a look of surprise on his smudged face.

— I think we should have the pen in the shop, said Deedee late one afternoon.

— Why?

— Well it's natural.

Jake felt the back of his neck prickle.

— I'll be in here more and more now he's older, Deedee explained. — Until you know, the baby.

— You'll hear him. If he wants you, he'll yell. You can go out. Jake stared at his son who was motoring around the playpen with more than usual speed.

Deedee turned to look at Jake, her face shocked.

— Don't you want him in the shop?

— Oh shit, Dee . . . Of course I want the little bugger.

— Jake!

The automatic buzzer sounded. Jake, who was leaning in the doorway to the back room, the giant liquorice straps of curtain streaming over his shoulders, leapt to the counter. It was only a packet of Rothmans but Jake greeted the defeated-looking man with enthusiasm.

— Certainly Sir. Just one was it? There y'go.

Deedee was sitting on the edge of the sofa when he returned, her eyes bright.

— I've already got Dad squatting there when he's not doing his Couch Potato act.

— What's that got to do with it?

— People won't like it, he tried.

— They will like it. They will. It's just what they will like, she insisted.

— You can't have the place cluttered up . . .

— Cluttered up!

They did like it. Jim Rollo they tolerated. Jason they loved.

Jake didn't take much notice of Darryl at first. He knew most of the kids in the area. Well not most, but a lot of them. Having grown up in the shop, seen them as babies, a combination of instinct and family histories advised him as to which ones to watch. All young kids pinch things, he knew that. He had himself, in Woolworths. They all did, with Deedee hovering at the door. He gave her a blue plastic hair slide he'd stolen, but she never wore it. They took anything which was easy, not necessarily because they wanted it. Once he pinched something when he didn't even know what it was. Deedee tried to snatch the pink elastic thing from him, her face scarlet. — That's awful. Awful! Give it to me. He caught the hot rush of shame. — It's for *girls*, she hissed. — I know that, but I thought it was a . . . — Give it to me! said Deedee shoving the thing in her school bag.

So he knew, as any dairy owner knows, to keep the glossy wrapped enticements of the Crunchies, Moros, Pinkies and Bounties behind him and the cigarettes in dispensers above his head. Only the spearmint leaves, wine gums, gobstoppers, milky chews — the kids' lollies — were displayed in their open boxes on the counter. He had stopped making up ten cent mixtures. He remembered himself. Half of it is the choosing. He was aware of the absence of some of the favourites of his childhood but arranged the survivors with care, keeping the boxes well filled so that his customers were not confronted by a few broken rejects beneath their sugar dust. — It's the little things that count, Deedee said, and Jake agreed. — Come and look, she said one Sunday. — Tom's made an effort with his weekend window. She took Jake's hand and led him to the butcher's shop next door. On a square of brown paper in the middle of the Snowline display cabinet stood two small black and white fibreglass pigs. One gazed straight ahead, bland and cheerful, the other, more suspicious, squinted upwards from beneath lowered brows. One non-biodegradable red rose lay between their tiny hooves, a wreath of white plastic daisies surrounded them.

— Isn't that neat. I like people who try. Like you, said Deedee, hugging his arm, her eyes on his.

— I better get back, said Jake. He opened another box of orange Jaffas and slipped it in the front row between the pallid sherbet lollies and milky chews for extra colour.

It wasn't only the kids who stole. He even had to chain the billboards to the front of the shop. A half-naked starlet you could understand, even Lady Di in a cowpat hat, but what sort of a wimp would want BROTHER CITED AS CO RE?

Darryl wasn't interested in the lollies or the billboards. He was a bright-looking kid, about nine or ten. Skinny, but boys are meant to be, with a wide grin. Whoever cut his tough blond hair had given up and cropped it close all over his head. He ignored Mr Rollo, but seemed pleased with the baby, whose playpen fitted neatly at the end of the canned goods row. Each time Darryl came to the shop he hunkered down to talk to Jason, encouraging him to undertake more daring playpen enterprises, extending one skinny finger through the bars as a prop. Jason beamed at him, a drool of saliva pouring down his chin. The boy picked up the spit rag and mopped.

— What's your name? Jake had asked, remembering how he'd hated being called son, or worse, sonny.

— Darryl. He clapped his hands at Jason, who hid his face on one knee in ecstasy.

— Got them at home, have you?

— Yeah.

He bought the usual things kids are sent to the store for: bread, milk, the staples. He always waved to the baby before skidding off at a barefooted trot. — See y'.

— How long've you been here? Jake asked next time.

— Not long.

— Where d'you live?

The kid gestured with his head. — Round the corner. Credentials established, Darryl poked Jason in the stomach. Jason gazed at his stomach with solemn interest then got the idea. He seized the finger, placed it in his mouth and chewed.

— I think Darryl's lovely, said Deedee. — He's the only one of kids who really cares. Mopping up, I mean. That's lovely.

Jake lay staring at the dark, the flutter of neon visible through the gap in the curtains. He tossed onto his side, then checked to make sure he'd avoided pulling the lot with

him, but Deedee was still covered. He lay very still. His head
seemed to be growing larger and larger, a vast hollow space,
expanding, filling the room, the street, the whole town. He
gnawed the inside of his cheek, swallowed, but the sensation
remained. He flung himself onto his back. It only seemed to
happen when he lay sideways. Think of something. Think
of something. He knew not to think about the shop. Figures
muddled and jumbled in darkness became nightmares. He
thought about Deedee, put out his hand to touch her. She
murmured and rolled away. He thought of Jason and how he
loved him. Of course he loved him but somehow he felt . . .
not cheated, how could he? Why? How? Not because Deedee
loved the baby and he felt left out. He'd read several articles
about that too. Some were quite firm. 'Remember,' warned
Women, 'to your partner, the father of your child, your son
is another male animal.' Again Jake knew he'd got it wrong.
His puzzled confusion was different. He had hoped the
arrival of the baby would somehow lighten things. Take off
some of the weight, not weight, there was no weight. But he
had assumed that Jason's existence would dilute the essence,
water down the concentrate of so much loving.

But Deedee's love, like energy from exercise, seemed self-
engendering. The more she gave, the more she had. It flowed
in endless draughts, more than enough for Rollo's three male
animals and the entire world.

— Of course you're young, Mrs Fussell told him early next
morning. — You and Deedee.
— You're bang on there, Mrs Fussell.
— But still it's long hours though, isn't it?
— Keeps us off the streets, Mrs Fussell. That's for sure.
Jake slapped the useless piece of thin white paper around

the half barracouta, sellotaped it, and put it in Mrs Bassett's spotless white cotton bread bag. Her pale eyes smiled at him. — I think you're just lovely, she said. — All of you. Her day enhanced by goodwill, she trotted off. Her small feet in their black cubans and white ankle socks reminded Jake of their counterparts next door.

He went straight to check the soups and meats. He didn't check every day, how could you, but just recently there was something odd. He could have sworn the rows of beans plus sausages were level yesterday morning and he hadn't sold any. Deedee had been on while he did the banking, but he didn't want to mention it to her at this stage. He took a rough pad from the counter, made a count, then hid the sheet beneath the till. What could you do? You couldn't search bags. Not in a dairy for God's sake. That would be the kiss of death. Rage swept through him. One sodding thing after another. Inflation. GST. Every move they made seemed designed to destroy him. And now this.

He looked up. Darryl was watching him. Bare feet planted wide on the pink and green Have a Nice Day, he nodded at the empty playpen. — Jason not up yet? he asked.

— Doesn't look like it, said Jake. Darryl grinned. He always acknowledged jokes.

— What can I get you?

— I'll get it.

Darryl walked down the canned foods aisle, the vinyl bag banging against his knee scabs.

Jake stood very still. He put down his ballpoint, crept past the deep freeze, down the cereals and baking needs and peered around the corner into the canned goods aisle. Darryl's vinyl bag was collapsed on the floor. One hand held a tin. He bent and put the tin into his bag, the movement silent and furtive. Jake leapt at him, a flying tackle which brought them both crashing to the ground. The corned beef tin skidded down the aisle, several others rocked on their shelves. Jake leapt to his feet and slammed the terrified child hard against the shelves. Three more tins rolled crashing to the floor.

Jake's heart was belting in his chest. His hand tightened around the skinny neck. He could kill him, kill him! Darryl's hands clawed at the huge one, his face contorted. Shaking, sweating ice, Jake loosened his grip and clamped the boy's wrist. — Why! he shouted. — Why! Darryl's eyes were dilated, his breathing chaotic and rasping, the free hand clutched at his neck.

I nearly killed him. God, I nearly killed him. Jake leant against the soups, his hand still clamped around the bony wrist, breathing in, out, in, out. He forced himself to look at the thief.

— Look, he said. — Look. This is my stuff! I work for it. I slave my guts out. His fury engulfed the glistening face. — I don't come to your place and pinch your stuff.

— We haven't got any stuff, whispered Darryl.

Jake exploded, his arms windmilling, legs flaying. — Get out of here! Get out of here, y'little shit. Get out!

Darryl fled. Jake picked up the vinyl bag and thundered up the aisle, snatching the corned beef as he ran. Darryl skidded on the mat, crashed to the ground, picked himself up and lurched out the door. Jake leapt onto the empty early morning pavement and heaved the bag and the tin after the fleeing boy. Darryl paused for a second, then, still bent double, retrieved them both and disappeared around the corner.

Jake leant against the end of the aisle, his heart thumping. He wiped the back of his hand across his eyes. From the blur beneath his eyes yellow shapes defined themselves. He stared as the familiar shapes of the playpen, the straight sides, the soft padded curves of the mattress, the chewed bears, surfaced into focus as though pushed from beneath.

— Oh Christ, he whispered. — Sweet Christ.

It Is Necessary I
Have a Balloon

— Well, it is my birthday, Tom said, leaning back against the heaped pillows, hers as well as his cushioning his back.

— I know. She continued folding the crumpled wrapping papers, aligning the sides with care, creasing the fold with thumb and forefinger, flattening the useless stuff against her jeans with brisk sweeping movements of her hand.

— Why do you do it!

— What? She glanced up, her face half covered by the huge fashionable glasses.

— Save the paper. He smiled. — You look like an owl, he said. — A Small Barn Owl.

She jumped up. His hand steadied the sliding mug as the tray bucked. She stood the cards upright on the chest of drawers. One had a rod and fishing gear draped around *Happy birthday, Dad*. Chosen with tongue-biting care for a non-fisherman by his daughters from the selection labelled Male. From depictions largely of manly pleasures, veteran cars, racehorses, balls, bats, pads, she had chosen a noble-headed lion. Its expression of benign autocracy was enhanced by a magnificent mane. Its eyes were kind. Under the inscription, 'A birthday card for you today, to say you're loved in every way,' she had written, 'Kind regards, Jan.' The joke had flopped.

He tried again. — So what about it?

She scooped the washing from the floor and clutched it lovingly to her chest. — Well it's just the kids, she said, wriggling a free hand in attempted clarification. — You know, your birthday ... She thought of the plump and gleaming chicken, the paper hats, the stricken faces.

— That's right! It's my birthday. Why d'y'think I skipped the wine tasting? And the dinner? His voice sharpened at the memory of his sacrifice. He saw Grant oiling alongside the man from Sydney as he left. Saw himself crouched in a purple bucket seat among the graveyard faces waiting for the last plane, the only energy that of two toddlers in red parkas who hurtled around snatched at by a distracted woman with spiked hair. The flight had been bumpy, the air hostess's farewell smile a rictus.

He took another swig of cold coffee from his birthday mug, replaced it, and put the tray carefully on her side of the bed. He kicked the duvet back with both feet, padded to the door and turned. His head lifted. She was reminded of the lion.

— I just want to go to the Molloy's party.

And so you shall Cinderella. But she was puzzled.

— Why do you want to? So much I mean.

He scratched his left buttock and yawned. — Carol'll be there. You know, Anna's sister. I want to dance with her.

— Why particularly?

— Because, he said, she dances with animal grace.

— Animal *what*?

— Grace, he said, his bare feet slapping the stained floor as he moved to the bathroom.

*

— It's Dad's birthday you see . . .

— We know *that*, said Rita, her round face stern.

— Yes well you see he wants to go to this party and we'll have his party here tomorrow night.

— Why? Implacable, squat as a lunch box in her yellow dungarees, tow hair bunched at right angles, Rita was unconvinced.

— Because he wants to dance with this lady.

— Oh for Christ's sake, he groaned from behind the *Herald*.

She swung at him, her arms stiff with outrage. — Well *you* get out of it!

He leant back and slapped the paper over his face.

— I can danth, said Jessie. She hefted her frock over the solid curve of her belly and stumped about shaking her bottom.

— So can I! Rita the ever competitive swung herself into the phantom beat.

— So can I! shouted their mother. They rocked and swayed and lurched about, enchanted with themselves and their dance.

— Give me strength! He flung his Docksides on the sofa to lie full length, his face hidden by news.

The balloons jerked everyone's eyes upwards. The Molloy's high-raked ceiling was awash with them. They clung in the steep angle of the beamed roof as though magnetised, their boiled-sweet skins ovoid and tight. Each had a streamer attached which drifted languidly in the currents and streams of talk, the shrieks of joy.

— Helium! cried Jan. She knew.

— Where did you get it? Tom asked Anna Molloy.

Anna's hair was sweet disorder, her mind racing. How had she got into this. Self inflicted wounds. Open the door. Go home, go home, go away.

— Industrial Gases, she screamed, handing Jan and Tom's coats on to ten-year-old Rob. Good God the Balfours. She swept to embrace them.

Rob's round-eyed gaze was solemn. — Dad knows a guy, he told them, hanging their coats with responsible care.

Jan's hair was falling down. She shifted her weight onto her other foot and gazed into the eyes of the man talking to her. She hadn't heard his name. His rust-coloured shirt was faintly pharmaceutical in design. It buttoned off centre, his neck rising from a stand up collar. If her chemist dyed his uniform in Cold Water Dylon he too could have one.

He dropped his eyes. They were blue; so strong a blue that if you saw him across a cafeteria you would think, That man has blue eyes.

— Well you did ask, he said.

— Yes, she said, wondering what.

His glance flicked down again. — Where are your shoes?

— I didn't want to come.

— Oh. The pause was too long. — I'll get you a drink.

— I'll get it, she said, but he was gone.

She turned to the anxious woman beside her.

— Balloon's are great, aren't they Margie?

Margie's eyes searched the room, checking each corner for secrets. Her lipstick was weeping, leaving sad imprints on the cold glass. — Nnn, she said. — Lovely party.

The noise level was increasing, the balloons drifting tails moved more rapidly in the warmer air. The room was full of people who cared about issues and were beautiful.

Tom stood by the door with Carol, his body canted in the drooping curve of a tall man talking to a small woman.

— Your husband's so good-looking, said Margie.

— Tom? Yes. Has been for some time.

A thousand years. Where was that rust-coloured clown?

Excusing herself to Margie, who looked as though she might howl at this defection, she slipped on her shoes and moved away.

The bar was a mess, sloppy and disorganised. Giant bottles of spirits stood in puddles, soft drinks were muddled beside used glasses. Cardboard wine flasks gushed and flowed. She tried to back out but was trapped in the crush of supplicants.

— Wine please, she said to the sweating boy whose T-shirt shouted obscenities at her. Holding her glass like a chalice she slid off at one side of the bar table. Someone turned on the stereo. *Flash Dance* surged and racketed around her.

People began to dance. Tom was quite right. Carol moved as though she was born for nothing else; her hair swung, her eyes were dreamy, her mouth slightly open.

Perhaps she could do something? Toss a salad? Hell bent on salad tossing, clutching a sticky glass, Jan stood staring at Carol and the balloons.

She moved from the living room to the passage. There were no balloons here. She missed their colour, their lazy completeness.

She trailed along the passage, opening doors. The master bedroom was pink. There was no evidence of Michael Molloy other than *Time* and a digital clock on the left hand table. Full-blown roses crawled across the double bed, mushroom pink lay wall-to-wall, pink ribbons ruched and fell from the lampshades.

Backing out quickly, Jan tried another door.

— Hang on! a voice cried.

Irritated, she retreated back up the herring-gutted hall. The sounds of the party swirled and stamped beyond the thin wall.

The kitchen door opened at her touch. Against the huge refrigerator Carol was flattened. Only the top of her head above Tom's shoulder was visible, and a drift of green polyester trapped behind his moleskins.

The door shut automatically as she blundered backwards. She clutched the arm of a man ambling along the passage from the bathroom.

— I want a drink.

— So do I. Wait here.

She stood staring, hypnotised by the row of coats. Each peg had at least six coats hanging from it. Some had fallen to the ground. She aimed a kick at Tom's tartan-lined raincoat but moved her foot quickly as the man reappeared.

— I've found a bottle and glasses, he said. — Do you drink whisky?

— Anything. Don't go in there.

— Why not?

— Yes, she said. — Why shouldn't you?

He looked at her.

— I've gone off the idea, he said. — But we need some water.

— Here. She opened the door next to the kitchen.

— Ah, he said, peering at the whiteware. He placed the open bottle on the window sill, then poured two drinks, adding water from the cold water tap above the tub.

— Here's to our side.

— Thank you.

— To hell with stomp and grind.

— Yes. She paused, the glass half way to her lips. — Excuse me, she said moving to the door.

— Where're you going?

— I'm going to chuck it at someone.

His face was shocked, his grasp on her wrist a manacle. — No, he said. — Not whisky.

She put the glass on the windowsill and turned to fight him. Average height, glasses, a thatch of black hair, a face that looked as though someone had pulled all the lines downwards, dragging fingers through plasticine.

Her shoulders shrugged. — OK, she said.

— What's your name? he asked, releasing her wrist.

— It doesn't matter.

— I don't suppose it does. No. Let's make ourselves comfortable.

He opened the clothes dryer and groped in its black hole. His hand appeared holding a blush-pink duvet which he doubled and spread on the floor.

— What a bit of luck. Good old Baby Doll Molloy.

They slid down onto its softness, then leant against the cool comfort of the Fisher and Paykel, the whisky bottle between his outstretched legs, a faint whiff of soap powder in the air.

— You're in such a strong position with your own bottle.

— Yes, she said.

Shoulder to shoulder they sipped their drinks.

The kitchen door clunked open, pushed from inside.

— Thank you, Tom, sang Carol. — If you'd just bring the salami.

Jan choked on her gulp of whisky. Shoulders heaving, eyes streaming, she snorted the stuff from her nose.

— I'm sorry . . . It's just . . . It's just . . . she panted.

Steadying the whisky bottle with one hand, he reached out and pulled her back so that her head lay on his shoulder. His arm slipped around her.

— It's all right, he crooned. — It's all right.

Her hiccough was doubtful but she lay back. — I quite like whisky, she said.

— Hang on. He freed his arm, moved the bottle, then removed his glasses and turned towards her again. — It'd be like antlers clashing, he said.

Eventually she pulled away from him. Her eyes stung with rage.

— Do you know what a glottal stop is? she said quickly.

— No, he said.

— It's in a book I'm reading. She keeps talking about glottal stops.

— Look it up.

— I can't be bothered.

Breathless at such wit, they sank lower on the blush pink, their arms entwined, the whisky bottle safely on one side. The beat of rock music pulsed through the walls and the floor beneath them.

— I can feel it in my bum, he said, pleased.

— Do you ever go to Kentucky Fried? she asked later, enunciating with care.

— Yes, he said.

— Who goes in and gets it?

— Hunh?

— You or your wife?

— Oh. He considered, his face more creased than ever.

— I haven't a wife at the moment. But I used to. Get it I mean.

She snuggled down on the duvet.

— Nice, she murmured.

— Come home with me, he said.

She shook her head and sat up, then rolled forward and clambered up. She heaved her skirt down, supporting herself against the gleaming washing machine. She observed the scene from a great height. He lay far below, crumpled, boozy, friendly, clutching his half-empty bottle, cradled in pink.

— No. I'm going home.

She bent down, kissed his glistening forehead, then stepped carefully over the wreck of his trouser legs and walked the few steps to the door.

His attempt to clutch her ankle was half-hearted. She turned and lifted a hand to him, then closed the door. The party racketed on, rock music thundered over the heads of the dancers, the eaters, the drinkers.

Her hair had collapsed completely, her glasses were crooked. She picked her way with care through the throng, very polite, very cautious as the dancers stamped and swayed about her. — I want a balloon, she told them. She reached the opposite wall and tugged a small table into position, then skirted the room and returned smiling with a small chair from the hall which she placed in the exact middle of the table. She kicked off her shoes, hitched her tight skirt up over her thighs and clambered onto the table, then teetered tiptoe on the fragile chair, her arm stretched upwards grasping for a balloon. The noise was louder still at ceiling level. Tom's head jerked upwards from the stomping haze below. — I want a balloon, she told the uplifted sweating face, the stunned mullet mouth. — It is necessary I have a balloon.

Subalpine Meadow

It beats in my head so I hear it although there is no sound. It doesn't match the rhythm of my painting hand. You'd think there would be a sweeping 'Dah, da DAH, da da da' sequence as I broad brush the mountains. Not the bounce and stump of 'One O'Clock, Two O'Clock, Three O'Clock ROCK', a tune which slots me in my slice of time. I am a child of the fifties.

I live with my mother and have no man to speak of, which seems an odd way of putting it. My mother's grace belies her age, I've been told. She has very little bust, but she is undeterred. She stuffs tissue paper down where it would be if it were larger, though lately she has given this up and who can blame her. Presumably she had more originally, it's not a thing we have ever discussed. It hasn't cropped up. I was amazed when I read that Julie Nixon was amazed that 'as a family we never discussed Watergate'. What did she expect?

My mother drifts through life. Moving languidly she trails through the days. Floating diaphanous fabrics, scarves, shawls and ribbons attend her. In the wind they get out of control and have to be constrained. Today she is swathed in beauty like a Byzantine Madonna. Long nosed, dark eyed, she appears on the back porch and clutches the wooden ball on the top of the newel post for support.

— What on earth do you think you're *doing* Kate! she screams.

I have been expecting this. I am cool. Cool.

— Painting the fence, I call merrily. Merrily, merrily shall I live now.

— Mad as a hatter, moans my mother.

I flick an upward curve to the stiff leaf of my Mountain Daisy. I have transformed the dull blue fence at the back of the section into a Subalpine Herbfield or Meadow, of daisies. Beneath the zigzag peaks of mountains their white slashes of petals spring from rosettes of flat leaves, or are glimpsed among tall spiky ones, easy to paint with a medium brush in St. Albans. I dream of the mountains. All the time. The daisies march half way across the fence. I wipe the brush on newspaper and stow it in a jam jar of turps before turning to my mother.

— Don't you like it? I ask.

I work at a sub-branch of a Diagnostic Laboratory out at Woolston. We all said we'd leave when they moved out there, but none of us did. A rottweiler tied by a running chain to the clothesline next door barks its heart out in endless despair. The Lab is housed in a former state house which they must have got cheap. It is surrounded by repeating images of itself which melt to the horizon. In rooms designed to protect, possibly even comfort, we spin urine in centrifuges, we count blood cells, we stain sputa.

I have been with the firm for ever. Unqualified, but good

at it, I am regarded as a fixture less exciting than the new microscope, but more reliable than the centrifuge.

On Monday Geoffrey our Senior is angry again. His shoulders hunched over the microscope reject us all, even Trudy. His beautiful head may be contemplated, the deep waves in his hair noted as they sweep back to tight curls at the nape of his neck. He probably doesn't know they exist and I have no words to tell him.

— You must've seen it on the direct slide, Trudy, he says at last.

— No, says Trudy our Junior. She unwinds one leg from around the other and places her shoes neatly together, toes straight ahead. She regards their pointed ends with affection, bending from her neat little bottom to get a better view.

Geoffrey swings around on his stool, snatching his spectacles from the bench. He looks so vulnerable, uncooked almost without them, I have to turn away till he has regrouped.

— Trudy it's not good enough, he says. He stands and leans over her, willing her, forcing her to understand the meticulous care required, the exact observation, medical ethics even.

— The plate's grown a heavy pure culture. Surely you must've seen *something* in the direct slide? he begs.

Her smile is a mirror reflecting unwanted junk.

— I just didn't I guess, says Trudy. Last week when Trudy misread a plate I explained her error tactfully. She looked at me kindly.

— So? she said.

Elaine in haematology is a horse of a different colour, a dark horse. Hunted, haunted, divorced, could have been the boss but isn't, she works meticulously and very very slowly.

Nothing disturbs her monumental disregard for the crises which occur daily, her refusal to accept one teaspoon of responsibility for which she has not been paid.

Elaine's hair is beautiful also. She sweeps it onto the top of her head, like a woman in an old photograph whose hand rests on the back of a chair on which a man sits encased in Edwardian trousers. Elaine is slim, her hair is the colour of ripe wheat, and if you've ever seen that you will know it is not gold, more a sunny fawn. Pieces escape from Elaine's bun so that she moves in an aura of floating wisps, as does my mother although different. Elaine's eating method has more appeal than most; it is as though she is unaware of her sandwich or pie until a piece has been bitten off and stored within her mouth for mastication purposes. Elaine does not tuck in. She *transfers* food, almost unknowingly. In this she resembles many fat women — but their seeming unawareness of food disposal is simulated, and stems from a different cause.

Harry, our Intermediate, does tuck in. He motors through food, and in fact life. His enthusiasm is at the ready like a towel at a waiter's waistband. He is not much older than Trudy, but he cares about the work very deeply. His tough brown curls leap from his bullet head, his step is quick as he moves with anticipation to the incubator each morning to get the culture plates.

— Come along gang, he cries in his Ricardo voice. — We are not here to make frenz.

Ricardo is our other staff member. He is the storeman, caretaker, the one who sterilises the rubbish in the autoclaves and bags it up. He comes from Venice; his English is not perfect like ours, so we laugh at it, and by extension, at him. This is harmless as we have nothing against Ric, nothing at all. We like him in fact, his neat movements as he tugs the stores about the shed, his lopsided smile as he greets us. — Good zay. I like him a lot.

But the Laboratory is not a Happy Ship. Hardly anyone likes anyone or else too much. Harry despises Trudy. — Heavy scene in the tearoom, Kate, he tells me at the end of the week. — Ah, I say. — Trudy threw a wobbly. — Not again? — Yeah. He swings around on his stool and aims a phantom .45 at me.

— Don't rap with the fuzz, kid, he warns, now in his Al Capone mode. He means don't tell the Boss in Town the Intermediate at Woolston has reason to believe the Senior is having it off with the Junior.

— Negative, I say, slipping another slide under my microscope.

My mother indicates the tangle of neglected garden as evidence that it's not as though the whole place isn't crying out. She then gives up on the fence. Having made her protest she withdraws in sighing disapproval. She gave up some time ago on my clothes. She is perhaps glad of signs of increasing eccentricity on the part of her daughter. It makes her more interesting, a fragile threatened creature trapped with some sort of familial nutter. I imagine her in the living room where she plays compulsive bridge. The curtains are drawn as the colours may fade, the chintzes are the deep purples, roses and buffs of corals bunched beneath shadowed seas. She tells Amy, Beryl and Con. — Sometimes I wonder about Kate. I mean seriously. But the Girls will reassure her, touching their lacquer for comfort. — Oh Kate's all right, they will tell my mother. — Don't worry about Kate.

*

Things are coming to a head in Woolston. The Laboratory situation approaches critical mass as Geoffrey is torn between his duty to sack Trudy and his need to cup her pretty buttocks in his large grateful hands. After her last serious error his eyes blinked tears, and even Trudy was not blithe. Harry steams in righteous disgust.

— Calls himself the Boss out here, he mutters. — Why can't he be a man? he asks, and sack the bitch?

But Geoffrey is, but Geoffrey is, and his hands hang empty with grief.

The rottweiler's agony is getting to us also. It now howls. We ring Noise Abatement, we whinge in sympathy with the dog's misery.

Elaine withdraws further, counting blood corpuscles at glacial speed. Ric remains cheerful. Dusty but calm he cleans out the storeroom. Hissing between his teeth as though grooming a horse, he stacks cartons of agar in segregated piles. He knows that this order, this clarity of intent, will not survive the daily scramble but does it anyway.

As the tension defuser, the one who can work with everyone, I become over-merry. Harry and I sing our Weepy. — Hush, not a word to Geoffrey, we moan. — He might not understand. Geoffrey does not smile, but Ric does. Like the deaf, the disregarded, or uncomprehending, he smiles often. When anyone laughs he smiles to indicate that he has not missed the joke. He smiles as he goes about his work. Some people in wheelchairs do this too. It is a signal, the opposite of Mayday.

Ric is good with the autoclaves. The snorting, belching things can be tricky.

— This one isn't constant at fifteen, Ric, I tell him one morning as I go to collect the fresh culture plates.

— Juz a lil juzzment, he replies and makes it.

— Tell me about Venice, Ric, I say.

— Your Venice is not my Venice, he says.

— I haven't got a Venice.

— You will one day. One day you go and you come back and you will say Ah Venice and everyone will say Ah Venice and you will not see the filth and the stink and hunger even. Venice! Take up it the ass!

I am enchanted. — Ric, I'm *mad* about you!

— Shuddup, he says. There is a pause as he heaves the tray of rubbish out of the autoclave. Steam pours out, as from a loco in an old movie. Ric dumps the tray and turns to me, still in his heavy gloves. — Why do you do it, like? he asks.

— The rubber bands?

— Hunh? My hair hangs either side of my face, Pocahontas with rubber bands.

— Oh. To keep it out of the way. The specimens.

— One real good thing in Venice is Titian, he says.

— Your hair is Titian. He slams the autoclave door.

— Rubber bands! I pick up the tray of plates and depart.

Despite my impatience to share the Venice one with Harry, I wait till we have finished planting out the swabs, as we both care and are good workers and don't chat on the bench. I don't begin until the cultures are in the incubator and the urines swinging in the centrifuge.

— One day you go and you come back and you will say Ah Venice and you will not see . . .

I am in good form. My mimicry is exact. Harry and Trudy are laughing so hard their fillings show, even Elaine smiles weakly before turning back to her unending thankless task.

— Take up it ze . . .

— Shuddup! shouts Ric from the doorway, his face

bleached, his hands shaking. I fall off my high stool.

— Ric . . . I start.

— Shuddup! he spits at me again. My shame is a dumper wave knocking me breathless. Ric slams the door and I am lost.

He still won't look at me. He cannot see me. I am the other side of the moon in darkness. The hissings and mutterings, the curses and bitches of laboratory unrest continue but I don't hear, don't care, don't jolly anyone, not even Harry.

— Stuff them, I think, as though it is someone else's fault I have betrayed my friend, and surely that is too strong a word and what does it matter. My Subalpine Meadow is no help. It no longer spins me into a mountain dream as I sit on the bus. Maybe I'll finish it this weekend and then it will be finished and so what. Will I even look at it much? — Forget it, forget it, forget it, I tell myself not meaning the fence, but the mind is its own bouncer and a tough one at that, and won't admit even vacant harmless amnesia without a pass.

I don't finish the fence. I hardly look at it and my mother says — Well are you going to finish it or not? and I say — I don't know, and she says — Merciful heaven, and glides to the telephone which is her lifeline to normal people who swim in her world.

I sit in the bus on Monday morning thinking of nothing. I watch two small boys across the aisle who are engrossed in conversation. One is very serious; he confides and explains at earnest length. The other shakes his spiky hedgehog head and laughs. He does not believe, will never believe, that life is anything but a laughing joke.

There are no cars outside the Lab, only Ric's pick-up truck.

I stump up one of the concrete strips of the drive, my thighs bouncing against each other. Three standard roses left by some previous owner struggle towards extinction. I push open the door and am astounded. The Laboratory has disappeared. I mean completely. The walls, the benches have been stripped, there are no stools, no microscopes, no bench racks, nothing. Nothing remains, not even the incubator or the centrifuge. The walls have been painted Arctic White, everything has been painted. There are no people. The ceilings, the walls, the window sills shimmer back at the emptiness.

I turn to see Ric staring at me from the doorway.

— What's happened? I gasp.

He is not impressed. — It's been painted, he says.

— But but . . . ? I start laughing. I drop my shoulder bag, my knees buckle as I weave around the room laughing.

— Nobody, nobody, nobody, I gasp.

— Didn't they tell you? On Friday?

— No, no, nobody. Nobody. I will never speak again. Laughter is the only thing. Laughter and oblivion.

— What a pack of bums, says Ric. Then he begins to laugh. Moving with the stately care of the very drunk, clutching the bench at intervals, we laugh and laugh and laugh.

Eventually Ric moans. — They had to tell me for the humping. Only the humping. We continue the gutwrenching catharsis of the untold, we beam at each other in the empathy of the excluded. Tears of joy spout from our eyes, we clutch each other. — No one, I pant. — Not one of the bastards.

— I'll give you a lift home, he says. — It's shut till tomorrow. All the days shut. I've got to put the stuff back.

I crawl upright from my bench. — I'll show you my fence, I say.

*

My mother is playing bridge at the Club. Shy as any Artist at an Opening, I lead the way around to the back, brushing past the papery hydrangea heads. Ric follows in silence. When I see the fence with his eyes I am seven years old and not happy. Still staring at it he takes the brush from the jar at the back steps, wipes it on the turpy rag, then sticks the handle in the back pocket of his jeans. He skips the lid from the tin of white paint with a screw driver, stirs it with the stick beside it, then moves down the rough grass springing from the soles of his beat up Adidas like a slow motion dancer on TV, the brush in one hand, paint pot in the other.

— Don't! I panic. — You don't know. How can he know?

It's all right. Mountain daisies sprout from his brush, his hand is sure, the white petals spike out. His strokes get faster, daisies leap across the fence, in clusters, alone, or in drifts that multiply.

I open my two green pots, grey-green and a small bright glossy, give them a quick stir, grab the brushes and am in business. Our brushes stub and sweep the fence.

— Middles. Their middles, says Ric. — Get the yellow.
Its my fence. And I'm busy.
— You get it, I say.
Ric flings back his head to laugh.
— OK, he says, and gets it.

School Story

The story begins in the staff room.

Miss Franklin has her knife deeper than ever into Miss Tamp. She has already flattened her over detentions, and she has not given an inch on parent participation which is a controversial topic in need of discussion.

Several staff members don't know where to put themselves. The blue, brown, brown eyes of Ms Powdrell, Ms Murchison and Ms Doyle (Sooze, Margot and Carmen) are wide with spectator interest. They are young. They climb up mountains and into deep valleys out of which they must scramble as best they can, their hearts bumping and their hands full. Our less experienced staff members Miss Tamp calls them. Shit, think Carmen, Margot, and Sooze, and Carmen's mind adds that Miss Tamp should sack the bitch. Who's Head anyway? Margot and Sooze, however, admire Miss Franklin because she is an excellent teacher and has iron control even in 4F though of course it is not called that now. Still even so, shit, they think. They see the handle between the shoulder blades and watch the blood drip dripping as in *Tess of the D'Urbervilles*. Margot's shoulders move in unconscious sympathy, Sooze wriggles lower in her plastic chair. Carmen lights a cigarette in the staff room smokefree zone and dares Miss Franklin with her young eyes.

— Put it out, says Miss Franklin without a please and Carmen leaves the table, her long plait leaping from side to side across her back with the impetus of her departure. Carmen is Phys Ed and smokes very rarely. Mr Tysler smiles.

The older members have seen it all before, but even so. Mrs Toon (Maths) gazes at the ceiling, her verruca is giving her gyp and she can't remember if she has another tin of Gourmet Beef and Heart in the cupboard above the sink. She tries to visualise the contents of the cupboard, her mind moving over the gaily labelled soups to the flat Herrings in Tomato Sauce to the small oval-shaped tin of anchovies left over from the time when she made her own pizzas and her youngest asked if those fish were sad. She thinks she has another Gourmet but it is better to be safe than sorry. Mrs Toon will stop off at the dairy.

Mr Tysler is Art and fed up. His face is rugged country. His beard is untracked bush. His body moves continuously, his legs writhe in a kinetic sculpture of frustrated boredom. His hands tap the table, his feet scrub the carpet squares. He hates Miss Franklin, he despises Miss Tamp. He has had it up to here with sodding kids and sodding females though he fantasises about Carmen. He aches for her as she flounces back to the table having finished her cigarette gesture and flops down muttering Sorry to Miss Tamp who doesn't know what to do. Miss Franklin knows exactly what to do. Carmen smiles back at the glare across the table. Her hands are folded in her lap. Her plait is still. She is a good girl again. Mr Tysler lifts his hands from the table and slams them between his thighs. He could weep. And weep.

— Can't we get *on*, he mutters.

The other more experienced staff members including Miss Hobbs, Mrs Benchley, Mrs Hopere, Mrs Medgley and the part-timers indicate their agreement. They nod, smile, scrape their chairs, sigh, look at their watches, shuffle papers, scratch about in their carrier bags, stare at the ceiling, bite the insides of their mouths, scratch about in carrier bags and clamp their lips tight as they role-play their role as a captive audience. Mrs Stillburn continues her abstract doodle. She adds a circle to the point of the middle pyramid, encloses this within another pyramid then shades in with quick decisive strokes of her Air New Zealand ballpoint. Mr Tysler has his head in his hands.

Miss Tamp has resumed command. Her face is stern, her complexion blotched red on white.

— Yes indeed, yes *indeed*, she says.

Ms Jenni Murphy who is vegan has discovered a small jar of bean sprouts hidden beneath papers in the bottom of her kete. She takes out the jar and inspects it with interest, shakes it, peers at it, then puts it back having resisted the temptation to take off the lid and have a good sniff as she would like to. She didn't know she had it she whispers to Mr Tysler who does not reply.

— Now the final item, says Miss Tamp. — Gowns at Prizegiving.

Gowns, writes the Head's secretary, Mrs Sinclair. She thanks God that she made the curry last night. The thought of not having to start from scratch is so comforting that she smiles.

Miss Tamp smiles back.

— Gowns at Prizegiving repeats Miss Tamp. — Several members of the staff, she says, glancing at the younger members, don't own gowns. Carmen returns a vigorous nod of encouragement. — They cost the earth she murmurs with downcast eyes. Margot and Sooze don't know where they are. Their smiles are non-commital. — So therefore, continues Miss Tamp speaking rather fast, I have decided that gowns will not be worn at Prizegiving.

Miss Franklin's voice slices out from an ice cave. — The last shred of dignity gone from what used in Miss Sargesson's time, to be a memorable occasion, she says.

— Jesus wept mutters Mr Tysler. Miss Franklin bounces round to face him. There is uproar at the staff meeting. There is agreement, disagreement, frustration, rage, aching boredom and a trickle of anarchy. Hands slam the table. A part-timer's chair topples as she leaps up. She is off. She has had it up to here. Her neighbour Mrs Sinclair lays a restraining hand on the day-glo track suit and whispers. The part-timer rights the chair and crashes back onto it muttering. Carmen reaches for her cigarette packet which she has left sitting with a Bic lighter on the table. — Ladies! Ladies! cries Miss Tamp.

Mrs Benchley (English) straightens her back. — Things have changed since Miss Sargesson's time, she says, brushing the front of her shell pattern with quick downward flicks of her right hand.

Miss Franklin bounces from Mr Tysler. Her hair is a white crest. Her hands clamp the table to hide their shaking.

— What do you mean!

Mrs Benchley is almost satisfied with her front. She picks a final fleck of white off and lifts her head to Miss Franklin's eyes. — Just that she was a thousand years behind the times, she says.

— If you consider . . . ! But Miss Franklin's rage has

trapped her subtle words. They cannot get out to fight. Mrs Benchley consolidates.

— The place was pickled in aspic she says. There are puerile sniggers of laughter. Miss Tamp's head swings from side to side. She is a trapped umpire.

Miss Franklin is on her feet, her hands reach out as she leans across the table to kill Mrs Benchley.

Miss Tamp resumes control. — Ladies! Ladies! she cries.

Now Mr Tysler's chair topples. The less experienced members of staff clutch themselves with delight as he storms from the room swinging his canvas bag up onto his shoulder in an enraged sweeping arc.

It is morning break next day. Sooze lifts her head from *The Population Explosion*.

— What've you got on? she asks Margot.

The yellow plastic spoon in Margot's hand is stilled. Her face is anxious. — Is it too strong? she asks.

It is but never mind. Sooze shrugs. — What is it?

— Stephanotis. Margot dips her head quickly to her shoulder and sniffs, testing for overkill. She sits on the large table between two piles of marking. Her soft red lace-up boots are on the seat of a plastic chair.

— I hate scent at work says Carmen. She tips her chair back. — What about last night though! She says.

Margot agrees with Sooze and Carmen that the whole thing was over the top. She adds that she liked Alec not being able to handle being called a lady for God's sake.

— Did you see his face!

— No one can see his face, says Sooze.

Margot continues shovelling shell-shaped pasta salad into her mouth with the yellow spoon. She is selective, she removes small pieces of chopped onion which she places on the lid of the container for later disposal. The pasta is decorated with cubes of red and green peppers but it still does not appeal to Sooze.

— Yuk, she says.

— He's not that bad, mumbles Margot. Sooze does not bother to explain as she doesn't have to eat it and she is now searching the numerous pockets of her stone-washed denim skirt. She knows she has a bus ticket somewhere which she wishes to use as a bookmark. She finds the small useful thing and is reassured.

— What we're talking about here, says Carmen, is a confrontation situation. The faintest shadow of golden hair is visible above her upper lip as she swings around to the window to touch a bud of the gift-wrapped cyclamen plant on the window sill. Mrs Sinclair had to dash out during her lunch hour yesterday because she had forgotten her aunt's birthday and then forgot to take it home but she has explained to Aunt. The puce buds hang like toy furled umbrellas, a green calyx frill at each throat. Aunt will be pleased thinks Carmen.

— Anyone who can control 4F, well whatever they are now, has my vote, says Sooze. She sees the rows of sullen faces, senses her failure, her occasional prickle of fear. What can she do. — It's not your fault, her lover tells her as she lies confiding in his arms each night. — It's not theirs, says Sooze. This she knows. She had thought this knowledge would save her. Sometimes Bryce feels as though he works at Girls' High all bloody night. He is getting hacked off. No one told Sooze teaching would be war. If they had she would not have believed them. Sooze is a good teacher, she knows she is a good teacher but how can she even get out the microscopes.

4F and microscopes! And they would enjoy, they should see the free-flow amoebae rolling along in a drop of ditch water, the paramoecia bumping about like ciliated Dodgems. It is all wrong. Sooze sees the chalk-strewn room, sees the still face of Mavis Kanji who waits stoically for the racket to subside so that Miss Powdrell can continue to teach her the Science she wishes to learn so that she can go to Training College and be a credit.

— Control is what she should be talking about, cries Sooze. Control! Not flaming Gowns!

— If we could just get rid of a few of the hell kids, says Margot. She tips the onion discards and spoon into the empty pottle, replaces the lid and holds the container in both hands.

Sooze agrees. — Jen Nation came at me with a chair yesterday, she says.

— Which is Jen Nation, asks Margot. Margot is five feet and slight.

— Huge! Punk. Sooze demonstrates Atlas without the world.

— Not Cissie Nation's sister?

— Maybe. Sooze shrugs. — Don't know.

Margot had a difficult interview last term with Mrs Nation who appeared at the door of the Clothing Room demanding satisfaction. She required to know why Margot picked on Cissie. If Cissie wanted to make pink taffeta dungarees she would make pink taffeta dungarees. Margot quite agreed. It was just that she thought the material mightn't . . . Margot could get stuffed. Mrs Nation loomed over Margot who was eye to eye with the tan reindeers on the heavy blue jersey in front of her and told Margo where she could put herself and all fucken teachers. Who paid them anyway. Who did they think they were picking on kids like Cissie. And she knew where Margot lived, she added over her shoulder as she departed tip tipping across the courtyard in her high heels and white hailstone-spotted tights.

— Alec Tysler kicks open the staff room door. His arms are full of Art which he dumps on the table. — Sodding girls, he mutters.

— Go to Boys' High, says Carmen turning from her study of the cyclamen.

— I don't like knives, says Alec.

— We have the odd knife here says Sooze.

They continue their sagas of in-school experiences. Survivors, they draw comfort from escapes, near misses. Carmen reties the cord at the end of her plait. Any moment soon, she thinks, we'll be talking about the one that didn't go off.

— Why did they appoint a wimp to a tough school like this, asks Margot.

Alex is about to ask her if she really thinks *this* is a tough school, but refrains when he sees from the look of polite interest on Carmen's face that she is waiting for this remark.

— She's not a wimp, says Carmen. — Franklin never gives her a chance.

— She shouldn't need a *chance*, says Sooze. On and on and round and round in endless grinding circles the subject is discussed. The bell rings. Margot tosses her pottle in the Non Biodegradable where it lies on the plastic liner beside Jenni Murphy's bean sprouts which have gone off after all. This is the story so far.

*

4F have suffered Sooze's carefully prepared lesson on the Carbon Cycle with comparative calm. Sooze likes the Carbon Cycle. It explains a lot. All living things, she tells 4F, are born, grow, reproduce, die, then are buried if they are lucky. They rot and fertilise new growth. Life, explains Sooze, goes round and round in circles, but no one smiles. When the bell goes Sooze shoots the Vistavision screen up behind the blackboard, unplugs the slide projector, stacks away the slide carousel and heaves the heavy case off the table.

— Open the door please, she mutters to Jan who shrugs pained shoulders but obliges. Sooze heads off along the shining corridor trailing a cord which has slipped. She is surprised to see Mavis Kanji coming out of the girls' toilet. She dumps the projector case on the vinyl. — Mavis, she calls. Mavis moves hesitantly towards her. Sooze, Mavis, and the projector case form an island buffeted by waves of yelling females.

— Why weren't you in Science, Mavis? asks Sooze.

Mavis bursts into tears. Oh God, thinks Sooze, placing one leg firmly each side of the projector. Why did she ask. Her free period is a melting treat. She heaves up the projector case from the floor. — Come over here, she says. They move into an alcove, a backwater designed for such sanctuary, and sit on the mock leather bench. — What is the matter Mavis? asks Sooze. Mavis's tears flow from a deep well of sorrow. Her brown eyes are awash. They drip. Eventually, Sooze slots the pieces of the story together. Mavis wished to give Miss Powdrell some Basmati rice. — Basmati rice is the best rice in the world. Basmati rice is long, fine, best tasting. Sooze nods. She knows about Basmati rice. — For you, gulps Mavis. — Well thanks Mavis, says Sooze, who bought some Basmati rice last week at the Indian dairy who have it occasionally. — I asked my mother, continues Mavis, but she said no so I took some. And then, and then . . . The memory is painful, the tears gush. — The big kids grabbed it from me like this, says Mavis snatching air with long narrow fingers, and poured it down the toilet. It is not funny Sooze tells herself but she knows Bryce will love it. — You shouldn't have taken your mother's rice Mavis, she bleats. — But it was for *you*, Miss Powdrell! Sooze touches the heaving shoulder. — It was a very kind of you Mavis. It is the thought that counts says Sooze who is smug about clichés. — Don't worry about it any more. You must get back to class. Mavis's limpid eyes are wide. — But it is still *there* she says. — Still sitting. I am trying to get it out!

— What!

— All through Science I am trying.

Mavis is in despair. She makes wooshing noises and wriggles a handle in the air. Her long hands are beautiful, the fingers skin and bone. — Oh God, thinks Sooze again. — Show me, she says. Together they move to the nearby toilets where paper lies deep on the floor and the graffiti is an open book.

Margot's Clothing period with 3G is going well. She teaches Home Economics which used to be called Home Science and is about to be called something else, but Margot teaches sewing and is happy to let it go at that. She demonstrates correct Cutting Out procedures. No hand is allowed to *touch* the giant scissors chained to the cutting table until Margot has checked Lay Out. Margot is meticulous, her small quick hands align, brush, straighten the length of printed denim on the table. — Always *check* girls, she says, that the pattern is printed straight on the material. However expensive the material . . . Margot does not finish the sentence. — Now the next thing is the darts. Margot likes third formers. Everyone likes third formers, or rather if they like any girls it is usually third formers or the occasional seventh former. 3G think Miss Maitland is neat which is a good description of Margot. She has the bobbing compactness of a scaup duck. She bounces back. All the girls are impressed by what Margot knows. They watch her. She knew when to stop, wearing heavy belts slung low on her hips. She knew when to discard the ties which knotted, the boots which clanked. Last week she turned her bright pink collar down at the back and buttoned the shirt to the neck like the lead singer in the Pet Shop Boys. She is thinking about removing her shoulder pads. The girls don't miss a trick. Margot's lover wears jandals both summer and winter. He is used to them he says, and so what.

Carmen has also had a satisfactory third period during which 5G played intelligent fast exhilarating netball. Carmen discussed strategy which is all important. She cannot understand why the fire of fifth form netball is so hard to maintain in the sixth and seventh forms. She would really like to know. Carmen is everywhere at netball. She leaps, blows her whistle, exhorts, seizes the ball in mid flight to demonstrate how Ema's shooting stance could be improved. — See! begs Carmen and Ema nods. The slack kids hide during Phys Ed and Carmen is damned if she is going to flush them out. Perhaps this is why Carmen is less impressed than Margot or Sooze with Miss Franklin's control.

Miss Franklin teaches French which makes it more amazing. She has the French stream of 4F this period. Sooze is still head down over the girl's toilet with Mavis weeping by her side. 4F is by no means silent but Miss Franklin is in control. When she tells Jeanine to stop talking Jeanine stops talking. When Jess answers a question in English Miss Franklin says — *En francais s'il vous plait*, and Jess stumbles into Francais. Miss Franklin's bright hair is a banner, her eyes are a beacon as she leads 4F. She will teach 4F and they will learn. One or two will share her love for what she insists is the most beautiful language in the world. Miss Franklin and 4F have had serious discussions about the *Rainbow Warrior* and the French. Francais survives. It would break Sooze's heart. Miss Franklin tells 4F. — When I was in Paris as a postgraduate student (no desk lid bangs, no one moans), we were each asked for *un histoire* to explain why we were angry. — In French? Miss Franklin is pleased. — In French, Bonnie. I explained to *le professeur* that I had received mail from New Zealand that morning and could be angry with no one. — And then what asks Bonnie. Miss Franklin tells them *en francais* and 4F get out their *cahiers* like lambs.

Miss Tamp sits in her office with the sun on her back. She studies a large chart of next year's timetable and wishes once again that she could manage without part-timers who make things so much more complicated. Miss Tamp's skill with timetables is legendary. She has the vision of a three dimensional noughts and crosses champion. She can *see* 4F at Science in the lower lab there, 5B at Social Studies here. The slight problem of the clash between Scholarship French and Scholarship Applied Maths leaps to her gaze. She finds the computer invaluable but likes to do her preliminary shuffling with felt pens and cardboard. It is a tough round but she is winning. Miss Tamp is very concerned about the situation *vis à vis* Miss Franklin. Last night was impossible. However she will worry about that later. At the moment Miss Tamp is in her element. She turns to the keyboard.

Mrs Sinclair in the outer office has snatched a moment to look at the Community College Winter Term Programme. She moves the vase filled with Iris stylosa which she brought from home, and spreads out the paper. She normally does something each Winter. She can choose between Patchwork and Patchwork for Christmas. Between Vegetarian Cooking, Chinese Cooking, Microwave Cooking or Cake Decorating. She can Keep Fit. She can try Living with Teenagers. Dressmaking for Reproduction intrigues her until she sees Porcelain Dolls on the next line. If she joins she must bring her doll on the first night. Assertiveness for Women. Stress Management. Mrs Sinclair sighs. She folds the paper and puts it in her bottom drawer. The hell with it. But she usually does something. She will show the newspaper to Una Benchley.

But Mrs Benchley does not want to be pinned down. She is quite dismissive when she comes into the staff room from Gate Duty in the southerly. — Oh Thea! she says. — Not now for heaven's sake. She flops into an easy chair and stratches about in her bag labelled *Loot*. She finds a plastic bag, unwraps the Gladwrap and munches her vegemite, lettuce and wholemeal, staring straight ahead as though stoned. Mrs Sinclair is left with the page hanging. She folds it. Each class is one and a half hours long she reads but she knows this already. Beauty Unisex Complex catches her eye. This is an advertisement for Swift Scissors Hair Salon. There are Winter Specials.

Carmen, Margot and Sooze sit at the large table where the younger members of the staff congregate. There is no

189

hierarchical seating structure in the staff room. It is just how things happen. Carmen is surprised when Miss Franklin, who usually occupies the third easy chair from the door, joins them, until she realises that the only vacant easy chair is beside Mrs Benchley. Carmen, who is convent-educated, moves a pile of books to accommodate Miss Franklin and offers her a chair. Miss Franklin thanks Carmen and gives her the smile of the ex-protagonist. Miss Franklin eats her Mealmates and apple. Carmen and Sooze, lean as Masai warriors, demolish greasies from the takeaway at the gate. Their precise polished fingers dip and pick. They lick their lips, suck their fingers, then scrub them with the scrappy paper napkins provided. Later they will wash. Margot, who wishes she had not eaten all her pasta salad at break, accepts some chips.

— How long have you been teaching, Miss Franklin? asks Carmen.

Miss Franklin peels her apple with spiralling expertise.

— Thirty years, she replies.

There is silence as this remark is processed. It will take longer than the greasies. Thirty years thinks Sooze. Jeeze. Poor old cow thinks Carmen.

— Why have you stayed so long? says Margot, leaning forward to select a well done chip. She hates the pallid floppy ones. — Teaching I mean.

Miss Franklin knows their thoughts. Her brown eyes snap with pleasure. Her air is triumphant. — Because, she says, it amuses me to combat ignorance. And suck on that one thinks Carmen. There is no reply to Miss Franklin's statement. It sinks, rocking slightly from side to side like a coin subsiding in a mountain spring.

Alec Tysler lies back flattened in an easy chair. His

outstretched legs impede progress to the coffee machine. There is some extravagantly high stepping. He stares at Carmen over the top of the *Dominion*. His eyes never leave her. He is ridiculous.

Carmen and Sooze go and wash. Margot makes do with a good scrub of tissues as she has not touched the chicken. The bell rings. The story continues.

Miss Tamp has put the timetable to bed, or rather to rest. There is only so much she can do at this stage. She sits very still at her desk gazing at one of the chimneys of the Old Block. The pot is the old-fashioned type, the smoke can go both ways. Miss Tamp thinks about Miss Franklin. Instinctively she reaches for her silver ballpoint and rough pad but they cannot help. What would she write. Friend of previous Head now dead. Wanted position herself. The cliché has been observed before and needs no clarification. There is no point in noting, Excellent teacher. Miss Tamp fingers the pencil. Destructive. Irrational. Impossible. Miss Tamp has tried everything. She has made allowances. She will not put up with it another minute. She is in the right and thus armoured. There will be no repeat of last night. Quick resolute thoughts shoot along Miss Tamp's nerve fibres. They leap the synapses. They stiffen the sinews. Miss Tamp reaches for the telephone. — Mrs Sinclair, she says — would you please get a message to Miss Franklin. Thank you. Ask her to come to my office, please, before she leaves school today. Yes. Thank you.

Miss Tamp leans back and twists Mother's garnet round and round her finger.

Miss Tamp's next concern is Fire Drill. She has decided, rightly, that advertised fire drills are not treated seriously enough. A slackness has crept in, not only, she fears, among the girls who linger and hide in the toilets. Midway though the last period Miss Tamp intends sounding the fire alarm. She has advised the Fire Service but not the staff. She looks at her Seiko and pushes her chair back. Miss Tamp leaves her office. She winks at Mrs Sinclair. They are conspirators.

The fire alarm shrieks through the school. Miss Tamp's heart is beating rather fast. She has always wanted to do that.

Sooze's wedge-cut hair swings back from her face as she lifts her head. Shit. Electrolysis of water is working perfectly. (Sooze is always grateful, surprised even, when her experiments work.) Oxygen is bubbling into one gas cylinder, twice the quantity of hydrogen is evident in the opposite cylinder. 3A are impressed. This is the real thing. I must have missed the warning spiel thinks Sooze who tends to think things are her fault. — OK girls. Sorry but we'll have to leave it she says, turning off the current. — Aw shit says Meryl. — Come along girls, leave your books. — They'll be nicked. — Leave your *books*. And hurry.

Margot is glad of the fresh air. Anything to get away from the combination of whooping chatter plus the buzz of the heavy duty machines which the kids foul up endlessly then scream for her to fix. — Amy! How many times! Press this *thing*, unravel the cotton, it's because you've put the thread around *here* instead of *here* . . . But Amy is itching to get back to her jump suit and wishes Margot would shut up and get off the chair. — Aw I get it, she lies. — And next time, says Margot, *don't* . . . But Amy is motoring. The Clothing Room is overheated. 5C are into being happy with their own

bodies. Deodorants are out. Stephanotis is overwhelmed.
— In order girls. Turn off the machines. In *order*. Margot
checks, turns off the lights and shuts the door. — Straight to
your *Station*. This way Penny. In Earthquake Drill Margot is
instructed to tell the girls to hide under their desks when the
plaster starts falling from the ceiling.

Miss Tamp and Mrs Sinclair take their own warning seriously.
They turn off, they shut down, they hitch their skirts high
and climb out the window onto the long vertical fire escape
ladder which they treat with respect, each foot groping with
care for the rung below. They are joined by Mrs Benchley
as she appears backwards from the staff room Fire Escape
window. She has had to clamber over a misplaced sofa. — I
thought I'd better come even though it *is* my free period she
tells Miss Tamp's departing hands. — But of *course*, Miss
Tamp replies to the behind above the Hush Puppies. — What?
— Oh never mind. There is an unexpectedly long drop to the
ground from the last rung of the ladder.

   Alec Tysler shepherds 4K from the chaotic Art room,
rounds up the stragglers, takes them to their Assembly
Station by the Library, discovers it's another bloody fire drill
and ditches them. He storms off across the hockey field to
the Sports Pavilion for a smoke. His narrow jeaned legs slice
the air as he fulminates with himself. What does she think
they *are*! No male would play games with his staff like that.
Treat them like kids for Chrissake.
   Alec bumps open the door of the Sports Pavilion with
his shoulder. Carmen turns, two panda netballs in her arms.
Alec flops onto the nearest bench. — What are you doing
here, he asks.

— I work here replies Carmen, stowing the balls into a locker which she locks with a key dragged up on a cord from around her neck.

— There's a fire drill says Alec as if it mattered. Carmen stares around her mote-filled empire.

— This is my Station she says. — I'm First Aid.

She could heal the whole sodding world. Alec moves to her.

Miss Franklin also dismisses her class as soon as she discovers the fire alarm is not genuine. The seventh form fan out chattering from their premature release, then, programmed as pigeons, swing back to the classroom block for their books. Miss Franklin is ropeable. Ropeable. What sort of a woman. What sort of a woman would *do* that. Lack of trust. Negation. Miss Franklin strides along the concrete path beside the hockey field in her ribbed *strumphosen*. She ignores the sun which shines through the few remaining leaves of the plane trees. She seethes beneath her lambswool then remembers. Tamp wants to see her. Good. Tamp will do that. Miss Franklin's pace quickens. She will cut across the hockey field to the Administration Block. She is on business bent.

She passes the Sports Pavilion. Miss Franklin inspects noise on principle. She tries the door handle then kicks the door open. Alec lies on the floor in the foetal position writhing in pain. A shaft of light from the skylight illuminates him, specks of dust are trapped in its rays. Carmen is against the lockers. Her face is scarlet, she is breathless and shaking. — He tried to rape me! she cries. Alec groans negation. Miss Franklin looks at the figure on the floor. Alec, speechless with pain, rolls his back to her.

— Come with me, Miss Franklin says to Carmen and they leave the Sports Pavilion.

And thus it is that Miss Tamp's interview with Miss Franklin is deferred. She has after all made notes, marshalled her resources. She is calm and very determined. She will deal once and for all with Miss Franklin whose behaviour is impossible. Things cannot and will not go on like this. Last night will not be repeated. Miss Franklin must shape up or ship out though Miss Tamp does not think in these terms. There is a knock on the door. — Come in calls Miss Tamp and in burst Miss Franklin and Ms Doyle whom Miss Tamp last saw in confrontation but who are now obviously united in their mission. Miss Tamp hears them out and of course agrees. This must be dealt with *now*. Where is Mr Tysler? asks Miss Tamp. — He was in the Sports Pavilion says Miss Franklin. — On the floor says Carmen. Miss Tamp picks up her bag. — He won't still be there snorts Miss Franklin. Miss Tamp sets off on principle. Her cubans click along the empty polished corridors and concrete paths till she reaches the still building. The door is open, the Sports Pavilion is empty, a dusty stowage area for shadows, a quiet warehouse.

There is no answer from Mr Tysler's home number when Miss Tamp tries from her office on her return. She will try from home.

Carmen is shaken, though not from danger averted. Carmen is fit, she has studied Self Defence and her kick was well directed, but something is wrong with her. She stands staring at the face in the staff cloakroom mirror after Miss Franklin has finally left her. She removes a couple of long black hairs from the handbasin in front of her and fills it with cold water which she slaps against her face. She tells herself again not to be such a bloody fool. She clenches her fists with rage as her eyes prick with tears. She could kill the shit. It was all quite heavy. She is glad that Miss Tamp gripped the situation with such speed. He's had it. Carmen has had men. Bad enough anytime, but straight after Barry . . . She scrubs her face again. Sooze and Margot will have gone long ago. Carmen collects her gear from the empty staff room, takes her orange helmet from her locker and heads for her Honda. She will go to the gym and call in on Sooze on the way home. Bryce won't be there yet . . . Her eyes sting. — Shut up. Shut *up*. Get to the gym. Get to the gym. Have a sauna for God's sake.

Sooze is defrosting the chicken which she forgot to take out last night. It sits solid as the rock of Gibraltar in a bowl of warm pink water on the bench. Sooze turns in surprise when Carmen walks in the back door, then takes her in her arms as she sees her face, her hands dripping on the black and white vinyl squares.

Margot arrives a quarter of an hour later for her Kaffe Fassett pattern and the story is retold. Sooze produces a wine cask and three glasses and she and Margot are supportive and loving to Carmen who is angry because she can't stop crying. Carmen, Margot and Sooze sit at the formica table and talk about rape, they talk about men, they talk about the school, they talk about themselves, they talk about rape, they talk about themselves.

Bryce comes home. He runs up the back steps two at a time and flings open the kitchen door. He takes a step back. — Hi, he says.

*

Aunt is delighted with her cyclamen. — The buds are like baby umbrellas she tells Mrs Sinclair. Aunt puts it on top of the TV as they like the warmth. Mrs Sinclair kisses Aunt's soft floury cheek and goes home to her teenagers and her curry which is still holding out.

Mrs Benchley stands at her kitchen bench on one leg and inspects the other, hauling it up behind with one hand and peering at it over her shoulder. She has just discovered that she has laddered her Columbines which were new on this morning. Bloody fire drill.

Mrs Toon did have a tin after all but it doesn't matter. She picks up Caesar and cradles him in her arms to love him. Caesar writhes and twists away to drop four footed on the floor, then rubs his hearth rug beauty against Mrs Toon's legs to love her.

It is six o'clock. Miss Tamp has lit the gas in the Hutt and pulled her curtains which show sailing ships butting across seas of blue glazed chintz. Miss Tamp loves tall ships. She stands by the small sideboard which sits against the back wall of her living room. There is a wooden cupboard each side and glasses behind glass in the centre. Miss Tamp bends for the square-shouldered bottle from the left hand side. She pours herself a gin, replaces the bottle and closes the door. The tonic is beneath a fizz saving cap in the Kelvinator. The kitchen is galley-shaped; not by Miss Tamp's design, it was like that when she bought the house, but it pleases her and works well. — It works, she tells visitors who admire its compact shape, its crisp white formica and navy blue cupboards. She adds a slice of lemon which makes all the difference to her gin and tonic. Miss Tamp has a businesslike affection for her one gin each evening. She regards it as a friend. She likes advertisements on hoardings of foot square ice cubes and liquids which swirl in six foot glasses. Good old gin, she thinks as she moves to the sofa and adjusts its many cushions around her. Her choice in cushions is eclectic; there are cushions made from scraps of Persian rugs, dark velvet cushions for comfort, a Victorian embroidered patchwork one which cost the earth years ago in Camden Passage but she is glad she bought it. Miss Tamp settles for the News and sips. Bubbles gather round a lemon pip and carry it up to the surface, its ascension as effortless as a soul escorted to heaven by angels. The bubbles burst at the surface, the pip sinks, the bubbles rush to its aid and the process is repeated. Miss Tamp is pleased. She was Science originally.

Her small pleasure is punctured as she remembers that she has not yet spoken to Mr Tysler. She remembers the extraordinary dream she had last night about Mr Tysler or rather about the back of his neck. She had a vivid glimpse of the tough wrinkled skin in which was imbedded a tiny blue iridescent gastropod shell. Flesh had grown up around it so that only half the base below the pointed tip was visible. Miss Tamp is not Freudian about dreams but she does find them interesting and inexplicable. She must ring the man immediately. Miss Tamp knows that the more difficult something is the more quickly she must deal with it. She does not have to move. She reaches for her stiff leather bag, finds her Collins diary, checks under Staff and dials from the telephone by the sofa. No reply, she will have to keep trying. Damn. And she must ring Carmen to see how she is. No reply. Miss Tamp takes another sip of gin and sighs. And Miss Franklin. She will make another apointment with

Miss Franklin tomorrow. Miss Tamp reaches for the tapestry footstool which repeats the nautical motif and heaves her legs onto it. She will never surrender.

Miss Franklin stands in front of a small oak table in her flat in Brooklyn. She enjoys the view though parking is a problem. In the centre of the table on which she has dumped 4F's marking is a brass tray with a sherry decanter and five glasses. Miss Franklin does not know what happened to the sixth glass as they had been in Jean's family for many years. The glasses are small hand-blown flutes. The decanter and each individual glass rest within a filigree silver holder. Also on the table is a photograph of Jean on the Milford Track laughing at a scavenging kea. Miss Franklin pours herself a Flor Fino from the decanter.

Jean died almost two years ago. Miss Franklin does not remember her as well as she used to. Or rather — she remembers everything she did and said. Every word of Jean's wisdom and ribald wit lives on, but sometimes Miss Franklin is surprised to discover how many hours can go by without a thought of her friend. She did not think this would happen. When Jean first died even making a cup of tea was a memorial. Miss Franklin remembers Jean, bright and sparky as chips, when she is in confrontation with the Headmistress whom Jean never knew. Miss Tamp is beneath contempt. But not quite. Each evening Miss Franklin tells Jean of every twist, every turn, every triumph in her continuing struggle with her friend's successor. She thinks of the scene in the Sports Pavilion. Of Carmen. She lifts her glass.

There is no end to this story.

Fast Post

— I've been thinking a lot about death, says my friend Sooze holding out her glass for more wine.

— Death, says her lover Bryce not wanting to commit himself.

— Why death, I say though of course I know. It's the sort of thing Sooze does.

My lover Cam doesn't say anything. He regards death as unacceptable for thought or talk. Cam is not interested in abstracts. His back is bent, his elbows jut beyond his knees, his hands hang dejected as he stares at the floor.

We are at Sooze and Bryce's bach. Her parents' really, but Sooze and Bryce live there because their last flat folded and they can't find anything because they have no money so they can't find anything. Cam tells me they don't try. I can't comment on that but it's nice for us. We pile into the Skoda after work on Fridays and slip out to the coast in the slow lane. We take food and wine and we lie about and talk and drink a bit. Maybe go for a walk. We read a lot. There aren't many people you can read with. Most people say
— Yes great, and you drag out your paperbacks and start.

Then they tell you bits from their books. — Listen to this, they say then they read it and you have to listen perforce. Or else they read for a bit then lie on their backs and say — Aaah, and you know they're bored and want to do something else and will suggest it soon, so you keep your head down and try and read your Barthelme faster which is unsettling because you can't do that.

It's not like that with Sooze and Bryce. We just read. Their son Jared who is measured in months not years lies around with us though of course we keep him in play. We more or less take it in turns. When it's Sooze's turn she props Jared up surrounded by cushions and holds one of his pudgy hands while she reads and kisses a dimple at the bottom of a finger occasionally to fool him. He doesn't mind.

— Death, says Sooze again staring at the sea.

— What about it, I say.

— Well what do you think about it, says Sooze. She wears a large sweater with a design loosely based on aboriginal rock carvings. The zigzag lines which go up are green, the zigzag lines which go down are orange, the small stick figures are red and the background is black. The aboriginal paintings I like best are the x-ray ones which show what the animal has eaten *in situ.*

— Or don't you, she says.

— Of course I do, I say. — What do you think I am.

— I don't, says Cam.

Sooze is incensed. — Why not.

— What's the point, says Cam.

— There's no point, says Sooze. — Except that it's inevitable.

— Right, says Cam so don't think about it.

— So doesn't it *interest* you?

People like Sooze think people like Cam are not as intelligent as they are. People like Cam don't care which would really surprise people like Sooze if they could believe it, but they never would so by and large it works out all right. People like Cam know about the shifting mud which can bury abstract thought and often does.

Enough, Cam thinks, is enough, and reality will be more than.

Bryce has made his decision. He puts out one finger and corkscrews a piece of Sooze's hair around it which doesn't work as it's straight. He picks up her hand.

— Why hon he says. It's inevitable. No problem.

What interests me I say, is why doesn't it worry us, I mean.

— It worries me says Sooze removing her hand.

Bryce really wants to know. He snatches both her hands across the table as though he's going to drag her into a square dance. — Why! he says.

— I mean when you think, I say quickly, that for thousands of years the best minds all over the world have fussed about life after death . . .

— And if you were a best mind and didn't you were burnt, interrupts Bryce.

— . . . so why don't *we* care, I say.

— I do says Sooze.

— But you're a scientist! says Bryce.

— Ha ha says Sooze who teaches it. — Oh it's not *that* she says. — I don't mind about death of the *body*.

— 'Change and decay, in all around I see', roars Cam who was a choirboy.

— What worries me is the *spirit*. The human consciousness continues Sooze. — Where does that go?

There is a pause. Cam inspects his jandals. Abstract thought has the same effect on him as pornography. He doesn't see the point and it's depressing. Cam is a builder. He wears short shorts at work, the front of which are hidden by a leather apron so heavy it looks like a costume prop for a medieval film. In it he keeps the tools of his trade to hand. — We're getting there he says, dropping onto his heels from a great height to hammer the floor. I still feel glad when I see him swinging up the street.

— It doesn't go anywhere hon says Bryce. — You've got to accept that.

— I can't says Sooze.

— That's why people invented religions I say. — Because they couldn't accept the death of the sprit, see.

— Well nor can I says Sooze getting up to go and check on Jared.

The sun is sinking but no one gives it a thought. Bryce tops our glasses then reaches up and scratches about with one hand in a top cupboard. — We had some corn chips somewhere he says coming back empty-handed.

Sooze also comes back and flops onto her chair. She puts both hands up and combs the fingers back through her hair. It looks better; the trapped air fluffs it up for a bit though the result was unintentional.

— OK? I ask.

Sooze puts her hands together and lays a sleeping head on them. — OK, she says.

I change the subject. — How're things going in the flat world I ask.

Bryce leans back tipping his chair, maintaining balance with one hand. Suddenly he is behind a large table top with desk furniture, a rock-a-bye blotter, an embossed leather folder, a paper knife. — We've been approached to house sit a place in Khandallah, he lets slip.

— Great I say. — I like 'approached'.

— Sounds as though they're on their knees says Cam. He removes a speck from his beer with his smallest finger.

Sooze smiles. She knows about Bryce but it's OK.

— Yes she says. — Aunty Gret was on the lookout.

We know Aunty Gret. She paints. She gives us muddy water colours called Zinnias or Dahlias at Christmas and is a good sort and gets on with it.

— We haven't seen it and all that. I mean they haven't seen us and then there's Jared.

— Jared's flat on his back says Cam. — What can he do tenant-wise?

Sooze smiles. — Some people. Kids. You know, she says.

— Some people. Houses. You know, he says.

She puts out a finger and circles the vaccination mark on his bicep which dates from our overseas time. He flexes just for fun.

— What about Voltaire says Bryce untipping his chair.

Oh God.

Cam's bicep flops. — Who he says.

Sooze turns very slowly to stare at Bryce. — What about him she says.

— Well he didn't get burned.

— Of course he didn't get burned snarls Sooze. — He was too late wasn't he. For burning.

— He was exiled though wasn't he I say.

That's the trouble. We don't know anything. Just snatches. — Have you got an Oxford Companion I ask.

Bryce yawns. — Not here.

— Pears?

He shakes his head.

— Voltaire said that if God didn't exist it would be necessary to invent him I tell Cam, as though the man is a new pleat for third form clothing instruction which I teach.

Cam likes it. — Good thinking, he says.

But Bryce won't let it go. — What did *he* think happened to the human spirit after death he says.

Cam bends down to pick up Jared's plastic rattle from his feet, examines it carefully, shakes it a couple of times and places it on the table out of harm's way although there is no harm.

— I reckon this Fast Post is a rip off he says.

And then we are fighting about Fast Post. Bryce says it's essential. He has a letter from Levin ordinary post which took five days. He slams the table, the rattle rolls onto the floor. — Five days he says. — From Levin. Give me Fast Post!

— That's what they want you to do. Cam is very angry. His mouth tightens, the skin around his lips is white. When he is eighty he will have deep lines, not fine bird track wrinkles like some old men. — Pay twice as much. It's a con!

I don't post much and I know nothing about it but that doesn't stop me. — We should boycott it! I cry.

Bryce wants to hit me. All of a sudden we are hating each other, snarling and snapping at each others heels, circling around the ethics of Fast Post.

Sooze is not interested in Fast Post. She has taken the lasagne from the fridge and put it in the oven. She has prepared the salad but has not yet tossed it. She has chopped the chervil we brought and removed the Bleu de Bresse from the top of the fridge where it has been ripening. Sooze presses it between the slats of its small wooden cage. She seems pretty happy with its condition as she releases and unwraps it. She rinses her hands and shoves her hair back before curling up on the divan to clutch a calico patchwork cushion she made years ago. The design is called Cathedral Windows, not easy.

— What I do believe she says over the cushion top, is that two thousand years ago a really good man lived and died and if we could all live according to his commandments . . .

Bryce has had enough. He is on his feet, a tormented big cat loping the few steps from door to table, swinging in rage to confront her. — God in heaven! he shouts. — What's got into you!

— I can't stop thinking about death, Sooze mumbles into the cushion. Cam is determined to help. He leaps up from the table and sits beside her, pulling the cushion from her face.

— Look Sooze he says. — There's nothing to it. Don't worry about it. He takes her hand. — I promise he says smiling. — I nearly snuffed it. Didn't I Margot. In Milan.

— Yes I say.

— All you feel is surprised. You know, like it's not happening. Death, Cam insists, is for other people and when it's you you're surprised. That's why they'll never stop the road toll. — Disbelief, he says. — That's all I promise.

Milan is a challenge. It doesn't lie back and welcome you like Venice say. You have to track it down, find the good bits, work on it. We headed off from the station with our packs.

It was one of those hotels which always surprise me by not starting on the ground. It was on the third floor, recommended by *Let's Go*. Ground floor was shops, first and second another hotel, and the Pensione Famiglia Steiner on the third. Space was used twice — coffee and rolls were served in last night's bar. The family, mother father and three dark-eyed bambinas watched TV at night lined up on straight chairs against the wall in the slit office space. You put down the lavatory seat in the tile-lined box and turned on the shower. In England where dirt cheap means it, it would have been filthy but it was clean, the cotton bedspread white white, the linoleum shiny, the paint scrubbed.

We had a coke in the bar when we arrived, dumping our packs in the space labelled Rucksack in six languages. I flopped down beside a man at a table while Cam moved to the self-service dispenser. The guy had one of those streetwise faces, blunt features, pointed ears set at the slope, quick eyes. His haircut and fingers were short and stubby, the rest of him long and lean and pretty to watch. Cam was having trouble with the machine. The guy was up, instant and agile as a gibbon. He demonstrated the thing to Cam who thanked him. — That's OK, the man said.

He came from Manchester, a male model. Milan was the place, even though the agents took half your fee in commission. Milan is the world centre of male fashion he told us glancing at Cam's jandals. Milan is the big time where it's at. He'd been there three weeks and was doing OK so far though the whole thing was a real hassle. You've got to sell yourself he told us. No one else will.

— Yeah said Cam. — Nice guy he said as we went to our room.

We flaked out on the bed and slept. They don't let you sleep on second-class Eurail. The bastards wake you all the time.

Cam came to first. Making love all over Europe is different each time; well surroundings, externals. The late afternoon sun fell through the net curtains. Cam's legs were pure gold. — Tea? he asked afterwards, lifting my foot to kiss a toe.

— Mmm I said, easy either way but why not. He hauled himself off the bed and assembled our survival equipment, our artifacts. A narrow little Cretan saucepan from the market in Heraklion, an immersion heater, adaptor plugs. Lying on my back I heard the familiar clanks and knocks of illicit tea making.

— Haven't met one like this before he said.

— Nnn? I said watching the patterns of light caught in the net.

The flash was followed instantly by Cam's naked body hitting the floor. He lay stiff, catatonic, every musde locked. The plug was smoking, the air acrid. I was on my feet leaping to fall on him. I yanked his head back chin to ceiling and cupped my mouth over his mouth and nose and breathed in, out, in, out. At first I was shaking so hard I couldn't breathe deeply but the rhythm took over. Breathe, look, breathe, look. It didn't take long, half a minute or an hour. Cam. Don't stop. Breathe, stop, look, breathe, stop, look. His chest moved slightly, stopped, then gradually rose and fell in beautiful repetitive movement. My breasts stroked him, his eyes opened. — Nice he said. I dragged him onto the bed and shook for an hour as I lay beside him, watching, holding him, being held.

He wouldn't tell the owner. — He'd kick us out. It wasn't the plug. My fault, no mucking furries.

Next morning we sat drinking coffee and holding hands, you can do it. The amiable hairy proprietor heated the rolls in a mini oven beside the coke dispenser. Last night's bar was dark brown, benches, walls, an old sofa. The air had been there for some time. The male model sat reading a torn copy of the *Daily Mirror*. Jerry his name was.

The most beautiful girl I have ever seen dumped an enormous pack in the space by the door and subsided at the other table. She was six feet at least and walked haughty, slender, breasts firm beneath a Benetton T-shirt, her hair a stream of silver down her back. — Hi said Jerry. She said nothing, but dipped her crisp profile in recognition. German she must be, German, an ice maiden from a schloss in the pines. Or Swedish, saunas and birch twigs. Cam's hand moved in mine. His eyes were feeding on her. We all were. Beautiful women slay me.

She ordered coffee from the owner who seemed calmer than the rest of us. She drank it staring straight ahead then replaced the white cup with precision, centering it with care on its unmatching saucer. She lit a cigarette. I let Cam's hand go. Jerry was trying not to look at her, riffling the tattered *Daily Mirror*, flinging it onto the floor, snatching another from the pile on the end of the sofa. He was a cartoon figure, an expectant father from the days when fathers sat in waiting rooms with discarded papers at their feet.

She ground out her cigarette, stood up and shouldered her huge pack with one dip and lift. Jerry was on his feet. — You're not going! he cried. — Now!

She nodded and walked out, heading towards the cage lift. Jerry leapt after her, they disappeared. The owner picked up her cup, flicked the table with a checked duster and headed for his operations centre.

— Jeeze, whispered Cam.

— So *beautiful* I gasped. What was their relationship? One night? Ten years? Nothing?

Cam shook his head. The square brown room smelt very used. We were in shock, bereft, sitting there staring at the space she had filled.

*

— So you see, says Cam now squatting on his heels, staring up into Sooze's face for added conviction. — It's nothing.

Sooze shakes her head in the slightest possible rejection but she is grateful and smiles to tell him so, her hand on his knee.

— It's not that Cambo, she says. She sits up busily and knuckles a finger against her nose. — Did you see Mantegna's *Dead Christ*, she asks.

— We tried says Cam who likes looking at paintings. — The place was shut. Marg got the time wrong.

I kick his behind which unbalances him into Sooze's lap. One of our failures.

— It's the foreshortening. Sooze moves her head in slower wonder. — Amazing, she says.

Bryce has been reading the *Evening Post*. He folds it and slaps it on the divan as he stands to refill the glasses.

— In the morgue, he says, stretching his arms way above his head then letting them flop, they tie your name on your big toe. The right one. For identification.

Sooze Cam and I stare at him in silence, then turn to the dark sea, listen to it roll.

— I'd hate to be buried says Cam.

The Westerly

There's not a lot of action round Hils' Haven Motel tonight. Slow, you could call it. Definitely slow. Only a young couple in the left front and a single out the back and two families up the far end of the pool. It would break your heart.

The Reception Area looks onto the road, straight at the corner they crawl round before dropping down to the town, or village more like. I want to leap up from my desk and rush out screaming and waving to stop the cars and the trucks and the buses even. 'Come in,' I'll yell. 'Come in and stay. It's good value. It's clean. We'll make you happy. Come in, for God's sake.'

What'll we do otherwise, Lloyd and me? What'll we do but I won't tell them that. I won't tell them anything, of course, but I'd like to, it's that frustrating. I see them coming and they slow right down and I'm willing them to turn in beneath the neon and draw up outside and the man to come in. 'Any chance of a week?' he'll say. 'You have! Great. Hear that, love? The lady's got one by the pool.' And all the kids pile out with their baseball caps on backwards and their bright baggy shorts if they're boys and it's summer, and all of them in T-shirts.

But then they drive on. Well, they don't because they didn't stop in the first place, but you know what I mean. Lloyd thinks I'm mad. He says I make it worse for myself. Maybe I do, but I can't help hoping.

'What's the point of hoping,' he says. 'If they stop, they stop, right, and if they don't, they drive on.' He doesn't mind really, though. He knows it's because I care. Not only the money, though that too, of course. We put our hearts into Hils' Haven. Both of us.

He insisted on calling the motel after me. Mum christened me Hilary but I was Hils right from a baby and all through Primary. When I got to High I wrote it with a Z for a while, you know how kids mess about with their signatures on assignments and things and I liked the fat tail on the Z. But I went back to S later.

I said to Lloyd when he suggested Hils' Haven, 'I like the name too, but not for a motel. Why not Ace of Spades or El Paradiso or Buena Vista even? Something sort of frisky to show they'll have a nice time. Hils isn't lucky,' I said without thinking.

His face went sad. 'I thought you'd like it.'

'I do like it but it lacks pizzazz.' I'd seen the word in my little weekly in an article about how Hollywood didn't have it any more and the great days were over. I was trying to get away from the unlucky aspect before he thought of the baby too.

That was why we started the motel, because of our little girl, Ilona. She was a dear little thing. I know all mothers say that but you should've seen her. I suppose she was more cute than pretty. She didn't have blonde curls or big blue eyes but when she snuggled up to me, clinging tight as a toy koala on a pencil, I could've died of happiness.

212

It was so sudden how she went. She had diarrhoea and vomiting when she was four and a half and I took her to the doctor and he said she must go straight into hospital because she was dehydrated. I'd never heard of it even. I didn't know that it meant she would be on a drip. The young doctor couldn't get the needle into the vein and I was trying to hold her still and her screaming, I can't tell you what it was like. But he got there in the end and she perked up quite quickly. I sat with her all day and coloured in with her and read a story about chickens, which was her favourite, and stayed while she slept, in case she woke up and was frightened. But at bedtime they said I had to go home. You couldn't stay the night then. I would've slept on the floor or anywhere, but no, they wouldn't have it. So I went home and they rang in the night to say she'd gone. She'd had some sort of collapse. They did a post-mortem. Yes. She had a weakness in the heart, they said.

I've still got her pencil case. I bought it for her because she was that keen to go to school. Kiddies had them months ahead, all ready for when they started. Not plastic fold-over things like nowadays but real cases made of wood and the top half swung out from the bottom and there was a special part hollowed out for the rubber in the top bit. The case was made of some sort of blond wood and had toy soldiers painted on the top with red jackets and those high bearskin hats. That's another thing they probably wouldn't have now — soldiers, especially for a girl. But it was so long ago and they were toy soldiers. She loved it, especially the place for the rubber. I remember the man in the toyshop saying they all like that.

She ran away to school one Saturday morning. We laughed later, but not at the time. Lloyd rushed off in one direction and me in the other and he found her heading through the gate to the local Primary. It was lucky she chose a Saturday. He could show her it was all empty and they came home hand in hand, talking it over. She wanted to learn to read, see, and we didn't know how to teach her.

She was so bright. I met her one day after Playcentre and she said, 'Trucks and lorries are traffic too, you know Mum.' It was the way she came out with it. She'd worked it out after Traffic Drill. I think of that as the trucks change down at the corner. They're traffic too, you know.

But we let her down. Both of us. Not being there when she died. I read a book later about how a mother had insisted on staying with her baby. She said she wasn't going and what were they going to do about it, call the cops? Then she lay down on the floor. Why didn't I do that. Why wasn't I there when she died. Probably nobody was. It was that unexpected.

Bronwyn, the Playcentre lady, said they were going to plant a rose for Ilona and they asked Lloyd and me to be present at the ceremony. So we went. It was kind of them. They were being nice. But when I saw all the kiddies I couldn't stand it. I just couldn't stand it and when Bronwyn handed me the spade, all brand-new and shiny and never used, and asked me to put the last earth around the floribunda, I couldn't and I sobbed, 'No! No! No!' and shoved the spade away. Lloyd picked it up and he finished the job and I clung to him, crying my heart out in front of all the mothers, and the kiddies with their mouths open.

And then Lloyd took me home. I felt I'd let her down again, not planting her rose. But I couldn't I just couldn't. I haven't seen it since.

We left Hamilton soon after. 'We'll get right away,' Lloyd

said. 'Make a fresh start.' He sold his share of the carrying business to Alan, his partner, and he bought the motel and we came up here to make a fresh start, like he said. I didn't care where we went. But he was right. We had to work so hard, see. There were just the two of us at the beginning and Lloyd kept thinking of new Room Projects, he called them. He'd always been a home handyman, and he had all these ideas he called Hils' Havens. At first I thought who cares, who cares where they sleep if only they can. If I could sleep I wouldn't care if it was in Hils' Haven, or Hils' Hacienda, or Hils' Hangar or wherever.

Lloyd did it all for me, as therapy. For him too of course, but at first all the ideas and everything had to come from him, as well as all the work.

Later I thought up some, like Hils' Hillbilly and Hils' Hideaway for example. In Hideaway the whole unit was done up like a cave. Lloyd did all the structural work required, including a rockface at the back of the bed, but he had to make a bedhead later after a guest flung himself on the bed with a drink, shouting, 'This is the life!' and there was blood everywhere.

We both did the painting and the wallpapering — the whole place was badly run down. I'll never forget how tired I was but it was good being too tired to think. That's why Lloyd insisted.

One of the things of course was finding the wallpapers and all the other things to get the decor right for each unit, but they'd just lifted import restrictions and we had the money from Lloyd's share in the business and there were some lovely things about in Auckland. As well as the rock wall in the Hideaway, we had that wallpaper that looks like rocks, you still see it occasionally in kitchens, and we had those white hairy Greek rugs, they're wilder somehow than sheepskins, and the vanity was hidden by a frill of polished cotton with brown and black cave drawings on it and we had one of those fake-fur covers on the bed. The picture above the bed showed a caveman, or rather lady, cooking over an open fire just outside the cave.

You can see the idea. It was fun to do, working each room out and then getting the decor perfect. We did get a sense of achievement. It saved us at the time. And people loved them.

And now look at it. I can't bear to see them getting run down. For Lloyd's sake especially. And they do need upgrading, there's no denying. The sombrero wallpaper in Hacienda, for instance, and the plastic cactus is shot.

The man had to ping the bell twice. I came to with a jump. He had on pink trousers tucked into flying boots not zipped up, his hair was parted in the middle and he looked angry, his mouth all twisted beneath one of those big moustaches that I think'll date.

She was a washed-out-looking little thing, thin as a wisp with long blonde hair. She wore a plaid jacket over a green cotton frock and jandals. It wasn't a cheerful plaid like a tartan. It was sort of mud-coloured and cream and so big I wondered if it was his. I couldn't imagine a young woman choosing a thing like that, even to keep the wind out, and tonight it was a westerly and hot.

'Got a room?' he said. I've never liked centre partings.

'Yes,' I said, smiling. 'Which one would you like?' I showed him the postcards mounted on the desk of the units we had vacant. It's always been a feature. People like to choose.

'I don't give a stuff,' he said.

I felt as though he'd hit me. Well no, not hit me, but it was a rebuff. I was glad Lloyd wasn't there. He was down town with the truck.

'Could we have Hils' Homely?' she said, pointing. Her smile was nervous, scared almost, as though there wasn't much chance.

It seemed so sad, someone dressed like her wanting to sleep in a cottagey decor, let alone with him. Hils' Homely is my favourite of all. Lloyd isn't so keen. Maybe the treatment isn't so imaginative, like he says, and he didn't have any input into the structure. It's more of a girl's room perhaps. Cottagey, It's all matching, pink and blue flowers on the bedcovers and the curtains, and lots of ruffles and the pillows have white eyelet work. If anyone's booked it I always put a posy on the TV. Pansies, for instance, though of course I hadn't this time, not knowing they were coming.

I gave her a big smile back. She made you feel like that. You had to help her. 'Certainly,' I said. 'Come and I'll show you.' I took the Homely key from its hook and the half-pint of milk from the office fridge, checked the till was locked and came round the desk still smiling.

He strode ahead of us with his behind rolling from one side to the other and she picked up their beat-up green suitcase. He didn't even glance. He knew she'd bring it, that's what got me. You get all sorts, there's no doubt about that. You can't let it worry you, you wouldn't survive otherwise, but I could've kicked him.

You could see straight away that she loved the unit. I knew she would but it still made me feel good to watch her. She stood just inside the door with her hands clasped to her chest like a skinny little kid. I opened the window. The westerly was more of a gentle breeze round this side and it lifted the ruffled Terylene between the floral drapes. It did look pretty.

I'd spent so much time on this room: the covers, the drapes, even the frill on the stool by the vanity. I'd made them all. 'Do you like it?' I said.

'Yes,' she whispered. 'Oh yes. It's lovely.'

'I'll bring in a wee posy,' I said. 'Just to finish it off. Would you like a few pansies?'

If you'd heard him. 'Not bloody likely,' he roared, laughing and slapping the front of his greasy jeans.

I'm not silly. I knew how he'd taken it, but it was awful.

'I'd love some.' Her voice was that soft I could scarcely hear. She took a step, just one step towards me. I put out my hand and she grabbed it and burst into tears; they were running down her face, splashing like a baby's that can't bear it another minute.

'There, there,' I said. I heard myself saying it. There there.

'Get out,' he muttered, not even looking at me. He kicked his second boot off and turned round. 'And stuff the pansies.'

I went. What could I do.

I told Lloyd when he came back with the truck but he didn't understand. Why should he. What was there to understand.

But I couldn't sleep that night. I couldn't sleep at all and the westerly was there again next morning, blowing grit and sand in through Lloyd's revolving door.

I don't like plastic flowers. I always have fresh on the desk. People remember, usually the ladies of course, but you'd be surprised the number of gentlemen who comment. I always have something in the garden I can pick, even if it's only red photinia leaves. There's always something you can find.

People remember the eggs too. Ever since we opened I've always put one egg per person in the unit fridge. Just the first night, but even so they always ask if they come again. 'Do you still have the eggs?' they say, and I say, 'Of course,' and we laugh. One lady said it was like finding a present from Santa. There's something about eggs, as well as them being unexpected in a motel. Now with the low occupancy I just run round with them later. But last night I hadn't.

I took two out of the office fridge. 'Lloyd,' I said, 'could you pop round to Homely with these?'

'Sure,' he said, and went.

It was the first thing she said next morning. She came into the Reception area and walked straight up to the desk. She was still wearing the same clothes, including that awful jacket, but her smile was beautiful. Shy, like I said, but beautiful. 'The eggs were lovely,' she said.

He was right behind her. 'Come on,' he said, without even a nod at me, and she scurried through the door with him pushing it at her heels. I couldn't tell if it was deliberate — some people never get the hang of revolving doors. But I felt it was, as though it was another way he could get at her.

'Had a nice day?' I said all smiling when they came back, and then I saw she'd been crying again and he was more angry than ever. I watched his bum jigging from side to side as he headed down the corridor in front of her. Macho. That's what he was. Macho and tough and violent, I shouldn't wonder.

I gripped the Formica tight, I remember that.

She scarcely glanced at me, just ran down the passage after him, her legs knock-kneed and pale above the jandals.

*

Lloyd took over at the desk at four-thirty. He's good like that. He doesn't leave me stuck there all day and night and anyway there's so much else for me to keep an eye on, like checking on the rooms. We've got a good part-timer called Gerri at the moment but you still have to check. And I pop into the laundry several times a day. You have to. You wouldn't believe the way they leave the irons on, to say nothing of the ones they pinch. I always check the plugholes as well. Nobody else ever deals with the hairs and the gunk and they do block up. So I had my rubber gloves on and my head down when she came in.

'Can I come in?' she said, all quick and nervous.

I jumped. 'Of course, dear,' I said.

She leant against the Bendix. There was a bruise on her cheek. I hadn't noticed it before. 'Can I stay here?' she said.

'Pardon?' I said. I couldn't take my eye off it. It wasn't purple or anything, just a grey smudge under her left eye.

'Stay here,' she said. 'Stay in that room.'

'I don't quite . . .'

'We're leaving tomorrow. He'll be watching me. But I could wait till he's drunk or asleep or something and hitch back. He'd never think of here. Never.'

My head was whirling. 'Stay on in Hils' Homely you mean?'

'Yes, oh yes.' She gasped. One skinny hand was at her mouth; her eyes never left mine. 'Please!'

'But dear . . .'

I had to say it. How could I not say it. Hils' Haven wasn't just mine, it's Lloyd's as well. And the downturn, the endless worry of it all. All that work and effort going down the drain and all the love we put into it as well and both of us trying to pretend there was any point in going on. So I said it.

'Have you any money, dear?'

She shook her head. She didn't say anything. Just shook her head.

We stood there. I pulled off my gloves. I could smell the rubber on my hands as well as the spilt soap powder on the floor and the scorched smell from the ironing board still warm from the last user. And that pinched wee face staring. But even so, even so. I said it.

'No dear,' I said. 'I'm sorry, but no. Things are that bad at the moment. Normally of course we could think of . . .'

She didn't wait. She just gave a sort of yelp and ran out.

When I can't sleep I think of her as well. In the westerly.

We Could Celebrate

Sooze who is my friend, and Bryce who is Sooze's friend, have lent Cliff and me their bach at Paraparaumu for the weekend. They have gone to the wedding of their friend Hester in Te Atatu. Cliff and I watched them as they loaded the car. It made me feel quite faint. All that mountain of stuff in the back is for a one-year-old, their son Jared; reusables, disposables, restrainers, containers, you couldn't see out the back window.

I was pretty thoughtful as they left and Jared waved a bear in a red jacket. So was Cliff. We didn't say anything as we walked back inside.

'Let's go for a swim,' I said, leaping to my feet. I like swimming in the sea. I always start off in my bikini so as not to startle the natives but take off the top and usually the bottom, because I like swimming like that, and in the part where we swim there aren't many people. In the surf you have to hook the straps round your arm then put the same arm through a leg of the bikini so you don't lose them. I did lose a top once but it's worth it for the feel. I don't like sunbathing unless I have a book.

Once, when I was in the Coromandel with an ex-friend of mine called Barry who ditched me, we walked miles and miles up a deserted beach. Right at the end there were three small baches beneath gnarled old pohutukawas in full bloom, it was lovely. But the thing I remember most was an old couple without a stitch on who sat reading in canvas chairs so low their behinds were almost on the paspalum. They were Pakehas but they were tanned mahogany and they just sat there after a quick glance up from their paperbacks and continued reading like a couple of bookish old pelts. I thought that was great and I'd like to have told them so but Barry was getting embarrassed so we walked on. Sometimes I think I'd like to try it but I suppose it only works when you're old, and only then if you've got the sense to play it your way and not fuss.

The shape of her, Christ the shape of her when she swims naked in the sea, leaping over each wave, her nipples hard with the cold, she nearly finishes me. And she has no idea, no vanity, when she's swimming she's swimming, that's what she's there for. She grew up near a good surf beach and still flings herself in front of an unbroken wave like a twelve-year-old, arms clamped to her sides for a good run.

Now I know Carmen, I can believe everything I've ever read or seen about 'the expense of spirit', the fever in the blood; Anthony, the poor wimp with the terrier who abdicated, Othello, the headmistress who killed the diet doctor, any of them. I tell you I could join them, count the world well lost for love and lust and it drives her insane. We have rows about it, flaming dirty gut-wrenching rows because I watch her, want her too much. She calls it eating her. 'Don't eat me, Cliff,' she says, but what can I do. I'm a painter, I look at things, I watch her legs, the angle of the knees as she folds onto the floor, the way she springs upright in one sinuous movement, shall we say. I can't stop watching her. I sketch her and she's not mad about that so I have to be quick to catch the angle of her moving arm, the curve of her bum. Hokusai said any artist should be able to sketch a man as he fell from a high window to the ground and I'm getting better. Her arms are the most beautiful I have ever seen. I watch her plait her hair each morning. She does it without a mirror, she bends over to brush it forward, then swings upright, her hands scoop the pale hair upwards to plait, her fingers move swish swish and it's done. I've got dozens of her plaiting her hair because she's concentrating then and doesn't notice me so much. And of her sleeping. She can sleep on her back, one hand under her head, her elbow in the air. Try it some time. Every movement she makes is graceful. Her toes are prehensile. When she leans her rounded arms over the back of a chair I am hypnotised and that's just her arms for God's sake. So what I do, to try and cool things so that I don't explode and wreck everything, is I clear off quite often. I get out into the Tararuas with my brother, who used to be a deer culler and still hunts. I don't shoot but I like the tracking and Gavin doesn't mind my help in lugging the stags back through the bush to the car.

And I'm working towards an exhibition, aren't I. Last week, on the hottest day for three years, I had two free periods from Girls High, where I teach, and I went round the galleries to show my stuff. I could feel my feet sweating in their canvas containers, which didn't help as I ran up the narrow stairs to the first gallery. The guy was small with a pink-and-white face and baby hair, and he was wearing one of those suits that dogs and bears wear in kids' picturebooks

— crumpled and sort of hairy, the colour of Scotch mist. I burst into sweat all over in sympathy but he was cool, very cool and sharp. He didn't say anything as he looked through the portfolio and very little afterwards, except that he'd let me know, and we talked about the art scene in New York and how would I know about that except in magazines and I don't see many of those. I left feeling sick, sick in the gut.

The next owner was a woman. She wore a black beret and it suited her, perched on the back of her head surrounded by curls. I wanted to ask her to take it off so I could see if she looked as good without it but I didn't feel I was in a position where I could make that sort of request. She was a nice woman and the gallery had a good light. She said she'd let me know. And it went on like that until my feet and I were really stinking and I went home to Carmen's where I live and fell into her bath which has claws for feet and damn near wept. Then Carmen came home from school and got in too though I told her I stank and things got better.

That's the trouble I suppose. Nothing else matters, though I'm painting better than I've ever painted because of her. I always wonder about poor buggers like Van Gogh who never sold anything or only one while he lived. How did he keep knowing he was good? I don't see much point in posterity. Did he know he was great or did he just slog on, obsessed with nothing but the next stroke of paint. OK, he had vision, but that doesn't answer the question. I'd really like to know the answer but there is no one to ask. I could ask the man in the suit maybe. He would give some sort of answer probably but we'll never know. Not really.

I touch Cliff's bare foot with mine. 'Let's go for a swim,' I say once more.

He looks up, blinking.

'Swim!' I demonstrate, clawing the air with my arms.

He swings his legs up on the sofa. Cliff has good legs, like Edna Everage and my brother Stephen, who says he has the best legs in Hawke's Bay.

Cliff drags up one foot to pick the big toenail. Toenail checked out, he sits up. 'I think I'll go to the store first,' he says.

'What the hell, we've just arrived.'

'Yeah, but that guy, the dealer guy, he said he'd drop me a card, care of the store. I said we were going to be here and he said . . .

'He won't.'

Cliff looks at me, not pleased. His mouth tightens. 'He said he would.'

'Yes, but people say, people say, people say!' My hands are all over the place trying to disperse my previous negative comment.

'It's not important to him, see,' I explain to my lover who is not in fact handicapped.

'It's only important, the speed, to you.' The sands of non-support move beneath me. I bog deeper in the mire of not understanding a thing about it.

'I'm going.' Cliff leaps to his feet and goes. I read the *Kapiti Observer*. I like the For Sales best. You can pick up anything.

He is back in five minutes flat. He leaps in the French doors and seizes me. He flings cushions. If he could do a backward somersault of delight like the decathlon man he would. He can't contain himself. He is beside himself with joy.

'Let's have a look,' I say, seizing the card. The man in the furry bear suit wishes to mount an exhibition of my lover's work.

I share Cliff's joy and all is harmony and better than that, I shouldn't wonder.

He stops in the middle of a strong clutch and pulls back. 'It'll be a ton of work,' he says. 'This guy's good.' He stares through my head. 'I'll need three nudes,' he mutters. 'Three at least, I'd say.'

His gaze refocuses on my face. He looks at me. 'Oils. Of you.'

I smile, muscles clench. 'Three?' I say.

'At least.'

'Let's go for a swim,' I say yet again.

And we go, leaping down the track, up the track, down the track through the marram grass; sand flying, wind tugging, tumbleweed on the scoot. We are yelling as we fall into the sea which can solve everything. All frustration, all longing, all despair, the sea can cure but only when you're in it. When I am old I will live by the sea and potter about poking at things with a stick and watching the young. When I am dead I will live in it.

We swim naked.

We make love afterwards on Sooze and Bryce's bed. The room smells musty, like the bach bedrooms of childhood when you brushed sand from the soles of your feet with flattened palms before climbing into your bunk.

Nothing wrong with the action though. Cliff is even is more charged with creative imagination than usual. I love him dearly.

'We could celebrate,' he says afterwards. He picks up my hand and inspects it. 'Celebrate,' he tells it. 'Make a booking at that restaurant in the village.'

I roll over to bite his ear. 'What's it called?'

'I can't remember,' he says.

But we remember later. We make a booking and we go clutching our BYO. The restaurant has a theme and the theme is sport. The wall by the entrance shows cricket memorabilia. An Edwardian child in knickerbockers presents a straight bat. There are framed and autographed photographs of other straight batters and strong bowlers. Several of them have moustaches. There is an old etching of the Hambledon cricket ground.

The other wall is rugby. More moustaches, photographs, deathless tries. I like sport, I'm not knocking it. I like playing it. It is just that here the images are trapped like beetles in kauri gum.

There is a mural in the main room. Pale mauves, lilacs and greens define shadowy figures, most of which are static. Men in white stand near the crease, sit in the pavilion with hats on, converse. Up the rugby end they tackle and fall on their faces. The heads of the figures are transparent, defined by outlines, you can see the dark or light green bushes through them. Cliff is interested in the murals, which he finds effective — as murals. He whips out his sketch pad and begins drawing.

I read the menu. I read that our hosts are called Trevor and Fay and that the restaurant is on the corner of Titoki and West Streets, which we already know.

There is a slice of lemon in the water carafe beside our bottle of Te Mata Estate White, which the waitress has opened. It is not full, the restaurant. One table has a lone male diner with fluffy white hair curling over the back of his collar. He eats slowly, entertaining himself.

Cliff has his pad beneath the table as he sketches a party, if you can call it that, of five. There are two middle-aged men, one handsome, one had it, who sits squeezed and bosomy inside a souvenir shirt labelled *Fiji* with a hibiscus surround. One woman's lilac spectacle frames match the blotched flowers on her frock. She tries to keep up with the men, who are laughing and having fun. The two women opposite have given up. One wears her hair screwed on top in American Gothic style. Flamenco dancers flaunt on her cream jersey silk. She is sick of being here. Gran tells me this happens when you get old. You get sick of it and wonder why you came, though this can happen when you are young and often does.

The rain is hosing down outside, water slams against the windows. The blades of one of the overhead fans on the ceiling move faster than the other. They must be on different settings.

'Well,' I say, lifting my glass to Cliff. 'Here's to the exhibition.'

Cliff has a beautiful smile. It happens comparatively rarely and it pleases me to watch the lips part, the dent in one cheek deepen, the eyes gleam. Rarity has value. People used to get excited when Dylan Thomas turned up sober.

'Yeah,' replies Cliff, lifting his glass to clink mine. He reads the menu. 'Do you want your oysters *en crêpe* or looking at you?'

'Looking at me.'

The door opens. Thundering past the memorabilia, damp with rain and slapping one another, comes a party of eight. They are drunk, these young men. Their faces are red, their clothes are a mess, their feet stumble as they weave around the table laughing and groping for chairs. They are happy.

The eyes of the other diners concentrate on their plates except for the lone male diner who has not yet noticed their behaviour. The waitress, smiling strongly, ushers them to a table alongside ours. One of the young men focuses on me. 'Shit,' he informs. 'Get a load of that lot.'

Eight pairs of glazed eyes turn in my direction. Eight drunken hoons gape, their mouths slightly open. They are not a pretty sight.

I order oysters *au naturel* and venison that something time-consuming has happened to. The waitress is very pleasant. I think she must be Fay because she cares so much. She wears the type of long apron worn by French waiters, which is not a good idea because her stomach sticks out and is clamped and bound by the stiff fabric. Periodically she glances at the hoons and gives a quick smile as though she meant them to happen. She takes Cliffs order and moves on to more dangerous territory. She is patient, amiable, she smiles into their stunned-mullet eyes in her attempt to pretend that all is well; that they are civilised welcome guests at mine hosts' (Fay and Trevor's) table. It is uphill work. She moves around explaining; smiling as they order, shout, hit each other, belch, drag bottles of wine from a chilly bin and slam them on the table. They make gestures behind her back to indicate that though she is old enough for kissing she is too fat to tango.

I am getting angry.

'Cliff,' I say.

He is sketching again, his hand moves with authority, he glances with swift stealthy up and downs of his head at the table of five. Even upside down I can see that he has got the spare dignity and resignation of the American Gothic woman to perfection.

'Nnn?' he says.

'Cliff!'

His hand is still moving. 'Yes?'

I wriggle my shoulders and indicate the table next door with a sideways jerk of the head. 'Drunk,' I hiss.

'Certainly looks like it,' he says, and carries on sketching.

My eyes meet those of the lone male diner. He picks up his lilac napkin and presses it against one corner of his mouth then the other. He returns the napkin to his lap, places his hands on the table and stares at them. He reminds me of something.

I remember. Barry who ditched me and I were staying in a motel in Tauranga where the dining-room invited us to enjoy our smorgasbord in a family atmosphere. The salads were inventive: kumara and bacon, tamarillo and red cabbage, brown rice. There was a lot of kiwifruit. There was kiwifruit in every salad, slices of kiwifruit decorated the plates of cold meat, the pavlovas, the fruit salads and the trifle. It was the ultimate kiwifruit experience. At a table beneath a firehose decorated with a frizzled tinsel wreath left over from Christmas sat two men, one older than the other. The older man's sparse hair was swept across his scalp. He had a tip-tilted nose and a gold chain. He was ashamed of smoking. He took furtive puffs behind one curved hand. He spilt ash and swept it from the table with quick brushing movements of the same hand. The young man's fingers fanned between their faces, dispersing smoke. The older man pressed food. The younger man ate. There was no conversation. The young man had a good haircut, his Docksides were splayed at ten to three. When he was not eating, his hands were clasped together or hung down in despair. He was offered treats, sweets for the sweet. He ate two helpings of trifle decorated with kiwifruit and they departed in silence. It was infinitely sad.

I smile at the silver-haired man. He dips his head but does not smile back. He raises his eyebrows in agreement. He does not enjoy the hoons either.

The noise is increasing at the table next to ours. One man, all red hair and ears, is telling us in song that there's a bridle hanging on the wall, there's the shoes that his old pony wore. If we ask him why those teardrops fall, it's that bridle hanging on the wall. A man with a mean moustache is telling a story with a lot of fucks and ducks in it. All the men are drinking like fishes, except that fishes are breathing when they gulp. Someone throws a roll. There is uproar at the table.

The good-looking man at the table of five summons the waitress, who is looking distracted. She spreads her hands wide in answer to his complaint. Her body language tells me what she is saying. What can she and Trevor do? They didn't know when they took the booking that they would be like this, did they.

His outrage informs her that someone ought to do something and smartly. 'The proprietor,' he mouths. She looks even more miserable but moves quickly to the kitchen, presumably in search of Trevor.

Trevor does not appear.

I am fidgeting about on the seat of my chair in rage and shame for them all. Cliff is totally oblivious. He is now sketching the particular way the silver curls fall on the collar of the jacket of the lone diner, who sits very still staring straight in front of him.

'Good one!' the table roars at the punchline of the fuck and duck story.

'Down trou!' someone screams. The redhead staggers to

his feet. Pale and sweating, his head down, he fumbles with his belt. His trousers and underpants fold about his ankles. His hairy white buttocks are presented for inspection two yards from my face. The table roars its approval.

I am on my feet. So is the lone diner.

I haven't been watching. I sense that Carmen is getting a bit toey but the sketch is going so well and I want just a few more minutes and then I'll stop sketching and we'll celebrate and rejoice in each other, which is what we have come for, I do realise that.

I glance up from my pad. The camp man with the silver hair has disappeared from his chair. The table of five is in shock, their knives and forks clutched in mid-air. Carmen has disappeared. There's a lot of noise. I see some guy's bum for a second before he pulls up his trousers amid thundering applause from the rest of them. Carmen and the old gay are standing side by side in front of the table. Carmen is flaming. Someone has lit her fire.

'Get out,' she hisses. 'Now!'

Their obscene comments on her beauty melt on wet lips. They stare. Their mouths are slack. The old man puts one hand on her arm.

'I think perhaps the young lady is upset,' he says gently.

He stacks their half-empty bottles upright in the chilly bin with care. He smiles at them all. 'Why don't you leave now,' he suggests. 'The kitchen will give you corks for the bottles. There's a good takeaway just round the corner on Highway One. And please,' he begs with clasped hands, 'please take taxis home.' He slips a twenty-dollar bill into the chilly bin beside the bottles. He looks at them benignly. 'You are too young to die,' he tells them.

Now they will kill him. There will be a gay bashing. I leap up ten minutes too late.

Not so. The table crawl to their feet and stumble out clutching their liquor. They do not say anything. They do not look at the old man or Carmen. I am still standing, one hand on the chair, the edge of the seat digging into the backs of my knees as they go out the door.

Carmen and the old man turn to each other. They shake hands. He waves one hand towards his table; he asks the jittery waitress for another glass. He holds the chair back for Carmen to sink into. He pours her some wine, showing her the label as he does so. They lean towards each other with their arms on the linen cloth. They talk together, nodding occasionally. They smile.

Living on the Beach

She stopped the car, climbed out stiffly and opened the gate. It swung wide, clunking against the radiator.

'Nearly there,' she said, backing the car away from the pursuing arc.

'Hh.'

He had an infinity of small sounds to express things he couldn't be bothered saying. Mind the radiator, about time too, or just a noise to indicate continued existence. He clung to the door handle for support as they bucketed up the gravel drive. The ngaios tossed and lurched in the wind, teasing the roof of the car, flinging leaves across the paspalum. The grass that saved the North, a man had told her years ago as they rolled in it. The old man began tugging as she switched off the engine.

'Undo me, Mary.'

'Press the red thing.'

'Where?'

'There.'

'Which?' A vague hand groped by his side, his eyes straight ahead.

She pressed the release and the belt sucked back.

'Oh.'

Her mind flicked to Maud and George, snug and smug in the Hutt. But kind, so kind, to lend the bach, dim faces beaming as they handed over the keys. 'It'll make a change, Mary.'

She climbed out and put the Yale key in the lock. It wouldn't turn. A prickle of panic brushed her as she flung herself against the paint-blistered door.

'Try the other key', he piped.

Sweating slightly, she did so. The door opened to reveal a concrete block wall, airlessness, and a flight of wooden steps leading above.

'I'll never get up those.'

'It'll be all right, Dad. Just wait while I unpack.'

Some cardboard cartons are better than others. Some are too deep, some, of course, too small. She dumped the sturdy Family Recipe Cake Mix on the sloping bench and stared around her.

The cottage was made of fibrolite flung together on concrete blocks. The main room had budded off four smaller clones, kitchen and bathroom beside the steep stairwell, two bedrooms at the other end. Two elderly armchairs, Maud and George, squatted either side of the doll-sized fireplace which was lined with yellow bricks. Above the mantelpiece hung a faded reproduction of an English wood awash with bluebells, a damp stain creeping down the pale mount. Beneath it a line of shells trekked across the shelf to the glass jar on which laughing peanuts played cricket. The cotton-wool heads of the harestail it contained were thick with dust. There were two more hardbacked chairs and an unyielding divan covered with a brown rug. An extremely dirty green carpet lay on the floor. The wind flung itself at the front of the house which faced the sea, the draughts making little puffs among the sand drifts on the sills.

But outside was the sea, from every window.

Mary dumped her bag in the pink shoebox bedroom. As she straightened up, she glimpsed her face in a square of mirror which hung from a nail beside the bed. Her hand moved to tuck a strand of hair behind her ear. She remained staring, searching that face.

The other room had two bunks and little else. She sniffed, then opened the window. The mouse lay in a corner, having chosen not to die in the open. Lifting it by the stiff tail, she threw the corpse onto the paspalum to await future burial.

'Mary.' The reedy cry echoed in the stairwell.

'I'm coming.'

First she heaved him out of the car seat, into which he seemed to have collapsed like a punctured beanbag.

'One, two, three, heave!'

'You heaved on three.'

Her laugh turned to a snort. 'I did not.'

I like snorters, the man had told her. Snorters enjoy life, he said.

She held the old man while he stamped some life back into his numbed feet. They were long and slim, their nails fortunately not horny. Then began the climb. She supported him from behind, pausing at each step as he fought for breath. 'Phrrr, Phrrr, Phrrr.' What little breath he had all seemed to puff outwards.

'I'll never make it.'

'Don't talk.'

They reached the top and he collapsed on one of the hard chairs, mottled blue face in his hands.

'Whisky.'

It was at the ready in the hutch-like kitchen. She slopped some into a glass, added a splash of water and placed it in the groping hand.

'Mad. Mad. Shouldn't have come.'

'You're here now. Don't worry.'

'Never get up there again. Never.'

'You won't have to. Look, there's the island. And the sea.'

They turned to watch their common interest, rolling and sucking at the sand below. The rough weather had tossed the sea into vast stripes of green, steel blue, and . . . ultramarine. Of course.

She had never seen him in the water. Childhood memories of learn-to-swim campaigns had never included his arms. He had loved to be in boats tossing in water which made her sick. They stared at the repetitive unforgiving sea.

'I can't see it,' he said.

She turned to him. He had recovered what little breath he had and sat sipping his whisky with dignity, long legs crossed above the knee, the upper hanging parallel. Not many men sat as well, she had noticed. Their crossed legs were a collection of protruding bits, no symmetry in the assemblage. His hands, like his feet, remained satisfactory. When he moved them, the long fingers often made an acute angle with the bony wrists. Flexibility remained there, and beauty. She remembered her mother saying so.

Mary moved about the cottage with precision, scrubbing the smell of mouse to extinction, making beds and stowing gear.

'You'll be better in here, Dad. The bunk's nice and low.'

'Where's the lavatory?'

Her arm swept in the direction. 'Here.'
'Where?'
She flapped her outstretched hand. 'Here,' she said.
'Miles away.'

Their days settled into a rhythm. Meals followed meals in an orderly procession, little nap followed little nap, much as at home. He appropriated the divan and its rug and lay staring out the window, searching for the sea. Or slept, a crumpled heap of brown. Occasionally he jerked, or gave a stifled yelp like an old dog asleep by a fire.

Mary lived on the beach. She could hear her future grateful voice as she returned the keys to Maud. 'I lived on the beach. It was wonderful.'

There were not many occupied baches, no store, all the children were back at school. She swam twice a day, her square figure encased in a bathing suit aglow with hot flowers, her head in an orange rubber cap. Every day she braced herself against the damp shock of stretch nylon, then ploughed through the sculpted sandhills to the waves. She floated over unbroken ones, or swam at them, head on, to surge over the top, defeating the crashing roar behind her.

After he was settled, a word often in her mind, she turned right and walked for miles along the beach, conscientiously adding to the driftwood pile by the back door on her return.

About a quarter of a mile along the beach to the right, a bach stood alone. Marram grass had been planted in the drifting sand in front, taupata and ngaios ringed the section — like the green scribbled hedge in a child's drawing. On the beach below the house, a man and his golden retriever played each morning. Except that you couldn't call it playing.

'Heel!' roared the man.

The dog responded by hurling towards him, flinging itself slobbering against the godhead, its tail a plume of gold.

'Sit!'

It dropped on its haunches, eyes beseeching the next clue, ears pricked, tail lifting.

It was usually 'Stay!', after which the man walked away from the quivering mass crouched on the damp sand. But at the slightest lift the man would turn. 'I said Stay!'

'He seems to enjoy it,' she said one day.

'It's obedience training.' The wind was blowing strands of faded red hair across his face.

'Oh. What's his name?'

'Rusty.'

She rubbed the dog behind the right ear. It opened its jaws wide, yawing at her wrist, trying to catch the agent of ecstasy. Its wet frilled black gums reminded her of the dark insides of a paua shell.

'He's very obedient.'

'Him! Lord no, he's only a pup. It takes months. Or years.'

She smiled a beach meeter's token smile and walked on.

The next time she stopped to watch, the man had a rolled-up newspaper in his hand.

'Down!' he yelled, hitting the dog's nose with the teaching aid. Then he called, 'Come on, you fool.'

Each day their walks became longer. The glistening hardness stretched before them as the dog gambolled, the only word. It chased gulls, which obligingly arced into the air. The oystercatchers could hardly be bothered, but at the last gasp they lifted from their fussy comic run into long straight flight along the tide line, screaming to each other,

Kee-eep, Kee-eep.

He talked easily. His wife had been a true blonde, never touched it, women always asked her what she used, they couldn't believe it was natural. It was though. After she'd died he'd felt completely lost. Completely. Mary told him little. There was little to tell and she was a reticent woman. She had taught English for many years, and now she looked after her father. Yes.

Companionable silences followed amiable comments. They agreed that a walk without a dog is not the same, that it seemed a pity that the best weather always came after the children had gone back to school. He told her about the time he'd been sent to the UK on a course, he'd been lucky to get it, and how he could hardly stand it, being so bloody lonely. There used to be a cigarette advertisement: 'You're never alone with a Something.' He couldn't even remember the name.

'Next day,' he said, eyes disappearing as he grinned, 'I went out and bought a packet of Somethings.'

The dog was investigating a dead fish, sniffing and barking at the mouldering carcase above the tide line.

'Heel!' Rusty lifted his head and careered towards them.

'Good dog.' His hand slid over the shining, sycophantic head.

'Now I feel like that about the sea,' he said.

She stopped, staring at him, the tide licking at her jandals.

'I must get back to Dad,' she murmured.

She tried to remember when the sun had shone so continuously. She had to go back to her childhood, to days of dried paddling rings around the scaly brown legs of endless summers. The weather broke but the walks continued, parkas dripping, rain spitting the sand.

He asked about her father.

'He's very old,' she said.

'Can I come and say Hullo to the old boy?'

She cut the walk short and stumped home, brushing the rain from her eyes.

'His name's Don McIndoe, Dad,' she said next day, checking his jersey for major spills.

'Hhh.'

But the old man was sitting on the straight-backed chair, waiting, when Don crashed through the front door in a scud of rain. It was the first time she had seen him without Rusty.

Talk immediately ballooned between the two men, fishing talk, shared memories of the Tongariro, the lakes, other rivers. Her father bummed a cigarette, triumphantly not coughing. He told Don that one of the pleasures of old age, almost the only one, Hh Hh, was remembering, in exact detail mind, almost every cast he'd made when catching a fresh-run hen, fifty, no sixty years ago, in the Major Jones Pool. It happened quite often, those sudden sharp complete memories. Don said he'd look forward to such pleasures. The old man grinned, his mouth a weathered slit. He gripped the edge of his chair, lifted his behind fractionally and jerked nearer his friend, his virtually blind eyes leaking with joy. They turned to rugby, controversial decisions, hard, bruising games, brushing aside proffered nuts as though they were uninvited flies.

The rain had stopped. A stream of dense grey clouds poured across the sky to the south. The low ones disappeared behind the island as though pulled behind a black cardboard cut-out. Time passed. She rose to fill the glasses again.

'I'll get Don a drink,' he said. Levering himself up, gasping slightly, he stamped his feet into action.

She sat down on Maud. The noise was only a dropped glass but the spell was broken. The old man shuffled back and collapsed on the divan, tugging at the fringe of the rug.

A sensible man, Don suggested leaving by the back door to avoid sand blasting them again with the northerly. She followed him silently downstairs and shook hands like a hostess. His skin was tough and dry, his eyes bright.

'Great old guy. If I can be like that at his age . . . See you in the morning, Mary. Thanks a lot.'

He ran off down the drive. She wondered for a moment if he would jump the gate, then remembered it was open.

She climbed the stairs slowly, pulling on the wooden banister.

She woke next morning and lay watching the sunspot reflection from the mirror jigging on the ceiling. One two, up and back, one two . . . She heard her father creeping to the lavatory, the clunking pull of the chain, the rushing sound of the water followed by the dragging whisper of his slippers' return. She pulled a jersey and trousers over her pyjamas and crept downstairs, opened the back door and floundered through the sandhills to the sea.

At the water's edge she turned left towards the river. Her hair streamed back from her face in permed rats'-tails as she quickened her pace. 'Frankie and Johnnie were lovers,' she bellowed. 'Oh Lordy how they could love,' she roared at the wind which snagged each word upwards, outwards, away, in snatches of diminishing sound as she strode along the beach.

The Right Sort of Ears

Why, thought the poet sourly, am I here? I should go home. 'Return to my mountains of light and mauve melancholy.' Just piss off.

He looked around him, glancing left, right, and left again beneath lowered eyelids. The effect was to make his face inscrutable, or rather more so. The expression on his well-planned face had been non-commital since early youth. The darting glances, the heavy lids, merely increased its air of detachment, almost, one could say, its reptilian aspect One would not have been surprised, or not as surprised as usual, to have seen a forked tongue flick lightning-fast then disappear. Such astonishments are seldom seen, but poets are different from others and this one was more different than most.

And why had the wretched people chosen this place for interrogation? Outdoors, shadowed by trees and deep in sparrows, crumbs, and clutter, the place left much to be desired. Pigeons, pigeons for God's sake, were swooping. The place was alive with hazards. A downtown café they had called it. A downtown café with knobs on.

He looked at the blackboard menu on the wall and found no comfort. Focaccia with hummus, beetroot, tofu and pan-roasted vegetables, smoked chicken and avocado salad, bacon, tomato and lettuce salad, cream cheese, kiwi fruit and God knows what salad. As always, there were repellent muffins; broccoli and feta cheese, cauliflower, brie and sesame seeds. And buns. Buns to the right of them, buns to the left of them. Bagels were present.

How had it come about, this dreadful food? he wondered. Why had he not noticed this infuriating lurch towards health and indigestible muck before it was too late? Where was the food of his youth; the chop and the sausage; the pie, the pea and the pud? The glories of the Pie Cart, the chips with everything had suited him well, and now look at it.

Recently he had attended a dinner after some Writers and Readers shindig and found, to his pleasure but not surprise, that he was seated next to the guest of honour. Miss Phoebe Glass was a poet of international renown, a woman of intellectual vigour and at ease with words. He had hoped for intelligent converse with this handsome being, an exchange of sentiments, a marriage of true minds to which no one would have the nerve to admit impediment. This had not happened. Miss Glass had talked about little else other than her indigestion. She did enquire, not tenderly, no one could call it tenderly, but at least she had asked whether he suffered from this complaint. When he said no, she had sighed, had left him sitting beside her belch-free and heartburn-negative, had picked up the conversational reins and cantered on. The pain, she said, the sleepness nights. She discussed alternative palliatives available and their comparative efficacy, she gave him names — Slowburn, Quickees, and all shades between. She couldn't, she told him, move without them.

She rummaged in her bag, produced a packet of tablets and sucked a couple before resuming her wistful poking at a side salad.

The poet smiled his reptilian smile. 'Bismuth before pleasure,' he murmured.

Miss Glass gave him a long cool stare and turned a shoulder.

They were late, these people. Americans are meant to be punctual, to appreciate, to astound you with the depth of their perceptions, their sensitivity to the more arcane aspects of your work. But above all to be punctual. Where the hell were they?

He gave more glances to right and left. Not a glimpse of them: no one beneath the artificial palm, nobody crouching behind the nude female statue who drooped beside a small and dingy pool.

The nude was made of concrete; the grey lumps of her breasts seemed to have been slapped on to the rest of her arbitrarily, without any reference or knowledge, let alone admiration for the female form. He could imagine the scene. A handful of concrete this side, Bong! And another over here to match, Bong! Now she's apples.

The result depressed him. These rounded orbs of beauty, these concrete hills of passion with protuberant mud-grey nipples, were as extraneous, as sexless and oddly attached to the torso as those of Michelangelo's figures of Night and Dawn in his Tombs of the Medici in Florence. He remembered standing before them many years ago, discussing the topic with his then wife, Mildred.

'Very odd. Do you think it was because he was a homosexual?'

'No,' said Mildred. 'I think it was because he couldn't do breasts.'

Nor could this one. Useless.

There were, understandably, not many other people in the place. Even waitresses were few and far between. One with an exuberant mass of yellow hair had asked if she could take his order. He had explained the position and she had departed, virtually skipping with the relief of it all.

In one corner sat two women, sisters without a doubt. Grey-haired, pleasant, and faded to monotones, they were sharing a large slice of carrot cake. One wore wheat on sand, the other pink on rose. They put sugar in their respective cappuccinos and giggled. The poet knew, as surely as though they had semaphored the intelligence to him with small coloured flags, that they did not normally take sugar, that this was a treat and why not. Life, they signalled, was for living.

At a table nearer to hand sat Father, Mother, and two small girls. Again the occupants of this table were neatly dressed and somewhat anachronistic in appearance. Both Father and Mother were bluff, portly, dark-suited and well shod. The twins, for such they must be, wore dresses which could have been designed for the little princesses Lilibet and Margaret Rose. They were blue, these frocks, they were smocked, they had bows. They were as identical as their blond-haired wearers who sat eating cake and being good. Their fork work was competent and their white socks had frills.

Nevertheless, they palled. The poet glanced at his watch. Bugger this. He had half risen to his feet when he was engulfed, overwhelmed by a tsunami of apologies which began at the door, surged forward and knocked him sideways. Harold and Bea Benderman couldn't begin to say how sorry they were. They had gotten lost, would you believe. Could the poet ever forgive them? They had walked to the Art Gallery and gotten lost. Their arms indicated astonishment, their knees, their whole bodies, begged for pardon.

'Not at all,' said the poet. 'Shall we sit down?'

They sat, they ordered, they smiled. Harold explained to the waitress that he wanted hot chocolate with water not milk. The young woman was puzzled. Even her hair looked startled. 'Like no milk at all?'

'Like no milk at all.'

'Not even cold?'

'Nope. Just a bagel.'

'Not even the marshmallow?'

'Pardon me?'

'You get a free marshmallow.'

Harold raised a hand. 'Hold it.'

She gave up. 'OK,' she said and drifted away.

'We can only hope,' murmured the poet, now grooming himself in preparation for questions. A hand wiped each side of his head, one carried on to smooth his front hair forward.

The odd thing was, he thought, his eyes still flicking and his mouth firm, that Harold and his sister, Bea Benderman, were so alike. The place seemed to be filling up with clones, twinned identikits, double-goers. Harold and Bea (first names, please) both had flat faces. They had flat little noses, flat foreheads and almost non-existent chins. Their ears were flat, their hair was fair and their eyes were small. The poet was reminded of photographs demonstrating the flat profiles of maggots; the straight fronts of railcars; the sliced-off ends of sidewalk canopies.

'Of course, Doctor,' said Harold, after some discussion had taken place, 'I'm thinking that your place in posterity is assured. There can be no doubt about that. And I'm wondering whether you would you care to tell me how you feel about this?'

Oh God. The poet gave a small crank-up cough. 'I have nothing against posterity,' he said.

Harold and Bea laughed merrily. Harold stopped first. 'Your body of work, its universal excellence, the respect in which your entire oeuvre is held throughout the world, both in academia, and,' a hand tossed, 'the general public. You even,' confided Harold, '*sell.*'

The poet stared at his boots. 'Yes,' he said.

Harold leaned forward. He wore a gold chain around his neck. Why would a man with a flat face wear such a thing?

'Can I ask a question?' asked Bea, her small eyes bright with daring.

'Please do.'

'Why is it, do you think, that your poetry is so universally admired?'

The poet glanced at the concrete maiden. The sands were running, the tide would soon be on the turn, there could well be whitebait. 'Summertime, and the livin' is easy.' Or should be.

He made a major effort, looked into her eyes and smiled. Her face, when he looked at it closely, was not as flat as her brother's. It was longer, finer, a serene medieval face with unexpectedly bright eyes. He looked with attention at her ears. As he had hoped, they not only lay flat against her head, but were lobeless. He had always had a weakness for lobeless medieval ears. He could not lie to those ears.

'Because,' he said, 'it's good.'

Bea clapped her hands, gave a little bounce. 'Sure,' she said. 'But why is it so good?'

'Because I can do words. I can find the right ones to say what I need.'

Her long neck drooped, a hand touched her mouth. 'Could you enlarge on that a little, Doctor? Harold and I have both always been so . . . well, it's just so mind-blowing to even like, meet you, let alone talk.'

There must be something sensible he could say. 'I do a lot of thinking,' he said finally. 'Is that any help?'

'To find *le mot juste*?' yelped Harold.

'Yes. And *la pensée*.'

It was now Harold who was bouncing about. '"What oft was thought, but ne'er so well expressed"?' he cried.

'If you say so,' said the poet. He smoothed his front hair once more. 'Nice word "ne'er", I must look it up.'

'It'll just say "poet or arch,"' murmured Bea.

She seemed to have gone rather wistful. He must help her. 'Tell me some words you like, Bea.'

'Sundance, quicksilver, heartsease.'

'For Chrissake, Bea,' snapped Harold, 'don't go all peasbody on us.'

The poet did not enjoy seeing a woman discomfited, especially a serious, gentle woman with the right sort of ears. He smiled at her. 'There's nothing wrong with the word "peasbody" as long as it is taken to mean the body of a pea. I can't say I care for it as a name.'

Bea smiled back. Between them, unexpected and munificent as light from glow-worms, flowed sympathy, understanding, empathy — all the good ones. Harold was on the outer, a dead duck in need of plucking.

'Tell me some words you don't like,' said Bea.

250

They were interrupted by a minor commotion from beside the pool. The two small girls were inspecting the naked lady. One of them put out a tentative hand to stroke a concrete breast. The other, overcome with giggles, snatched it away. 'Mummy,' she squealed, 'Ella's going to touch the lady's boosies, and she shouldn't, should she, Mummy?'

Ella gave the sneak a passing swipe and danced back to the table.

'Rosie,' called Mother. 'Come here.'

Rosie went.

The poet put one hand over Bea's long, tapering fingers. 'Boosies,' he said, 'is a disaster. Promise me, Beatrice, you will never use the word "boosies".'

'I promise.' Beatrice glanced at their hands for a second and laughed. Her voice lightened, her bright eyes snapped. 'Tell me more words,' she said. 'All the words you know. Tell me.'

I Thought There'd
Be a Couch

Dr Celia Crowe is switched on and well presented. A super-slim Rolex hides her left wrist, a small-linked gold bracelet lies alongside, an antique watch-chain circles her neck, the toggle lying in the dip at the base of her throat. Her skirt is not visible below her desk but her legs are. Close together, slanted side by side like the Queen's, they lie pale and interesting in 15-denier. Her feet are small, hidden inside black patent-leather shoes with mini heels and flat grosgrain bows. They are so shiny you could see her pants in them, but this Standard Four vernacular is forgotten. The caramel linen jacket she wears is pleated and padded on the shoulders like that of a Samurai warrior. It fastens with brass buttons. When Dr Crowe stands it hangs well below her hips and she looks fashionably top heavy. She wears her hair pinned up during consultations. When she loosens it, leaping black curls spring from their confinement. There is so much to stow away that the effect, when she is working, is of exuberance controlled but not repressed.

Dr Crowe used to be an active feminist but after fifteen

years of slaving night and day to attain her position as a psychiatrist in private practice, sisterhood has gone down the tubes. Dr Crowe is an Uncle Tom; one of the boys, professionally speaking.

Mr Huxtable has never been one of the boys. He sits very still in one of the uncomfortable chairs in Dr Crowe's waiting-room. They are so overstuffed, so unyielding, that he feels like a pea on a drumhead.

The colour scheme is grey and darker grey plus silver with touches of flamingo pink. The knobbly carpet is the weary grey of old porridge, the walls are silver grey, the chairs are dark grey, the scatter cushions are flamingos ranging from palest blush to dark salmon. (Well-fed flamingos, whose diet includes shrimp-like shellfish, are a deeper pink than the disadvantaged.)

The pictures on the walls are reassuring and calm. The one directly in front of Mr Huxtable has splashes of pink flung against what looks to him like wet sand at Waikanae when the tide is out. There is the same sheen, the same silver streaks at the tide line, a black outline which may or may not be Kapiti. Mr Huxtable shuts one eye in his attempt to make a decision. He thinks on balance it must be.

The other picture hangs beside the reception area. A sign saying RECEPTION stands on the bench beside a cardboard cut-out of a red rose on a long stalk, the base of which tells him this is a smoke-free zone. Mr Huxtable turns his attention to the picture. Here silver nymphs dance, silhouetted on the skyline against a huge full moon. A weeping silver birch stands to one side of the last leaping nymph. There is a satyr or two; the procession is led by a round-bellied infant playing upon a medieval musical instrument, the name of which escapes

Mr Huxtable, though he did know it once. Trump? Timbal? Not that. He will have to look it up. How though? How will he start when he knows only the shape, which is that of an elongated horn.

Mr Huxtable has been waiting a long time. He looks at the young man opposite him, who is reading what must be a piece of in-depth journalism as he has not lifted his head for forty minutes.

'They think you've got all day,' says Mr Huxtable gently. The young man lifts his head in fright, nods and dives back into his article. His jersey is sage green, his chubby face is pale, his hands fumble as he turns a page.

Mr Huxtable picks up the morning paper. The front page has a photograph of a proud young policeman after his graduation ceremony. He holds a sleeping baby bundled in his arms. The previous week he supported his wife throughout her long and difficult labour. It was thirty hours, he says. He wouldn't have had it any other way, he says. Mr Huxtable sighs. He knows the cop means he is glad to have supported his wife, not pleased her labour was difficult. Don't they hear what they say? Another photograph depicts a doctor on an offshore island which has inadequate consulting-room facilities. One of these days, warns the Doctor, we're going to lose someone we needn't have. Mr Huxtable sighs again, puts down the paper and rubs his knuckles in his eyes. He picks up an Australian magazine which shows red-capped lifesavers marching, places it on the table, lifts his feet onto it and closes his eyes.

'Dr Crowe will see you now, Mr Eddy,' cries the nurse from behind the glass which defines her territory.

The young man ditches the magazine, scrambles to his feet and lopes to the door indicated by Nurse Mollet. He wears boots which Mr Huxtable's reopened eyes do not recognise as either farm or army. They are tidy boots of quality, but not fashion. They are workmanlike, the laces twist from knob to knob up his ankles, the toes are blunt and bulbous. They nail Mr Eddy's fantasies to the ground.

'Good luck,' calls Mr Huxtable.

Mr Eddy, appalled, backs through the door. Mr Huxtable shuts his eyes again. Nurse Mollet stares at his feet but says nothing.

Mr Huxtable opens his eyes slowly as Nurse Mollet shakes his shoulder.

'You were asleep.'

His eyes are clear, blue, rimmed with pink lids. 'I'm not now.'

His bald head is freckled and sun-pocked, his curls have retreated to a ring of grey fluff above his ears. Hair sprouts from his nostrils, his ears, from beneath the worn cuffs of his grey cotton shirt.

'Dr Crowe is a very busy person,' says Nurse Mollet. 'Especially taking over Dr Grigg's list like today.'

Mr Huxtable agrees. His voice is soft as he confirms her statement. 'Well, you can see that, can't you,' he says, 'otherwise we wouldn't be sitting round here all day.' He nods at Nurse Mollet's pink-and-grey head and heaves himself out of the chair. The seat of his woollen work trousers hangs in folds about his shrunken old-man's buttocks as he moves to the door. Nurse Mollet recalls the same grey slackness at the zoo as Kamala lurched away, one manacled foot clanking behind another. Her grandson Errol's wave from the swaying howdah was nervous.

Kamala is dead now. Opportunists wanted the ivory but

Mr Gartrell the vet insisted the tusks remain intact, buried with the rest of the corpse.

Celia took her car in first thing for an oil change. Margie followed to provide a lift home.

Celia's instructions to the mechanic are quite explicit.

'And make sure you put one of those things on the steering wheel,' she says.

'What things?' asks the blank moustached face.

Why do they always wear white? Like the blood-smeared overalls of late-night meat deliverers. Mad.

'Those things to keep the mess off the wheel,' says Celia, nodding at his blackened hands which tighten around the cheesecloth.

'OK.'

'Last time it was all over me.' Celia flings quick hands at her hair, her chest, towards him, palms wide in demonstration.

'I said, OK.'

Celia gives him a winning smile. 'Five-thirty,' she says. She turns on her heel and marches out of the cavernous clanging dump, past the oil-slicked puddles to Margie's Mini.

They have been friends since Grammar and started Medical School together. Margie and Rob dragged her from beneath the dissecting table when she fainted. The cadavers were memento mori carved from mahogany, the formalin stench all-pervading. It got into your clothes, hair, fingers. Cameras were forbidden but later Rob took a snap of her dissecting out Bert's laryngeal nerve. Rob was also on Bert. Some of the men were full of innuendos and sexual cracks during dissection. Not Rob. He appeared in third-year after a year off to sort himself out. He spoke only when he had something to say. People found it disconcerting. He's hard to know, they said.

The three of them went to pubs together, handed on news of the best takeaways, op shops, likely exam questions and model answers. Rob had an old Escort and Margie sat in the front passenger's seat. One day she found herself in the back and Rob and Celia have lived together ever since. Six months ago they bought a house in Mount Victoria and one day Rob will unpack completely. Celia realises he is swotting but God in Heaven, can't he see she can't live like this? Not when it's their own house. Rob is at Public and is about to sit his surgery finals for the third time.

Margie leans across to unlock the passenger's door. The parting between the red-gold curls is bright pink. Celia's mother disliked red hair. Her redheaded sister, Celia's Aunty Bet, fell in the sheep dip when she was eight and Celia's mother laughed and laughed.

Margie is in general practice. Her surgery is near Celia and Rob's house and she has agreed to take Celia back to pick up the Honda. Celia has taken the day off to work on a paper entitled 'Sanctuary: An Outdated Concept?' which she is reading at a forthcoming psychiatrists' conference in Queenstown and is worried about.

Celia opens the yellow door of Margie's Mini and ducks in. Her legs swing in in a united sweep. 'Surly brute,' she says.

'Oh well,' says Margie. She leads the gear lever by the hand, her fingers resting on top of the round knob through first and second, beneath to slip into third, on top again to sweep down into fourth. Margie is a good driver. She and Celia have a game called What I am good at. Celia is good at having legible writing and a sense of direction. Margie is good at driving. And she answers letters. Not everyone can play this game. I'm not good at anything, they say, thereby missing the point. One of the talents Celia and Margie share, for example, is for scrubbing floors. They both use plenty of good hot soapy water, get right into the corners and take a pride in doing so. Such shared minor talents increase their empathy and make them laugh.

Margie stops for a red light, her head high. Women, especially women with good profiles, look better driving a car. The world is their oyster. Women don't look so good driving a car with children, as their eyes have to glance about, even with seatbelts, and the alert questing look is dissipated.

'I've thought of another game,' says Margie.

Celia has discovered a hangnail on her thumb. 'Oh, What?'

'What's the main thing you knew during the first seven years of your life? Your main feeling about it.'

Celia gives up trying to snip it off with her front teeth.

'You mean the Jesuit bit? First seven years stuff?'

'Not necessarily Jesuit.'

'Why seven then?'

'All right,' Margie's right foot is down, she is leaping away. 'Make it six if you're fussed.'

'Six. OK.' Celia knows immediately, but two can play at this game. 'What's yours?'

'I'm working on it,' says Margie. 'Tell me yours.'

'I knew they loved me,' says Celia. 'That I was special.'

Margie changes down and swings into Majoribanks Street which can be either Marsh or Marjorie.

*

Celia has been working in the spare room for a quarter of an hour. The floor is bare. Rob's stuff is piled beneath the double-hung window; clothes are bundled into cartons, old textbooks lie about. *Medical Jurisprudence* is open at putrefaction, a New World plastic bag contains mixed shoes, two sleeping bags are dumped beside his squash racquet, which has two small white feathers caught in its stringing. An Agee jar contains a Citizen diver's watch without a strap, a ten-trip bus ticket, a blue ballpoint, an old comb, a red pencil-sharpener shaped like a die, assorted keys and a twenty-first wallet. Rob works in the living-room in a cane chair with a piece of board across his knees and his books in a wide circle around him. He can only work like that. Celia's table is an old flush door on trestles, both of which she bought at a Rotary auction. She gave the door several coats of gloss polyurethane and its dark shining surface pleases her. She is working on her statistics, getting them in order to put them through the practice's computer. The figures look weird. She picks up her pocket calculator as the telephone in the hall gives its muted ring.

'Celia Crowe,' she says, squatting down to its level.

'Celia? It's Jenny Mollet.'

'Yes, Jenny.'

'Dr Grigg has flu. He says can you do his surgery list?'

'Oh, *Jenny*.' Celia rolls onto her behind, cradling the receiver against her face as though she loved the bloody thing.

'Well yes, I *know*,' the voice wheedles. 'But he's got a full list and there are some urgent repeats.'

Dr Grigg is the psychiatrist with whom Celia shares consulting-rooms. He is an elder statesman, a bosomy cuddle-bunny of a man well loved by his patients.

The soundproofing at the rooms is not perfect. Each day Celia hears Dr Grigg's soothing murmur through the wall, though she doesn't hear the words as he questions, diagnoses, explains and cares for his patients. Celia finds the sound distracting but the architect says the proofing is as specified, no one queried it and Insulfluff wouldn't help. Celia thinks Dr Grigg is dependent on his patients' dependence, but he and Celia respect each other and have an arrangement whereby each will mind the shop for the other in a crisis. Not long-term treatment; just urgent repeats, a hand on the pulse, a keeping of despair at arm's length, or bay if possible. New patients can be a problem. Are they to be returned? This is open for negotiation, but defections are usually accepted with good grace by the absent member of the team.

Celia glances at the large sheaf of papers in her hand. Shit. 'OK, Jenny I'll have to get a taxi, my car's in dock.'

She throws the papers down on her work table. They are abandoned, adrift on a bronze sea. She returns to the hall and punches the taxi numbers with a stiff middle finger. She'll ring Margie from the rooms to change the pick-up arrangements.

The taxi arrives promptly and Celia scrambles to change from jeans to skirt and snatch her briefcase, bag and jacket. She usually has plenty of time and emerges trim as a marching girl in garments assembled from the floor. Rob can never understand why this is different from his mess and Celia thinks his lack of perception is endearing.

The taxi smells of nicotine and a synthetic rose which seeps from a deodoriser attached to the dashboard. The thing is nearly defunct. Only a half moon of pink deliquescing substance is visible between the slots of white plastic. Celia opens the window.

*

Last night Margie arrived at Celia and Rob's house with greasies, having got fed up. They ate them sitting on the new wall-to-wall carpet in front of the TV, their backs lined against the pastel weave of the six-foot sofa. Three people on a sofa is more of a straight line than three people on the floor in front of it. People on sofas are framed by sofa, cut off.

There is not much in the room apart from the carpet and the sofa and the cane chair, which has padded cushions aglow with hibiscus and is large and designed for relaxation on patios. Rob's board leans against it and his current textbooks lie open or shut around it. There is a bay window and a mantelpiece of three curved pieces of wood like the Pink and White Terraces before eruption. Rob thinks it's Art Deco. Celia isn't sure but will find out. The curtains which loop and fall are unbleached calico in profusion. There is a leather pouf which Celia's mother was glad to get rid of, stereo equipment, speakers, records and CDs piled high. On the mantelpiece buds of Japanese iris, long and tight and enclosed, reveal slashes of deepest blue at their tips. The heavy glass vase which holds them was Margie's last birthday present to Celia.

Margie has just told them something they hadn't heard about the National Women's Hospital Inquiry, but nothing would surprise them now.

The TV sits on the carpet, blinking through lack of aerial. Periodically, the two doomed whales in Alaska which have captured the attention of the viewing world surface on the screen. A snout appears, breaking the surface of the water. The mouth gapes, the whale gives an ineffective blow, then, infinitely poignant, the blunted snout sinks once more. Inuits and cameramen stand silent about the hole, another snout rises, lifts, then slowly disappears. President Reagan appears on the screen, his eyes sad as he promises that America will do all it can.

'No one would give a stuff if it was three Eskimos,' says Margie, her hand on the Cerebos.

'Two,' corrects Celia.

Margie's eyes shut briefly. 'More salt?' she says to Rob.

'Rob shakes his head. 'What did you expect?'

'You're not having more salt?' says Celia.

'A lady doctor like you,' says Rob.

Dimples are evanescent. They appear from nowhere like mushrooms, sometimes before the smile. Margie sprinkles salt, replaces the Cerebos and leans back, still smiling.

'These chips are good,' she says.

'Where're they from?' asks Rob.

'The usual.'

'I thought they'd changed hands,' mutters Rob.

Margie shakes her head, her mouth full.

'Did you see *Nanook of the North*?' asks Celia.

Heads shake. Hands select, abandon, stow.

'They really did ditch them, you know. Old people.

'They did in the film.'

'When they had no teeth, wasn't it?' says Margie.

'Whatever,' says Celia, rolling fluff from the new carpet into a ball with her fingers.

'Because they couldn't chew, I mean,' says Margie.

'Somewhere in Kurdistan the nomads just leave them on the other side of the river,' says Rob, scrubbing his face with a paper napkin. 'When you can't make it across you just stay on the wrong side.'

'Of course you'd be conditioned to it,' says Celia. 'I mean, as a child you'd see Granny left, then Grandad. I mean . . . Well, you'd know.'

'Yeah,' says Rob. He glances from one face to another, 'Any more?' Margie and Celia shake their heads. Rob screws up the remaining chips inside the paper and stands. From their angle his head seems to touch the light. 'But I reckon however conditioned you are it would be different when it's you.'

'Well of course,' says Celia. 'But you'd still accept it.'

'I wouldn't.'

'Nor me,' says Margie.

'Remember when I had that tendon?' says Rob.

'Yes.'

'I felt like saying to the guy, "This is not some hack you're dealing with. This is me." He pauses. 'Bugger it, I wouldn't accept anything.'

'You'd have to,' says Celia.

'Yeah, you'd have to but you wouldn't,' says Rob. 'Not when it was you.'

'They put them on icebergs, didn't they?' says Margie.

'Floes,' says Celia.

'Go with the floe.' Rob turns at the door. 'Nescaf OK?' Margie crosses her legs beneath her and is on her feet tugging at her skirt. 'I'll bring the plates. Hang on.' Rob waits at the door.

Celia comes to with a slight jump. The taxi man is talking, He is Greek. Every morning, he tells Celia, he has instructed his grandson to come to him and say, 'Grandad, remember Roger Douglas.' This is so the driver will not forget his morning hate against the Minister of Finance who ruined the country. A fifth-century BC Persian king, says the driver,

slowing for the lights, ordered one of his officers to recite to
him each morning, 'Remember the Greeks.'

'But you're teaching your grandson to hate,' says Celia.

The large handsome head nods, the eyes in the mirror
are calm, dark as Kalamáta olives. 'That's right,' says the
driver.

Celia has prescribed a repeat of lithium for Miss Cullen's
chronic depression and a repeat of Serenace for Mr Jiles's
psychosis. She has reassured Mrs Goodman that constipation
is one of the normal side effects of Sinequan but this can be
dealt with, and she will give Mrs Goodman a note for the
chemist with the name of the laxative that she is sure Dr Grigg
would recommend, though, as Mrs Goodman is probably
aware, laxatives are no longer on the prescription list. Yes,
it is unfair. She thinks probably the reason Dr Grigg didn't
warn Mrs Goodman is that it's not always a side effect. She
has suggested to Mr Eddy that he should ask Dr Grigg about
group-counselling therapy, which she has found helpful for
patients of hers with similar problems. Mr Eddy's white face
tightens. He says he'll think about it and leaves quickly. Celia
makes another note.

A young woman in a denim miniskirt hops on one leg with
glee as she leaves the Medical Centre next door. Pregnancy
test negative? Or positive perhaps? A child in a padded
yellow anorak and minuscule jeans pads past attached to an
old woman with pink-tinted hair. The child points. The pink
head nods.

Celia turns back to Mr Eddy's mental history. Her writing
is blue-black italic, modified for speed. She spent hours at
Grammar sitting in the back row perfecting the narrow
upstrokes and wide downward sweeps which give style to

her hand. The rest of Five A thought she was mad. Her pen came from Henlow and Jenkins of Jermyn Street. J. Fyfe pp James Spence despatched her black Mont Blanc. He enclosed a typewritten note suggesting she stick to Quink. The pen's shape is that of a small fat torpedo and cost the earth.

The door opens and Mr Huxtable enters. Celia sees a small unknown man and registers the secret 'new patient' snip of pleasure. She smiles at Mr Huxtable and stows Mr Eddy's notes away.

'Mr Huxtable,' she says. 'Do sit down.'

Mr Huxtable remains standing in front of her. He stares gravely around her pleasant consulting-room, which is Edwardian in concept. There is a large wooden cabinet which houses exotic shells collected in Samoa by Celia's Uncle Ted. An antique grandfather chair upholstered in dark green Dralon awaits the patient. A round footstool embroidered in white, grey and black beads sits beside it. The carpet is grey. The desk is new. There are no pictures.

'I thought there'd be a couch,' says Mr Huxtable.

Celia's bottom teeth are visible as her smile widens. 'Did you?' she says.

'You haven't got a proper desk either.'

Celia's hand touches the blond laminate. 'This is a desk.'

Mr Huxtable shakes his head. 'I thought you'd have a big couch and a proper desk and I'd . . .'

Celia's hand touches the wooden knob. The Roll-easy drawer slides out, its passage smooth as that of a coffin's sinking to cremation. 'Look,' says Celia, shooting the drawer in and out.

Mr Huxtable nods without conviction. Celia glances at his face and straightens quickly. 'Do sit down, Mr Huxtable,' she says, demonstrating with her palm on the desk top, as though Mr Huxtable is a small animal under instruction.

Mr Huxtable lowers his arthritic hip into the grandfather chair. He drops the last few inches from stiffened knees and waits to be told what to do next.

Celia picks up her pen. 'Well, Mr Huxtable?' she says. 'How can I help you?'

Mr Huxtable drags his eyes from the invisible couch and shifts the weight from his hip.

'I'm not happy,' he says.

Celia glances up, her eyes round. What on earth's he on about?

When Celia found herself in the front seat of Rob's beat-up Escort the world leapt into sharp focus. It was the first time without Margie. The leaves of the silver poplars beside the shingle road snapped green, grey, green, grey, as the felted undersides appeared and disappeared. Rob slowed down, pulled the car onto the grass verge and switched off the ignition. One small branch was outlined against the sky. Its leaves moved and shimmered, were blotted out by his head. 'Hullo,' he said.

Mr Huxtable sits with his back to the window. Celia gives him her full attention but the butcher's shop across the road is visible over his left shoulder. The marbled reds, the rosy pinks of the different cuts are an indistinct blur, but Celia knows they lie on white plastic trays divided by inch-high fences of imitation parsley. The meat is good, the service quick, the owner Terry is obliging and will leave Celia's order with the dairy next door if she is held up, as she often is.

Margie and Rob stand side by side looking at the meat, their backs to the road. Margie's head touches Rob's shoulder for a second as she points at a tray. Their attitude, their bodies, are relaxed, connubial. They are lovers. They will choose the chops, the schnitzel, something quick, easy, and take it to Margie's flat. After Margie has driven Celia to collect the Honda she will return to the flat and they will cook the meat, eat it and fall into bed. Or before. Tonight is Rob's squash night with Des Carnihan. Margie's bright cloud of hair lifts as she turns to Rob. They enter the shop.

Mr Huxtable waits, his eyes on hers. They are old, kind, blue as her dead grandfather's. His hands nest in his lap, their skin tucked and pleated, slack and extra as lizards'.

Celia releases her fingers from the underside of the desk and presses them on top as she leans forward. There is a lull in the traffic, a screech at the lights. She stares at her patient as if he knew something important, something he could tell her. A child props a red bike against the plate-glass window opposite, balancing it with care.

Real Beach Weather

I used to be a nice woman, kind and pleasant, a dear girl once, I swear. When I was young; younger.

My husband, Derek, works in town during the week and comes to the beach only at weekends. He will be here on Friday, as the night the day. Nothing is surer. Nothing.

I, on the other hand, sit in a deck chair in the cool of the evening with Mrs Clements and her daughter who are both reasonably amiable people, especially Isobel. I am offered Twiglets, sip vodka with lime juice and tepid water and find fault in everything. I clench my fist to prevent myself shouting 'Stop talking,' at Mrs Clements, who is explaining with much detail and many diversions how she came across the vodka. She was down on her benders this morning making sure there was enough beer because if there's one thing James hates it's a drought. He is not a toper as we know, but, like all young men, he likes his beer. So there she was, head down bottom up, when lo and behold she came across this old bottle. Goodness knows where it came from. But now she comes to think of it the Parkinsons might have left it when they stayed that time before Harold died.

'Heavens above,' she cries, 'that's about, six, seven years ago. How old is Charlie now, Lorna?'

'Five,'

'Is that all? I suppose it seems longer because of his foot. Anyway, I thought we might as well try it.'

'Yes,' I say.

Warm vodka will probably be worse than warm beer but at least it will be different. It will make a change. I would like a change very much. Even the sea is boring, which I would not have thought possible. It is flat, oily, calm and predictable. The rock face of the Island beyond is stark and white as a tooth snapped from the mainland. On the seaward side of the Island, they say, are trees. Trees would be nice.

Cushioned by hillocks and dusted with sand my younger children, Ann and Charlie, loll on the couch grass in front of the verandah. They lie torpid, sated with sun and sea and glad to be here. Occasionally one of them lifts a hand in a doomed attempt to swat a fly.

The flies are bad this year, but then we say that every summer. They are large these flies, sticky-footed beach ones which cling and bite. Like children, they cannot be flicked away or ignored. Ann is now making a fuss about them, slapping arms, legs, whimpering. She has not had time to get used to them yet and will have to do so. I open my mouth to tell her so, but shut it again because I see Mrs Clements' pale eyes watching me and I don't want her to hear me being irritable. I treat Mrs Clements with respect, which is the wrong word because there are aspects of Mrs Clements which I do not, nevertheless she is a woman of great presence and I am aware of this. She is a large, well-powdered woman, not shiny with sweat like the rest of us.

Perhaps you sweat less when you are old but more probably

it is because she keeps well away from the coal ranges and heated flat irons of beach life when the temperature is in the high nineties, as it has been for weeks. What are daughters for, and Mrs Clements has Isobel.

We talk about the real beach weather we have been having, we tell each other it is more comfortable in the sea than out. The nights, we say, bring little relief. The children mutter in their sleep as they toss in their bunks without a stitch of cover.

Mrs Clements says that James and Isobel were just the same at their age.

Isobel, lean and sharp-kneed, her eyes gentle behind steel rims, sits on the steps and strokes Charlie's pale hair. She has strong features like her brother who is the most handsome man in the Bay by a long shot, but a large nose and strong eyebrows are no help to Isobel. Her hair is thin and black and clamped to her head with bobby pins, not flopping in chestnut waves like James's.

Mrs Clements says yet again that this is a pity and that Isobel should have her hair permed, that she won't *try*. Isobel says No. She refuses, she likes to be free. She swims without a bathing cap, her seal head ducking and diving beneath the waves, her spectacles at home.

Charlie is now almost asleep against her angled knees. Isobel's head is bent to his. Mrs Clements hisses in my right ear, 'Poor Isobel, she's potty about that child. Of course she'll never have one of her own.' She sighs.

Some childless couples in Malaysia, I am about to tell her, adopt orphaned baby orangutans. They shave off their body hair to make them look more like human infants and dress them in appropriate clothes and are happy. I open my mouth, and, thank God, shut it again.

When I was a child my mother stressed the importance of the sorting house which, she told me, lies between the thought and the tongue. If I remembered about the sorting house I would not make gaffes like my remark at the School Sports to Arthur Smedley who was coming in last as usual — 'Come on Arthur, you'll win if you don't lose,' I cried in a loud voice *in front of everyone.*

Nowadays I have given up on the sorting house. I will say anything for a laugh and often do, but I am glad the orangutans are safely stowed.

Their story does not end there. When the orangutans are about three years old they become obstreperous and violent. Some surrogate parents hand them back to the forest rangers from whom they came, whereupon the doubly orphaned *Pongo pygmaeus* cry day and night and refuse food for weeks. Other parents abuse them or hack them to death in despair at their recalcitrant behaviour.

Mrs Clements thinks, and I know she thinks, that Isobel's fondness for Charlie is because of his foot. But I know that both Isobel and Charlie are made of sterner stuff. People stop Charlie on the beach. They ask him where he lost his foot. 'I didn't lose it,' he says. 'They cut it off.'

His left foot went the wrong way. It was all they could do.

It is essential for him to be tough and he is, thanks to me. I have made him so. Somebody had too.

I sip vodka. I have not had it before and I find it agreeable.

James Clements reappears from the back door. A small child with school sores has brought him a telephone message from the store. The Rowans up on the hill would like him to have a meal with them next Thursday. There's some cousin from Somerset and would he ring back.

James leans against the verandah post and rubs his back against it like some large and beautiful animal. He is incapable of making an ungraceful movement which is unusual in so tall a man. Even the way his heavy cotton shirt hangs from his shoulders moves me. It is James I come to watch. He is the author of the heaviness in my chest, the tightening in the groin. Even, perhaps, the clenched fist.

James is not pleased by the Rowans' invitation. 'Put on a tie and drive for miles in this heat for dog-tucker mutton! Let alone with some dim Rowan cousin. Bugger that.'

Mrs Clements smiles. Her grey curls frame her face like the frill of an antique bonnet.

'Then don't go, darling,' she murmurs.

James tells us that even the thought of trailing down to the store to tell them so makes him feel tired.

His mother is delighted at such indolence. She knows James doesn't mean it. That he will be there and back in a flash. 'Don't forget the bread order,' she laughs.

I've done that,' says Isobel and Mrs Clements nods.

I want to tell Mrs Clements to stop being ridiculous about her son. That she is spoiling him rotten. What would she do if she had Charlie; she would ruin him, turn him into a cripple. She has already squashed Isobel, or thinks she has, but not from kindness. Mrs Clements did her best for Isobel when she was younger. She told me so herself. Take the evening shoes. There were no size eights to be had then, let alone without heels. Mrs Clements bought a pair of men's leather slippers from the Farmers and Isobel painted them gold for the Ball Season.

Isobel and I met at a dinner party before the Black and White Ball, which my father called the Tight and White. Mrs Newman, our hostess, was large and golden and loved fun and games. She was an icebreaker.

I was a flapper by instinct and conviction, one of the first in the Bay to bob my hair. Straight shifts, shingled hair and high heels suited me. I was a success.

Isobel wore a long frock of some dark crêpe. Her hair was shorter than mine and better cut. She stood tall and straight and told me she wished to be elsewhere. That she had hidden the invitation, but that Mum had found the wretched thing and there had been a stink. She laughed, and watching her, I wondered at what stage slim like me becomes skinny like her. I thought she looked good. Different, certainly, from the rest of us Cuddlepots and Snugglepies, but good.

After the meal Mrs Newman gathered us together to tell us her plan for breaking the ice. The girls would each throw one shoe into the centre of the room, then sit down carefully so as to hide the still shod foot. The boys would then come in, choose a shoe and come to find its mate, thereby claiming their partner for the first dance. I was not pleased. The second best-looking man in the Bay (James had not yet returned from the War) had insisted on the first dance and I had hopes of more, many more.

We tossed shoes. Among silver pumps, louis heels, neat little brocades and pale satins, Isobel's gent's leather lay like a gilded cattle truck.

There was an embarrassed pause, a titter truncated by Isobel. She flung back her head, her short hair tossed as she laughed and laughed and laughed. I laughed too, seized her hand.

And then the men came in; and we stopped.

Mrs Clements has now given up on Isobel. For a time before she lost interest she scared the wits out of the one or two young men who hovered briefly and were never seen again. They were, she told us, unsuitable.

Sweet as a nut, I was once. Lorna Brownlee, who loved old dogs and children and was kind and patient with incontinent old men in Men's Medical.

I'm sorry, Nurse. I done it in a fit. I'm sorry, dear.'

'Don't worry, Mr Spence,' I laughed, game as Ned Kelly with sodden sheets.

So what changed?

I had been engaged before the War, long before I met Derek, had written to my fiancé Corporal Alan Webster every week while he was overseas. The troopship berthed in Wellington and I was given special leave from the Hospital to go down to meet him. I can still hear the nagging of the train. 'What're you doing, what're you doing, what're you *doing*, you fool.' I stood on the wharf staring up at the face of the stranger beneath his lemon squeezer hat and panicked. I ran, fighting, struggling my way through the crowd pushing against me until I reached the entrance to Queen's Wharf. I arrived at the hotel, sobbing. The receptionist thought my fiancé had died en route and I wished he had, though not really.

That was when I began cheating.

A girl who jilts a wounded war hero at the moment of his triumphant return to his homeland has to start somewhere. My friend Nan said when she took off her corsets at the beach and flopped about, the sheer, physical joy of relief, the release from tension, reminded her of the first time she saw William again, alive and in one piece after the War.

Not so for me. My downhill course began with that sick scramble among the hooters and streamers and the crowds in hats waving and shouting and senseless with happiness. It was then I learned I was bad medicine. Alan Webster told me I so.

Lorna,
I cannot call you dear because you are no longer. Little did I think as I gazed at the snap I wore next to my heart all those years that you were bad medicine. I used to think that you had kept me safe. Safe for what? You are heartless and fickle. You can keep the ring. I could not take it back if you paid me.
Alan.

And I didn't mind, you see. I was glad, yea glad with all my heart to have got rid of him. Which shows there was something wrong, does it not, with both me and my heart.

I had boyfriends. Pretty girls did then, plain girls didn't, it was as simple as that. I also had a reputation. I was now flighty, if not wild. Mothers throughout the length and breadth of the Bay cautioned their sons, who took no notice. They flocked, we Charlestoned. I was fun.

I did not go to bed with these young men. They were too young, too gauche. Their hair was plastered with Brylcreem and their hot dancing hands were encased in white cotton gloves to save us from sweat marks on our dresses. Their programmes, their wee gold pencils and their groping, now gloveless hands, bored me beyond words.

The man I did love was married. We spent our time together at an hotel in Waipawa with no lift. There was a sign in the lobby saying, *Commercials Welcome.* The bottom of the dinner menu read, *Fruits in Season.*

You do not need the name of my lover. He is dead now. His shell-shocked mind caught up with him and he blew his brains out in the station woolshed not long afterwards.

I had not told him I was pregnant. What could he have done, out on the coast with his new bride and baby son and his whole life ahead of him.

Derek was slightly younger than I, and a friend of my brother's. Like Ian he had been too young for the War, a dubious privilege in the twenties. He worked in Dalgety's Stock and Station Agents and studied for his accountancy examinations at night, and had admired me from afar for years, he told me.

I smiled and said Thank you and yes, I would be happy to go with him in my new apricot cloche to the Autumn Meeting. I like racing and I sat on the steps of the Members' Stand and took covert glances at Derek's profile as he stared at the field through binoculars. He was not a bad-looking man. He had a moustache but he did not, as it were, use it much. It was just there.

He held my hand. I moved it to my knee. He glanced at me, his smile one of radiant surprise. I removed it as Mrs Cyril Bradshaw ran up the steps to tell me that people below could see my knickers, and the race began.

I knew I was pregnant, I knew what I was doing. I was bad medicine. 'You must have fallen on your wedding night,' they said when my elder son Duncan was born prematurely. He was a beautiful baby. His father had been a fine-looking man.

You must understand that, like Mrs Clements, I did try. I did not love Derek Dobson but I was grateful to him. And at least I told him. 'I cannot marry you, Derek. I am pregnant. The father is dead.' I could not have made it clearer. He was shocked, deeply shocked, what young man would not have been.

But, and this perhaps is why I married him, he looked me in the eye and told me that he loved me and that if I married him he would give the child a name.

I wept. I don't think I had wept before. The baby has a name, I said, he or she has my name but not his father's because his father is dead and what about his poor little wife out at the coast, so tragic. And I meant it. It was tragic, tragic. I did nothing. It was the least I could do.

Derek, obviously, was a good man. He was also a hard worker and determined to do well. He saw his own brass plate shining before him like a vision at the end of a long uphill slog. *Derek Dobson, A.C.A.* Something he would win and lay at my feet for me to scuff.

I knew I was cheating and still do. I know.

Ann was born two years later. A solemn baby and easy after Duncan who was difficult. Babies were either easy or difficult, as girls were pretty or plain. I had to watch Duncan as a small child and still do. He is very quick.

I look around, leap to my feet. 'Where's Charlie?'

James grins at me. 'He and Isobel have gone to the store.'

'To give your message, I bet,' I say, teasing, flirting, oh the wit of it all to disguise my anger.

He smiles, nods. 'Aye,' he says. 'We all take our pleasures differently.'

And what has all this nonsense to do with me? Why do I rage inside because Isobel, who is plain, has seen fit to walk to the store to decline an invitation for her beautiful brother, who has no wish to eat tough mutton in the hills with Garth Rowan, his pigeon-toed Midge and a cousin from Home.

The Rowans for God's sake. Why should I fuss because

Isobel, who has not been included in this gaiety, has acted as James' runner? She is an intelligent woman, Isobel, as well as a good sort. Besides, as James so rightly says, she will enjoy her time alone with Charlie. I see them walking in single file to the store where the beaten track through the bleached grass is thinnest, side by side where it widens. Charlie will be telling her things, he is a talker. He will be swinging himself along on his crutch, his face glancing up at hers to make sure she has got the full impact of his favourite story from his weekly comic, the one called 'Betcha Barnes and his One Wheel Wonder', which his father will bring out on Friday. He will also bring liquorice allsorts. Charlie doesn't like the black rubber ones but Annie does and she lets him eat her hundreds and thousands which fall off.

Charlie has been known to hang around outside the beach store. He leans on his crutch, his eyes sad beneath his floppy grey sunhat, which all children wear this summer because of the polio epidemic, and stares at strangers as they come out clutching Frosty Jacks or Eskimo Pies. His eyes widen as he stares at their bounty. 'Just what I like,' he murmurs, and they rush back to Mr Girlingstone sweating behind the counter to get something, anything, quickly, for the waif at the door.

I checked when Duncan told me this story. I spied on Charlie and told Derek when he came out at the weekend.

'Ten out of ten for initiative,' I laughed.

I do that, you see, I do it all the time. I exaggerate my lack of moral tone so that Derek will overreact, will respond with pompous platitudes and I can laugh at him.

I stoke him up. He never lets me down.

Nor did he this time. He told me that there is initiative and initiative, called Charlie to him, sat him on his knee and explained to him that he must no longer ask people for ice creams at the store.

Charlie explained that he didn't ask for them, that people gave them to him.

Derek said he realised that technically this was so, but in actual fact Charlie was begging for them and this must stop.

Charlie said he liked ice creams.

Derek said he realised this but that Charlie was exerting moral blackmail and this must stop.

'How?' asked Charlie.

'Well, just stop,'

'No, I mean how blackmail?'

'Well you look sad and ...' Derek waved a worried hand.

'The foot, you mean.'

'Yes, well ...' Wretched, out of his depth, Derek sat silent.

Charlie looked thoughtful. 'Oh,' he said.

I laughed.

'Charlie, don't you see,' persisted Derek. 'We are lucky. I have a job, so many people still have no jobs, their children have no money for ice creams.'

'Annie gave one of her dolls away,' offers Charlie. 'At school.'

Derek's face, Derek's happy face. 'Did she?' he breathes.

'Did she say why?'

'The girl didn't have one. She had plaits.'

'The little girl?'

Charlie's white-blond head moves. 'The doll. Elsie.'

I bite my lip, literally bite my lip but the sorting house fails again. 'She didn't like Elsie much,' I say.

Derek's face.

Charlie is a truthful child. 'She did, Mum,' he says. 'She liked her a lot.'

Derek's eyes shut briefly. He tries again. 'Yes, well. So you won't do it any more?'

'Would it be all right if you didn't have a job?'

'It would be . . . it would be more understandable.'

Charlie swings around, looks up at him. He trusts his father. 'What about the foot though?'

Derek buries his head in the curve of his son's neck. His voice is muffled. 'No,' he says, 'the foot doesn't count.'

Charlie swings off Derek's knee. He picks up his crutch, grins at Derek as he scoots out the door. 'OK,' he says.

I keep my eyes, which are damp, on the fly paper hanging from the light above the table where we eat. It is black with dead and half dead flies, one still waving.

'I lied,' I say. 'Annie did like Elsie.'

'I know,' says Derek and is silent for a moment. He stands, looks at me sadly and delivers his verdict. 'You really must stop the children saying OK all the time, Lorna.'

The evening breeze stirs the tamarisk. The breakers no longer roar, their sound is muted as the waves retreat, are sucked back, return with more water. I don't believe the moon controls the tides. Waxing and waning, all that. It seems very far-fetched to me. On moonlit nights when we swim naked phosphorus sticks to our bare flesh. Phosphorus is mysterious, inexplicable as moons and tides, all that.

James lights a Craven A and hands the match to Annie to blow out. She does so but James has got it wrong. It is Charlie who enjoys blowing out matches. Ann teeters on the brink of becoming one of the big kids like Duncan, and there are things she has put aside.

The smoke rises around James's shadowed head, the light is fading. His face is all angles, hollows, manly beauty at dusk. I think of the *Indian Love Call*, 'When I'm calling you, ooh-oo, ooh-oo,' and wish to do just that. I wish Mrs Clements and Isobel would go away and I could make things clear, or perhaps clearer, to James. I am not a good woman, though presumably even a good woman may feel this clench, this awareness that her heart is beating and has been for some time.

James leans forward, plants a hand on each knee and tells us his news. 'I'm going to make a film with my movie camera this summer,' he says. 'Cowboys and Indians, goodies and baddies, that sort of thing.'

Mrs Clements and I are impressed. Movie cameras are new in the Bay and much desired.

'Acting, you mean?' says Mrs Clements finally, as though trying out a new word.

'Yes. You can ride, can't you, Lorna?'

'Yes,' I whisper.

'We'll have to get another cowboy from somewhere and two men, both bareback riders preferably, for the bad guys. Dark sinister-looking coves.'

I inspect a loose board on the verandah. 'Isn't that a bit obvious,' I mutter.

'Cowboy flicks are obvious. That's the whole point. Their conventions are as rigid as morality plays.'

'Who wears the white hat?' I ask, knowing already.

'Me,' says James.

'Yes,' says Mrs Clements. 'But who will work the camera?'

'Bel.'

'Ah,' says Mrs Clements and rearranges her skirt.

There will be parts for all of us; Mrs Clements will run a Wild West gambling den. There is a Madonna-of-the-plains type part for my friend Nan Lane next door.

Her husband William is Maori and can also ride bareback, which will be useful in the action scenes like the thundering chase along the surf beach.

Mrs Clements says that she'd always been interested in charades and dressing up, pretending to be somebody else, that sort of thing. She tells us she was a fairy once at school and what was James looking for? A tough egg. Well, she could try. But she wouldn't ride bareback.

She has an idea. 'James,' she says, 'do you think any of the men at the pa would be interested? William could ask them.'

James face is now in deep shadow at the back of the verandah but you can hear him smile.

'Local colour, you think?'

Mrs Clements laughs.

The tide is out on the beach below. Maori men and women dig for pipis, their children roll on the shining pewter sand. Somebody calls. The sound echoes, cuts across the car noises coming from Ann who is now pushing Dinky cars around tracks made through the rough grass.

Duncan's father told me once, and he was right, that every person in the world when shown a group photograph, looks for themselves first. Besides, I want to change the subject.

'What's my part?'

'Yours?' James looks at me as though I already knew. 'Oh, you play the bad girl. The harlot with the heart of gold.'

'How do we know,' I gasp, 'that she has a heart of gold?'

'She saves me at the end. From certain death.'

I see Mrs Clements' pale eyes on me. She is no fool, Mrs Clements.

I'm going to find Charlie,' I cry.

But Charlie and Isobel, hand in hand and still talking, are coming through the gate past the hole for rubbish which James digs every year. No wonder there are flies.

I leap up. 'Thank you so much, Mrs Clements.'

'Hardly a party, dear, just informal drinks.'

An informal ex-peanut butter jar of warm vodka.

Mrs Clements is congratulating James. She thinks the film will be a triumph. She loves the idea of the Wild West gambling den. Does James remember the poem his father used to recite? More of a ballad really. Something about Winifred the Wonder of the West and how people said she had a hairy chest. And James has written the story himself? She shakes her head in wonder.

Isobel tells us that Yes, James has asked her to be the cameraman and she would like to. She smiles her slow smile. 'Rather fun.'

'Beat you home,' I call to the children and we scramble through the broken-down fence at the place where Charlie can slide through. I swing him upwards, hug his brown thinness, kiss his salty ear.

'Oh Charlie,' I say.

Ann and Charlie have extended the Dinky car tracks among the long creeping roots of the couch grass in front of our bach, which is next door to the Clements'. There is now a hill town and a town on the flat, garages burrow into hillsides, a hospital marked with a wilting yellow gazania indicates where you are taken when you crash. As well as the cars there is a pick-up truck, a London bus and a milk van. Each child operates three vehicles, leaving two stationary as they brrm off with the third as required. The school bus has broken down. Brrm, brrm.

The thing I like best is their concentration, their complete absorption in the realities of their invented world.

Powered by Ann, an ambulance ploughs to the scene of a major crash. Invisible men jump out.

'Is he dead?' asks Charlie.

'Nearly. This may be a case for Betcha Barnes himself.'

'Betcha,' squeaks Charlie, 'but we haven't got a One Wheel Wonder.'

'We have! Look!' Ann snaps a minute tyre from a red car. Charlie is suspicious, looks doubtfully at his plundered Austin. Betcha Barnes is his, not Annie's. She has pinched him.

'You're not allowed. They get lost. Mum says.'

Ann's bare feet wriggle deeper in sand. She does not like interruptions. 'Do you want a One Wheel Wonder or not?'

'He's mine,' mutters Charlie.

'He can't be yours. He's in *Rainbow*. He's everybody's.' She trundles the wheel towards the yellow gazania. 'See. Now, he's rescued the man. He's all bleeding and Betcha's whizzing him to the hospital and . . .'

'No!' Charlie snatches the tyre and flings it into his mouth. He coughs violently, tears spurt from his eyes. I leap from the verandah, seize him above the knees to up-end him, beat his back. He coughs, splutters, sobs with fright as I beat and beat and beat.

'Is he going to die?' yelps Ann. The tyre shoots from Charlie's mouth.

I hold Charlie, swing him upright. I tell him it's all right, all right, it's all right.

Ann, shivering with fright and white to the bone, tells Charlie he shouldn't have put the tyre in his mouth.

'He's mine,' gasps Charlie as the Buick turns into the open gate and Derek toots the horn in greeting. He has arrived bearing basic provisions and fresh meat, beans from the garden, and treats as well. Watermelon and a tray of white-fleshed peaches from Morley's orchard, Rainbow and *Teddy's Own*, the week's mail and two yellow Gollancz detective stories for me.

'Charlie nearly died,' says Ann and picks up the sticky wet tyre.

Derek wants details. I give them. He takes Charlie from my shaking arms, asks him why he put the tyre in his mouth. Daddy has told him a thousand times not to put things in his mouth. Charlie, limp with exhaustion, opens his eyes. 'Have you got my *Rainbow*?'

Derek tells Ann that this must be an example to her. He has told all you children not to remove the tyres from Dinky toys. They get lost and as this incident has shown they can be very dangerous, though why in the name of Heaven a big boy like Charlie should swallow a toy tyre is beyond him.

Charlie closes his eyes. Ann says how could she know Charlie was going to go all dopey and swallow it.

Derek looks at *Brave New World* lying face downwards in the sand where I must have flung it.

'Were you reading?'

'Have you any objection?'

'No, but . . . No.' He pauses, looks around. Is unhappy. 'Where's Duncan?'

'With Mike from the store.'

'Where?'

'I've no idea.'

Derek puts Charlie down. 'I think I'll have a look around first before I unpack the car.'

'Where're the sweets, Dad?' cries Ann, scrabbling in the boot of the car.

'Yeh!' cries Charlie flinging himself around Derek's suited legs. He sees the wreckage beneath the town shoes; the collapsed towns, the hospital. 'You've mucked it all up, Dad,' he wails. 'Look, all our roads, everything, all busted.'

'Sometimes,' says Derek, glancing around as though Duncan might pop up from a nearby sandhill, 'I wonder why I drive over that filthy road every Friday night and back every Sunday.'

Charlie has found his comic. He pats Derek's leg kindly. 'To bring *Rainbow*,' he tells him.

And to make love to his wife on Saturday night. Derek is a meticulous lover. Normally he rubs and squeezes and twiddles and asks me whether I like it and I say yes and I fear he does not believe me, and nor do I. But he tries. And so do I. Sometimes he asks me if I would like to try another way and I say how and he says backwards and I say no thank you as I have said many times before, so he pumps away and I help. 'Help me,' he says and I do.

But tonight is different. He is excited, perhaps, by the heat, the blackness, the slick of sweat. Union is achieved, fulfilment is given, need assuaged. I have no longing afterwards, as I sometimes do, to leap from the sagging bed and the dead mattress and rush into the still night and scream for a man, any man, to finish me off.

At home it is the milkman. At the beach it is James Clements or occasionally Chris Appleton who is a strong swimmer but leaves the water when people start fooling about beyond the breakers because why should he risk his life.

I roll over. My hand brushes Derek's back.

'Dear heart,' he murmurs. 'I do love you so.'

'Yes,' I say. 'I know.'

Balance

In that drift of time between awake and dreaming, Tommo comes back. I see the shape of his back bent over the slides, or the way his hand moved, a wave from the morgue. I haven't been back for years. It was only a temporary job.

He was still shocked when they brought him in to hospital. He could hardly speak, or wouldn't, except to tell you his name. 'Tommo,' he'd say, staring through you as though you were Perspex. He wouldn't talk about the War. How long he'd been sick. What had happened. Anything. They tried to make him, they said he was bottling things up. He must learn to verbalise to release the trauma, they said.

I never heard him verbalise. Not once, all the time he was in the ward. If they pressed him too far he'd heave himself up, bend his head as though he was getting a medal from a general and hobble away.

Every morning I'd swing the chair into the day room to collect him for his session with the consultant. Tommo would put down whichever ripped magazine he'd been stroking, then lever himself up with his stick and stand waiting. Above the collarless grey dressing-gown, the back of his pale neck was naked and vulnerable as a boy's. He had a walking plaster so he didn't really need the chair, but it made things easier. I took him to Physio in silence. I took him back to the ward. Until the day he disappeared.

I found him in the cemetery which spills down the hill behind the hospital, in terraces like in photos of Japan. He was sitting on a concrete-covered grave in his faded hospital pyjamas. The cords of hospital pyjamas are always unravelled and he was playing with them while the tears ran down his face. When he saw me he picked a handful of white marble chips from the grave. He sorted them carefully and gave me the largest.

'Thanks, Tommo.'

He wasn't violent, not ever, but it was unnerving trying to get through to him. It was worse of course for his wife June. She had shiny dark hair and she used to clutch the sleeve of my uniform and ask, 'Why's he cry all the time?' Then she would tell me how he used to laugh. He was so funny, he made everyone laugh. Everyone. Why's he cry all the time?

After a few months they thought they'd have to send Tommo down the line for specialist treatment. There was nothing much physically wrong with him now and they had given him a smaller plaster. Dr Lee disagreed. He was young and he didn't mind the tears and the patients liked him.

'Go a couple of rounds this morning, Mr Johansen?' he'd say to some old wreck on a drip, and the old man would suck his remaining teeth and say he'd come out fighting if Doctor would give him another pint like the one last night. The other patients in Men's Surgical would grin at each other, comforted.

Dr Lee must have persuaded the consultant. The best

course was for Tommo to go home and cry if he wanted and no more questions. Time the great healer, said Dr Lee.

So Tommo went home to June and the baby, and Dr Lee was right again. The baby was a help. It didn't ask questions and it took up a lot of time and it laughed all over the place, especially when Tommo blew on its stomach or took it for walks in the cemetery. I used to meet them there sometimes on my way to afternoon duty. Tommo would be propped against a weathered tombstone while the baby inspected the rough grass between the graves and the pink and red valerian stirred above their heads. The baby and Tommo had the same hair. Thin and so fine it lifted in the breeze like pale silk.

If Beach the Head Porter wasn't on I'd stop for a while. Tommo talked more every time I saw him. You could see why he had a nickname. A man to pass the time of day with till dark. A yarner.

'The Catholic padre was the only one who was any use, and I'm not a Mick. "Hasta mañana, Madre, adiós," he'd say. Every night he'd say that.'

'Why, Tommo?'

'God knows. But the tomorrow sounded good.' His eyes followed the bird sideslipping the cliff above us.

'Wouldn't it be terrible to be a bum seagull?' he said.

'What?'

'No poetry of motion. Shit. And you'd starve too.'

'You'll have to get a job soon,' I said the next time I met them. Jealous. Him lying there.

Tommo picked a piece of lichen from the baby's mouth. 'Kee bor bor! Dirty. Pooh!' The baby looked at him like a blank pudding. Tommo stared up at me.

'Are there any orderlies' jobs going?' he said.

I shut up then. There was a job going, but it was a special. Mortuary porter. You need a lot of balance for that job and I didn't think balance was Tommo's strong point.

I retrieved the po-faced baby from the top of the grave and, hooking my little finger, dug a marble chip from its mouth.

'Kee bor bor,' said Tommo automatically. Still staring at me, his eyes calm.

'You'll have to ask old Beach.'

'OK.'

I didn't say anything to Beach. What could I have said? Don't take him . . . He used to cry. And I liked Tommo a lot more than that walrus-moustached sod. Every time Beach had a cup of tea he'd stir the spoon round and round and round and round. I always meant to time him. I'd feel myself sinking into the middle of the middle ring beneath the spoon. His wife used to stir his sugar in at home, he told me.

There's a curve outside Physio where the trolleys start to waltz. I met Tommo there a week later, pushing the mortuary pie-cart on his own. He was concentrating so hard he didn't see me at first. The pie-cart is realy a two-man affair. It was lunchtime and the corridor was full of the crashing rattle of the ward trolleys as they lurched against each other like steel dodgems on a gleaming surface.

'You got the job then, Tommo?' I said, taking evasive action from the unattended end of the pie-cart.

Tommo kept pushing. 'Yeah.'

'This your first trip?'

'No, I was lucky the first time. I had Nick. Death's part of life,' said Tommo. 'Nick said that.'

Nick was a huge man. Even his eyelids seemed heavy as

they sagged low over his eyes. His friend Theo was nimble, a quick darting performer who swirled the sacks of dirty laundry about the polished floors in sweeping curves instead of just kicking them along. Their meetings were rituals, right hands chopping down to shake the other, left hands embracing, slapping each other's backs as though they'd won again by meeting, indifferent to the currents of people streaming either side. They didn't give a stuff.

Tommo settled quickly into the routine. He was hardworking, neat and respectful to the quick and the dead, and the morgue had never looked better. The stainless steel had always gleamed but Tommo extracted an extra shine with Brillo.

The pathologist, Dr Klaus, liked him and promoted Tommo to assisting with the post-mortems. They were a good team. Tommo told me that Dr Klaus would come in, take off his lab coat, bow from the waist and put on the gear. 'If you are ready, Mr Thompson? Thank you.'

Tommo had a little workshop behind the p.m. room, which he kept as spotless as every other place in the department. The shelves were lined with bottles, beneath whose ground-glass stoppers specimens floated; some unrecognisable, some joltingly familiar. I never knew what was going to peer back at me from Tommo's shelves. His attitude to the bits and pieces was as caring as their original owners'. He was proprietorial about them too. Took a professional interest in size, shape, number. Though he wouldn't talk about where or who they came from. No gossip, nothing juicy. Jeeze, the stories he could've told from that place — murder, rape, self-inflicted wounds, you name it.

I tried hard enough.

'Come on, Tommo,' I'd say, waving a jar with something

pale and grey drifting about in formalin. 'What does it matter? The guy's dead now. Was he a boozer? You can tell me.'

But no. Never. He wouldn't.

Dr Klaus wouldn't have stayed in a town as small as ours if his English had been better. He taught Tommo how to prepare the specimens right up to the final staining of the slides. I used to envy the assistant as I crashed about the place, heaving and tugging and having to be cheerful to boring old buggers in pain. Tommo was always pleased to see me. I would lean against the incubator smoking, while he bent over the staining bench, the shape of his shoulder-blades visible beneath the white coat. Sometimes I'd wait for him to finish. He always left everything ready for the morning. It saved time, he said. Then we'd walk together through the cemetery, past the old house I had known as a child, down to the pub which clings by its eyebrows to the edge of the hill. Tommo and June lived further down the valley in a yellow cottage below the road.

The Lab was next door to the mortuary and the technologists liked Tommo as well. He stuck the tissue sections onto the slides with egg-white, and when necessary he would ask one of the girls to separate it from the yolk. Whichever one he asked would leap up from the bench, laughing. They all asked after the baby but it was Tommo they were talking about. As June said, he could make them laugh. Yarners can. And he could dance. At the Christmas Dance, hot and steaming in the Nurses' Social Hall, the streamers limp and the fruit cup spiked with lab alcohol, the girls fought to dance with Tommo. One small black shoe out, gentle and slow to the beat, then swirl, his hand low on her curve and around. Oh shit, I could've killed him as their hair swung around their damp little faces and they danced. June was quite happy and the baby slept soundless in the room with the coats.

I left at the end of that summer. I called in to Tommo's room at the end of my last shift. He placed the stained slides in the incubator to dry overnight then washed his hands, slipping the green soap from palm to palm. The overhead light shone directly on his head and I could see the pink scalp beneath the pale hair. He locked up and we walked down through the cemetery past the old house on the corner.

The old house had been beautiful once. Lack of paint had leached the walls to silver and the whole place shimmered in the late afternoon heat, outlined against dark macrocarpas. I had played on that sagging verandah, my nose level with the lowest streams of nutmeg-scented wistaria. Terror had stained the ground beneath those trees when I'd trodden on a rusty old coil of wire and it had struck my leg like a snake in fury.

The owner had sold the house to a small silent widow named Mrs Wellers. The house settled down around her, still and quiet as its new owner.

She had been found dead that week, slumped on the verandah in her nightdress, the bleached boards cool beneath her.

There had been an inquest of course, and a police post-mortem. A reporter had attempted to interview Dr Klaus.

He escorted the young man to the door, asking in his careful English, 'Is nothing sacred in this country?'

'Did her post-mortem show anything suspicious, Tommo?' I said as we passed. 'You know? Violence or anything?'

Tommo glanced at me. 'God, you're a weirdo,' he said, and ran down the steep path.

One of the things I like best about a pub, especially that one, is the first surge of light and sound as you push open the door. Shouts and laughter splintered to the roof and echoed back from the barman's armoury of glass and light.

'I'll get them,' I said, shoving forward to the bar.

I carried the glasses high, working a path back to Tommo through the curses and spills.

'Here, Tommo.' He took the glass and stared into it as though he could see something in it other than the beer which sloshed over the side as someone knocked his arm.

There was a long silence, I remember, then I said, 'You know something, Tommo? I don't reckon I could do your job.'

Tommo lifted his eyes from his glass and stared at me as though I was something uprooted from the tartan carpet.

'No,' he said. 'You couldn't. And I'll tell you why you couldn't. Because death's a part of life, and you've got no respect for either.'

Then he put down his glass and turned to the door. The window was open, there was a breeze from the sea. Above the roar of the bar noise I could hear his feet clattering down the concrete steps as he ran.

The Grateful Dead

First thing I remember knowing was not some lonesome whistle blowing or a young 'un's dream of growing up to ride. First thing I remember knowing was that my father liked my mother a lot but my mother didn't like my father. Hardly at all, not even at Christmas.

'Not another stupid vase,' she muttered, poking a stiff finger at a large vase-shaped parcel wrapped in red and green paper with reindeer.

I put my hand on her knee. 'This one'll be nice, Mum,' I said. 'Truly.'

'Huh,' said my mother and left the room. I stroked the parcel, put it down carefully.

'You're a lucky girl, you've got the prettiest Mum in town,' the butcher told me, the liver in his hand bleeding tears of blood onto the sawdust beneath. He slammed an inadequate piece of paper onto the scales, laid the liver to rest and peered at the reading. Both hands stroked the skirt of his striped apron, leaving tracks.

'Wouldn't mind being a number two then, Fred?' enquired

the baker, who had popped in from next door for a bit of shin on the bone.

Fred grinned at the baker and winked at me to show that the baker was a caution and I mustn't mind. I didn't. Like much in life, the baker was inexplicable.

I imagined the butcher choosing his weekend joint with care; furrowed brow, lips pursed, pork fingers clutching the edge of the chilled display cabinet as he leant over to choose from the red rounds of beef, the forequarters of lamb, the legs. How did he recognise the very best one of all? Even better, presumably, than the one he saved each week for my mother. Marbled flesh I knew about, but what were the other signs of grace?

'Are you going to be as pretty as your Mum when you grow up?' asked the man who made Christmas candles in his shed at the back of his section. I had called in for some gold ones on the way home. I laughed once more to show I knew it was a joke and didn't mind, but I was full of doubts.

My father was interested in grammar. He said I didn't have any. He sat at one end of the table and told me not to say 'got'. 'I *have* ten biscuits, not I have got ten biscuits.'

I was allowed only one biscuit but knew the fact was irrelevant.

My mother sat at the other end of the table and said nothing. Her hair was coiled around her head. There was not a hair out of place.

'Your mother never has a hair out of place,' marvelled the ladies in the town.

'I know,' I said with pride. I watched her doing it. Brushing and brushing then both hands snatching to twist slam bang and stick with pins as though she hated it.

I longed for plaits. 'Please, Mum, please.'

My mother said no. Plaits were untidy. They came undone.

I put posies of rosebuds and gypsophila on her dressing-table all summer. I was good at posies. I won a prize in the Children's Section at the Agricultural and Pastoral Show. My daisies and cornflowers with red geraniums for contrast sat in a regulation vase in the Produce Shed alongside a stiff yellow card. Highly Commended, it said.

My father played bowls. Bowls made him happy, even the thought of bowls made him smile. He forgot about 'got' on Saturdays and strode down the concrete drive in long white trousers and white shirt and white shoes with no heels because of the turf surface, his bowls in a domed case and gladness in his heart.

He met Mr Duras at the Bowling Club and brought him home. Mr Duras was hail-fellow-well-met. He said so himself, in our living-room.

'Call me D,' he said, holding out arms which I avoided.

How could I call him D? He was grown-up and unknown. And how did you spell it?

Mr Duras made jokes and my mother and father laughed as the late-afternoon sun fell through the plane trees and warmed their backs.

'Shall we have a drink?' said my father, looking at my mother to see if it was all right. My mother nodded. Not a hair moved.

Mr Duras sprang to his feet. 'Good thinking,' he cried. 'Let me help you, Douglas. Can I call you Doug? Let me help.'

'No, no,' said my father. 'You keep Ella happy.'

My father asked Mr Duras and my mother what they would like to drink and Mr Duras looked happier than ever and said, 'Brandy, thanks, Douggie. And ginger ale.'

My mother said she would have one too, why not, and I sat on the floor and coloured in the pictures in Flower Fairies of the Spring with my crayons because my mother said I could. I never went over the edge, even when doing the hard bits, like eyes. I was very careful.

Mr Duras came after Bowls and sometimes during the week. He gave my father lifts to Bowls and then had to bring him back. 'Beauty,' said Mr Duras as he slammed the door shut on my father's side and ran round to his side of the De Soto. 'Beauty.' My father called Mr Duras Mr Beauty for a joke, but my mother didn't laugh and my father stopped.

I ran up the hill to my grandfather's, an over-sized Little Red Riding Hood bearing gifts. I took bits of pudding in plastic bowls with frilled plastic hats to stop them spilling, left-over bits of casserole, slices of meat on a covered plate. All these I took in a flat basket so they wouldn't spill. If the puddings were sloshy I walked.

The smell of lysol was evident long before you saw the monkeys in their cage at the Zoological Gardens next to the men's lavatory. The monkeys took no notice of me and my basket. They were small with bright pink behinds and they curled side by side and hid their eyes behind their arms when they were not leaping about shrieking, or hunting for fleas in one another's fur with long snapping fingers.

'It'd be a million times easier if he'd live with us,' my mother told people about her father. 'All this endless ferrying of food. There's plenty of room but he won't. You know what they're like,' said my mother.

My grandfather played Harry Lauder records on his old wind-up gramophone and laughed till he cried. 'Stop y'tickling, tickle ickle ickling. Stop y'tickling, Jock,' piped

Harry Lauder, as the tears ran down my grandfather's face.

'Won't you come and live with us, Grandad?' I begged. 'Please.'

He shook his head and reached for his smelly old pipe from the ashtray with shells on it. 'Not likely,' he said. 'Not likely, sweetheart.'

I stopped on the way home to check on a small white magnolia in a park near our house. I liked the thick torn-paper petals, the furry grey of the tight buds, the heavy scent.

Mr Duras was sitting by himself on a wooden seat beside the bush.

'Hullo, D,' I said, proud of my casual use of Mr Duras's Christian name, if it was.

A bud brushed the brim of Mr Duras's hat as he jumped. 'Hullo,' he said.

'What are you doing here?'

Mr Duras coughed. 'I like these things' smell,' he said.

Perhaps I had got Mr Duras wrong. I sat down beside him. He took my hand. I removed it.

'Don't say anything about seeing me here to your Dad, will you, girlie?'

'Why not?'

'It's our little secret. You like secrets, I bet. All little girls like secrets,' said Mr Duras, jumping about on his bottom with excitement.

I hated secrets. Secrets were exclusion.

'All right.' I stood up. 'I've got to go now, Mr Duras.'

He nodded. 'Don't forget,' he called after me as I belted home with my empty basket.

Mr Duras appeared as usual on Saturday to pick up my father. We had had a scratch lunch, my mother called it. Cold meat and pickles and bread because she had been making chutney all morning and had had it up to here with food. The house sang with the scent of spices.

'Pickle factory,' snorted my mother.

She was standing halfway up a small step-ladder, stowing the full jars away when Mr Duras arrived. 'Beauty,' he said, clapping his hands as he often did when he said it. 'Beauty.'

My mother's smile, even to Mr Duras, was brief. 'And who's going to hand them up?' she said, snatching a warm shining jar of peach chutney from my father's outstretched hand.

'I will, Mum,' I cried, pink with excitement at the thought.

My mother laughed. I had been known to drop things.

My father looked miserable.

Mr Duras knew my father had a needle match at two. He had a solution. He saw it in a flash. He handed his car keys to my father. 'Take the De Soto, Douggie,' cried Mr Duras. 'I'll walk round when I've handed up this lot. Do me good, lovely day. Lovely.'

'No, no, no,' said my father. 'I'll take the Dodge, but if you could give Ella a hand with this lot, that'd be grand.' He slapped Mr Duras on the shoulder. 'Thanks, D.'

'Byebye, darling,' he said.

'Goodbye,' said my mother.

I watched my father out the window. He ran, almost skipped down the drive, the domed bag swinging in his hand. 'Bye,' he called again.

Mr Duras and my mother were silent. My mother smiled down at Mr Duras, whose hand was sliding gently down her leg.

Day Out

About three times a year my friend Ruth and I drive over the Rimutaka Hill to see our friend Lindsay, who lives in the Wairarapa. We would like to make it more often and so would Lindsay, she says, but you would be surprised to find how difficult it is to get three women organised for the same day, same time, weather permitting.

This is because we are busy. We are not proud of this fact. When people ask us how we are we do not reply, 'Busy.' Busy is not how you are. Busy is what you do with days.

Nevertheless, we are.

One of the reasons Ruth is busy is because she and Tom are good grandparents and either she is visiting grandchildren to the North, or the South, or locally, or they are coming to stay.

Ruth and Tom like this and know how lucky they are. Ruth is also an ace cook and hospitable as well. Twenty-four for Christmas dinner, you know the type. Her daughter cooked the turkey this year. But even so.

Ruth also does good by stealth and is funny with it.

When I say weather permitting, I mean it. Who would

302

want to drive over that hill in a gale? I don't enjoy it in fair weather with a following wind, but Ruth likes driving, which is lucky for me. I'm not bad at the wheel, I have never had an accident but don't quote me. It's just that either you're keen or you're not. I've never been a bags-I-drive kind of girl. Or indeed bags-I-anything much.

Our friend Lindsay is also a busy woman. She cooks and sews and reaps and hoes and her husband, John, is not getting any younger. Lindsay also has grandchildren; older, busier, coming and going they frequent her days. Her daughters are busy too. Astonishingly busy. Lindsay doesn't know how they do it, and nor do I. Most people in the Wairarapa are busy. There is not much ambling or rambling: except, of course, on the Wine Trail.

Ruth tucks two or three cushions underneath her so she can see over the wheel, and we're away. We cruise along beside the Hutt River. We note the debris from the last flood, the broken branches, the silt piled against the willow trunks. Goodness, we say. We talk all through Upper Hutt, which, as always, goes on for longer than you expect. We sail over the first group of small hills which are a preliminary hurdle before the five-bar of the Rimutaka itself.

I realise I am exaggerating. There's nothing wrong with the Rimutaka Hill and it's better than it was. I know a young woman who drives a twenty-six-wheel articulated truck over it twice a day and loves every minute. During the First World War when the men had finished their training in Featherston they marched, in full kit, up and over the Rimutakas to Wellington.

Nevertheless, I still don't like it. It is covered in bush and scrub. 'Its cliffs are sombre and its defiles mysterious,' but the road is too near to both.

Ruth is unperturbed. Before long we are up and over, have passed through Featherston which is the Gateway to the Wairarapa and are creaming down the straights towards Masterton. The power lines are singing along beside us and we are still talking.

To our left lie the mountains, but Ruth can only glance.

Shadowed with clouds and wreathed in mist, their leviathan shapes of blue, grey and purple roll on forever. They are mysterious and unknown, and likely to remain so.

We agree with the psalmist who wrote, 'I will lift up mine eyes unto the hills, from whence cometh my help.' We nod our heads in unison. However, we are not convinced that our help cometh from the Lord, let alone that He made Heaven and Earth.

Ruth adjusts one of her cushions with a quick heave and says that if the help which cometh from the hills doesn't come from the Lord, where does it come from? That we can't have it both ways.

I say that's not the point. We can get a sense of numinous awe from the sublime wonders of Nature without . . .

'What's numinous?'

'Spiritual, awe-inspiring.'

'Like God.'

'Well, a local deity, perhaps. Small g.'

'Like the Maoris?'

'No, but . . .' I see the sign in the nick of time. 'Mushrooms!' I shout, and we turn onto the side road and head for the farm.

'How do you feel,' I say later when we get back to Ruth's car with our five-dollar trays of mushrooms and what good value, 'how do you feel about us lending fifty-seven million

dollars to help bail out the financially embattled South
Korean Government?'

Ruth resettles a large, fresh, pink-gilled mushroom.
Mushrooms are fragile and she does not want any to spill
or spoil before we get home. She gives a smaller darker one
a reassuring pat before getting back into the driver's seat.
She snaps her safety belt, plumps her cushions. 'I can see
why it makes sense,' she says. '"Major New Zealand trading
partner, fifth largest market, vested interest in its recovery."
All that. But . . .'

'The Minister of Finance says that the chances of getting
the loan back are "very high".'

'"Very high",' says Ruth, 'is not high enough.'

We are silent as we drive through Carterton, which
goes on longer than the previous village, Greytown. One
is considered more desirable than the other but I can never
remember which.

'The Accident and Emergency Department,' says Ruth
suddenly, 'is so run down there are holes in the linoleum.'

'I know.'

'However, my main problem at the moment,' she says
after a pause, 'is my funeral.'

I give her profile one startled glance, then calm down.
Ruth, her eyes focused on the road ahead, is not thinking
about the immediate future. Ruth is onto abstracts, the
practicalities of these abstracts are giving her concern.

'In what way?'

'You *know*,' Ruth says you *know* quite often, and pokes
you for emphasis, though not at the moment. 'Being Jewish,
going to an Anglican boarding school, marrying a Welshman.
I feel I've lost my *roots*.'

I take a quick peek over my shoulder to check the

mushrooms. 'What's that got to do with your funeral?'

'Everything,' says Ruth. 'Who's going to *do* it?'

'You don't have to have anyone now. Not a professional. You can get a co-ordinator. A sort of MC.'

'Who?' says Ruth, staring sourly at the straight black asphalt unrolling before her and not another soul in sight.

'Anyone. A family friend. Marriage celebrant. Some vicars don't mind no God now.'

'But which *sort* of vicar.'

'What about a rabbi?'

Her glance withers. 'I don't belong to the Jewish faith. I never have. How can I start at this stage?'

'You could read it up.'

'*Read it up.*'

I know what she means. I had a T-shirt once. *So many books, so little time.*

'And anyway,' she says. 'I don't know that I want to.'

'Then why fuss?'

Ruth sighs. 'There're some peppermints,' she says, 'in the glove box.'

They are large peppermints, dusted with soft sugar; good of their kind, but cumbersome.

We take one each, suck in silence. 'It's because,' she says eventually, 'I'm scared of death,'

'I can't see for the life of me how the sort of funeral you have is going to help that,' I say. 'You're putting the cart before the horse.'

'Well, they'll have to do something,' she says. 'Won't they?'

'Yes, but why should it worry *you*? You'll be the last person on earth to be taking an interest.'

'It's all very well for you,' says Ruth.

This is true. As with everything, death only matters if you care. I am rather a chucklehead in this regard, but again, don't quote me. I try harder.

'How about the Salvation Army?' I say. 'You've always been a great supporter.'

'You can't just bail up a uniformed officer and ask him or her to take over your funeral. You're no *help*.'

'Well, then, try your local talent. The clergy.'

'I don't even know who they are.'

'Then find out. Patti, you know Patti?'

'Yes, indeed.'

'She tracked one down. Nice man. Quite young. She asked him round for a cup of tea, explained her position frankly and asked him if he would be prepared to take her funeral service at a later date. He said certainly, that was his job, or one of them, and that it would be a pleasure, or words to that effect. They had quite a merry time, Patti said, working things out, choosing this and that, getting the whole thing teed up and a rough draft down on paper, and then he had a sherry and a few nuts and departed. Patti was delighted, so pleased to have the whole thing organised. It had been hanging over her, she said.'

Ruth laughs and laughs. 'You have to hand it to Patti.'

'Yes. Except the poor man dropped dead next week.'

'How *terrible*. What?'

'Coronary.'

'So then what?'

'I'm not sure. I think Patti sort of lost heart.'

'Tt,' says Ruth. 'What a dreadful story.'

'Yes.' We are silent for a moment or two.

'I don't like those ones, do you,' I say, 'when the

congregation are invited to come up and share their own memories of dear old Ralph?'

'Not much. Not when they talk to the box.'

'You can see why, though. It's all a matter of personal preference.'

'Yes,' says Ruth bleakly.

I have been tactless. 'You'll be all right,' I say quickly. 'Why don't you have one of those no-God ones and a family friend co-ordinating and a few people asked to speak. And beautiful music. You're musical. Some of those ones are lovely. You could decide the music now. That'd be something done.'

'So could you.'

'No. The *Cow Cow Boogie* wouldn't get me anywhere.' I think about it for a while then perk up. 'There's the hymns though. And those wonderful old prayers, psalms, the old words. Glorious. Restore your faith in anything. You can't beat them, really. I've been to some inspirational funerals with God and hymns and the old words.'

Ruth turns into Lindsay's carport and switches off the ignition.

'But *which* God?' she snaps.

Lindsay comes to greet us. She is pleased to see us and vice versa. She declines mushrooms. No, no. She can get them anytime. She stands beside Ruth and tells me she is half an inch taller than her, though this is a moot point.

If you boiled the three of us down you would get three average-sized women happy to be together again.

'What've you been talking about?' says Lindsay as we walk into her house which is filled with light and warmth and welcome.

'We've been working,' I say, 'on our funerals.'

'Oh good,' says Lindsay. 'Where've you got to? Which sort? Let's have a glass of wine.'

Ruth shakes her head. 'Not for me, thank you,' she says sadly. 'I'm driving.'

The Peacocks

It's the peacocks, you see. I think about them all the time, she said. I can't stop. Even when I'm talking they're there. In my head, if you see what I mean.

Dr Mayer put down his ballpoint pen in silence, then picked it up again before lifting his eyes to meet those of Miss Dallas.

He was too late. Hers were now fixed on his suede shoes, innocuous and comfortable beneath the desk. She sat crouched on the edge of her chair staring at them, her thin fingers laced together.

Dr Mayer shifted his feet slightly.

'Peacocks,' he said, reaching for his ballpoint to fill in the 'o' of the word 'Choice' imprinted on his blotter. *Lactine, the Drug of Choice for the Something Something.* She couldn't read it upside down.

'Tell me about them,' he said.

So she told him. How she couldn't stop thinking about them. How even if she was laughing and talking with the other girls in the cafeteria they were there, inside her head.

How she could see them, pecking and strutting with their tails up, or moulting or ruffling their feathers.

Or flying up to roost in the macrocarpas, their blotched tails hanging. At first when she'd started thinking about them it hadn't worried her. Why not? There were worse things to think about. But then . . . Well, it never stopped. They were there always, inside her head, like she said. Sometimes she woke up at night and click they were there. Instantly. How could that happen? Click. Like that. Before she even knew she was awake. And she hated the way she couldn't think about anything else because of the peacocks.

She used to love this time of the year. She walked to work each morning, and she used to look down on the sycamore buds in the gardens below the footpath. Bright red, lying beside the green. Tight. And the Virginia creeper. Had Dr Mayer ever noticed how the leaves opened like tiny rust-coloured fans? He shook his head. He hadn't. No.

But all that wasn't any use now. The peacocks mucked everything up. You couldn't really enjoy anything if you were thinking about them, if they were there in your head all the time. There was no point in going to a film or anything. You couldn't forget yourself, just relax and enjoy laughing, or crying if it was sad, or being scared even. You'd just be paying money to sit there thinking about the peacocks till you could scream.

Dr Mayer redistributed his weight on the chair and leant forward.

'Can you do your work?' he asked. 'Or do the peacocks . . . ?'

No, she could do her work. You had to concentrate. She was on B Bench now, in the Bacteriology Lab at the Hospital.

311

It was a good job and she liked it, though she couldn't stand Janice who was in charge. She picked on her, but then she picked on all the juniors, expecting them to know everything. 'It's just,' she said. 'It's just the peacocks, see.'

The other funny thing was that her writing had packed up. She used to have lovely writing. Clear and easy to read, and it looked good too. The other girls always used to get her to write the farewell cards and things. Now it had gone all funny. Tiny and scribbly. All over the place. Could it be the peacocks? How could the peacocks mess up her writing?

She stared at him, her eyes dark pools, her hair the black of a burnished shoe. One hand moved to her lips as though to make sure they were still there.

Dr Mayer shifted miserably from one buttock to the other and breathed out. Christ Almighty. He leant back in his chair and told her that this was quite a common condition. It was called rumination. Lots of people had things they couldn't stop thinking about. Not necessarily peacocks, but other things. Some people washed their hands all the time; they were obsessed with cleanliness; some people became anxious if their routine was upset. They felt threatened. Some people . . .

Her fingers moved. Hers was peacocks. He nodded. Yes, he knew hers was peacocks and he would give her a note of referral to a very able colleague of his, a psychiatrist called Dr Howarth, who was an expert in this field.

He was quite sure Dr Howarth would be able to help her. He had no doubt at all.

She stood up. At the door she turned.

'It's just the peacocks, isn't it?'

Her eyes moved again to his shoes. She'd feel silly going to a shrink. As though she was some sort of nutter. It was just the peacocks.

He found himself on his feet, beyond the safety of his desk. He wanted to take the skinny child in his arms, to make it all better, to keep her warm. To stop her shoulderblades sticking out in that obtrusive way.

He opened the door, smiling.

'Just ring Dr Howarth's nurse for an appointment, Miss Dallas. As soon as you can.'

'Yes.'

The rain had stopped and the sun was hot, causing the puddles to steam. She looked at a small one by her right foot. Soon it would have dried out. All that remained merely a slight depression in the asphalt, a puddle waiting for existence next time it rained. Lots of things were like that. Seeds, for example. She remembered silly little experiments in the third form with seeds on blotting paper. Just water, warmth, absence of light and the seeds got on with it. That was all they needed to start.

She had almost reached the bus stop. A few yards from its shelter she stopped abruptly.

The peacocks had gone.

Her teeth closed over her lower lip then moved to release a slow smile. The bus arrived and, holding her smile carefully as a shared secret, she climbed sedately on board, bought her ticket and sat down in the front scat.

She stared at the passing scene. She wanted to clutch the arm of the sour-smelling man who had dumped himself beside her, to show him the wonders of a world without peacocks. To tell him to look, look over there. Watch how that man in the woolly hat rides his bicycle, his knees high like a circus clown, his hat the colour of a clown's nose.

How good that is. Or see how the plump knees of that woman jogging blush with shame at their exposure. What courage though, to jog, if your knees looked like that. But then that was probably why she did jog. So that they wouldn't. Or have you noticed, you smelly man, how toddlers in plastic-sided pushchairs look as though they're in mobile oxygen tents pushed by unconcerned parents?

Her sigh of pleasure was as deep as the burp of a replete baby.

When they weren't there in her head, like now, she felt as though she could almost split with joy. Perhaps even be strong enough to touch the peacocks for a second with her mind, then flick away like a tongue from a sore tooth, or one of those roughcast tubeworms in childhood rock pools unfolding its chimney-black lashes slowly when the danger was past. So strong, so calm she felt, that she began remembering the peacocks as though she were someone else idly thinking about them. Their owners, for instance.

Their name was Dyson, Nancy and Merv Dyson, and they ran the country store near her grandparents' dairy farm. The dirty Dysons, her grandfather called them. The place was a shambles. He said someone ought to put the District Council onto them. Her grandmother said she'd rather have a store which was dirty but open, than clean but closed.

The peacocks were a problem, though. You had to watch where you put your feet. They roamed wild on the baked earth where the trucks and cars parked beside the single petrol pump. Sometimes they appeared inside the store. If someone left the door open they would slip in, stepping delicately down the aisles with lifted heads and quick nervous pecks before being chased out. Disgusting really, Gran could see that.

There were three peacocks and one peahen. Periodically, in the breeding season, the peacocks shook themselves, rattled their back feathers, then, whirring their tails into a fan, trod the stately movements of display on scaly legs. Completely ignored by the indifferent hen, they circled. You learnt not to run around the front. It was better to wait until the peacock had turned slowly around and you could sink into the iridescent shimmer of blue-green light. Feasting the eyes, Gran called it.

She thought of the shimmering colours, clung to the memory when she heard, hiding behind the sofa, that her mother had killed herself. Whenever Dad said he was coming to see her and then didn't, she thought of them.

So it was a shock, well, more than that if you were honest, when she came home from Girls High for a long weekend and the peacocks were shut up in the dank stinking shed behind the store where Merv killed the odd ewe.

She remembered begging. 'Merv, you can't keep them there! They can't fly, they can't roost . . . anything. They won't put their tails up, Merv.'

'It's that or the chop,' Merv had said. 'I've got enough on my plate, Denise. Looking after Nance. She's never been the same since that last operation. And there's the shop. What's a man to do? I haven't the time to be hosing down peacock crap all day long, and who else is going to?'

The bus stopped at the Hospital. She climbed out and drifted up the steps, then made her way along the shiny corridors awash with people, some striding along, some, like the porters with trolleys, navigating with difficulty.

At the Lab she changed into her uniform and adjusted

her name-tag. Denise Dallas, it had said, but she had put some sticking plaster over Dallas. All the girls did that. Some of the young doctors did too. She'd seen one the other day saying Bronwyn. It was more friendly and no one could call you Miss Dallas, which she hated.

Her dazed smile widened as she reached B Bench. Janice couldn't snarl at her for being late. Not when it was the doctor. You were allowed time off for the doctor, and she'd told her yesterday, anyhow. So she ignored the look, and took over the staining of the slides from Claire, stood watching the swirling rhythms as the decolouriser swept across the gentian violet. She was good at stains. You just had to concentrate. It was basic, really. You'd never get anywhere if your slides weren't stained right.

The bunsen burner hissed as the organised progression through B Bench's morning work continued. She loved it, always had, right from the start. Identifying the cultures from the plate, picking them off, staining to check and double-check the organisms visible on the slide beneath the microscope. Every step required meticulous care. All was observation, order, routine. There was always an answer. Even if Janice didn't know, the books would. Or if Janice was really stuck, she could take it to Dr Blackmore. Someone would know.

There was a large pile of bright red blood agar plates waiting to be looked at. They'd be flat out to finish by lunchtime.

She gazed at the bunsen burner. Three parts it had, or was it four? You had to watch it, though. Several of the girls had singed their hair, and Claire her eyebrows once. You had to be careful.

She rinsed the slides with water, then lifted them onto the blotting paper with care. At the final blotting her expression changed. Her head jerked backwards.

Nothing else changed on B Bench. Janice remained crouched over the microscope and the other girls worked steadily as the quiet flame flickered. But now she was staring straight ahead, her eyes wide with fright. Her hands flicked to her head as though her hair was on fire, or she was listening. Her right arm shot out and swept the pile of untouched blood plates onto the floor. The tops fell off the plates; the exposed cultures lay gleaming. The other girls leapt to their feet. A high stool fell to the floor as she clutched Janice, her rigid fingers denting the smooth arm.

'They're screaming,' she gasped at the gaping moon face. 'Tell him they're screaming! In my head. They're screaming.'

Glorious Things

Autumn. No doubt about it. Dew on the grass, nip in the air. Pale sun.

Clive Harper sniffed the sparkling air. He liked autumn. It had a certainty about it which pleased him. You knew what would happen next. The stroll down the concrete path to the letterbox, the knowledge that the milk would be in the billy, the paper alongside, all pleased him.

The milkman was reliable. Very. And the paper boy.

Clutching his goods in one hand, Clive turned to a dazzle of reflected light. A burnished brass garden tap flashed back at him from the hydrangea bed. Why the hell did she polish that? He was used to things gleaming inside the house, to wood and linoleum shined to mirror surfaces. Now his mother's obsession with buffing up seemed to have moved outdoors. He glared at the thing; banged the paper against his thigh with quick irritated whacks. She would have had to force her overalled bust (*Fadeless florals, 4s.11d. Variety bewildering*) through waves of mop-headed blooms to reach the thing, apply polish and then, grunting with effort, remove the stuff and back out. There was no room to turn. If she believed in an all-seeing God he could understand it. (*I shine for Thee.*) But she didn't, not a word of it, though she loved the hymns.

'*For all the saints,*' she'd bellowed in her cracked contralto that morning after dumping his Cremoata in front of him, '*who from their labours rest.* You can just see them, can't you! Lined up in rows. Serried, that's what they call them, serried rows.'

Her tongue flicked her upper lip, her hands crashed down on the yellow-toothed old Bently and she was off again — singing her heart out, giving it wings while Clive went for the paper.

'Hand us the ads, boy,' she called, heaving herself up from the Bently. '*Avoid shoe shame. Use Nugget.* What do they think we are! And look at this one. *The acid in your stomach would burn a hole in the carpet.* There's even a picture. See the wee hole?' She sucked her teeth with delight at the find.

He could never work her out. Never reconcile her passion for making anything shine that could shine, for hunting dirt like a beagle on scent, for rubbing things and scrubbing things, with her total lack of concern for what anyone else in the world thought or did or said. She had no hesitancy, no apprehension. Mothers were meant to work you out, to understand you, but she'd never bothered to do that. He existed, he was there; a man going on thirty-three with slicked-back hair and crooked teeth, a two-pack-a-day man who didn't say much. What was there to say? He'd given up begging for reassurance long ago.

'Do I look all right, Mum?' he said, his hands sweating with fright before the Sixth Form Social.

His mother flapped her arm in dismissal. 'Of course you look all right. Off you go. And leave the billy in the letterbox.'

Clive had begun training as a motor mechanic when he left school, under the personal supervision of Jas Henry (*Moderate charges, Carlyle St Petrol Station*). He gave it up when he developed sore knees from kneeling on the concrete all day. He had been lucky to find a job in the china department of the Farmers' Co-Op.

His mother had been unimpressed by the change. 'You could have got a cushion,' she said, peering vaguely around the dining-room. A heavy oak sideboard supported a blue-and-white biscuit barrel, an equally empty fruit bowl and a pair of electroplated candlesticks from which the silver had long since been polished. Framed in gilt, Napoleon on horseback reared above. Clive had been disappointed to discover others had it too. He thought his hero was his alone.

A red plush cloth edged with bobbles covered the table; yellow camels trekked across red velvet cushions brought home from Cairo years ago by Clive's father, a gaunt wreck of a man who lay about for ten years after Gallipoli and then died. 'The Harpers are like the potato family,' said his widow. 'The best of them are under the ground.'

Nothing in the house was ever altered or discarded. Even the well-wiped aspidistra in its brass pot had belonged to his grandmother. His mother didn't care what anything looked like as long as she could clean it.

There was a lot of reading in the *Clarion*. Even the headlines took him quite a time. *Hitler at War with Pope*. The Pope kept the names of persecuted Catholic youths in a White Book in the Vatican and had remonstrated with the Führer.

Where is Jardine? The question was intriguing India. Was the MCC Captain still tiger-shooting? Ten days ago he had shot an old tiger in the Mysore district, told a relative he was after a better specimen, and disappeared into the jungle.

There was a photograph, but not of Jardine. A local landowner had recently shot his second bull moose in Dusky Sound.

Clive turned the page. His hands tightened. Mary Boyle was advertising. *Miss Boyle. Dressmaker, Costumier, specialising in matrons and outsizes, hem-stitching 4d. Upstairs, Farmers' Bldgs.* There had been no money left, everyone knew that, after her father had drunk himself into the grave. Sometimes Mary had come to help him home from the Criterion at six o'clock. Jenson, the bull-necked proprietor, would telephone her. 'Sorry, Miss.' Clive had seen her a couple of times from the window. She stood calmly by the door, seemingly unconcerned by the uproar within, her face blank as she waited to prop her father on her girl's bike with its skirt-shield, and wheel him home. Clive had hidden behind his paper. He could have helped her. He should have helped her. He'd known her since primary school, since she was tiny. She was still a slip of a girl, five feet at the most, and here she was specialising in Matrons and Outsizes. More money perhaps. Clive reached for his smokes.

'Tennis on Sunday?' called Dr York, from across the hedge. Clive liked his neighbour. Dr York was an amiable man. He was large and cheerful and specialised in obstetrics. He had brought Clive into the world at Sister Fahey's Nursing Home. His mother had given him details: the gas heater hissing, the nightie and booties laid out warming.

'The usual four?' continued Dr York.

'I wondered . . .' said Clive.

'Yes?' Was the poor man blushing?

'I wondered if I could ask one or two ladies, say.'

'Ladies?' Dr York snapped an escallonia twig between his thumb and forefinger and gazed at its small red flowers.

'We, well, that is, you, could ask the White girls and Mary Boyle.'

Forceps delivery, thought Dr York automatically. The baby's head had been a real mess at the time.

'Arthur Boyle's daughter?' he said. Comment on Arthur Boyle, even in the deceased state, was not easy.

Clive nodded. 'I believe,' he said, the tide of red still surging up his neck, 'that she plays a very good game. In fact, I know she does. She was runner-up in the mixed doubles at Tikokino.'

'Ah.' Dr York squeezed a leaf, sniffed the aromatic sharpness on his fingers. 'You'll have to ask her,' he said. 'Them.'

Clive's adam's apple rose and fell. 'Yes,' he said. 'Yes. I will.'

Mrs York watched from her kitchen window as Clive adjusted his bike clips at the gate. 'Poor Clive,' she said. 'There's always been something, I don't know . . . something sort of, you know, squiffy about him.'

'Clive's all right,' said her husband, wishing they could have hot milk with their breakfast coffee like he'd had at the base hospital in France. Mrs York said it wasn't worth the effort. It boiled over in a flash and she had better things to do.

'You think everyone's all right.'

Dr York unfolded the paper. 'He's a little . . .' Dr York

waved a large hand. He didn't know what he meant himself. Shy, perhaps? More than that.

'He's all right,' he said again and changed the subject. *Renew that graceful figure, he read aloud. Naturettes, the non-fasting, non-exercising and safe way to reduce superfluous flesh will make today's form-fitting frocks a realisation for you. Naturettes dissolve the flesh and improve health. 17 days' treatment 7/6. Money-back guarantee.* Dr York snorted. 'Now that's something I do know what I think about.'

'I'm thinking of asking Mary Boyle to play tennis on Sunday,' Clive said, putting out a hand to the upturned cup which was skidding around on soap bubbles. 'And the White girls.'

'You've taken my leaner.'

Clive replaced the cup. 'Sorry.'

Mrs Harper leant a saucer on it. It fell off and lay flat, bubbles frothing around its rim. She stared at it. 'See that? That's the sort of thing that makes me not believe in God. What's the point in that happening? If there's a God, there's meant to be a reason for everything, isn't there?' She glared at Clive above her steamed-up glasses. 'Hairs on the head numbered, things of that nature?'

'Not for physics and stuff. Not for surface tension.' Clive knew he was on shaky ground. He'd never done physics or surface tension. He just wanted to shut her up.

'Surface tension,' she murmured. 'Is that right? Surface tension. I'll remember that.'

'On Sunday,' said Clive, 'I'm going to ask Mary Boyle and the White girls. For tennis at Dr York's.'

Mrs Harper flipped the end of her nose with her newly dried hand. 'Why?'

It was always the same. Always. He heard his voice. 'I thought it would be, you know . . . Nice.'

'You'd better put citric acid on the order then,' she said. 'There's no lemon drink.'

Clive left the order at the grocery section of the Farmers' Co-Op next morning. The wide wooden counter stretched the width of the shop. Behind it, white-aproned assistants were ranked in strict hierarchical order. Ken Bates, the manager, was on the left; the most junior lad far away in the shadows beside the storeroom on the right. Ken was one of Dr York's regular tennis four and had put in a word for Clive at the china department. A fine player and good at his job, he was considered to be on his way up. He was pleasant and efficient as he sliced and weighed and wrapped with speed. And popular. A bright-eyed, recently married charmer. The local farmers' wives, perched on long-legged chairs across the counter, were flattered by his attentions, his cheery grin. 'Basics first, shall we, Mrs C? Flour? How're you going on flour? Butter? Why not? Make it five, shall we? Six? Right, you're the doctor.' He slapped a hand against the dark hide of the rolled loin in the slicer beside him. 'And bacon? Lovely piece, this one. Lovely.'

The china department was less fun. Clive spent a lot of time dusting crystal bowls, Dresden ballerinas standing on one toe and mugs with rabbits selling parsnip wine. He didn't see how he could ever get on in china. Miss Kirten, the supervisor, was lean and tough and obviously would live for ever. It worried him.

He jumped slightly as a customer shoved a cut-glass decanter under his nose. 'Sorry, Mrs Stevenson. Oh yes, certainly. For the Crayford wedding, was it? Yes, of course.

I'll wrap it straight away.' Clive took a deep breath. 'If you were going up to the tearooms, I could bring it up. Save you waiting and that.'

Mrs Stevenson looked at him, trying to put her finger on it. Straight-backed, a polite young man, but . . . A light flicked inside her grey head. She almost told him. Young man, you are too aware of yourself. Real men, she could have told him, don't notice themselves. 'No, thank you,' she said, tugging on a glove. 'I'll wait.'

'Right you are, then.' He had hoped to slip upstairs with the thing and knock on Mary Boyle's door on the way down. He couldn't ring from work and the telephone was beside the piano at home. Last night Mrs Harper had got stuck for hours on 'Glorious Things of Thee Are Spoken'.

'That's it then, Clive,' said Miss Kirten at five-forty. 'See you tomorrow.'

He grabbed his bike clips from the hook beside the till, ducked out the back way through hardware, dodged the buyer with a neat sidestep and ran up the steep stairs to the offices above. The pseudo-marble clattered beneath his toe plates. His hand flicked the Greek key pattern of the dado. The Farmers' Co-op had been built to last.

He stood panting outside the door. It was unmarked except for a small card, 'Mary Boyle, Seamstress'. She probably couldn't afford a gold-lettered job. Clive knocked. There was a pause. He knocked again. Mary appeared, her dark hair held back by a velvet band, her small face startled. 'What is it, Clive?'

'Can you play tennis at Dr York's on Sunday?'

'What?'

'Would you like to?'

She shut the door and stood beside him in the corridor,

her face smiling. She had something exciting to tell him. 'I've got Mrs Earnshaw in there,' she whispered, jerking her head towards the door.

'Oh,' said Clive. He knew Mrs Earnshaw by sight. She often sat overflowing the chair opposite Ken Bates. Mr Earnshaw's acres were broad. He was a racing man and his brood mares were renowned.

'So I'll have to go.' Her brown eyes were sparkling. For him? For her client? 'Fifteen minutes?' she said. 'Downstairs?'

'OK.'

Clive waited outside the office exit. He sat slouched over the handlebars, one foot on the pavement, the other in the gutter. A man waiting for his girl after work. His girlfriend.

Mary came running down the stairs. 'Fancy me having Mrs *Eam*shaw! She's ordered a wool georgette for spring. From *me*.' Her feet skipped on the dusty pavement, triumphant as a child after her first high dive.

Clive beamed at her. 'Good on you.'

'You know what?'

He shook his head.

Her eyes were snapping, sparking with her secret. The impact of the tennis invitation, if it had ever existed, had disappeared. Her voice dropped as she glanced over her shoulder, checking for eavesdroppers.

'She says if the wool georgette's any good she'll tell all her friends. Mrs *Earnshaw*.'

'It will be,' he said.

She frowned slightly. 'Don't tell anyone.'

He shook his head again.

She snatched off her hair ribbon to retie it. The Farmers' corner caught every breath of wind. Dark hair blew across her face. She tugged it back with both hands. 'Don't,' said Clive. 'Leave it!'

She glanced at him, shy once more. 'What time on Sunday?'

'Two o'clock.'

'OK then. Thanks. I'd like to.' She turned to go.

'Have you got your bike?' asked Clive.

'Of course.'

'I could wait. Ride home with you.'

'But I'm way up Pakowhai Road.'

'I know.'

'Oh. Oh,' she said again. 'All right.'

They said little on the way home, the wind in their teeth, her hair all over the place. Clive could feel his heart, knew where the thump was located.

He clutched the sagging gatepost of the old villa where she lived alone. 'See you on Sunday, then.'

'Yes.'

He lifted one hand. 'See you.'

'Glorious things of *thee* are spoken, *Zion*, city of our God,' he yelled to the tossing wind on his way home. The words flew upwards, disappeared beyond the line of poplars.

Mrs Harper dumped a large yellow jug on a rickety table beneath the phoenix palms next door and departed.

Mrs York, after vague welcoming gestures towards Mary and Babs and Muriel White, had also disappeared. She had views about silly old buffers bounding about with bare knees.

'Ken's not bald. Or Clive,' muttered her husband.

'Clive might as well be.'

*

327

Tim Bartlett, the chemist, and Ken Bates were happy to be invited to play at Dr York's. The court had a good surface and Clive did all the work, mowing and rolling and trundling along behind the little white marking cart.

But there was no hostess, no other woman to sit with the spare girl during mixed doubles. No one to ease the strain for Babs and Muriel and the specialist in outsizes when the men's four bounded about within cooee of apoplexy, the sweat running below the white flannel bands around their scarlet foreheads.

The tennis was good. Inspired even, in patches. Babs and Muriel were not bad at all and Mary's classic style was pretty to watch. She wore a white pleated skirt, her ankle socks were white, her knees pink. Her fuji silk blouse came out from her skirt as she flung the ball a yard above her head and slammed the racquet down at the right moment. Her forehand was deep and true, her backhand not so good. Clive watched, absorbed by her every move. She became pinker and pinker, happier and happier, dancing around beside the White girls, who were good sports and known to be so.

'Tea,' called Mrs York. It was served in the dining-room and was always the same. Sandwiches which leaked tomato or cucumber and Mother's cut-and-come-again sultana cake.

The players were happy, relaxed, reached for more cake and thanked Mrs York's departing back. Clive looked at them all fondly. I, he thought, am entertaining. I am entertaining girls. He straightened his shoulders, reached for Mary's hand beneath the table cover. She edged away. Ken Bates smiled down at her. 'About your backhand, Mary,' he said.

'I know,' she murmured, gazing up at him in sorrow, 'it's terrible.'

'I could fix it in half an hour.'

'*Could* you?'

Mary wouldn't stay after tea. 'I've got to do Mrs Earnshaw's buttonholes,' she told Dr York, her eyes troubled. 'Bound buttonholes. She insists on them, even for little wee fiddly . . .' She shook her head. 'And it frays too, wool georgette.'

Clive said nothing. He could think of no word of comfort.

He wheeled her bike to the gate. 'Well,' he said.

She put out her hand. 'Thank you. I know it was you, really.'

The small hand lay in his. The formal gesture dismayed him. They'd got further than that. Hadn't they?

Husband and Wife's Handbook by *Dr Hector Cole*, he read. *A concise treatise on a subject of vital importance to married persons and those intending to marry, together with our book on Appliances Free.*

His mother toiled in from the kitchen, bearing sliced tongue.

Clive sat very still, the newspaper hiding his crotch, his face tense. 'In a minute,' he said.

'Now!' His mother waved her free arm. 'There's flies.'

Oh, God. 'In a *minute*, I said.'

Her face was the same pink-purple as the tongue.

'What's up?'

'Nothing! Nothing.'

She put the plate on the table and slid into her chair, both hands flat on the table for support. 'Well, then,' she said, the serving fork poised. 'There's cake for afters.'

*

Roland Young, as advertised, was without peer in *Blind Adventure* at the Cosy. Clive and Mary sat in the warm fug with fingers entwined. They were together, at the flicks on Saturday night, eating Jaffas and smiling at each other occasionally in the dark. Mary jumped slightly, then moved Clive's hand from her thigh, her eyes straight ahead on Roland Young in his unusual role of cat-burglar. The rejected hand lay in his lap, extra and unneeded as a spare limb.

'Next Saturday,' she said as they rode home against the head wind, 'it's *His Grace Gives Notice*. I'd like to see that.' He could see the gleam of her teeth beneath a street light. 'It's all about a duke pretending to be a footman.' She paused. 'And it's the Show soon.'

So it was all right then. She was happy to go out with him, to progress from biking home, to Saturday flicks, to going to the Annual Show together. 'Will you marry me?' he gasped.

She stopped pedalling. 'What?'

He braked in the middle of the road. 'Marry me.'

She stopped, adjusted her headlamp. 'Come in when we get home.'

'The thing is, Clive,' she said, handing him milky tea in an octagonal green cup. 'The thing is . . .' He felt cold; there didn't seem to be a heater. Bare scrim hung on the walls in patches where the wallpaper had peeled off. He lit a cigarette. No ashtray either.

Mary sat on a large cushion at his feet, her back to the empty grate. She leant forward, trying to explain, to make him see. To understand without pain. 'You're different,' she said.

Despair, familiar-since-childhood misery, clenched his gut. 'How?'

Her hair was loose around her shoulders, her eyes wide, begging him not to mind. 'It's not that I don't like you.' She paused, licked her lips. 'It's all right, going out and that. The Show even. But . . .'

He ground his cigarette out on the saucer. 'I'm not a pansy, if that's what you mean.'

She blushed scarlet. 'Oh, no. No! I didn't mean . . .'

'Or a mother's boy. You needn't think that. If you want to know . . . I hate her.' He paused panting. 'Hate her,' he gasped.

'Don't,' she whispered.

He wiped one sweating hand beneath an orange sateen cushion on the ancient sofa. She was so little, so gallant, with her no-hoper father and her Mrs Earnshaws and their bloody wool georgettes. 'I'll look after you,' said Clive.

'I've looked after myself since Mum died when I was ten.'

He leant back, reaching in the pocket of his grey flannels for his smokes. 'You'll have to marry someone,' he said.

Her head lifted. 'Why?'

'Well, because,' He was begging now, his hands clenched. 'So why not me?'

'No,' said Mary. 'I'm sorry, but no, no.'

'I'll wait.'

'No!'

She refused to see him, to answer the telephone. She ran for cover when he appeared.

He begged her, beseeched, mowed her lawns, bought her presents she tried to return; a pink quilted nightdress case with 'Nightie' stitched in blue; things for her glory box which made her weep; an organdie throwover, embroidered

331

hankies, a golden toilet mirror and a salt and pepper set of red-nosed gnomes.

He hung around, persisted, would not go away. How could he possibly go away?

Ken Bates appeared at the china counter. He picked up a jam jar with a china strawberry on the lid, put it down again. 'Where's Miss Kirten?'

'Lunch.'

'I want a word with you, Clive. I'll make it quick. If you don't stop hanging around Mary Boyle I'll knock your block off.' His voice dropped. 'No flannel, I mean it. And it's a criminal offence. I'll put the cops on to you. Get it?'

Clive's hands clutched the counter. 'Offence?' he gasped.

'Like I said. Harassment.'

'But I love her.'

Ken Bates smiled his wide smile. His eyes crinkled. 'You, Clivey?' He shook his head sadly. 'What would Mum say?'

Clive snatched the jam jar, flung it at the tanned laughing face. It crashed to pieces, blood spurted, the strawberry rolled across the counter. 'Get out,' he screamed. 'Get out, y'sod!'

Mr Ken Bates, the popular manager of the grocery department at the Farmers' Co-op, has been selected for higher management training at Head Office, Wellington. Mr Bates and his family will leave the district next week.

'We'll be sad to leave our good friends here,' laughed Mr Bates, 'but promotion's promotion.'

*

She stood beside him at the bike racks.

'Hullo, Clive,' she said.

He swung around in astonishment, the chain of his padlock clanging. 'Mary?' She looked terrible. Ugly, almost. There was something wrong with her. Something had gone wrong.

'Are you all right?'

'Of course. Why shouldn't I be all right?'

'Yes, but . . .' Her eyes were black holes, pee holes in the snow. Ken Bates had said that, not about her, not about Mary at all. Someone else entirely. Clive was breathing hard. 'You look . . . you look sad.'

'Sad?' She ducked her head. 'Why would I be sad?'

'I don't know,' he muttered miserably.

She smiled up at him, put out her hand. 'Perhaps I'd cheer up if you'd bike me home.'

He stared, felt the tears in his eyes. 'OK,' he said. 'OK.'

The church was tastefully decorated by friends of the bride in belladonna lilies and lycopodium for the marriage of Mr Clive Harper to Miss Mary Boyle last Saturday.

The bride was beautifully gowned in white satin cut on classical lines, the yoke being trimmed with hand-made leaves and orange blossom. The bride made a charming picture as she entered the church on the arm of Dr York, a family friend. There was no train.

The bride was attended by her cousin, Miss Hazel Neltey, dressed in pale pink frilled organdie, with large organdie hat trimmed with deeper pink flowers. Frilled organdie gloves were worn and she carried a shower bouquet of pink carnations, dahlias and belladonna lilies and wore a rose quartz necklace, the gift of the bridegroom.

*The reception was held at the Cornwall Park Tearooms.
The bridegroom's mother, Mrs Harper Snr, acted as hostess.
She wore brown figured crepe de chine and a brown hat and
carried a bouquet of dahlias and carnations to tone.*

*The bride's going-away outfit was a cinnamon-brown
suit with hat, shoes and gloves to tone. The honeymoon
will be spent in Nelson. The couple's future home will be in
Hastings.*

They lay awake in the dark, rigid, scarcely able to breathe.
Clive held her hand. 'It'll be all right,' he said finally. 'You
know . . . later.'

Mary's hand moved in his. 'Yes.'

'You'll be tired,' he said hopelessly. He rolled towards her.
'Mary?'

Yes?'

'It's probably that thing.'

'The frenchie?'

He lay still, startled by her knowledge.

'Why did you use it?' she whispered.

'Well. I mean we don't want a baby straight off, do you?'

She flung herself at him in the dark. 'Yes. Yes. I do.'

'Well, then, I'll just . . .'

She was sobbing; fierce, gulping angry sobs. 'No. No.
No.'

He held her in his arms. 'Don't cry, don't cry. We've got
plenty of time.'

'Yes,' she gasped.

'I love you.'

'I know,' she said. Her hand touched his hair. 'I know.'

He flung himself to his side of the bed, one hand groping
for his smokes and matches.

Mrs Harper telephoned Dr York to tell him, her voice calm, almost brusque. She had always told Clive about smoking in bed. She'd told him and told him and told him.

Dr York spent a sleepless night, his eyes open as he waited for the morning newspaper. He spread it flat on the scrubbed-pine table in the kitchen and he read each word of the report with slow care. There was little detail.

Honeymoon Tragedy. Local Bride Dies.

A popular local bride and seamstress, Mrs Clive Harper (née Boyle), died in a hotel fire in Nelson last night. Mrs Harper and her husband were honeymooning in the South Island after their marriage in Hastings last week.

The fire is understood to have started in the bridal suite. Mr Harper, who was found unconscious in the corridor, is under sedation. Other guests were unharmed, but the hotel was extensively damaged.

A spokesman from the Fire Brigade said that rescue operations had been hampered by a strong wind.

Funeral details for Mrs Harper will be published in the Obituary Column of the Clarion at a later date.

Dr York put his head in his hands.

All right. So what would you have done? . . . Told him? What good would that have done? He paused. And if you've any decency at all, make sure there's no postmortem.

Mrs York appeared at the doorway. She stared at her husband's grief. He looked so old, so cold. She put her arms around his shoulders, kissed his bald head.

'There's no point in being morbid, George,' she said. 'That won't help anyone.'

Dr York moved his head slowly from side to side.

'Poor Clive,' he said. 'Poor, poor Clive.'

'Clive's all right,' snapped Mrs York. 'What about that poor child! What about Mary?'

'Oh yes.' Dr York's hand shook as he adjusted his glasses. 'Yes.' His head moved again. He raised myopic eyes to the white sky beyond the kitchen window, the bare branches. 'But poor Clive.'

So Lovely of Them

George had always been sure of himself, had known he was right, had made quick decisions and stuck by them. How else could he have been so successful, have had his own factory at thirty, made his first take-over at thirty-nine. A self-made man and proud of it, as who would not be. A good boss, they said on the factory floor, tough but fair. You knew where you were with him.

Except, thought Mavis, slipping out of striped cotton in the motel bedroom after lunch, that you didn't. Not in the home you didn't. Not in the home at all, and never had, and getting worse day by day in front of your very eyes.

It was understandable, of course, now he was retired. Quite understandable. One minute you were saying unto this man Go and he goeth and unto this man Come and he cometh and then overnight you're rattling around the house with a wife of thirty-five years and not another soul now Tom had gone to Melbourne. It was probably just that he was bored. No coming, no going, just Mavis to put through the hoops of punctuality, tidiness (lack of), powers of concentration (failing). Memory, he told her, is mind over matter. Muddle, he said, is trouble.

Mavis shook her head in quick dismissal. Such thoughts are not for weddings and she was glad they had come to Tony's. Her favourite nephew after all, and Fielding such a pretty little place in the spring. All blossom, catkins and lambs, it had been a lovely drive up. And fun being part of it, staying in the same motel with the bridegroom and the rest of the wedding party. 'Are you part of the Wedding Party?' the lady had asked. 'The rest of the Wedding Party are at the rehearsal.' Things like that. It made you feel welcome even if you had given the happy couple their third travelling iron which had seemed such such a good idea at the time with them both going off for three years. He and Betsy had been sweet about it. Still . . .

The wedding was timed for three at the Presbyterian church. Mavis and her sister Bet had agreed they would have time to put their feet up before starting.

Not that they got much rest. The bridesmaids ran along narrow corridors shrieking with laughter and looking for the laundry and a quick press. Someone had mislaid a belt, two cousins had swapped hats, the groomsmen were yahooing around the place trying to find the Going Away Car so they could mess it up with confetti and stuff like they do at country weddings, though less often now.

Just as she was nodding off George appeared from the en suite clutching the *Dominion*. You either do or you don't read the newspaper in the toilet and she had given up on the whole thing long ago. But it seemed worse somehow when it was right next door, the cistern rushing and clanking and all so immediate.

He dropped the paper on the candlewick bedspread. 'I'm going to do a recce,' he said.

She edged away from the thing. 'What for?'

'The church. We don't know where the church is.'

'Bet and Doug'll tell us.'

'Time spent on reconnaisance,' said George, 'is never wasted.'

She knew this. She also knew that a good man leads from the front and that if you have time to spare you should go by air. Mavis smoothed flesh-pink nylon over her front with one hand and closed her eyes. Mad, she thought dreamily. Quite mad.

He arrived back in good spirits having found the Presbyterian church. It would be no problem. All would be well.

Mavis, now dressed and preoccupied with her hat, made small encouraging noises. She had made an effort with the hat, had gone to Mercer's in her blue, had sought advice from the young woman with the teeth who had suggested eau de nil to tone. The hat now sat on her head like a pale green meringue, its white silk daisies wreathed in tulle. It refused to settle, to become part of her. It remained perched, disparate as a seagull on the bronze head of Sir Keith Holyoake's statue in Molesworth Street.

Mavis turned for help. 'How do I look?' she asked.

George glanced at his watch. 'Gone in fifteen minutes.'

'Fifteen!'

'It's right the other side of town.'

'But this is *Fielding*.'

'I've just been there, haven't I? And we want a good park.'

Why, she wondered, remembering not to panic at the

unexpectedly shortened time did they need a good park? There would be a church, there would be room to park. Why a good one? In Fielding.

She moistened her lips, gave her image a small tentative smile. The stranger's lips moved in response. The face looked tired, its normal pink now tinged with green beneath fluorescent light and tulle. There were strange bruised shadows beneath the eyes.

'Pull yourself together,' snapped Mavis at the defeated-looking thing. It knew as well as she did. It's simply a matter of doing the best you can with what's left.

'Coming, George?' she called.

George reappeared. He was still a good-looking man, a well-dressed man at ease with himself and destiny. He glanced in the mirror, smoothed his hair. 'Don't fuss, woman,' he said. 'We've got plenty of time.'

They drove through Fielding in silence. Neat houses sat in rows surrounded by well-mown lawns. Roses were in full bloom, an occasional rampant climber waved high in triumph. Sharp green foliage covered old trees, the roads were wide and empty.

'It seems a long way,' she said.

'I told you.'

'Yes.'

They pulled into the churchyard, parked the car beside the small white church and sat silent.

'There's nobody here,' said Mavis finally.

He checked his watch. 'There should be.'

'Well there isn't.'

George lifted his eyes to the pointed wooden spire. 'They'll come.'

Mavis leaped from the car.

'Where are you going?' he cried.

She clutched the iron ring of the church door and rattled. The door was locked. She beat on its wooden panels with both fists, a supplicant begging for sanctuary. There was no reply. The air was warm and heavy, the silence unbroken except for the soaring song of a skylark and the frustrated bellow of a nearby bull.

She ran down the steps, flung open George's door.

'It's the wrong church!'

He waved a hand at a nearby hoarding. FIELDING PRESBYTERIAN CHURCH, it said. The Minister was named, the times of service, the extramural activities. All were welcome.

'You wanted a Presbyterian church. You've got one.'

If only the bull would shut up. 'There — is — no — one — here. There must be two.'

'In Fielding?'

There had been a time a thousand years ago when she had found that slow smile endearing. Mavis could feel her heart, hear her deep rickety breaths. 'It's a quarter to three,' she shouted. 'And there is *no one here.*'

He lay back in the seat and closed his eyes.

If only Tom were here. He could deal with his father, has always been able to from an early age. Had refused to be reduced to pulp by imbecility, to be bullied by irrational behaviour. But Tom, good staunch Tom was doing very well in the bank in South Yarra and he and Sue were looking forward to seeing them both next month, in fact they could hardly wait.

Mavis gave a small strangled noise and spoke to closed eyelids. 'I'm going to find the other one,' she said.

'Do that.'

She slammed the door and set off, wobbling across small stones in her new navy courts, sweat dampening her face, her hat slipping. Rage impelled her, marched her swollen feet forward and carried her onto the grass verge beyond the church gates.

'Excuse me,' she said to a young man standing thoughtfully beside a large freshly dug hole in the middle of his front lawn. Foundations? Sewage? An ornamental concrete pond with bridge? All, all were irrelevant.

'Can you tell me where the *other* Presbyterian church is?' asked Mavis. She gave a light laugh. It could happen to anyone, she intimated, part of the human condition, here a church, there a church, you can never be sure till you ask.

He pointed. 'First right, first left, and right again.' He glanced at her feet. 'It's quite a long way.'

'Thank you.' She gave a quick backwards movement of her head. 'My husband will be coming soon.'

The young man lifted a hand in salute. 'Go for it,' he said and resumed his silent contemplation of the hole in the ground.

They had had a wonderful time in Melbourne with Tom and Sue fussing over them, such a welcome and so kind. And Jamie a real little boy now with that haircut, and fancy him remembering. And their idea, their lovely idea had left Mavis, and George as well, quite speechless. It was so kind, so generous, so, so well . . . loving.

A booking had been made for them both for a night in a first-class hotel on the Bellalarine Peninusula; dinner, bed and breakfast for two and see a bit of the country at the same time. An early Christmas present, all paid in advance. They would get the train from Spencer Street, the bus from Geelong. They would have a ball.

And so they had so far. George was good at journeys. Things which involved timetables and keys, departures and arrivals pleased him, especially when the transport was punctual. Mussolini, he told her, had made the Italian trains run on time. Mavis nodded. 'I read somewhere,' she said, 'that the bodies of Mussolini and his mistress. Carla someone . . .'

'Petacci.'

'Yes, well . . . they were shown to the crowds hanging upside down. Someone had tied her skirt around her knees, but even so . . . The misery he'd inflicted, the misery of course, for so long. But upside *down*. Like being buried standing on your head. Not that it would matter, I can see that, but the idea appals me.' She stared over flat dry plains, shaking her head at tin sheds and sparse scrubby bush. 'Appals,' she murmured.

'You're all over the place as usual. I'm talking about *trains*.'

'Yes.'

They clambered from the train at Geelong. Tom had given them directions. They read them carefully. 'Get bus to Queenscliff at Station.'

George strode off purposefully. Mavis followed. It was very hot. Thirty-five degrees the man had said, and more to come. Trickles of sweat ran down the back of her knees, slid between her breasts as she headed towards the bus park to the right. George strode straight ahead. Mavis put her grip down. 'The bus park,' she said, 'is over here.'

'It's this way.'

Gentle Jesus, meek and mild. 'George,' said Mavis, 'I can see the *signs*.'

'I'm going this way,' he said and did so.

Mavis stood watching his straight back, his decisive stride into nowhere. He stopped beneath a wattle tree and a sign for a local bus stop. Mavis picked up her grip and walked over to the sign labelled *Queenscliff*. The next bus was due, she read, at twelve-fifteen.

Primary school children passed, hatted like miniature French Foreign Legionnaires. Old women toiled by in tied-on straws. A shop window advertised cotton jamas with racing cars. Perhaps she could get a pair for Jamie. No, no time.

She felt curiously empty, devoid of any emotion, either of empathy or distaste. A hot hatless old woman waiting for a bus. She looked over at George standing upright and resolute in the wrong place. She was not concerned. No sweat, as Tom might inaccurately have said. The Queenscliff bus would arrive, she would climb in. George would abandon his heroic stand on the wrong deck and come to join her. Not a word would be said.

Mavis stared straight ahead. At the far end of the square two young abseiling workmen were engaged in mounting a giant roll of white plastic sheeting to the blank wall of a multi-storeyed building. They pranced about its vertical face, their rubber-shod toes bobbing and leaping on French Vanilla stucco, their harnesses suspended from steel ropes far above. Their neat rear ends were safely strapped, their hands free. As she watched, each one swung to an opposite side to cut the bindings of the roll.

Its descent was dramatic, instantaneous and complete. Its message was proclaimed in Christmas Tree shape, in letters of foot-high green.

FED FAX
Wish all their customers
a VERY HAPPY CHRISTMAS
and a PROSPEROUS NEW YEAR
YOUR FUTURE LIES WITH FED FAX
THRU
1998
1999
2000
and the Rest
of the
MILLENNIUM

The word made visible, the mission statement confirmed. There was a sense of proclamation, of Hear Ye, Hear Ye, flapping gently but securely at the end of the square. The two young men descended at speed, unbuckled, and disappeared in a flash.

Mavis stared at it.

The news brought her no redress. The rest of the millennium. Dear God, what a thought. A thousand ages in thy sight may well be like an evening gone. I understand that, I'm not disputing it for a moment. But not for me, God. Please, Sweet Christ, not for me. Her eyes filled, tears welled over, unbidden and inevitable as overflow.

Half blinded, sweating, Mavis mounted the steps as the bus arrived. There was no hand free to wipe her eyes and anyway what did it matter. Look at the rest of them; the fat angry driver, the little woman with the tic, the old man with his strange basket. Where on earth did they think they were going and what in Heaven's name did it matter if there were tears or no tears.

George strode across the parade ground. He climbed the steps and called to her. 'Have you paid?'

'Not for you.'

The driver took his money with a wink.

George stowed his bag and sat beside her in silence. She turned her sodden face to the window and mopped. Be still, be still.

After some time she faced the front, her expression, she hoped, non-judgmental, but how could you know.

His voice was startled. Mavis was weeping. Mavis never cried, never, let alone *wept*. 'What the hell's wrong now?'

'Wrong how?'

'Why are you crying, for God's sake? We haven't even got there yet.'

'Oh.' Mavis drew a deep breath. She was now crying loudly, uncontrollably as a small child. Tears sprang from her eyes to splash unheeded down her face. 'That's just it,' she gasped. 'I was thinking,' she hiccupped, 'thinking about Tom and Sue. It's so lovely, so lovely of them. So generous,' she bawled, mopping and banging about with a screwed-up rag with polka dots. 'So lovely.'

George drew a clean white handkerchief from his trouser pocket and handed it to her in silence.

Gasping, sobbing, clutching at straws, she took it.

He put a large freckled hand on the knee beside him and squeezed slightly.

'You'll be better when we get there,' he said.

Peppermint Frogs

I'm glad you asked me about my 21st. It's not a topic which crops up often, in fact I don't think it ever has before.

21st birthday recollections don't have the starkness, the where-were-you-when-it-happened impact of global tragedies — that day in Dallas, that car crash.

Nevertheless, memories surface, and strangely vivid they are too. Looking back I see the day itself, and more especially the day before I came of age, with detachment. This was not so at the time.

I cannot include memories of my 21st among such joys. The celebrations were muted but emotions ran high.

At the age of 20 I was teaching Science at a Girl's Boarding School. I was, in fact, Head of Science. Science, in that school, was me.

As well as teaching Forms Three to Seven I had, like all the residential staff, extra-curricular responsibilities. These were a mixed bag and revolved mainly around the Boarders: House Duties with the Boarders, Dining Room Duties with the Boarders, Prep Supervision with the Boarders, Church Attendance with the Boarders, and, finally, Lights Out for the Boarders. Yippee — but softly. The Staff House held perils of its own.

A responsibility which was mine alone was the restocking of the Science Cupboard. This stood at the back of the laboratory where I taught, secured for safety yet still threatening, like some large and famished animal snarling for food. I did toss it some copper sulphate occasionally ('Chile, girls, is virtually a mountain of copper') but remember little else.

For some reason this task alarmed me more than most. More than Full Day Sunday Supervision with the Boarders which included Ballroom Dancing with the Seniors in the Hall after tea. Not more, certainly, but almost as much as the importunate clamour of my alarm clock each morning and the strictly hierarchical queue for the geyser-equipped bathroom in the Staff House.

I can still see the dressing gowns: the plaids, the camels, the florals and the sad. And the waterproof sponge bags creaking in the hands of First Assistant, English, Maths, French and so on down the line. Physical Education and Science tossed for second to last.

There were power cuts that year I began teaching. I had bought a radio shaped like a miniature caravan with my first pay cheque, and listened each morning to Morrie Power's session on 2ZB. Morrie was a cheerful man, or appeared to be so, and I would like to take this opportunity of thanking him for my morning laugh. At 8.30 each morning he would intone, 'Ladies and gentlemen. On behalf of my brother, Vital Electric, please turn off your radios.' I thought this very funny indeed and so did Val.

*

Val (Phys Ed) was 21 and blonde. She danced and leapt about the school, glowing with health and easy on the eye. I can remember thinking at the time that working in an all girls' school seemed rather a waste of Val's more obvious attributes. Our other friend, Woody (Beryl Woodhouse, Geography), had been teaching for years. Val and I took her breakfast in bed on her 30th birthday. Woody, attractive warm-hearted Woody, sat up in her bed and wailed, 'I don't *want* to be 30.'

Val and I stared at her. What could we say, what could we possibly say to our friend Woody who was 30, still teaching, still living in the Staff House, and not married.

We came to, prattled on: 'Look Woody, bacon *and* fried bread. Presents! And your favourites, peppermint frogs. And we're taking you to *The Best Years of Our Lives* tonight. And The Green Parrot after. We've got it all worked out.'

We had, hadn't we? Yes, we had indeed.

Val's boyfriend was now working in Auckland. Mine had left university unexpectedly and was mustering in the High Country. I still find that phrase deeply romantic. As one of Janet Frame's characters says, 'I should like to have lived in a house whose tall windows face the mountains.' Or think I should. I enjoyed Stephen's letters and his tall tales from the hills. Also words of affection and praise were more than welcome in the chilly atmosphere of the Staff Room.

However, I realised that I no longer loved their writer. Stephen wrote to tell me he was coming up for my 21st. We would, he told me, paint the town red. I wrote to him immediately, saying, 'Don't come. It's over,' though more kindly and with grateful thanks. I still remember the relief. I practically levitated about the Staff House singing Val my new song which I had set to the tune of an indecent tramping song about a maid in a mountain glen and a fountain pen.

'I'm out of love, let's all cheer,
The turtle dove has shot through here.'

My birthday coincided with Easter Monday that year. Val and I, mostly Val, had organised an overnight tramp in the Tararuas with the left-over Boarders. Most girls and staff high-tailed as soon as the appropriate bell had tolled on Maundy Thursday. There were 12 stragglers left, girls ranging in age from 13 to 17, who, for various reasons, were stuck at school. The Headmistress and the cook were delighted with Val's enterprise and we set off, like Belloc's firemen, with courage high and hearts aglow.

Val was an experienced tramper and had access to one of the huts. The weather was fine, the beech trees sparkling in the sun and the girls delightful. My sense of freedom soared to euphoria. The next day, appropriately tired but happy, we caught a nearby bus back to school. Val, I remember, taught me the words of 'The Martins and the Caugheys, they were reckless mountain boys' en route.

We handed over our charges to the French mistress who was Sunday House Duties and thus also pleased with us, trailed back to the virtually empty Staff House and sat on the verandah, drinking tea and counting the treats in our working lives. We came up with three. A cup of tea, a hot bath (if and when the geyser behaved itself) and the Sunday Request Session.

'Well, we've got that later,' said Val, pushing back the hank of blonde hair which fell across her left eye. I asked her once why she didn't cut it off. She replied that the boys liked it. I understood immediately.

'And there won't be a queue for the bath,' I said. 'Toss you.'

Val won the toss and I went to my room which was small and dark and much loved. There was mail from home and, lying on top, a note from the Headmistress. 'Dear Miss Wright. Please come and see me in my study as soon as you return.'

Why on earth? I changed into a skirt, brushed hair, washed hands and set off. The Headmistress was working. She never stopped working. There are many types and conditions of women whom I admire but headmistresses of girl's schools, particularly boarding schools, come high on the list.

Miss Grainger looked up, smiled her anxious gentle smile, asked for details of our expedition, then corrected herself. She would speak to Miss Rowland and me after Assembly on Tuesday morning and hear all the details. She was glad it had been such a success. The girls had been very fortunate and the school was grateful.

She stopped, looked at me even more anxiously. She had a message for me. From a young man named Stephen something.

'Bamber!'

'Yes. He has been trying to contact you all weekend.'

'Where?'

'Here, of course. He seemed very surprised you weren't here. Very,' she murmured to her fingernails.

'But I wrote to him. Ages ago.'

The Headmistress's hands moved quickly. She didn't want to hear the details. Anything but. She handed me a piece of paper between thumb and forefinger. 'He's in a hotel in town. Here's the number. Perhaps,' said the Headmistress, 'you might care to contact him.'

'Yes, yes I will. Thank you, Miss Grainger.'

'Not at all.'

I rang Stephen. I saw Stephen. Stephen told me he had never received my letter telling him that our romantic attachment was at an end. He showed me the ring he had brought up from the south. The ring he had hoped to place on my finger as a token of our everlasting affection and regard for each other. I stared at the high-domed blue-velvet-covered box, at the bright golden circle with a diamond winking from ruched white satin and burst into tears of shame and guilt. Stephen wept too. He asked me if there was any chance of my changing my mind. I said no.

He asked me if he could kiss me goodbye. It is always a mistake to ask and I bawled louder.

Finally, thank God, he got angry, told me what he thought of me, snapped his little box shut and departed.

He married a girl called Bobbie not long afterwards and lived happily ever after.

The next day was my 21st. Morrie Power wasn't on that morning. I sat up in bed and opened birthday presents from my family and friends. Val and Woody brought me breakfast in bed and sang Happy Birthday, dear Barbara, Happy Birthday to you.

They had booked tickets for *In Which We Serve*. And we would go to The Green Parrot afterwards. There were peppermint frogs.

I didn't tell them, of course, but in fact I preferred chocolate fish with pink insides. And still do.

The Daggy End

Noeline had been at the pharmacy for yonks, having, as she said, worn out two bosses in the process. At first she had hoped to qualify as a pharmacist like the Careers Adviser at High had suggested, but Mother had always been frail, and besides the money was impossible.

Mr Raven was the first boss, a tall silent man with a pince-nez, the only one she'd seen in life though she had met them in books. He had the right face for it, they all thought that at work.

On the tenth anniversary of Noeline's first day at work he dropped dead at Griffin's Shoes while trying on a new pair of brogues.

She hadn't liked to produce her anniversary cake after someone had rushed across the road with the sad news, but later, when the staff had recovered slightly, she offered it round. In the circumstances no one had liked to take a second slice so she had plenty to take home to Mother as well as the drama.

Mr Raven had been a fair boss but had little impact on Noeline, nor, it seemed, on anyone else. He had no wife or

children, and even the obituary in the *Tribune* found little to
say about him except the pharmacy and his pince-nez.

Noeline did mention having planned to qualify to the new
owner, Mr Newtown, but he said forget it. Girls came and
went, he said, some qualified, some not, but someone like
Noeline who knew the stock like the back of her hand, was
always willing, helpful and reliable . . . well, she was worth her
weight in gold. He ended by saying he was sorry he couldn't
give her a rise at the moment but he would bear it in mind. In
the meantime how would she like to go on a training course
with *Touche Magique* cosmetics in Auckland? She could still
remember his praise, his concern, the whole thing had left
her grinning like a twit. She would love to go on the course,
she said, providing Aunt would come over to mind Mother.
'Love to,' she said again.

It was wonderful, quite wonderful; Auckland itself,
humming in the upbeat eighties, the traffic so fast and endless
and the hotel in Lorne St where Mr and Mrs Newtown had
spent their honeymoon, slightly run down perhaps, but the
staff so kind and helpful.

The course itself was inspirational. The lady instructor
was professional, calm and smart and the other girls young
and keen as mustard, but again friendly. One of them, Toni,
curled her eyelashes. She showed Noeline the little clamp
thing she used, quite easy she said when you got the hang of
it and the boys were mad about it.

Noeline came back to Havelock with her red *Touche
Magique* badge on her uniform and her Certificate in her
hand. She put up a small display of the products at the end
of a counter and demonstrated with patience to some of the
older ladies who were inclined to muddle the moisturising
process with the nourishing, and who couldn't get the hang

of how cells could absorb the vitamins, or the rejuvenating creams get rid of their wrinkles or not, until Noeline explained about the amazing skin technology now available from *Touche Magique*. She also made it clear that the routine must be carried out each night before retiring.

Sales went up. Mr Newtown was pleased. So much so that Noeline suggested facials, but Mr Newtown thought that might be going a bit far and they hadn't got the space.

They hadn't either. The place was packed to the gunwales according to Mr Newtown who had been in the navy during the war. The trouble, in his opinion, was that pharmacy as a career had changed; things had crept up on him, that was the trouble. It had been an excellent profession all those years ago when he trained in the hospital, but look at it now. Gone were the days of pestle and mortar, of lubricating unguents and soothing emollients made up by hand. Most things now were prepacked, preprepared. Little remained of the wise, the skilled apothecary.

It had affected the medical profession too, he said. They used to have their favourite prescriptions, things they swore by, their cure for anything and everything including hair on the chest. Now it was 'Keep on with the pills and ointment' from docs wooed and chivvied out of their minds by drug companies and their miracle pills. No variety. No vision. Pharmacy, said Mr Newtown, had lost its soul.

'Worse than that,' he said, mopping his spilled tea with a nearby Wettex, 'is the other change. "Nature", as you girls know, "abhors a vacuum." "Work expands to meet the time available." Both true, and the result is we've filled our time and shops with trinkets. When, at what precise moment, did pharmacies become gift shops? Soaps, toothpastes, trusses, shampoos certainly, but look at all this . . .' He waved a wide inclusive arm at psychedelic bubble baths, furry green teddy bears and gorilla-shaped bath gels.

Pharmacists, he explained, had once been a trusted source of advice to a grateful public, still were to a lesser extent. 'But now we're inclined to grab the appropriate pamphlet from the stand and hand it over grinning like those clowns on TV. *Nappy Rash, Frequency, Athlete's Foot*, you name it. One stop shop, that's what pharmacies have become.' He sighed deeply. 'But don't let me put you off it.'

Mr Newton retired a few months after Mother died. Noeline had thought of making a cake for his farewell party but decided against it. Mrs Freebaker, who had also been at the pharmacy forever, might recall the unfortunate timing of Noeline's cake shout twenty years ago, and besides, the new girl, Maggy, had ordered one from De Luxe Cakes which certainly looked more professional if a little dry.

Mr Newtown thanked them all, told them they would like their new boss Warren Havill, thanked them again and disappeared to the coast of Coromandel and his new lifestyle, his sharp blue hills, and his wife Ina.

Noeline was sad to see him go. He had been especially kind lately. Well, everyone had, his wife, and the other girls and her friends at the bowling club, but there's not a lot anyone else can do when your mother's dying. Except of course Aunt.

Mr Havill was tall and clean-cut, with alarming eyebrows. Black, scowling and unruly, they leapt from his forehead as though accusing you of some crime of which you were innocent but unable to produce the required evidence to prove it. The first thing he told his staff was that his partner's name was Honey. The second that they must call him Warren. 'None of this "Mister" crap. Warren for God's sake.'

The first change he made was the uniforms. Baby blue replaced black. Maggy looked even more fresh and beguiling, Mrs Freebaker and Noeline less so.

The next was the stock.

'And who's the buyer for all this?' he said, glaring at a shelf with Piglet hot water bottles and rattles with bells.

Mrs Freebaker's head lifted. Warren smiled. 'Ah, you, Freda. How about a little chat in the back room when you've got a minute? Thanks.'

Mrs Freebaker came from the tea room with her size eighteen baby blue straining across her front and her face daubed with red blotches. She marched to the dispensary area, hissing to Noeline as she passed, 'Honey's going to do my Extras. Apparently,' she said with a sniff, 'she has an eye for the upmarket.'

Then came the windows. 'Who does the windows? Oh yes, of course, Noeline isn't it? Got a minute, Noel? Thanks,' he said striding towards the back room. 'And how long've you been here, Noel? Thirty years? Wow. That's longer than Freda Freebanker.'

'Freebaker'

'Whatever.'

She watched his eyebrows heaving about his forehead.

'Let's sit down. Right.' He sidestepped two unpacked stock cartons to reach the Formica table, hooked out a chair with his foot and collapsed onto it.

'Now then. How can I put it to you about the window? Let's focus a little, eh? What's the first thing a man, or woman, either sex, child even, what's the first thing they see when they're passing. It's the windows, right? Or in our case, window. That's the bit that shouts, "This is us." "Come on in."'

Noeline stared at her new shoes. They had a strap and button like a pair she'd had in Form One. Things do come round again. Some things. She wished he would shut up.

'And what have you got?'

'Pardon?'

'In your window, right now, what've you got?'

'Well there's *Recharge for hair* and cough mixture . . . I mean I'd have to think.'

'Exactly, exactly.' Warren was now on his feet, jumping around in the limited space available. 'It hasn't got an image, has it? No impact. No focus.

'I'll tell you what you've got in your window over there. First you got *Recharge for hair*. And how's that turkey advertised? Photos of the back of a guy's nut with a bald bit and another alongside with the bald bit gone smaller.' Warren shook his head in sorrow. 'Before and After images went out with the Ark. And what else've you got? You got coloured ads for kids' cough mixture with them all honking their heads off. You got *Granddad Stokes* in an old-time hat offering *Granddad Stokes for Smelly Feet*. It's all negative, see, negative as they come, losers, losers all the way. That's not the demographic group Honey and I'm targeting, see what I mean.'

Noeline gazed at the black hairs on his ring finger trapped beneath the gold wedding band. She said nothing.

He collapsed on the chair again and stared at the threadbare carpet.

'You could trip on this y'know,' he said finally. 'Yeah, there's a lot to do. It's a prime site, that's why we bought it, but it reeks of *déjà vu*.'

'What?'

'*Déjà vu*. Old-fashioned if you like. Cluttered, like the window. We want clean modern lines, new, top of the range. That's what we're after, get rid of the daggy end.'

Her voice sounded high, cracked. 'People have things they're worried about when they come to pharmacies. They want help in, in, intimate things.' She tried to meet his eyes but they were on the carpet again.

'Yeah, yeah. You didn't meet Honey last week did you? Friday. Yeah, Friday.'

'I had asthma. Mr Newtown always said if my peak flow was under 200 I wasn't to come in. I did ring.'

'Yeah, they said. Pity really, your not meeting her then, you'd know what I mean. Anyway we discussed the window *in situ*, decided it'd be better if she took over. Make it more,' he snapped his fingers, 'NOW! Laid back. Cool if you like.'

Noeline's stomach tightened against her spine. Something felt odd, dizzy. She lifted her head and spoke carefully. 'Of course, I understand what you mean but . . .'

He slammed his hands on the black stuff across his thighs and jumped up. 'Good on y'Noel. I knew you'd get it. Honey'll have it fixed up this Sunday.'

The following Monday Noeline arrived before Warren was due to open up. She wanted to inspect the new window in detail and by herself, before Freda Freebaker arrived with her *And what do* you *think?*

It was certainly different.

Two cut-out figures, you couldn't call them mannequins but they were definitely formed, held centre stage. One bulged at the breast line, the other at the crotch; both were made of some grey textured substance which gave them a strange distinction. Their faces were ill-defined but the breasted one had thicker lips. She wore a golden mini bikini, he a snatch of blue stretch-nylon.

Behind them stood a cut-out palm tree to the right, above it a laughing cardboard sun hung high, all fiery rays and beaming smiles as it shone on the couple exchanging toiletries from the Male and Female Range. She was handing him an impressive looking glass container labelled *Stag*, swapping it with his equally well presented offering of *Lady Jayne's Body Butter*.

Display shelves behind them carried more, each product handsome and well lit. Even the sun lotions and packets of Wet Ones seemed carefully chosen.

All of which Noeline noted. She had sometimes felt things had got a wee bit crowded in her windows. She had mentioned this to Mr Newtown but he disagreed. 'No, No. Give it the lot, Noeline, give it the lot. We've got to get rid of it somehow.'

She didn't like the grey people, who could? But yes, the window was striking. And Honey's attention to detail, just look at the floor for goodness sake. It was covered, not with ordinary sand, anyone else would have pinched that from Westshore, but not Honey. She had gone to the trouble of finding that crumbly whitish stuff people used to have for drives though Mother never liked it. It got inside, she said.

Honey, however, had focused, had acquired pale sand, the type where beautiful, languid, grey strangers could luxuriate at their ease.

Noeline remained staring, occasionally stamping her feet on the frosty pavement as she stared at the window; its impact, its clean lines, its oomph.

She could learn from Honey, improve her own style like a true professional.

Another thought surfaced. A thought astonishing yet possible. Her fists clenched inside Mother's blue woollen gloves. I am a free agent. I can go myself, why not.

Her father, Tom Webb, had remained a shadowy figure to his daughter. Her main memory, or rather lasting impression of him, was of bad luck. He had spent over a year in the TB sanatorium in Waipukurau and shortly after he was discharged had been killed in an industrial accident at the canning factory when Noeline was four. Mother kept the ribbons from his wreaths and sometimes Noeline had been allowed to play with them, but gently, and not for too long.

His other legacy was more robust. He had kept his father's collection of R.M. Ballantyne's *Adventure Stories for Boys*. Her grandfather had scribbled in pencil 'Rattling good yarn' on the flyleaf of her favourite, *The Coral Island*.

She read it over and over, was *there*, a castaway in the blue Pacific Ocean with Ralph and Peterkin and Jack, as brave as them when confronted by pirates, as resourceful in finding food and lighting fires. Lying on the floor behind the sofa she practised her diving, made excursions among the coral groves at the bottom of the sea *where lurked the wonders of the deep*. She could still remember quite long bits.

What a joyful thing it is to awaken, on a fresh glorious morning, and find the rising sun staring into your face with dazzling brilliancy! — to see the birds twittering in the bushes and to hear the murmuring of a rill, or the soft hissing ripples as they fall upon the sea shore.

And she would go, go now. Use some of Mother's money

and ask Aunt to feed Smoochy for a week or so and go. There were specials everywhere now and she had some leave due. The thought weakened her knees.

'Good heavens,' said Mrs Freebaker appearing beside her on the pavement. 'Give me strength.'

'I think it's lovely,' said Noeline. 'Ah, here's Warren.'

Honey was a surprise. Unexpected for her name anyway. She was small and neat and her hair, which might once have been honey coloured, was now light mouse.

She had been nice about Noeline's comments on the window, so nice in fact that Noeline found herself telling her successor why it had made such an impact on her. How she had always longed to go to a coral island, how she had had a thing about them ever since she was a child and how, although Honey's interpretation was wonderfully way-out and modern, it had given her, Noeline, a kickstart into getting to one as soon as possible. Had Honey been there?

Yes, she had, and it was heaven.

A loud shout came from the back. 'Coming,' cried Honey. 'Thanks for the feedback, Noel.'

And off she ran. 'Coming,' she called again.

That was another thing about Honey. Not only was she friendly to one and all but she deflected the heavy hand of Warren, his tendency to have what Mother used to call her temper tantrums. She had them quite often but she always said sorry afterwards and gave Noeline a cuddle to cure her hiccups which she always seemed to get on these occasions.

Aunt, if present at the time, always cuddled Smoochy. 'He just loves it,' she said, 'when you tickle behind his ears.'

Honey's method of dealing with such situations was different. When any staff member was under suspicion of incompetence she would appear beside them, smile her gentle smile, touch her husband's arm and defuse things.

'Needs his bloody rattle,' said Maggy who didn't give a stuff and was going up North anyhow.

Noeline, in a funny sort of way, could understand. Warren wanted the pharmacy to be perfect, was determined to make it the most successful in the district. And yet there he was, frustrated by what he saw as the hopelessness of others.

Noeline chose her island — *'The Friendly Island lives up to its name,'* said the brochure. It also said the island was casual, relaxed, had free snorkelling equipment, children's rates were available.

Kay, one of the girls at the bowling club, wanted to know if she was going alone with an emphasis on the 'alone', which spoke volumes, or would have if Noeline had allowed it to. 'I'm a people person,' she laughed at Kay's caring powdery face. 'I love people, and islands. And I'm going to snorkel.'

'That mother,' sighed Kay to Jan in the cloakroom. 'All those years.'

The rain fell in strong drenching sheets day after day. Noeline was glad of her jersey and the golf umbrella hidden at the back of the bure's cupboard, something not mentioned in the brochure but essential as you sloshed along the streaming paths to the restaurant area.

Her bure did not help either. Made in traditional Fijian style with thatched roof and low eaves, it was designed to cut down the glaring sunlight, to offer a cool dim oasis for repose, not for a curl-up with a book alongside a notice advocating the usage of 30-degree strength sun lotion.

Most of the other guests were straight-backed men and women with cheerful children having fun at Wet Weather Pursuits and not grizzling.

The family in the next bure, for example. They hadn't had a chance to exchange names, but had smiled and waved from the concrete verandahs beneath their dripping eaves, exchanging calls of *Better tomorrow* and *You bet*.

Noeline thought they were Australians at first, so athletic looking, no hips and legs for miles. But no, *New Zealand*, they shouted through the rain, *North Shore*.

On the third day Noeline faced facts as she sat surrounded by drips, staring at the grey choppy waves on what was meant to be a calm blue lagoon. There were four more days, certainly, and she had never been a pessimist, but there seemed no reason why the rain should stop, in which case the coral island experience had been a mistake, and an expensive one at that. Once again the sea was too rough for snorkelling and she had almost finished her P.D. James which she had thought would be long enough to see her out.

She woke next morning to stillness, no wind, no rain, no drips. She ran to the door to see sun, real sun, low in the sky, and the tide high on the lagoon thirty yards away.

The next-door family were already there, ducking and diving and calling, 'Come on in.'

One of the disappointments of the past few days for Noeline was that she had had little chance to join in. She knew she was friendly and cheerful. Mr Newtown had told her so. And lovely with children, not that he had mentioned that, but she knew how much she would enjoy adjusting a small tricky flipper, or lending a beach towel to a shivering toddler.

She had joined in with the Oakleys next door in the few

occasional gaps between rain squalls. Had joined them playing volleyball, coconut-throwing, or touch football, like the Kennedys. All of which had been organised by magnificent and endlessly patient Fijians.

Now, however, she was, as it were, fulltime — smiling, ready-for-anything Noeline minding the smallest, Rollo, when he strayed too close to the volleyball or too near the lagoon. Leaping up laughing, 'Here I am Roly Poly,' when he lisped, 'Weth Noeline?'

They were the nicest family you could meet. Don and Vicki and their two older girls and Rollo. She could hear herself telling Kay so. 'I supervised the little ones in the kids' cafeteria occasionally. It gave Vicki and Don a break.'

Another pleasure was the friendly Fijian staff. The way they called 'Bula', wherever and whenever you met, smiling all the time and so happy. So much so that it looked quite odd when one of them didn't smile. They only got three days off the island once a fortnight but she would never have known unless she'd asked.

The best thing of all, as she had expected, was the snorkelling. She could have stayed out at the reef all day, but one of them had to keep an eye on the children and Don and Vicki were such expert swimmers you felt they should never leave the sea. They did though, they were fair, more than fair, and Rollo was inclined to be miserable when Noeline left him.

But oh, the joy when you got the hang of the mask and the flippers fitted and you glided among hillocks of pastel corals, sadly dying apparently, but surely not here where the orange, pink, green, black and yellow fish were sweeping by, darting this way, that way, the midget psychedelic blues her favourite. She was back in *The Coral Island*, but better, infinitely better, with gear unknown to Edwardian boys. She drifted head down, mouth closed, across a world of shimmering movement and colour. Wonders of the deep indeed.

On their last night the Friendly Family of Friendly Island put on a Fijian feast and concert. A good note to leave on, as Don said. As always children were welcome, sitting spellbound on the floor as the drums bonged and bronzed warriors in grass skirts leaped and whirled and waved spears inches from their beaming faces.

Then came the feast; yes, well, the feast was a bit of a disappointment, but the wine and the Fijian beer flowed, though not for the Fijians.

'Let me bed the kids down, Vicki,' said Noeline, jumping to her feet, 'seeing it's the last night. Why not kick up your heels a bit?'

Don thought it would be a great idea as long as she promised to be back soon to dance with him. The oldest girl, Holly, was quite old enough to take charge once Rollo hit the scratcher. Vicki said it would be lovely and thanks a lot.

It took quite a time for Rollo to settle. *The Rabbit Who Fished Up the Moon* was read and reread till the black eyelashes faltered and finally closed. The two girls, prone on their beds, noses deep in fiercely guarded issues of *Girlfriend*, lifted a hand to wave goodnight.

Noeline ran along the well-lit path, stopping briefly to sniff the fragrance from some unknown plant. It was all so different, so gloriously different.

She would come next year, next year and forever till Mother's money ran out. Perhaps the Oakleys might come sometime, though it was the place, the island itself which was magic. Everything about it delighted her, the languorous warmth, the coral strand, the snorkelling and its magic new world.

She saw Vicki and Don across the bright dining area, their heads close together.

Noeline stopped, smiled and headed for the shadowy bushes surrounding the dining area to the bar, ordered a bottle of chardonnay, gave directions to a waiter and continued her way around the outskirts to surprise her friends on this dark and scented night.

Don's face was scarlet at close range. He was leaning forward clutching a wine glass and wagging it at Vicki.

'I know she's OK, Vick. I never said she wasn't OK. That's not my point. My point is she's always bloody well *there*. You can't move, turn round and she's yoo hooing . . . charging about, romping. She's too old to romp . . .' Vicki murmured something.

Don downed the glass, rocked his chair back and forward, back and forward. 'I know, I know she's lovely with the kids. That's not my point. My point is some people get on your wick and . . .'

Vicki put her hand over his. 'Be nice. It's only till tomorrow.' The waiter appeared at their table bearing a bottle on a tray.

'No thanks,' said Vicki with a pretty little flutter of negation. 'No more for us, we've had plenty.'

'It is from your friend,' smiled the waiter, nodding his head at Noeline. 'Your friend in the bushes.'

The Man with the
Plug in His Nose

The bus drew to a halt beside a large weather-beaten shed. The man in the aisle seat turned to her. 'D'y'want to go?'

She looked at him blankly. They hadn't spoken before. 'Go? Oh, *Go*. No. No thanks.'

'Nor me,' he yawned, ambled down the aisle. 'Stretch the legs though.'

Yes of course, that's what she must do. Stretch the legs, breathe in the sharp air, stare at the mountains and think. Get rid of the fug, this bewildering fug in the brain.

She followed the man, standing aside at intervals for elderly passengers who had made it to the Comfort Stop before the first rush and were now tracking back to flop stiff-kneed onto their seats. Two gnarled old men in striped beanies were discussing mileages. A red-faced woman and her friend were congratulating themselves at their decision to get in early. Neither of them liked a scrum.

The shed stood four square, surrounded by seas of tussock grasslands. A large sign on the roof said it all:

JOSH and JUDE'S
GAS / FISHING LICENCES
TOILETS

There was little else to see other than a few stunted pines, wasp-waisted steel pylons marching into the distant mist and patches of scrub leading up to the blue folds of the mountains. Stark, definitely stark, the Desert Road, and beautiful. Nothing to see but endless skies and blues and golds and snow on the mountain tops if you were lucky.

As she watched the clouds darkened and swirled across the mountain tops obliterating them completely. A pity not to see them. But then you can't argue with nature as Clark always said and presumably would continue to say. After all a leopard cannot change its spots.

Oh, for God's sake, woman.

She drew a shuddering breath of crisp air. You could taste the stuff, feel it going down.

The driver's call was a not a question. 'Coming, lady.'

'Sorry.' She scrambled up to censorious stares from the old and masticating jaws of the gum-chewing young.

'Thanks,' she said as the man stood up for her to slide past.

'Not at all.'

An odd way of putting it. Archaic. For the first time she focused on him. Late forties, fifties, neat features marred by a blood-stained wad of cotton wool protruding from his right nostril. A nosebleeder then, probably a bad one. Like Clark had been when they were first married. Her mouth twitched. Clark would have disliked appearing in public looking slightly nuts for twelve hours. A quick flash perhaps, but no not all day.

Paula had no complaints. The bus was warm, its passenger list harder to trace and she had longer time to think. All she had to do was to sit beside this seemingly amiable man and work out what to do when she arrived in Wellington.

Her brother Bill had said that Clark's nosebleeds presenting themselves so soon after matrimony were the result of overexcitement. Clark was not amused. His bleeds were serious, they involved flinging himself on his back and requisitioning iceblocks, clean towels and cotton wool plugs. Plus concern from all around. His newly acquired relatives stood gazing at his supine body, their faces reminiscent of gentle cows surrounding a newcomer to their paddock.

The whole thing was a bit of a bore in retrospect, though no one said anything at the time except for Mum, who finally suggested that perhaps the sunporch might do next time as the Bremworth was only a year old.

Bill also said that their children would have enormous teeth if parental genes were anything to go by. Again Clark hadn't laughed. Why should he.

No children had appeared, so nothing could be established one way or another. The jury was out on that one. One of his useful phrases.

She missed Bill.

The man swung his nose at her. 'Have you ever lost your passport?'

'No.'

'I wondered what the procedure is here?'

'You go to your Embassy. And the police.'

'I guess. Yeah.' He nodded at the window. 'Look at the mountains.'

The clouds had lifted, Ruapehu's summit lay glinting in

the winter sun, high above subalpine meadows and purple foothills. They watched in silence as the bus slid by.

'Fight,' said the man suddenly, tapping the wounded side of his nose. 'I lost. Had to run for the bus. They cleaned me up while I was waiting. At the depot, I mean.'

Bill would have liked this. 'Good service,' she said.

'Yeah, or else they didn't want me to mess up the bus. They'll take your cash however you look.'

'Where do you come from?'

'Canada. Cold Lake.'

'Is it?'

'Very.'

They exchanged tentative noncommittal smiles. 'It'll be a mess if someone's pinched it,' she said after a pause.

'Pardon me?'

'Your passport.'

'Forget it.'

She looked at him with interest. What a sensible approach. People fuss so. Or rather start fussing too early.

'Tell me about the fight.'

'I told you. I lost.' He yawned, murmured, 'Pardon me,' and fell asleep, tidily, instantly, out like a light. She lay back.

His voice woke her. 'Jeeze. Pardon me, but you're killing my arm. Wow. Gee. Cramp.' He jumped into the aisle, swung his arm around, rubbed his left shoulder with vigour and sat again. 'Right,' he said.

'I'm terribly sorry,' she said, 'I'd no idea . . .'

'Don't fuss, lady. You can't go through life apologising for your existence. If it hadn't been you someone else could have crashed on my shoulder. *Everybody's got to be somewhere.* Who was that old guy?'

'Spike Milligan. As Eccles.'

'Whoever.'

She looked at his bloody nose with respect. He didn't give a damn, didn't have to be right about everything. Spike Milligan, or not Spike Milligan. Let it ride. Relax.

'What's your name?' he said.

'Paula.'

'Bill.'

Her smile widened. 'I had a brother called Bill.'

'You don't say,' he drawled.

'I mean . . .'

He sighed. 'You're allowed to have a brother, even one called Bill. Why are you here? What're you doing?'

'Going to Wellington.'

'Why?'

'I'm leaving my husband. Left.' That'll shut him up.

'So there's some guy in Wellington maybe?'

'No.'

'Got a job?'

'No.'

'No guy, no job. Got anyone to bum on till you get organised?'

'I'll worry about that later.'

He grinned, gave an approving nod. 'Good thinking,' he said.

The bus swung in a wide arc and drew up in the courtyard. 'COME ON INN,' said the sign. The driver began his usual spiel on Food, Toilets, Time to reboard.

Bill stood, scratched his left cheek through his jeans. 'Another comfort station.'

'Food, this time.'

'Good.'

Once again they stood aside as the Seniors charged to the front then headed across the concrete. Followed by still-chewing boys with swinging hips and girls retouching their lip gloss.

Bill said as they entered, 'Grab a table, what d'y'want?'

'But I must . . .'

'Yeah, yeah,' he said flapping a battered menu at her. 'You can pay me later.'

'Poached eggs, thanks.'

He joined the slow trudging line, waved a hand.

After some time he appeared holding an infant-sized gumboot with a red H painted on its side and a handwritten invoice sticking out the top. Bill was delighted, thought the boot was both witty and innovative. 'Good PR.'

I know what it is, she thought, touching the boot with one finger as if it were dangerous, he enjoys small things. That's the trick. And no fussing till you have to.

Their arrival in Wellington was cold and dark. The driver flung luggage about, people groped and clawed amongst suitcases and packs, snatching the wrong bags with snarls, or the right one with effective speed. 'Where's the cabs?' said Bill.

More waiting, more shuffling, more dead-eyed faces. He nodded towards the piecart, a warm, well-lit, steaming haven. 'Like one?'

'I'll get them. You join the taxi queue.'

'OK.'

It was not till she walked back clutching two greasy bags that it occurred to Paula that this cooperative partner-like behaviour would have to stop soon. Standing in the cold eating steak-and-mushroom pies with a wounded stranger minus his passport was not her usual evening routine. Slippers and a book, more like it, when all was clean and tidy and stowed away for an early start. *An early start.* Sweet Christ. She stood rock still with pies, surrounded by chilly space.

She knew why she had married Clark, had known for years. It wasn't as if you were expected to marry in the seventies. Anything but. Women were liberated by the pill, were they not. Many were busy making love not war as the Vietnam War dragged on and on and on. She believed in Women's Liberation, went to meetings and worked for the cause. But like a rudderless dinghy she had drifted away. Nursing had palled after a few years and she was tired of liaisons with trainee doctors, keen trampers and a taxi driver. What she wanted, all she wanted, was to find a decent man who wanted her and loved children. Lots of children.

If you want to make God laugh, tell him your plans. A Yiddish saying. And right on the button.

Paula went back to nursing and later trained as a Special Needs Teacher. She worked hard and cherished her students' dogged determination, their achievements.

Clark prospered in his branch of the firm. Days, months, years passed as their marriage became more and more moribund, that was the word, moribund, as in 'lacking in vitality'. They talked less and less. Soon, she felt, they would communicate in grunts. The time had come to leave. She should have left long ago, taken the blame and beat it, but was restrained by guilt. She was at fault after all. There was nothing wrong with Clark. He was a decent man. They both knew that. There was no hatred, no unfaithfulness.

There were emotional farewells with her students. Yes, of course there would be another nice lady, and Paula would write to every one of them and they would write back wouldn't they? Yeah. OK. Cool.

She also knew that after the tumult and the shouting had died Clark would feed himself every night, help himself to a brandy and sink in front of SKY to watch documentaries like *The Last Days of Hitler* or *How the War Was Won*, with endless black-and-white explosions of buildings, doomed ships, wounded aircraft spiralling downwards and war refugees fleeing.

'We could sit down,' said Bill ditching their paper bags in a nearby bin.

'No,' said Paula with sudden decision. 'This queue's impossible. I'm going round the corner, there's another rank there.'

Bill leaned back on the wooden bench, stretched his arms along the back and looked up lazily.

'I want to go to . . . sleep,' she said, dropping 'bed' at the last minute.

'Yeah, but look over the road. A Backpackers.'

'I haven't been in a Backpackers for years.'

'There's no age limit. There was some old guy of ninety in the paper the other day. Bunks down all over.' He stood up. 'Let's give it a go.'

'OK . . .' She stopped, banged a fist into her palm. 'No. We can't. You haven't got a passport.'

'You've got yours.'

'Of course. You don't leave home without your passport. But yours . . . ?'

He groped around beneath layers of clothing, produced a

body bag at his waist, rootled around inside and drew out a passport.

Confusion is worse in the dark and the cold. 'You said you'd lost it.'

'No. No. Let's get inside for God's sake. We can fight it out in the bar.' She watched him as he hefted on his pack beneath the street lamp. Thin, quick on his feet, blue eyes and pale hair above the stoppered nose and lopsided grin.

Of course I will go. She grabbed the handle of her suitcase and trundled across the pedestrian crossing. A wheel snagged in the gutter, he booted it out.

The Backpackers was little different from those of the past. The ghosts of a lover or two followed her up the steps into the brilliantly lit foyer. Different faces and races milled about, dumped packs, picked them up, barged about, or came and went across the red and green tartan carpet to confer with fellow citizens in corners.

On every flat surface lay coloured pamphlets on the *Scenic Wonders of New Zealand*, from *Extreme Sporting Activities* to the peace and cathedral glory of the *Southern Beech Forests*. She picked one up, stood dreamily beside Bill at Reception.

The young woman behind it was dark, luscious, and half asleep. She went through their registrations with the exhausted competence of a zombie.

'Passports OK. Double Room?'

'No. Female Dormitory.'

'Male Dormitory.'

'OK. Both on Floor Four. There's a Safe Room for gear and the Special's still on. *One night Dormitory plus one breakfast $29.* How many nights?'

'Seven,' said Bill.

'And me.'

The young woman yawned so widely her back fillings showed. 'Yah,' she said, 'And the bar closes at midnight. Yah.'

The bar was packed. They leaned across the rickety table to talk.

'Why on earth don't you take that thing out of your face?'

'I thought I'd leave it till I hit the sack. It might gush all over the place.'

Paula nodded. They could gush. Gush and gush and gush. She felt lighthearted, nothing real. Just — well, agreeable.

'Why'd you ask me about passports?'

'I thought it was a good way to start the conversation.'

'And the fight was true?'

'Hell, yes.' He tapped his nose.

He picked up her hand from the table, inspected it, turned it over and kissed the palm.

'Thank you.'

'Not at all.'

He was an engineer. Engineers tend to crop up in cold places. Cold Lake, Alaska, Antarctica. They need people to keep the engines going, otherwise the whole place would fold. Hot places too of course. The world was an engineer's oyster, especially if you liked going places. Did she like travel?

Very much, mainly on her own. And why was that? Clark (she couldn't keep calling him her ex-husband) didn't enjoy flying long distances, the sweat of the whole thing, all that standing around, luggage. And now terrorism. He'd rather have a golf tour to Australia.

'Pardon?'

'Keen golfers from here go and play golf against Australians. Then the keen Australians come over here and they do it again.'

'I get it.'

They discussed places they'd been to. Favourite ones cropped up, ones they loved, had missed or never heard of. Had she been to Machu Picchu? No. In Peru. Amazing place. They were expert stone masons, built enormous structures hundreds of years ago, moved some for miles. They could go sometime.

She would read up about it. She liked books about places, did he?

Travel books? Couldn't stand them, rather just go.

So what books did he like?

Quite a few. They discussed them, agreed, dissected, disagreed. And what about Proust. Unreadable. Shock. Horror. And how about that new American? Couldn't stand the guy, and his wife was worse.

She snorted, groped for a nonexistent tissue then flicked the drip with the back of her hand.

The barman was waving his arms across the empty room. 'Closed,' he yelled, 'we're closed.'

They stepped out of the lift at the fourth floor. She walked into his open arms as they kissed, exploring, seeking and greeting as they moved together. His arms tightened before he let her go and they stood gasping, watching each other, smiling. Finally Bill lifted a hand. 'See yer,' he said turning away.

'Yes,' said Paula and headed towards the Female Dormitory. At the door she stopped. Partners? Wives? Not a mention. Oh well.

Her key opened the door to blackness and the whistling

snore from one of her room-mates. She groped around, found an empty bed, fell back onto it and lay there grinning into the darkness.

'So what,' she murmured. 'Don't fuss lady.'